FORBIDDEN FIRE

FORBIDDEN FIRE

HEATHER GRAHAM

OPEN ROAD

INTEGRATED MEDIA

NEW YORK

Cover design by Mimi Bark

ISBN: 978-1-5040-5236-8

This edition published in 2018 by Open Road Integrated Media, Inc.
180 Maiden Lane
New York, NY 10038
www.openroadmedia.com

This book is dedicated to "Sister T"—
Teresa Sutton—
With lots of thanks, affection
very best wishes,
and good things, always.

FORBIDDEN FIRE

PROLOGUE

Yorkshire, England
March, 1895

The first time Marissa saw the stranger, she was not quite ten years old. But she knew from the moment she saw him that she'd never forget him.

It was cold that day. It was always cold in the small coalmining town, for the fires were meager, and they never seemed to warm the little one-room hovels where the miners lived. Or maybe it was cold because there was no glass in the windows—they were covered in the winter and spring with whatever newspaper or sacking could be found.

And spring had brought heavy rain that year. But not even the rain could wash away the continual pall of black that seemed to hang over the town. The coal dust from the mines seemed like a miasma that clouded just the land that belonged to the mine. To Marissa, the very color of the air was different, and where the black cleared away was freedom. A different world. And her whole meaning in life came to a longing to escape the cloud of black.

The rains merely turned coal dust to mud.

On that day she saw the stranger for the first time, she had donned a clean dress and a pinafore she had studiously scrubbed herself, determined that it would be white. And she had brushed and braided her hair. It was wild hair, a deep red blond in color. Uncle Theo said it was like a sunset, but when she had first come to the coal-mining town, the children had laughed and called her carrot top. She was as tough and determined as any of them, and they'd eventually come to respect her, but they resented her, too. She was an outsider, and she could read and write to boot. She'd put on airs, Uncle Theo had told her.

Well, she'd had the right. She was the daughter of a Church of England minister, and she'd spent her early years in a far different life. She'd seen enough of the great manors to know that she longed for the life of a lady. Longed for it with every breath of her being. Marissa clung to her pride and her dreams as if they were floats and she were adrift in a vast ocean.

On the day she met the stranger she had just been coming from Petey Quayle's house. His mum had been down with the ague, and Uncle Theo had sent her over with his special chicken soup. Mrs. Quayle had been grateful and very kind, but Petey had determined to plague her silly. She had barely walked out of the house before he had come running up behind her calling out her name. Turning, she knew that he meant to knock her into the mud, and so she had started to run.

It was all the stranger boy's fault. It was, it really was. He came striding around the corner of the pony shed, and Marissa barely had a moment to glance at him before she plowed straight into him. But that one glance burned itself on her memory. He was so perfect. A boy, but a very tall one. Years older than she was. Maybe even a man. He was certainly tall enough. Tall, but very slim. Perhaps eighteen or nineteen. And impeccably dressed in clean fawn trousers, a cranberry vest and a light brown jacket.

She was running too fast to stop, but just before she hit him she met his eyes. He might have been young, but they were a curiously disturbing blue. A blue that stared and probed, and looked into the heart. And his hair was black. Jet black.

"My word!" someone at his side snapped.

Marissa didn't see who it was at first. She had lost her balance and was falling straight into the mud that she had been trying so very hard to avoid.

"Here, let me help you up!" the boy said, reaching for her.

She glared up at him, knowing how filthy the mud had made her. "You knocked me over!"

"I most certainly did not, young lady! You ran straight into me."

"Out of the way, you little coal rat! How dare you speak to a young gent so!" the other voice snapped. It was Mr. Lacey, the manager of the mines. Short and portly, he was also excessively cruel. She sensed that his cruel treatment of a people doomed to work the mines from birth stemmed from his hatred of the wealthy shareholders he was forced to report to.

Lacey and the young man were not alone. They were accompanied by an older man, white-haired and genteel, with the same blue eyes the boy had.

"Here, here, Lacey!" he protested. "There's no cause to bring the child grief!"

He seemed a nice man, but Marissa saw a pity in his eyes that cut her to the quick.

"I'm no coal rat!" she seethed, determined to rise on her own. As she did so, she made certain that the mud flew and that a few big globs hit Lacey. Lacey swore vehemently.

"Father," the boy protested, "I think this man's language quite unnecessary before a child."

"She's a trouble-causing coal rat, whatever her airs!" Lacey insisted. "And if you cause any more trouble with these fine people here, I'll take a switch to you myself tonight. And see that old uncle of yours thrown out!"

The white-haired man stiffened. "The girl can cause no more trouble. I'll not invest here. I'll not invest in human misery!" He walked away.

Lacey stared at Marissa furiously, then ran after the man. "Wait, sir," he called.

But the boy stayed. There was pity in his eyes, and Marissa couldn't help it, she hated him for it.

He tossed her a coin. A small gold one.

It would have probably fed them for a year.

"Buy yourself a new pinafore," he said.

He turned his back on her. Dismissing her.

After all, she was only a coal rat, needing a handout.

"Take this back!" she spat furiously, and she threw the coin at him. She fled home, very nearly in tears.

That night, when she went out to get water from the well, Mr. Lacey had caught hold of her. Before she could struggle free, he'd thrown her over his knee and given her several good stripes with a hickory switch.

With tears in her eyes, she bit him. Bit him hard. He screamed, and she was free.

Marissa never told her uncle.

Neither did Lacey.

And Marissa didn't even hate Lacey anymore than she already did. She understood Lacey. He was certainly no better than she was.

But she hated the boy.

She hated him for being impeccable. And she hated him for being handsome. And she hated him for his deep, rich voice with its American twang.

She hated him because he was free from the black miasma that hung over the town.

September, 1904

The second time she saw him was almost ten years later. She recognized him immediately, even though he had changed immensely. But it would be nearly another whole year before she would know his name.

And his place in her own destiny.

She had changed, too, of course. She was full grown. And she was no longer living in the coal village.

The thing she would remember most was his impatience. He was impatient even before he entered the house.

Leaving the squire's library with a tea tray, Marissa heard a thunder of horse's hooves on the driveway leading to the house. She had known that an important American acquaintance was coming to see the squire, but she had expected him to arrive in a carriage, or perhaps one of the new motorcars so popular among the fashionable and the rich. She certainly hadn't expected him to come tearing along upon the back of a big brown horse.

She paused to look through the ancient bay window of the manor house, and so she first saw him. He was very tall, and sat the horse well, and dismounted from the animal with an equal flare. His dark well-cut hair was wild from his ride. A waving lock of ebony curled over his forehead as he dropped the reins of the horse and nodded curtly to the squire's stable boy. He headed for the house with long, confident—no, arrogant!—strides, and his impatience was also visible in those strides. He was handsomely dressed, hatless, but wearing tight fawn riding breeches, a crimson vest and navy riding frock along with his high black boots. Marissa stared at him, remembering him, until he disappeared from her view as he leaped up the porch steps and rang—no, attacked!—the doorbell.

Katey, the squire's slim, elderly housekeeper, arrived to open the door. Marissa was left standing in the shadows outside the sliding doors of the squire's library. Poor Katey was nearly swept from her feet as the stranger stormed in. She stepped back hurriedly, and still he did not pause.

"Sir Thomas is expecting me," he said, his accent very much that of a Yank.

Marissa didn't wonder at that, for Sir Thomas had a multitude of friends and associates who were Americans, many of whom came to see him at the manor, but most of his friends were older men. This stranger was not old. Even his voice indicated that he was in his prime. It was deep, rich. The type that when spoken low still seemed to reverberate and take command.

And somehow enter into the body and soul. Marissa felt that voice, deep and masculine, as if it touched her like a fingertip, rippling along her spine.

It was the boy, she realized. The boy from the coal town. He, too, had grown up. He was very much a man, and had been for many years, it seemed.

As he strode past Katey, she must have moved in the wrong direction or made some other fateful mistake, for a second later, he was plowing into her. The tea tray went flying, and Marissa was thrown against the wall.

She cried out in distress, knowing the cost of the Chinese porcelain tea set.

Damn the man! He seemed ever to be her downfall!

She expected him to push past her, but he didn't. He paused, reaching not for the tea set, but into the shadows to touch her arm and pull her out into the light.

She stared into his eyes. As she remembered, they were very blue. Dark blue. Startling, striking, against the strong, tanned planes and angles of his face. A clean-shaven face, with a hard-set jaw, and a curious fire burning deep in the centers of those eyes. Eyes that roamed over her hastily, from head to toe, assessing her, she thought, as he would soon assess the tea service.

For damage only.

"Are you all right?" he demanded crisply. There was no recognition of her in his eyes. Who would remember a little coal rat from all those years ago?

And now she was merely the maid.

She nodded, jerking her arm free from his touch, suddenly nonplussed. Her heart was beating too rapidly, her breathing was coming too quickly, and although he was showing her—the maid—a definite courtesy, she resented that very concern.

Or did she hate the fact that he was looking at her with such detachment? Or that she was wearing a starched white apron over a very plain gray day dress and that what she considered to be her crowning glory—that carrot red hair turned into a headful of wild, red-gold hair that tumbled to her waist in long, thick waves—was completely hidden by her matching starched white cap?

She resented the very beating of her heart, the way his hand had felt upon her arm, hot, strong. She didn't understand any of her feelings, but she resented him from the depths of her heart for them all. For the way that his eyes flickered over her with that curious fire. For the way that they, like his voice, seemed to touch her, and send a lap of fire racing down the length of her spine.

Pride, she thought mournfully. Everyone told her she had too much of it. Her father had said so, her uncle, Sir Thomas, even Mary, who could find fault with no one.

"I'm fine!" she snapped. She realized that his gaze was locked with hers. He seemed, at least, intrigued with her eyes. To her discomfort, she flushed. She had been told that she had fine eyes. Green eyes, cat's eyes, so said Sir Thomas. Eyes with a startling rich color, darkly lashed and just slightly tilted. Eyes that demanded a second glance, Mary had once informed her. Far too imperious and flashing for a maid, and far too . . . well, sensual, Mary had also commented. Eyes that could arouse far too many emotions, too many passions, Sir Thomas had warned her.

Well, not in this man. Aye, he still stared at her. But there was nothing other than that flicker of fire and impatience in his own gaze. The lean, rugged planes of his face remained hard.

Then for a moment, it seemed that something flared between them. Something hotter than the fire that lurked in the deep recesses of his blue stare. Something that left her completely breathless, trembling, and angrier than ever.

No, she thought, and she didn't know what it was exactly that she denied.

But it didn't matter. Something harsh and cold and perhaps even anguished extinguished the fire in his gaze. He stepped back.

He has changed, she thought. The boy had not been so hard. This man was steel.

Despite herself, she wondered what had changed him.

Then she worried about herself once again.

She knelt to pick up the tea service. To her surprise, he knelt beside her and impatiently began picking up the pieces along with her. He was brisk. Before she had loaded up two pieces, he had the tray nearly loaded.

"I shall inform your employer that this was my fault," he said.

It was something, Marissa admitted grudgingly. But it *had* been his fault, completely, and she thought that she detected just a bit of condescension in his tone. She should have said thank you. She did not.

"As well you should," she said softly.

He had started toward the doors again. He turned and stared at her. Into her eyes, maybe really seeing them for the first time. Then he laughed. "Perhaps they do breed little tigresses here in the old English countryside, too. You should be in America, girl."

That blue gaze swept over her, then dismissed her, and then he was gone, striding into the library, closing the sliding pocket doors behind him.

Marissa swore softly beneath her breath and swung around with the shattered tea service. She paused, as did Katey, as they heard the stranger's voice rise and then fall. Katey smoothed her hands over her apron. Marissa offered her a wry smile, one that condemned the stranger. No one had a right to argue with the squire. No kinder man existed on the earth.

The exchange between the two men continued heatedly.

The doors slid open once again with a vengeance. "All right, all right! Have it your way—it will be as you wish!" the stranger exclaimed.

Now he was angry as well as impatient. He swept past Katey and Marissa without a backward glance, then paused in the hall, stiffening his spine and squaring his shoulders. He strode to the open doors of the library and stared in at the squire. His voice lowered, but none of the passion had left it. "All right, Sir Thomas. As God is my witness, I'd never cause you distress. But I warn you, sir, that you have gained little in your bargain. Little but the bitter shell of a man."

"I have gained you, my friend," the squire replied, his voice very light. "And that is all that I ask. I know the man." He smiled. "I'll see you at the club before you leave."

The stranger started to speak again, exploded with an impatient oath, then grinned. "Take care, you old goat," he said, and there was affection in the tone. He swiveled and was gone, out the beveled glass double front doors.

Katey and Marissa stared after him.

He left the door open and mounted the brown horse in a leap, that curl of ebony hair still haphazardly hung over his forehead.

And then his eyes touched Marissa once again. He inclined his head gravely, and a taunting smile seemed to curve his lip.

She wanted to scream. She wanted to race to the doorway and swear that she'd not end her days as a maid to be so easily disdained. She'd rise above them all, above everything. She'd die a lady, greater than any they had ever seen.

"Marissa, my dear. Come here, please. I'd dearly love it if you would read to me now. Something from Dickens, I think."

It was the squire calling her. The one man who could make her swallow her pride and bitterness and her longing.

"Aye, Sir Thomas. I shall come," she agreed quickly. But she was still staring at the door as Katey closed it.

Her lips tightened. Aye, she would die a lady, she swore it. She had already come far, she assured herself, and she brought her fingers before her face. Her hands were clean. They were not covered by the coal dust that had left her dearly beloved uncle hacking away night after night. She lived in the manor where brass and wood shone. Where the air was clean.

And she read. She read the classics, and she knew the great operas, and she could speak in a voice to mimic any woman who claimed to be her better.

"Marissa?"

Katey came for the tea tray and Marissa smiled gratefully. Then she entered Sir Thomas's study.

She tried to unwind her clenched fingers, to smile. But somehow, the stranger had left daggers in her heart. She wanted nothing more than to find some form of retaliation for the way he had made her feel.

I will rise above him, I swear it! she promised herself. I will be a lady so great that I can secretly smile and laugh at his discomfort.

But neither before nor after the time she spent reading with him did the squire mention the stranger. And by bedtime, when she could allow her lashes to fall over her eyes, she could still see his eyes upon her, the handsome bronzed and arrogant face. The curious touch of pain that had so briefly come to his gaze.

I will show him, she thought.

She was as determined as she had been as a child.

But in the morning, she smiled at her own foolishness. She'd never show him anything. She'd most probably never see him again.

But she would. Fate was destined to bring him back into her life. And indeed . . .

She would show him.

CHAPTER ONE

London, November, 1905

He's coming!" Mary cried with distress. She allowed the heavy velvet drape to fall into place over the window and looked anxiously at Marissa. Mary's pretty face was pale, and her warm brown eyes seemed huge against the narrow contours of her face. She had lost too much weight, Marissa thought.

It had been a terrible time for Mary, for the squire had died just a month previously after a long, painful illness. Both girls had spent endless hours at his side, doing whatever they could to ease his discomfort.

No matter what their differences, Mary had loved her father. Marissa, too, had loved the squire. They both missed him.

We loved him, we miss him! Marissa thought wryly. And here we stand, determined to undo his dying wish.

"Oh, my God!" Mary moaned, nervously lacing her fingers together. "Are you sure you will be all right?" she anxiously asked Marissa.

Marissa wasn't sure at all. Her breathing was coming too hard and too fast, and butterflies the size of the Jabberwock were flying pell-mell through her stomach. But she'd faced far harder tasks in her life, she was certain. And she had been told that for a brief and shining season, her mother had begun to rise as a young actress upon the London stage. Marissa knew she was a gifted mimic. The act she played today would be for Mary's benefit.

"I'm going to be fine," Marissa assured her friend.

She caught a glimpse of herself in the hotel suite's elegant free-standing mirror.

She would be fine. She certainly looked the part of the lady today. She was clad in one of Mary's beautiful white silk dresses. The tiny buttons were shimmering little pearls that ran from hem to throat and from wrist to elbow. Her skirt was floor length and in the height of fashion, narrow, conforming handsomely to her figure. Her petite boots were beige leather, and buttoned all along her ankles.

Her hair was swept up off her neck and held in place just above her nape by a gold barrette that matched the brooch at her throat.

She was elegant in the most casual way. Mary knew clothing.

Marissa folded her hands negligently and managed to smile at Mary. A tea service was already set on the oak coffee table for her convenience at the arrival of their guest. And she and Mary had played at tea for a long time now.

A very long time.

When Marissa's father, the Reverend Robert James Ayers, had been alive, Mary and Marissa lived close to one another. Robert Ayers had been the vicar at the beautiful old medieval church in the squire's parish.

Marissa had loved and admired him greatly. He had been destined for the coal mines like his brother Theo, but he had proven such a promising child that the vicar of Leominster parish, twenty miles away, had taken him in. Robert had loved to study, and he had grown to love the church, so he had taken his benefactor's place when Father Ridgefield died.

As the child of the local vicar, Marissa had enjoyed many advantages. She had been brought to the manor house for tea on her sixth birthday. Poor Mary had been forced to entertain her. Marissa had

presented herself as Miss Katherine Marissa Ayers of Leominster
Parish House, and had grown furious when she had seen the other
girl laughing. She had hopped up, ready to forget all about being a
lady and tearing out a bit of her hostess's hair, when Mary giggled
anew and held out her hand in protest of violence.

"I'm not laughing at you," she said. "Truly, I'm not! It's just funny,
that's all. You see, I'm really Katherine, too, Katherine Mary Ahearn.
Oh, don't you see. Our names are so very alike."

Marissa tossed her head. "I'm known as Marissa."

"And Father calls me Mary, so we shan't have a bit of confusion.
Please, I'm really glad that you've come. I'm so very lonely so often."

Marissa had played with Mary often enough, but then her father
had died. And with his death she also lost Mary, for she had gone to live
with Theo in the mining town. She had hated her new life, but she had
loved Theo, a wonderful man, uneducated, unable to read, but with a
charming smile, laughing eyes and a way of telling a small girl a story
that could make her smile and fall asleep curled into his strong arms.

Life was much worse for other children, Marissa knew that well.
Especially orphans. Many of them were beaten and abused by their
relatives or stepparents. She had known nothing but kindness.

Kindness . . . and coal dust.

She had wanted to repay her Uncle Theo in any way she could.
And so she had swept and cleaned and cooked, and had done her
very best to keep his clothing laundered and mended, and to make
their small cottage a home. But when her lessons ended she had
known she would soon be sent off to work, for there was no other
way for a child of her class.

During the days, though, she had dreamed.

Especially after she had seen the strange boy with his impeccably
clean clothing.

She had dreamed of the grand manor where she had studied
with Mary. And she had remembered Mary's delicate white hands,
and the furniture that never reeked of coal dust.

And then one Sunday, when Uncle Theo and she had been able
to borrow a pony cart and had taken the long drive to Leominster

instead of attending the small chapel in the coal town, she had seen Mary again. Standing by the squire's side, she was tall and lovely with her burnished brown hair and warm brown eyes and her beautiful fur-trimmed winter coat. She had grown up. They had both grown up, into young women. They were nearly fifteen.

Marissa looked at her hands, curled around her prayer book. Her nails were broken and ugly, her hands chapped.

And she knew that Mary's hands would still be small and elegant and lovely.

When the last blessing was bestowed, Marissa turned to flee. She did not want to see Mary.

But it seemed that the squire had seen her, for she had barely exited the ancient church with its spires and saints and gargoyles when his hand fell warmly upon her shoulder.

"Why, 'tis you, Marissa, child! We were heartily bereaved at the death of your father. And we missed you dearly, Mary and I. How have you been keeping yourself?"

"Quite well, Squire, thank you," Marissa murmured, wishing she could run. But Mary was behind him. Marissa thought she would lift her elegant nose and turn away from the coal child Marissa had become. But Mary stepped forward and hugged her enthusiastically. "Marissa!"

Before the day was out, Marissa and Uncle Theo had been taken to the manor for tea. Uncle Theo had stared around uncomfortably, and he had spilled his tea and used all the wrong silver, and the blackness of coal that the years had etched into his long bony fingers was glaringly dark against the Ahearns' elegant china, but it didn't seem to matter. Marissa could remember having tea as a child, and then she was ashamed that she could judge an uncle who had been so very kind to her. And seeing Sir Thomas and Mary, she swallowed hard and thought she had truly learned a lesson. Class and elegance did not lie in upturned noses, but rather in the graciousness inherent in these people. When she said thank you and goodbye to Mary and the squire, Marissa came as close to being humble as she had in all her life.

Three days later, the squire visited them in the squalid little coal town, and he suggested that Marissa should come to live in the manor house. Theo refused charity, but Sir Thomas promised that she would be a maid and earn her keep—and her education.

"I cannot give me niece away," Theo said with deep emotion.

"And would you have her grow to womanhood here, marry a miner and watch him die of the black lung only to struggle on to raise an army of little ones herself? I don't ask you to give her away, good man. I ask you only to give her a wee bit of opportunity. I say it from my heart, for my daughter and myself. And in memory of your good brother.

"Good Lord, man! Would that I had authority over this place! I despise the way it is run. But Ayers, man, I can help your girl. Perhaps I haven't the power to change the mine, but I do have the power to change her life. And we are still close enough that she can see you often. She loves you, and she will not be far."

Theo hesitated for only a moment, seeing the earnest appeal in Sir Thomas's eyes. "Go on out, Marissa," Uncle Theo told her. "The squire and I have much to discuss."

When she came back, a bargain had been struck. She would live at the manor during the week, she would work, she would receive a salary, and she would resume her education.

There was nothing like it. Nothing like it on earth. She moved into the manor, into a room in the attic. It was a small room, but it was hers—all her own. Six days a week she worked and studied, and on the seventh, the Sabbath day, she went to church and then she went home to her uncle. She never went empty-handed. Thanks to the squire, she brought hams and fowl and fruit and vegetables and fresh-baked breads. And Uncle Theo would have his friends over, and they would all share in the largesse. She would read to Theo and his cronies, and sometimes she would try to teach some of the little blackened urchins of the other mine families, and she knew that her uncle was very proud of her, and she was proud herself.

She had escaped the coal dust.

Living with the squire and Mary was easy, despite the fact that she worked very hard and studied even harder in her determination to become a lady. Most of the time, she was happy. Very happy. Mary was her employer, but she was also her very best friend. They dreamed together, Mary of love, Marissa of riches grand enough to feed the entire mining population. Marissa learned her mannerisms from Mary, and she copied Mary's accent. She excelled Mary in their history classes, mostly because she loved the tales of brave seafarers and pilgrims and the London Company and all those others who had set out to forge a new life. She was also exceedingly quick with mathematics, since math was useful with money, and she knew that little could be done without that commodity.

She had always thought that the town by the manor was so big, compared with the small community of the village. With Mary, she traveled farther, to the county seat of York. She was fascinated to see the wall that the Romans had built still standing, and she marveled at the magnificent York Minster Cathedral, awed by the age and grandeur, so close to the squalor in which she had lived.

It was as if the cloud that hung over the coal village had been a prison of a kind. It had kept her from viewing anything beyond it.

The years had passed, and most of the time she was pleased. And proud.

Most of the time . . .

Marissa frowned, wondering what uncomfortable thought hovered in the dark corners of her mind. Only upon occasion did she feel any less the lady than Mary herself. She could hold her head high in any company, and she had been attending the opera and the theater with Mary and certain acquaintances to perfect her current masquerade.

But every once in a while . . .

Then she remembered. Blue eyes touching her, racing over her, seeming to see her for what she really was. A British maid graced with a burning will to succeed, and a kind-hearted employer and the friendship of his daughter. Those eyes had made her feel so uncomfortable. Vulnerable and naked, as if they could strip away every pretense. They had done so to her when she had been a child, and when she had been a woman. They had made her feel hot and flushed and uneasy. And even now, when she most needed her confidence, they seemed to intrude upon the moment.

"Mary, maybe we're making a mistake! Maybe this fellow is kind, and we should be honest and truthful. Maybe he wants a ward even less than you want a guardian! You should deal with this man Tremayne yourself," she murmured suddenly.

Mary's dark warm eyes clouded with pain. She hurried anxiously across the handsome Victorian parlor of their suite. "Guardian! And I'm nineteen already. How could my father have done such a thing!"

"He loved you very much, Mary," Marissa supplied gently. "Truly, I don't think that he meant to hurt you. Mary, your health has never been good, and you've always been so kind and compassionate. I'm certain that your father was afraid that perhaps a fortune hunter might take advantage of that very loving nature of yours. And he might have swindled all your money from you. And left you. Oh, Mary, he was mistaken, but he was a good man. And he did love you!"

"If only I had told him the truth!"

Marissa didn't think that it would have helped any for Mary to have told her father the truth.

Mary was in love, and she had been in love for well over a year. The problem was that she was in love with a young Irish clerk named Jimmy O'Brien.

Marissa liked Jimmy, very much. If she hadn't liked him so much, and liked him from the very beginning, she wouldn't have helped Mary this far.

Though indeed, there were times when Marissa still considered Mary to be a fool.

Jimmy was a fine man. He was a struggler, a survivor, like Marissa was herself. He had left Ireland with little more than a good head for figures and a determination that no more potatoes could be eked from his meagre portion of land. He had a sense for fine wools, and he had managed to obtain a good, decent job with a fine merchant. He bought for his employer, and his eye was keen, and the merchant's shop was doing much better under Jimmy's care.

Mary and Jimmy had met, and fallen in love. The words of warning that her father would never accept the hardworking young merchant had not done a thing to turn Mary aside from her reckless affair. She had never told her father about Jimmy O'Brien, and Marissa had covered for her again and again when she had left the house in sunshine or twilight to carry on her liaison.

"Mary!" Marissa had warned her repeatedly. "You've grown up with everything you might wish handed to you on a very elegant silver platter! You're accustomed to servants and ease. Mary!" She had grabbed Mary's small delicate hands with their silk-soft flesh. "Mary, life cannot be so easy if you elope and marry this man!"

"You don't understand what it is to be in love, Marissa," Mary had assured her. "I would work for him, I would die for him!"

Such vehemence and passion from shy Mary were quite impressive. But Marissa merely replied, "And you don't know what it is to watch children starve."

Their argument became moot, for it was then that they discovered the squire was ill. And it was not too long before the doctors informed Mary that there was no hope, her father was going to die.

That night she and Marissa had grown closer than ever, crying, hugging one another through the night for what little comfort they could offer one another.

Mary never told her father about Jimmy O'Brien. There was no need to distress a sick man so. When the squire had whispered his last goodbye and Mary had learned to live with the loss, then someday she would marry Jimmy. And in the meantime, Jimmy O'Brien stood by her side. In those weary hours when Mary's father's illness was greatest, Marissa would tend to the squire, and Mary would disappear with her lover. He gave her a comfort that not even Marissa could provide.

Squire Ahearn breathed his last on a beautiful late summer morning. The sun was shining; the daffodils were in full bloom. Both Mary and Marissa had sat beside him at the huge bay window, and he had breathed in the fresh scent of the day, closed his eyes and died.

And three days later, after a very proper funeral, he had been laid to rest in the bosom of his ancestral tomb. Despite the knowledge of certain death, Mary and Marissa had grieved deeply, barely managing to speak to one another for days.

Marissa's Uncle Theo had been heartily worried about her, and so, when Sir Thomas had been dead about ten days, she had left to spend time with Theo at his cottage. She had cleaned away more coal dust, and she had convinced him that Mary was raising her to an income so high that Theo no longer needed to work in the mine. His cough was bad, hacking, almost a continual thing, and Marissa could not bear it. She had just watched Sir Thomas die and she was not about to let Theo follow him. She knew that she told the truth. Mary would be a wealthy woman now, and she could provide for herself and Jimmy and, in truth, offer Marissa a very fine salary, indeed.

But when Marissa had come back to the manor, she had discovered Mary as pale as death, sitting before the fire in her father's library, staring at the flames but not seeing a thing. She had rushed to her friend in fear, and had found Mary's flesh as cold as ice despite the warmth of the fire. Marissa had cried out, hurrying for the sherry. She had forced a sip through Mary's lips, and her friend had looked at her at last, huge teardrops forming in her eyes and falling down her cheeks.

"Oh, Marissa!"

"What, Mary, what is it? I am here!"

"Oh, my God, Marissa! How could he!"

"How could who do what?"

"Oh, Marissa!"

"Mary, Mary, calm down now. Please, you must tell me what has happened! It's Jimmy, is it? What has he done? Why, if he's hurt you—"

"Jimmy would never hurt me!" Mary cried.

Marissa breathed a sigh of relief. "Mary, then please, what has happened?"

"It's father."

But the squire was dead and buried, and Marissa could not begin to understand what had happened.

"Mary—"

"Oh, how could he have done such a thing to me!"

"Mary, what in God's name has he done!"

And at last Mary began to talk, trying to explain the substance of her father's will. Mary had not yet reached her majority. And so her father had arranged for a guardian, someone to control her fortune until she had reached her twenty-fifth birthday. Someone Mary did not even know, one of his American associates. And there was even more to it than that.

"What?" Marissa demanded blankly, trying to assimilate everything Mary was saying.

"He betrothed me to this man!"

"No one can force you to wed this man, Mary."

Mary groaned anew, burying her face in her elbow where it lay upon the arm of the chair. "Marissa, if I do not wed him, he is free to control my money until my thirtieth birthday! He will be free to take over the house—everything!"

"It can't be so!" Marissa assured her, and Mary looked to her with hope. "We'll talk with your father's solicitors and they'll fix things for you."

"No, they won't! They'll be loyal to my father. I don't even know any of his solicitors. Father never involved me with business, and I never worried about it."

"We'll fix things."

"I can't talk to his solicitors."

"I can. I'll call them, and say that I am you!"

Marissa did so, and she was heartily disturbed. Everything that Mary had told her was true. They were in a desperate situation.

The squire had even arranged for a special marriage license from the Archbishop of Canterbury. No banns needed to be cried if Mary chose to marry her guardian. The deed could be done immediately so that the man need hardly stay away from his business in America.

To Jimmy O'Brien's credit, he swore that night that the money meant nothing to him, nothing at all. He loved Mary. His place was nothing but a hovel now, but he would work hard, so hard, and he would save the money to buy his own shop. He would live with Mary anywhere, and with their faith in their love, they would survive.

The two held hands before the fire in the squire's library and stared into the flames, bliss in their eyes. Marissa, with her own problems facing her, left the two of them alone.

But by the next week, Mary had caught a fever. She was desperately ill, and Marissa spent all her time at her bedside, bargaining with God, pleading, promising that she would do anything to save her. Jimmy, too, sat by her bedside.

Mary had not just rescued Marissa from the coal dust. She had been her friend. Marissa had never forgotten the bitterness of those years, or ceased to long for something better for the poor people there. She was afraid that she would carry some of the bitterness and hatred to her grave. But Mary had given her hope, and allowed her dreams to fly.

There was little that Marissa would not do for her.

Mary took a turn for the better. The doctor warned Marissa then that Mary was not strong, that she needed to take the gravest care. She must avoid chills, she must not work too hard.

Jimmy and Marissa were desolate. Jimmy did love Mary, enough to give her up. There was no way for Mary to go and live in a hovel—whether love flourished or no.

"I can't have her, and I can't give her up," Jimmy said, his freckled face lean and haggard and anguished. "I can't leave my Mary!"

"I can get a new job, I can do something—" Marissa began.

"And support us all?" Jimmy scoffed. "Ah, Marissa, you are spirit and strength and wonderful courage and beauty, and I love you as deeply as does Mary. But Marissa! You've your uncle to care for. There's nothing left to be done. Aye, but there is! I shall wait for Mary if needs be until we both be forty, fifty or sixty! I'd wait until my grave!"

Marissa almost smiled, he was so earnest and so dramatic.

"Jimmy, that much waiting would do in us all! No, there has to be some way, something that we can do!"

They didn't come up with any conclusions that night. And Marissa went to bed wondering once again how the squire could have promised his young and beautiful daughter to some old and withered crony, no matter how wealthy and prominent the man might be.

It was the next day when the idea—outrageous as it was—occurred to Marissa.

Mary lay in her bed, silent, her face pale, her cheeks gaunt. Jimmy idly stood by the fireplace, teasing the flames with the poker, and Marissa sat by Mary's bed, silent, too, no longer pretending to read.

"Mary! I can do it!"

"What?"

"I can be you!"

"Oh, my Lord!" Mary breathed. Jimmy stared at them as if Mary's fever had caused them both to go daft.

"Oh, my God! Could we pull it off?" Marissa demanded.

"I know we could. I've never met this man. He's a Californian, or something American like that."

"But everyone here would know us—" Marissa began, then she laughed. "Mary! The solicitors already think I'm you. Oh, we can do this! We'll plan very carefully. We'll go to London! We'll meet him in London."

"Can we . . . ?"

"Yes! We'll start right away. We'll agree to the terms with the solicitors. We'll sign everything here, in York. And then we'll keep the solicitors out of it when we meet this American in London!"

"And our names are so very close!" Mary laughed. "How convenient!"

"What are you two saying?" Jimmy demanded.

"Marissa will take my place!" Mary explained happily.

"No, we can't have Marissa marry some ancient old being for ourselves, Mary. We can't," he said. And he was firm.

"I don't have to marry him, Jimmy," Marissa said calmly. "Just be a dutiful ward. Mary's allowance will be released to me until her thirtieth birthday. And then Mary will receive her inheritance and everything will be fine."

"Will it?" Jimmy demanded, walking over to Marissa. "And what of you? Will you spend ten years of your life alone? What of love for yourself, Marissa? What happens when you meet the man who can give you all that your heart desires?"

Marissa felt a coldness seal itself around her heart. "Jimmy—"

"You know nothing of love, as yet," he interrupted her softly.

"I know a great deal about hunger and death," she reminded him. "If I can take care of Theo, then I will be fine. And, Mary willing, we can even provide a small school there so a few other children may escape. Jimmy, I will be fine!"

Jimmy never was pleased with the plan. He fought it night and day. But Mary and Marissa had made up their minds, and the plan was put into action.

When they received the first correspondence from old Ian Tremayne—a short, curt missive to inform Mary when he would be coming—they were ready with their reply. Mary and Marissa composed it together, and Marissa wrote out the note in her flowing script. They had decided it would be necessary for Mr. Tremayne to become accustomed to Marissa's writing. Miss Katherine Ahearn fully understood the conditions of her father's will and was ready to abide by them upon her guardian's arrival.

The solicitors were informed that Miss Ahearn would abide by all her father's wishes, and Marissa and Mary learned that it wasn't necessary for Mary to sign papers—only Ian Tremayne's signature was necessary to release her funds. Mr. Tremayne already had her funds in his trust, and all other papers.

The solicitors indicated that they were more than willing to be present for her first meeting with Mr. Tremayne, as they fully understood the awkwardness of the situation.

They were impressed with the calm, cool maturity of the young lady who informed them that it would not be necessary at all.

And that was how they came to this day . . . now . . . waiting.

There was a knock at the door. Mary stared at Marissa in pure panic, and Marissa managed to smile at last. "It's all right, I promise, Mary. Think about it. I have always been able to charm old men. Mary! We made it past the solicitors! Now go on with you, get into the bedroom."

Mary sped past her, still white.

The knock came again, louder. There was an impatient note to it.

Then Marissa heard the voice. Deep, resonant, confident, the kind of male voice that spoke of authority and power. The kind that could enter the lower spine and send spirals racing up and down the back.

"Miss Ahearn! Are you there?"

The first twinge of unease seized her. She knew the voice. Knew it very well. It had even haunted her dreams, it had intruded upon her spinning her golden webs of aspirations, her hopes of glory.

She did not touch the door, but suddenly it burst open.

Him . . .

The tall stranger with the startling deep blue eyes. The eyes that touched her the way his voice touched her. Raking over her with a blaze of fire.

Arrogant, powerful, sharp. How could she possibly play out a deception upon this man with his hardened gaze, his determined manner, his ruthlessness? No anger or impatience with herself could quell the trembling at the pit of her stomach.

It was the surprise, she assured herself. The surprise and the fear. He would know her, he would remember.

"Miss Ahearn! I am Ian Tremayne."

Impatience flashed through his cobalt gaze when she still failed to reply. "I have come to fetch you home. Is something wrong? Are you all right?"

No, no, no! She was not all right at all! This was not an older gentleman to be twisted and swayed to her own will.

This was the lad who had carelessly tossed a coin her way. The brash man who had sent her tray crashing to the floor, who had laughed and told her that she should come to America.

This was the stranger who had broken into her dreams and reminded her that beneath her veneer she was a little coal rat.

The stranger had a name at long last.

Ian.

Ian Tremayne.

And already, his sharp blue eyes were narrowing. With recognition? She could not tell. Oh, no! He could not remember her! She had been a child that first time! And later, she had been a maid in a shadowed hallway. He could not remember, he could not!

"Miss Ahearn?"

"Yes, yes! I—I am Katherine!" she said, having found her voice at last. She struggled for a smile, but it eluded her. She managed to raise her hand, and he lifted it to his lips and brushed it with a cordial kiss.

A kiss that burned her fingers. That brushed and yet seared her flesh.

"Please sit down, if you will, ma'am. We've much to discuss of your father's will. We shall try to handle this all amicably since I guarantee you it was none of my own doing."

She was still standing in front of the settee. She seemed unable to move. Suddenly his hands were upon her shoulders, pressing her down to the settee. Then his voice came so close to her ear that the whisper of his breath touched her flesh. "It was not of my doing, but I gave Sir Thomas my word that I would carry out his wishes. And I intend to carry them out, my dear, I feel obliged to tell you. And I will do so, Miss Ahearn. I promise, I will do so."

CHAPTER TWO

He was sitting beside her, easily, relaxed, staring at her pointedly, rudely, with no apology. She might still be trembling inwardly, but Marissa would be damned if she would let him intimidate her again. She lifted her chin slightly to speak. She remembered the mannerisms of every one of Mary's rich and imperious friends, and she spoke softly, yet with her own form of arrogance.

"Mr. Tremayne, no one was more shocked than I that my father should have made such an arrangement. We were very close. Obviously, I have no wish for a guardian. Any more than you, sir, seem to have a wish to be one. With a minimum of effort, I'm sure we can reach an amicable understanding."

His brows arched with a certain amusement, then the curl of a smile suddenly faded and he was frowning. "Didn't we meet before?"

"No, Mr. Tremayne, we did not. I was not at the manor the day you called."

"How do you know I called?"

"I—I assumed you called upon Father some time—he had not left this country for years before his death."

"Ah," he murmured. Then he was up, striding the small parlor once again. "I shall wish to return to San Francisco as quickly as possible. Is that agreeable with you?"

She shrugged. "If it's necessary. Of course, I understand that a young woman could be quite a burden to you. If you wish, I've no problems with the idea of your administering the estate from America while I remain in London."

He smiled again, slowly, and for a moment, there was a certain tenderness about his gaze that softened the rugged planes of his face and made him appear very handsome. "My dear Miss Ahearn," he murmured softly, "I did not wish this responsibility, yet I take it very seriously. I would not dream of leaving a young lady of your tender age in such a city unattended."

"I would not be unattended. I have very good friends."

"So I imagine," he said wryly. Then he paused once again. "Are you sure we have not met?"

"Quite sure," Marissa said, locking her teeth against the sudden bitterness that filled her. No, he would not remember her. She had simply been the dirtied child in the mud. The maid with her hair pulled back and her face in the shadows. She was safe.

But a small tremor shook her, and she lowered her lashes quickly. "I can assure you, Mr. Tremayne, that I am a very responsible young woman, independent and able to care for myself. You could leave me with all good conscience."

"No," he said flatly. She raised her eyes to his cobalt blue ones and found them hard and emphatic. She suddenly longed to throw something at him. He brooked no opposition to his will—indeed, he would not even listen to reason!

But that was all right. They had all agreed that they would move to America if necessary. Jimmy could start up his business in California. They could live very near; it would work out!

"If you intend to argue with me further, Miss Ahearn, please save us both the time and effort. I had not expected a wayward child, yet if you persist . . ."

He was threatening her! she thought. His tone was low and

pleasant, but there was definite threat behind it. If she persisted, what? she wondered indignantly.

Once again her chin rose. She wanted to argue for the sake of argument, just to prove to him that she'd be damned if she was about to follow some Yank's orders.

But it probably wasn't the time for an argument. Discretion, Sir Thomas had assured her, was often the better part of valor.

"I had thought to make this as convenient as possible for both of us," Marissa said sweetly. "But if that is not your wish . . ."

"Girl, this hasn't been convenient from the start," he said impatiently, then exhaled slowly and apologized. "I'm sorry. I'm sure that this is a shock for you. You have recently lost your father and been informed of a guardian. And of course the terms of his will were quite stringent." Once again, there was a slight glimmer of compassion and tenderness in his eyes, yet it seemed quickly to be gone. Once again, despite her own predicament, Marissa found herself wondering about the man. What had given him that edge of hardness, and even ruthlessness, when he could be so gentle at times?

Times when he was not crossed, she reminded herself. She would have to take great care with him.

She found herself studying him again. He was tall, very tall, and well built, with broad shoulders and lean hips. He wore his clothing with a casual flair. Today he was in black boots, form-hugging black riding breeches, crisp white pleated shirt, black velvet jacket, silk vest and cravat. His body, she was certain, was well muscled beneath the fabric, yet it was his face that made him so imposing a man. His features were handsome, well-drawn and well-defined. He was clean-shaven with arched, clean dark brows, and his chin was firm while his cheekbones were high and well set. His mouth was generous and full, a sensual mouth when it curled to a smile, a forbidding one when it was set in a line. His eyes were his greatest power. They seemed to carry endless years of wisdom. Sometimes weary, sometimes as cold as ice, sometimes alive with a hint of humor, but mercurial, ever changing. He was somewhere around thirty years old, she thought, yet his eyes were much, much older.

"Stringent, indeed," Marissa murmured.

"And I repeat, very definitely not of my choosing," he said. His gaze left her. With his hands locked together at the base of his spine, he paced the room once again. "I cannot be gone long. My business concerns are varied and demanding, and it was not easy to get away. I plan to head back as soon as all necessary arrangements are made. You will be more at your leisure, and I do understand that you might need time to say your goodbyes to friends, to close up the manor and—and to move to a place nearly half a globe away. I think, however, that once you have made the move, you will find yourself pleasantly surprised. My house is large and spacious, I am nearly never around, and when I am, I have a tendency to keep to myself." The last was said somewhat bitterly, and again she found herself wondering about the man. "There is nothing I can do about the fact that none of your money is to be released to you unless the terms of the will are carried out exactly—"

"What?" Marissa was instantly on her feet. "What are you talking about?"

"I thought you understood. Your funds are to be held in trust until your twenty-fifth birthday should you agree to the marriage, and held until your thirtieth birthday if you should not."

"Yes, yes, I do understand that! But there was to be an allowance!"

He shook his head impatiently. "The allowance holds true only if you choose to marry. I'm sorry. I thought you understood that. But I am a wealthy man, Katherine, and I do not intend that you should suffer."

Taking anything from him would be suffering, she was certain of it. She was already deceiving him. If he ever discovered the truth . . .

She sat, suddenly so weary that she could not stand it.

What now of Jimmy? He was a good man. With a little help, he could have been a fine merchant, perhaps a wealthy man in his own right.

And what of Uncle Theo?

And Mary . . . Oh, dear God, could Mary bear another shock?

"There must be something wrong. Terribly wrong. I have seen the lawyers—"

"You must see them again if you still do not comprehend the will," he said, irritation touching his tone. "I shall try to explain it very simply. If you agree to the marriage, your allowance is to begin upon the date of the nuptials, and you will receive the bulk of your inheritance upon your twenty-fifth birthday. If you choose not to marry, then your allowance will begin upon your twenty-fifth birthday, and the bulk of the inheritance will become yours upon your thirtieth birthday. Do you understand?"

"I cannot live like that!" she gasped.

He paused, staring at her, and one of his ink dark brows raised high. "You will have to, Miss Ahearn."

"But I cannot! I've my personal expenses—"

"You will be provided with a home, and I shall, of course, do my best to see to your needs."

"I don't want your charity!" she exclaimed. "Oh, dear God!" she murmured suddenly, and sank back to the settee. That she had even tried to be decent to this man when everything was a disaster! She looked up at him sharply. "We must break the will!"

"There is no way to break the will, I assure you," he said calmly. "The squire was entirely of his right mind throughout his entire life."

"How could he have done such a thing!" Marissa whispered.

Ian Tremayne sighed, and she thought that he was very carefully swallowing his impatience and irritation. He came to the settee and sat beside her. He took her hands in his and for one wild moment she wanted desperately to snatch her fingers free. There was so much power in his touch, so much heat. And he was close beside her, his knees touching hers, his breath once again fanning her face with warmth, his eyes seeming to blaze through her and read her heart. Could he see the deception there?

Did it matter anymore?

"I believe, Katherine, that your father thought you were involved with a rather inappropriate young man. He was worried about you. He felt that your health was weak, that you might destroy your own life."

"He knew!" she gasped, and then she colored, because he was staring at her again, and she realized that he thought *she* had been involved in an affair with an inappropriate man.

Well, it wasn't her, and Jimmy was far from inappropriate! Fury filled her because she was quite certain that he was condemning her with his dark blue gaze.

He dropped her hands and stood. "Yes," he said wryly, "I believe he knew something. Is your affair over?"

Her cheeks flamed once again. It was none of this man's business. Well, at least she could tell the truth.

"That is none of your business whatsoever, Mr. Tremayne."

"If not now, Miss Ahearn, it will certainly be so once we travel to the States."

She didn't respond, but sat stiffly. "I don't believe that we shall be doing so now," she said at last.

"I beg your pardon, Katherine?"

"Marissa," she said. She smiled tightly. "It is Katherine, initial M, Mr. Tremayne, and I am known as Marissa."

"Marissa," he murmured. She was surprised at the soft way her name whirled upon his tongue.

"There is no reason for me to come with you," she said wearily.

"There is every reason for you to do so. I am your guardian. And I command it."

She looked at him with a certain amusement. "And do you intend to shackle me to your side, Mr. Tremayne? To pull me across the ocean in chains?"

"Trust me," he said pleasantly. "I shall see to it that you come, one way or another. It seems ever more important that I attend to your father's trust in me."

"I cannot go!" she whispered almost desperately.

Once again, he spoke gently. "It will not be so bad. As I have told you, I am scarcely about. I've my own past to live with, and I am not a man anxious for company. I will see to your needs—"

She was on her feet once again. "How could you ever agree to such a setup!" she demanded furiously.

She heard the sharp intake of his breath and saw the angry narrowing of his eyes. "I agreed to take on a guardianship. I knew nothing of the stipulations of the will. Yet I have told you—"

"You agreed to a betrothal."

"Yes, I did, for your father seemed desperate. But he knew that I had no intent of marrying again, that I wanted nothing to do with a new wife. Perhaps that was why the stipulation. He assumed you would be quite safe in my care until you reached your own maturity. And as I have said, it is inconsequential. I can provide—"

"But you cannot provide!" she interrupted him on a husky note, and then she fell silent as his sharp gaze queried her. She could not tell him that she didn't want to accept his charity with one breath and then inform him with the next that she was afraid his charity would not be sufficient to cover her needs.

What in God's name was she going to do? It seemed they were all doomed. Even playing this elaborate pretense had not altered their situation.

"Miss Ahearn," he said, suddenly very impatient, "I am afraid that I am tiring of hearing what you can and cannot do. I have stated the facts to you and they are what they are. Dear Lord, but this could have been easy, and here I am bickering with a whining child—"

"I have never, never whined in my entire life!" Marissa spat out, her hands clenched at her side. And then she realized how close she had moved to him, and felt again the sizzling heat that seemed to emanate from the man. She saw the furious tick of his pulse against the hard cords of his throat and felt the cobalt blaze of his eyes hard upon her. She wanted to back away. She dared not show such a sign of defeat, and yet she wished desperately that she had managed to handle things with more cool dignity and much less drama and passion.

"Nor," she said softly, "am I a child."

"Well, we shall see, won't we?" he asked her quietly. "I pray that you are right."

"And what, exactly, does that mean, sir?" she demanded coolly.

"It means that you are exasperating me beyond all sensible bounds, young woman. I have business in the city. And at this moment I'm afraid I need to bind you to my side as I go about it, for my fears concerning you—Sir Thomas's fears—seem quite justified."

She realized suddenly that he was serious, that he seemed to think she might be ready to run off with the lover she had seemed to admit that she had. She shook her head vehemently.

"You need fear nothing concerning me."

"Needn't I?" He walked around her once again, and she felt his eyes surveying her as he did so. "What guarantees do I have that you will not run the moment my back is turned?"

"There is no guarantee," she said softly, uneasily, whirling to face him. Then she smiled bitterly. "Truly, I have nowhere left to run."

"Make things difficult for me, Miss Ahearn," he said in a tone so soft it might have been gentle, "and I swear, I shall hunt you down. I've neither the time nor the inclination for this, and if you force my hand, I swear that it can be a ruthless one."

"Of that I've no doubt," Marissa murmured.

"Good," he said after a moment, "then we are understood." He headed for the door and paused before opening it. "I will be back tomorrow evening. We will finalize our plans then."

He did not say goodbye. He exited, closing the door firmly behind him.

Seconds later Marissa heard Mary's cry of anguish coming from the bedroom, then her friend rushed out, pale, nearly hysterical.

"Oh, Marissa! What shall we do now? There is nothing left to do. Dear Lord, I must find Jimmy! I must marry him immediately before he finds out! I don't care about the future, oh, I swear! I can live anywhere, I can do anything. I can find a position as a governess. That would not be too taxing upon my health. I will live in a cottage or a hovel or a one-room flat, I will scrub it, I will—"

"Die in it, most likely," Marissa said bluntly, wearily. "Mary, stop. Take hold of yourself. You are barely over your last bout of fever. You are talking nonsense, and Jimmy loves you far too much to allow it."

"I won't let him know!" Mary cried passionately, her warm brown eyes glistening with the hint of tears. "I love him, Marissa! There is nothing else to do!"

"Mary, listen to me! Your health—"

"No, Marissa, you listen to me!"

"You've lost touch with the realities of life—"

"No, Marissa, you have! Life cheated you when you were a child, so now you would cheat it. You truly don't understand what it is to love someone. Oh, Marissa! I would rather have one moment of ecstasy with Jimmy than a lifetime of mediocrity with any other man. Oh, don't you see that!"

Mary sank down on the settee facing Marissa. The tears streamed down her face. "There is nothing left, nothing left at all!" she said.

Marissa found herself patting Mary's shoulder as her friend sobbed.

"We've lost," Mary groaned. "We've lost everything." Then she added passionately, "I hate my father, oh, God, I hate my father!"

"Mary, hush! The squire is dead, and you loved him dearly."

"I might as well be dead."

"Don't say that!"

"It's true."

"No, no, there is a way out of this, I know it," Marissa assured her. But Mary was so desolate that Marissa sought desperately for some further words of encouragement. "We must call the solicitors again in the morning. I'm sure Tremayne must be wrong about this allowance stipulation."

"Father knew about Jimmy!" Mary whispered. "And he had no faith in me!"

"Let's have a sherry, shall we?" Marissa said. "And we'll work on this in the morning."

It took her some time, but she coaxed Mary into taking a drink, and then into bed. Late that night the proprietress of the hotel tapped on the door to say that there was a phone call for Miss Katherine Ahearn downstairs.

Marissa checked to see that Mary slept peacefully, then she hurriedly descended the stairs to reach the establishment's single phone. The connection was very bad, but at length Marissa heard Jimmy's voice.

And she lied. She told him that things were fine, she had met Tremayne. She told Jimmy that the man was young and gentle and very kind, and that she could foresee no difficulties. "I can take care of things, Jimmy, I promise," she vowed.

Then she wondered what she had done, for there was no truth to her words.

"You mustn't sacrifice so much for us, Marissa Ayers," he warned her firmly.

"Jimmy, I'm not sacrificing anything." He didn't believe her. "My Uncle Theo is at stake here, too, Jimmy. My own livelihood."

He laughed softly. "I don't think so, Marissa. You've incredible strength and will. You put the lot of us to shame. And I will not have you doing anything to hurt yourself, and neither would Mary."

"I won't do anything to hurt myself," she said.

"You don't owe us this."

"But I do," she murmured. Jimmy might not understand. Maybe there was no one who could understand.

Mary and Sir Thomas had taken her away from the coal mines. She owed Mary everything. "Jimmy, please be patient. I'll be in touch soon," she promised vaguely.

She stood against the wall, the ear piece still in her hands. For a moment she glanced at it, marveling at the ingenuity of Mr. Bell, who had invented the amazing piece of equipment.

Then she replaced it and grew amazed at herself instead.

Why had she lied to Jimmy?

Because she could not bear that they could not make things work. Nor could she listen to Mary's dreams of ecstasy. She was the one living in the real world, and she knew it.

She had seen the brutal cruelties of that real world often enough, and it seemed that the best way through them was to keep one's gaze ever upward and climb over them.

She sighed and closed her eyes. There had to be a way to make it work.

Moments later she opened her eyes and resolutely made her way up the stairs.

Aye, indeed, there was a way to make it work. And so help her, she would see that it did.

She had to. She loved Mary; she loved Jimmy.

And she could already smell the scent of coal dust sweeping around her ankles.

It was very late when Ian Tremayne at last rode through the almost silent streets near Hyde Park to reach the boardinghouse where he was staying. Most carriages were already off the road, and he hadn't seen a single motorcar.

The vehicles hadn't caught on as quickly in London as they had in the States. Of course, in the States, things were still in a mess because of the growing number of horseless carriages and more traditional transportation. Just before he had left home there had been quite an accident on the street down the hill when a horseless milk truck had collided with a horse-drawn ice cart. Suddenly every vehicle on the street—whether motor-powered or animal drawn—had collided into something. Motors had died, horses reared, and ice had melted all over the place. Once it was ascertained that no one had been injured, the spectacle had been rather amusing. Ian smiled with the memory. Diana would have loved the sight. She would have laughed with delight.

But then his smile faded as he dismounted from his rented mare before the boardinghouse and walked her to the gas-lit carriage house. It was a typical London night, filled with fog. And the fog somehow seemed to shroud his heart, letting more painful memories rush upon him.

It had been like this the night Diana had died. A night when the fog had rolled in from the Bay. He had sat with her upon his lap, and they stared out their balcony window, watching the mystic beauty of the fog. She loved San Francisco as deeply as he did, and in those moments, it seemed that their souls touched. She pointed out the stars, disappearing in the fog. And he said that it seemed they sat in heaven, where they were. She rested her head upon his shoulder and sighed softly, and it was several moments before he realized that she had breathed her last. Diana, so fair and fragile, with her delicate features and soft gray eyes. Listening to him build his dreams, listening when he ranted and raved about his buildings and his frustrations with the city. Always there, his support, his life, beside him.

Beside him no more. She was gone, and had been gone nearly two years. Though he would never forget her, never stop loving her, he knew that he had to find a way to keep her from haunting his dreams and his thoughts. She was with him almost always. And the pain of her loss was with him always, too.

Except tonight.

Well, he had to give credit to Sir Thomas's wayward daughter. She was so proud, so damned argumentative and so sure-fire irritating and troublesome that she had made him forget—if only for a little while.

Ian unsaddled and unbridled the mare and led her into her stall. Absently he checked her feed and water, patted her nose, then left the carriage house. He paused outside, his hands on his hips as he surveyed the night. He could scarcely see the park down the street. The fog was coming in, ghostly, eerie.

But he saw no ghosts as he quietly entered the pleasant boardinghouse and strode to his room. There he closed the door carefully behind himself, stripped off his jacket, cravat and tie, and loosened his shirt before falling into the comfortable armchair behind the wide oak sailor's desk. He opened the bottom drawer, drew out the brandy and took a swig.

Indeed, she had intrigued him, this child of his old friend.

Those eyes . . .

He could swear that he had seen them before. Green eyes, haunting eyes, eyes that flashed fire and warning and pride. Spitfire eyes.

He leaned his head against the chair. She was very beautiful, he thought. And despite his impatience with her—and his annoyance that the task of guardian should have fallen into his hands—he had wanted to see the hunted, haunted look disappear from her eyes. Well, he had tried, damn it. Really, he had tried to be courteous, sensitive and patient. The girl simply didn't allow for it.

Anger stirred within him again as he remembered how the wily old Sir Thomas had extracted his promise to care for her. He had harped upon his friendship with Ian's father, he had reminded him that he had stood behind his decision to become an architect, then he had coughed and reminded him that he was going to die.

Ian hadn't really believed him at the time. And it had been his turn to remind Sir Thomas of a few things. Such as the fact that he had so recently lost his wife. That he was an American, with no desire to be anything other. That he must take a young woman far across the sea if he was to be of any assistance to her at all.

And he had reminded Sir Thomas that he had become a harsh and cold and bitter man, and Sir Thomas had merely smiled. "You will promise me, Ian. You will promise me."

And somehow, he had promised.

So now here he was in London, when he should have been home.

Oh, it didn't hurt to come to England. The Tremayne stores always cried out for English goods. But Ian's interest was not in the stores.

The Tremayne dynasty had been founded by Ian's grandfather, a wily Scot who had spelled his name the old way, Iain. He had made his fortune in the gold rush, and had started the emporium. His son James had inherited the Scots business acumen, and the stores had prospered.

James had assumed that his son Ian would love the business as he did. But another fire burned within the son, the fire to build. He loved his city, loved the Bay, loved the fogs that rolled in, loved the coolness and the rugged, beautiful terrain.

It had been Sir Thomas who had written to James over fifteen years ago that he'd be a fool not to allow his son to follow his dream. There was no reason that Ian could not keep the family fortune in balance with the stores and study this new trade.

So there was much that Ian owed Sir Thomas. And his own father, he thought affectionately. James had succumbed to pneumonia five years ago, but he had lived long enough to admire some of Ian's projects. He had lived long enough to meet Diana, and to believe that his father's dreams of a great merchant empire would live through his progeny.

No more, Father, he thought. I have lost her, and there will not be another.

A few women entered into his life, but none that he allowed to touch his heart. San Francisco could be a very progressive city, and he had discovered after the first bitter grief had faded into the depths of his heart that he was still alive, still healthy and still in need of physical companionship.

It always seemed to be available. And he was careful never to whisper words that he did not mean or to issue promises he would never keep. He drove himself with his work, he knew it. But it seemed to be all that was left for him. The child he and Diana had both so longed for had died with her, and he had cast himself into not just the dream of a particular building, but into a dream of building a city.

He meant to pull out a glass for his brandy; he did not. He drank deeply from the bottle, leaning back. His thoughts, which had been on his wife, strayed.

Damn the girl with her green cat's eyes. She was trouble. He didn't dare leave her here on her own. He'd meant to make arrangements and hurry back without her. She could come over at her leisure. Now he didn't dare. As her father had feared, there was clearly a lover in her life. And she seemed willing, no matter what her promises, to throw away her inheritance to have this man.

Ian swallowed deeply again, then set down the bottle and leaned back. He felt the liquor sweep warmly through him. He closed his eyes.

He did not open them again that night. He stretched his legs out on top of the desk, loosened his shirt and dozed with the sheer exhaustion that came from traveling from continent to continent.

He heard the rap on the door, but he had told the proprietor of the boardinghouse often enough that he did not wish to be disturbed.

He opened his eyes and stared evilly at the door, but he did not hasten to rise, nor did he reply.

To his amazement, the door opened.

And to his further amazement, he saw that his early morning visitor was none other than his new, wayward ward.

She was elegant this morning, more beautiful than she had appeared last night in the gaslight of the prim Victorian parlor.

She wore a soft blue day dress with a low-cut bosom and a small, very fashionable bustle. She carried a parasol, wore immaculate white gloves and small elegant boots that just peeked out from beneath the hem of her gown. A matching brocade jacket covered her shoulders, but was fetchingly cut to offer both modesty—and the hint of a very fine cleavage.

She wore no hat, nor had she pinned her hair up, and it fell over her shoulders in sweeping waves like the rays of the sun. It was wonderful hair, hair that rippled and cascaded and fell to her waist, red and gold, fascinating.

She entered the room, and her eyes widened as she saw him at his desk with the brandy bottle before him, his shirt opened all the way down the front and his legs carelessly tossed upon the desk.

He did not bother to move. "Well, well," he murmured. "To what do I owe this honor?"

"I need to speak with you," she murmured.

"Obviously."

She didn't make a move, but seemed frozen against the door. He smiled slowly, wondering if he admired her or disliked her intensely.

No, he did not dislike her, he realized. He disliked what she was doing to his life. He wanted her to be passive and well-behaved and to follow him home and live quietly in her room, so docile that he could forget her.

Cared for, yes, cared for well. But so quiet and well-mannered that he scarce need know she was there.

He would know she was there, he thought. He would always know she was there. She was beautiful, and she must be well aware of it. She had already cast herself into the disgrace of a lover, and in honor of Sir Thomas's memory, he must make certain that she not do such a thing again. She was hardly quiet, and the furthest thing in the world from docile.

Those eyes . . .

She could tempt and taunt like the most practiced vixen, he thought, and was startled to realize that she had annoyed him last night and annoyed him now because she need only stare at him with those fascinating eyes and he felt the stirrings of longing, hot and pulsating, within his groin. He inhaled sharply, and exhaled, and spoke to her far more harshly than he had intended.

"What? You've come. You've entered unbidden. Speak!"

Green eyes flashed with fury. He was certain that she was going to turn and leave the room. And then he would have to chase after her.

But she seemed to stiffen and lock her jaw. She did not move. Her gaze swept over him scornfully. Her eyes locked upon his bare chest, then rose once more to meet his. She appeared to fight for nerve, then found her courage. She raised her chin, and once more her gaze was imperious.

"I wish to follow my father's will to the letter, Mr. Tremayne. I wish—" She hesitated only the flicker of a second. "I wish to—to marry you."

CHAPTER THREE

$\mathcal{Y}$ou what?" Ian's feet hit the floor. His eyes narrowed sharply, and his voice rang with surprise.

For a moment, Marissa couldn't quite catch her breath. The man seemed to be more formidable than ever. No, he had made a promise to Sir Thomas, and he was merely irritated with her attempts to thwart him. His voice could be gentle; he could be every inch the gentleman.

He didn't look much the gentleman at the moment. He looked every inch the rogue. His chest was nearly naked, very hard muscled and thickly matted with crisp dark hairs against which a gold medallion of St. Luke rested. He was scowling crossly, and a lock of his near ebony hair was dangling haphazardly over his forehead. He had spent the evening drinking brandy, so it appeared.

He was still a gentleman, she assured herself, despite his appearance.

After all, Sir Thomas had trusted him with his daughter's future. And still . . .

Deep within her, tremors had begun. To her dismay, she discovered that she was frightened, but also excited. There was something decadently tempting about the taut muscles that formed his chest. Something that made her long to touch . . .

And then start to tremble anew.

No, no, she didn't want to touch anything. She had to make that clear. Abundantly clear. But just thinking about it made her feel a curious unease.

He didn't want to marry. He had said that he had no intention of marrying again. So he had been married. She had to convince him that . . . that they could marry one another and lead separate lives.

"I want to marry you," she managed to repeat.

"Whatever for?" he demanded crossly.

"That's entirely obvious, isn't it, Mr. Tremayne?" she said with exasperation. "I need my allowance."

"I am willing to care for you."

"I don't want charity. I want what is mine."

"You don't want charity—but you're willing to marry a stranger for your allowance?" A single dark brow was raised high with incredulity. "Excuse me, Miss Ahearn, but I would think that marriage to a near stranger would have to be less appealing than the simple acceptance of the stranger's largesse." He was amused again. He was not in the least taking her seriously.

"Mr. Tremayne, this is important to me."

"It seems that our newly entwined futures must be important to us both. I am serious, too, Marissa. Marriage is a contract, legal, binding."

"Yes, I know."

"It is also much, much more," he reminded her sharply.

"It wouldn't have to be like that," she said hastily.

"Like what?" he demanded. He was taunting her, she knew. Baiting her, purposely. He was angry, and he meant to draw blood.

She pushed away from the wall, moving into the room at last. But then she paused, for he was now standing. He moved around to the front of the desk, crossing his arms over his chest.

Awaiting her.

She was silent, and he sat back comfortably on the desk, smiling suddenly. "Pray, do enlighten me, Miss Ahearn."

Enlighten him! She longed to smack the amusement from his face.

An ill choice of action, she decided, if she was to coerce him to her will.

She swallowed her anger and tried to speak intelligently and with dignity. "My father's will has devastated me, Mr. Tremayne. There are certain—charities to which I am deeply committed, and I would use my own funds for these expenses. You—you said that you did not intend to marry again. If we marry one another, then you will not have to marry again."

A quizzical expression passed over his face, then he laughed out-right. "Obviously. I shall be married to you."

"But not really."

"You cannot collect your inheritance by going through a pre-tense of marriage."

"No, no, I will marry you, really—"

"I don't wish to marry."

Marissa exploded with a sharp oath of impatience that brought amusement to his eyes, and both his brows shot up. "Mr. Tremayne, you have told me that you are not averse to accepting certain advances from certain women. I can only assume this to mean a certain kind of woman, sir. Harlots and whores, Mr. Tremayne, if I do comprehend your words correctly. I—"

"And dance-hall girls, Miss Ahearn," He added. "We do have some very fine establishments in San Francisco."

"Excuse me. And dance-hall girls. They can be very amusing, I'm certain—"

"Oh, much more than amusing."

"But what of the nights when you might wish to entertain at home? When you need someone to welcome important associates? When you wish to play the gentleman, Mr. Tremayne, which I do assume you do upon occasion!"

"And you are the epitome of graciousness!" he snapped suddenly.

She was silent for a moment, then murmured, "And you, Mr. Tremayne, seem capable of being a master of cruelty."

He sighed softly. "Marissa!" Curiously, her name sounded almost like a caress. "I am sorry, truly. I never meant to be cruel. I wanted this all to be as easy as it could be."

Marissa lowered her lashes, unnerved by his sudden gentleness. "There is no way to make this easy!" she whispered vehemently.

"Do you know what you're asking me?" he demanded.

"Yes!"

"I don't want a wife," he said harshly.

"You don't wish a wife to whom you would be obliged to offer affection!" she corrected him.

His startled look gave her a sudden advantage, and she determined to pursue it. "That is why it is all so perfect!" she exclaimed passionately. And once again, she stood before him. Too closely before him. Her hands rested upon the desk and she stared into his eyes, nearly pleading. He was still smiling. "Oh, don't you see!" she moaned.

"I do apologize, but your logic simply eludes me."

"I wouldn't expect you to—I wouldn't expect you to behave as a husband."

"Ah. And how does a husband behave?" he queried her.

She pushed away from the desk and strode with agitation across the room. Then she realized that she was facing his bed and she swung around, her cheeks flaming. He was taunting her. He knew darned well what she was saying.

"Mr. Tremayne, we could form a marriage in name only. I could receive my inheritance, and in turn—" She paused.

"Yes, well, it's that part I am interested in hearing about," he said dryly.

"I could protect you."

"You could protect me?"

"From unwanted advances."

He burst into laughter. All the grimness left his mouth, and a sizzling sparkle touched his eyes. If nothing else, she had amused him.

"You're being very rude," she informed him coolly.

"Oh! Do forgive me, Miss Ahearn. It's just that, though I do not wish to marry again, there are certain, er, advances that I rather welcome, if you know what I mean."

Her cheeks flamed and she willed herself to betray no emotion, no anger, no embarrassment. She tried her very best to stare at him with nothing more than scorn and to speak as softly as she could. "You would be more than welcome to your diversions, Mr. Tremayne. That is my whole point. You could wander at will, and be plagued by no woman, for you would already have a wife. A wife to whom you owed nothing at all, a wife who would stay out of your way, I might add, and in her gratitude, make your life as comfortable as possible."

"Comfortable?"

She gritted her teeth. "I make a very good hostess for business dinners and all social occasions," she assured him primly.

"Oh, I'm sure that you do!" he said.

She had no further arguments for the moment, and he was still staring at her without replying.

"Well?" she prompted him irritably.

"Well?"

"Have you an answer?"

"I'm thinking," he told her.

"You at least knew something of this arrangement!" she reminded him with a flare of anger.

"But I knew nothing about acquiring a wife," he murmured. "And if I am about to find myself with this wonderful hostess and entertainer who will boldly stand guard against all mamas who wish their daughters married, I am still afraid that I might have a few requirements of my new paragon of virtue."

"Such as?"

"Well," he drawled softly, his blue gaze sweeping over her with a lazy regard, "I would like her to be just that—a paragon of virtue."

Marissa gasped, infuriated. "Just as you are a paragon of virtue, Mr. Tremayne."

"Sorry. I am afraid that it is still required much more of the female in this day and age."

She swirled around, heading for the door. He watched her without protest. Her fingers closed over the knob.

She turned, quivering with anger, but very aware that she was the one playing for the high stakes—he really did not want a wife.

"What do you want out of me?" she demanded.

"The truth."

"Why?"

"You're asking me to marry you," he said harshly. "I want to know something about my future wife."

"Such as?"

"What of your young lover? I'll have no man trailing after you to my home. And I'll be damned if I'll ever give any woman my good name for her to make a cuckold of me by playing at any game with another." She realized then that he was amused, but he was also angry. Very angry. The open shirt displayed the pulse against his throat, and muscles bulged on his naked chest as his arms almost imperceptibly tightened over one another.

She leaned against the door and moistened her lips. Her eyes met his.

"I have never had a lover, Mr. Tremayne," she said flatly.

"You admitted it when I spoke of your father's fears," he reminded her.

"No." Her eyes fell from his, and she shook her head. "I admitted that I knew a man, but . . ." She forced her eyes to meet his. To offer the honesty that was still a lie. "He was never my—lover."

He rose from the desk and walked to the door. She was tempted to throw it open and run.

She held her ground. His arms came around her as bars on either side of her head, his hands flat against the panels of the door. "I wonder if you are telling the truth. I wonder if you are capable of telling the truth."

"What difference would it make?" she cried out passionately. "I want no real marriage. We could put it in writing, we could—"

"No!" He seemed to thunder out the word, sharp and savage. "You are not listening, my lady. I'll not have my name abused. And I'll have no contract for pretense written down upon paper. And neither will I make any damned agreements about what a marriage will or will not be. One a hostess, the other the provider of an income."

"It is my own income!"

"Not without me."

Oh, please! she thought. She could not face him much longer without screaming. His sudden change from laughter to passion and anger was unnerving. She could not bear it.

"I have told you the truth, I swear it!" she cried suddenly. "There is no man, there has never been a man. I plan to play no games, I just wish to live with a certain dignity—"

"And what, pray tell," he demanded savagely, "if you should discover yourself falling in love again elsewhere?"

"I will not fall in love elsewhere."

"Ah, how assured you are for one so young!"

"Well, you are certain you've no wish to marry again, and you are not yet decrepit!"

"Ah, but I have known love, my lady, and there's the difference," he said, his tone suddenly, deceptively soft.

"Please—"

"What are these charities of yours?"

"They are personal."

"Perhaps a young man is included in them?"

"No!"

He pushed away from the door, turned and paced across the room. A moment later he pulled out the chair at his desk and sank into it. "How strange. I don't see you being such an incredible philanthropist, Marissa."

"I told you—"

"Spell it out!"

"I—I have a maid. No, she is no longer really my maid. But she wishes to be married. They are both young and poor and her health is failing, and I want to bring them both with me. She has been a dear friend all her life. And there is a small mining town I wish to help—"

"And certain miners?" he inquired politely.

"I tell you, sir, that my intentions are entirely honorable!"

"Are they?" he mused, and he sat at the desk, idly tapping his fingers against the wood as he stared at her. He threw up his hands. "Lady, you did not want a guardian, and yet you would accept a husband!"

"I have explained—"

"Ah, yes, well then, let me explain." He leaned forward, folding his hands upon the table, his eyes seeming to impale her as his temper rose with his every word. "I am not an easy man, Miss Ahearn."

"You said that you are often gone—"

"But when I am home, I can be a tyrant. I am demanding and exacting, and I have a horrible temper."

"Indeed? What a shock!" she said with wide eyes and sweetly dripping sarcasm.

"You are asking for this," he reminded her.

"Pray, go on, Mr. Tremayne."

"Bear in mind that I've no wish to marry."

"So you've informed me."

"That I shall go my own way."

"That, sir, will give me the greatest pleasure."

A long finger was suddenly pointed in her direction. "While you, my dear, will be that wonderful paragon you have promised. And you will be at my beck and call for whatever social amenities I might require."

Her heart was hammering. It was a devil's bargain, made in hell. But she had already known that she would pay nearly any price to make this work.

She had paid part of the price, for the lie she was already living was agonizing.

"You make it sound like torture," she murmured, her lashes falling over her eyes.

"On the contrary, I do not beat or abuse women, Marissa." The harshness in his voice had suddenly faded, and she opened her eyes to his once again. "I have merely tried to show you your folly."

Again she moistened her lips to speak. "I came here, sir, with my mind set."

"There are times," he said quietly, "when you may think I resent you just because we are married."

She frowned. "I don't understand—"

"Never mind. There is no way to explain." He rose suddenly. "And I make no promises, no agreements. That is understood?"

She wasn't sure; she really wasn't sure what he meant at all, but she nodded, wondering if he was going to agree, or if this was all a charade to humiliate her.

He stared at her hard. Then he muttered a harsh, "Damn you, girl!"

And he reached for a handsome overcoat, and touched her at last, taking her arm to draw her away from the door.

"Where are you going?" she cried.

He turned to her. Once again, his blue eyes seemed to impale her beneath the rakish fall of the black lock upon his forehead. "I am going for a registrar, my lady. If we're going to do this thing, we'll do it now, and be done with it all. I've got a license. All we need is a registrar."

The door swung shut in his wake. Marissa gasped. Her knees were beginning to buckle and she braced herself with her hands against the door.

What had she done?

He had agreed. He had agreed too swiftly! He had given her no time to plot and plan, to find a way to make it all false or to make it all real.

But he had agreed. He was coming back with a registrar, and she must do something, she must . . .

Marry him.

A coldness settled upon her, and the words kept repeating hauntingly in her mind. Help me, God! she thought. But surely God would not help a liar playing such a deception as she played.

There was no choice, she assured herself. No choice at all. She had won, she had come here wanting this, and now, surprisingly, she had gained what she wanted.

But very soon, she knew, he would come to the room with a registrar. And she would stand there and vow to be his wife. His wife. Irrevocably tied to the man.

She started to tremble and closed her eyes. She didn't dare keep thinking, and yet she could not stop. What would happen if she were found out? The knot was tangling more viciously with every turn. . . .

Maybe he didn't mean to go through with it. Perhaps he had gone out to order a tray of tea and crumpets. He did not really mean to marry her; he just wanted to agree to give her the chance to realize what she was saying, to back out of it herself.

Which she could do. If she and Mary were caught perpetrating this deception it would be disaster.

He was letting her escape.

Perhaps she did block out her thoughts, for it seemed that he had barely left before he was back. At his side was a stocky little man with wispy gray hair. Behind the man were two women—a small, pert maid in a white cap and apron and an older woman, also in a cap and apron.

"My dear," Ian said, still appearing very much the rake, his shirt opened at the neck, his coat haphazardly over his shoulders and a night's stubble upon his cheeks, "this is Mr. Blackstone, the registrar. And this is Meg, and she will witness the ceremony for me. And this is Lucy, who will also witness the marriage. We *do* want it to be legal."

He was not letting her escape.

Marissa tried to smile. She needed to be gracious, to extend her hand to the two women. She couldn't speak. She had barely managed to move away from the doorway at their return. She stared at Ian with wide eyes.

His mouth was set in a grim line, and his eyes were hard upon hers. He said nothing to her, but she knew what he was thinking. She had started this. And now he would finish it.

He would give her exactly what she wanted.

"It will be just a minute here now," Mr. Blackstone was saying, setting his briefcase upon the desk. "I need the proper legal documents and my seal. Mr. Tremayne?"

Ian went to the desk and produced the license.

"Oh, this is so exciting!" Meg said.

"Thrilling," Ian agreed wryly.

"Did you wish to, er, tidy up a bit, sir?" Mr. Blackstone asked Ian.

Ian rubbed his cheeks. He offered Marissa a smile that didn't touch the fire in his eyes. "No, thank you, Mr. Blackstone. My wife will be seeing this Yankee mug every morning of her life from here on out. She doesn't mind it a bit, do you, my dear?"

Marissa smiled at last, as sweetly as she could manage. She touched his stubbled cheek and assured Mr. Blackstone. "I can't tell you just how charming I find Mr. Tremayne to be. Kind, solicitous— absolutely charming. With or without the stubble. It's such a noble face."

"She adores me," Ian told Mr. Blackstone.

Meg sighed. Lucy giggled. Mr. Blackstone seemed uneasy.

Ian snatched Marissa's hand and drew her to his side. "Can we get on with this?"

"Yes, yes, of course. My papers are now all in order. I think . . ."

He started to speak the words. Slowly, very slowly. Marissa did not hear them. She felt Ian Tremayne's hand locked around hers, large, warm, powerful.

She was building prison walls around herself, she realized. This was very real. She would have to travel across the globe with him. Live in his house. Answer to his beck and call.

"And do you, Ian Robert, take this woman to be your lawfully wedded wife, to have and to hold, to love and to cherish, from this day forward, till death do you part?"

Marissa couldn't breathe. He would protest now. He would say that it had all been a lark and that he hadn't the least intention of marrying her.

"I do," he said firmly.

"And do you—" The registrar paused for a second, squinting at a paper.

"Katherine Marissa, Mr. Blackstone," Ian supplied dryly.

"Yes, yes, of course. Now do you, Katherine Marissa, take this man to be your lawfully wedded husband, to have and to hold, to honor and obey, from this day forward, till death do you part?"

Death? she thought vaguely. It seemed drastic. He hadn't stopped it; she had to do so.

She almost cried out at the sudden pressure upon her hand as his fingers wound tightly around it in warning. "I do!" she gasped.

Then Mr. Blackstone was talking again, and she really couldn't hear a word he was saying. Moments later Ian was raising her hand, and something cold and way too large was slipped upon her finger.

Mr. Blackstone pronounced them man and wife, and nervously suggested that Ian might like to kiss his bride.

"Kiss my bride," he muttered, and she wanted to wrench away at the bitterness that tinged his voice. For a moment she thought he meant to thrust her far from him. He did not. His hold upon her was very firm. And she was suddenly pulled tight within his arms, and her mouth opened in protest as she saw the intent within his eyes.

No sound escaped her.

His lips touched hers. She expected violence from the way he held her.

But there was none.

His mouth formed over hers with a fierce demand and pressure, but there was something more. Perhaps it was something practiced . . . something innate within the man.

Whatever it was, she could not think once his lips molded so securely over hers. She felt the brush of the stubble of his beard, she felt his hold, his pressure, his undauntable determination. And yet she felt the seduction. The slow, almost lazy coercion. Her lips were parted beneath his, the startling, damp, heady warmth of his tongue filled her mouth, tasted and explored. Leisurely, and yet with such purpose. The fingers of his left hand entwined with the hair at her nape, holding her still to his thorough exploration. His other hand lay upon the small of her back, holding her close to him, so very close that she felt the pulse and tension of his body, the hardness of his build, and the heat that lay within, simmering, fusing, touching her in a way she had never imagined being touched before.

The tip of his tongue skimmed over her lips, delved deep within her mouth once again, endlessly deep. Her fingers wound into his shirt, for she was certain that if he moved, she would fall. All the fire had seemed to enter into her from his body. And a trembling that was rich with newborn sensations, making her both hot and cold, furious and . . .

And fascinated.

She should protest. . . .

She could not.

Dimly she heard Mr. Blackstone clear his throat; Meg and Lucy sighed very softly in unison.

And then, at long last, Ian Tremayne moved his dark head, lifting his mouth from hers. His cobalt eyes seared into hers for a long moment, and she could not draw her gaze from his. He touched her lip with his thumb, rubbing the remaining moisture from it. And still his gaze touched hers, yet she did not know what emotion lurked in his eyes. She thought that he was still furious with her for testing his hand. Yet he was the one with the sudden determination at the end. He had taken her course of action and flown with it. In a sudden impetuous heat? She was sure of it, for already she sensed a withdrawal. His touch fell from her face, and he was gazing at Mr. Blackstone again.

"Well, the papers, then," he said flatly. "We should keep this legal."

"Yes, Mr. Tremayne! Most certainly."

Mr. Blackstone pushed the license across the desk. Ian Tremayne leaned low over it and scrawled his name. It was barely legible.

He thrust the pen into her hand. She stared at him. The anger was back with him. "Sign it," he told her. She kept looking at him. "For the love of God, Marissa, sign the damned thing."

She hesitated a second longer. Which name did she sign? Mary's? Would things be legal then? Perhaps not. But if they weren't legal, things would be better if they were caught!

"Marissa!" Her name seemed to be an explosion of impatience. She started to write with trembling fingers, scrawling out her name in a far worse manner than he had done.

She stared at it. It was very nearly illegible. But she knew what she had signed. Katherine Marissa Ayers. At the last moment, she had signed her own name. He would never know. "Ahearn" and the "Ayers" were close enough when written with fingers that trembled as violently as hers had done.

Meg and Lucy stepped forward and signed the wedding license, then Mr. Blackstone did the same, and blotted all the signatures.

"Shall I get some champagne?" Meg suggested, and Mr. Blackstone looked up eagerly.

"Champagne?" Ian mused. Marissa bit her lip in silence. "Champagne. By all means. What is a wedding without a toast?"

"My own sentiments exactly," Mr. Blackstone agreed jovially.

Meg left the room for the champagne and Mr. Blackstone sat behind the desk, finishing with the forms. Marissa and Ian stood in silence. Waiting.

Then Meg burst through the door. Ian took the tray with champagne from her, setting it upon the desk. He observed the label with a critical eye, then shrugged and popped the cork. Champagne bubbled out, and he quickly began to pour it into the five flutes upon the tray.

He handed one to Marissa. Her fingers curled around it. He smiled, grimly. "Till death do us part," he said.

"Hear, hear!" Mr. Blackstone agreed. He lifted his glass and sighed. "To many years of marital bliss!"

"Oh, many years," Ian said wryly.

"To a huge, full, wonderful family! Strong, handsome sons and beautiful daughters!" Meg cried, well into the spirit of the thing.

Did neither she nor Mr. Blackstone see the hostility that lurked in Ian Tremayne's eyes?

They did not, but Marissa did. In silence, she sipped her champagne, then tossed her head back and swallowed the contents in a gulp. Ian's lip curled as he watched her, and he poured her another portion of the vintage, then added to Mr. Blackstone's proffered flute.

"Well, then!" Blackstone said with a sigh as he swallowed his down and set the glass upon the tray. "The very best to you both. To you, good sir, and you, too, Mrs. Tremayne."

Marissa's head jerked up. Blackstone locked his briefcase and lifted it from the table. Ian Tremayne opened the door for him. Blackstone bowed to Meg, and the little maid smiled and said good-bye and good luck once again and left. The more sedate Lucy followed quickly behind her. "Again, the best to you both," Blackstone said, bowing just before he exited the room.

Ian closed the door behind them. He leaned against it and stared at her.

Once again, she saw the curl of a mocking smile touch his lips. "Ah, yes. Don't look so startled, love. You are, you realize, Mrs. Tremayne. Just as you wished."

She started as he pushed away from the door and came toward her, catching her wrists, pulling her hard against his well-muscled form. "Yes, my dear, you've gotten exactly what you came for. Marriage. Are you happy?"

She tugged uneasily upon her wrists, frightened by his sudden hostility. "Mr. Tremayne—"

"So very formal, Mrs. Tremayne."

"But I'm not really—"

"Oh, yes, you see, that's where you are mistaken. You are really my wife, Marissa. My wife," he repeated softly.

Then he dropped her wrists and headed for the door, pausing with his hand upon the knob. His crooked smile curved his mouth and he repeated the words once again. "I've a wife. Dear God, whatever possessed me? May heaven help us both."

And then, with no explanation, he was gone.

CHAPTER FOUR

$\mathcal{Y}$ou did what!" Mary gasped with horror.

Marissa, hearing the tone of Mary's voice at her casual announcement that she had gone ahead and married Ian Tremayne, grimaced. She was in the parlor of their suite, trying very hard to be calm and casual while her heart beat a rampant pulse of uncertainty.

Ian Tremayne hadn't returned. He would have to do so eventually, Marissa was certain, because he had left all his things. But she had paced his room for half an hour, trying not to look at those things that seemed to be so personal to the man, growing more and more restless. The room made her uneasy. The desk was filled with business papers, with letters, some addressed in smooth, flowing scripts that could only be feminine. There was his bed. And there was his shaving equipment, a fine ivory brush and cup, his razor and strop.

She couldn't wait any longer. She didn't know if he had expected her to wait, he had slammed out so quickly. She had left the boarding-house, hailed a hansom and returned to Mary's suites.

There she found Mary awake and pacing the floor, worried about her.

"I married him," Marissa repeated, sinking down on one of the stiff needlepoint chairs that faced the settee over a heavy Persian rug. "We married him, I guess. I don't know. I used my own name. I signed my own signature. I think that makes it legal. The marriage, at least."

"Oh, Marissa!"

Mary hurried to her side and hugged her tightly. "What made you do such a thing? You shouldn't have. We would have survived somehow."

"Mary, nothing is really any different."

"Nothing is different!" Mary exclaimed. "Oh, Marissa! Don't you know what married people do?"

Marissa cast her a quick, narrowing glance. "Of course I know what married people do!" she said indignantly. Honestly, Mary could be terribly annoying. "But it's not going to be that kind of marriage."

Mary sniffed. "Any marriage is that kind of marriage. Oh, of course, he is very good looking."

"How do you know?"

"I was peeking out the bedroom door last night. He's handsome. Very attractive, really."

"He had you in fits last night."

"Oh, but that's because I couldn't begin to deal with such a man. He's such a tremendous presence, demanding. But I think he could be charming."

"Charming. That's the word," Marissa said sweetly.

Mary stared at her, hurt. "I only meant—"

"He is charming, Mary. Completely," Marissa lied. And he could be charming. When he wasn't snapping and snarling. "Mary, it's an arrangement, nothing more. If you were peeking last night, you must have been listening too. He was married before. He didn't want to be married again. So I'm really just going to be a guest in the house, and then, because he's already married, no one will bother him to get married. Understand?"

"You made him understand this?" Mary said, confused.

"Yes. Mary, it's going to be all right."

"No, it's not! And I can't believe that you went off and married him without a word! Marissa, you didn't give yourself time to think! Maybe we could have come up with something else—"

"With what, Mary?" Marissa asked wearily.

"I don't know. Something."

"Mary, I didn't think he'd really do it. I had all these wonderful plans and arguments. Then I assumed that if I did get him to agree, we'd make plans for later. The next thing I knew, a registrar was in the room, and we were married."

"Oh, Marissa!"

Mary hugged her tightly, then released her. She stared at her with such mournful, miserable eyes that Marissa patted her hand and rose, determined to cast aside her own fears to reassure her friend. "Mary, you musn't forget that I have my uncle to care for. Actually, it's everything I've always wanted. Mr. Tremayne's home will be very grand, I'm certain. I'll see the opera, the theater, and I'll be a gracious hostess for countless balls and dinners. I'll be in my glory."

Mary looked at her with a sad wisdom that was unnerving. "A house doesn't mean anything, Marissa. It's brick and stone and wood. And you've entrusted your fate to this man—"

"Our fates, Mary. We'll be together, at least."

"We've traded places, remember?" Mary murmured softly. "He's not going to let you choose your friends from among the poor immigrants."

"We're going to America, Mary. The land of opportunity! And equality."

"Equality takes a long time in coming," Mary said softly.

"Don't worry. He's not going to rule my life! Oh, Mary, don't you see, it will be all right. He didn't want a wife. I'll be an ornament upon occasion. And when I'm not, nothing will change. You'll have a beautiful little home nearby, Jimmy will work, and I'll help you with whatever you need. It is going to work out. It's going to be exactly like we planned. There was really just a minor hitch to our plans, and that was it."

She hiccuped suddenly. Mary stared at her.

"Champagne," Marissa offered. She grimaced. "We celebrated."

"You celebrated!"

"Of course. Remember, I told you," Marissa said blandly. "He's charming. Completely charming." She smiled. "Like a wolf!" she muttered beneath her breath.

"What?" Mary demanded.

"Nothing. Really. Nothing at all."

There was a soft rap on the door. Mary hurried over to it and opened it, then gasped.

Jimmy O'Brien was standing there.

"Jimmy!" Mary said.

"Aye, love, I'm here."

"But you were going to stay away until—"

"Until, love, that was the problem," Jimmy said, taking her hand and moving into the room. His young freckled face was serious, his eyes were grave. He nodded to Marissa then told Mary, "I have to admit, I did not trust the two of you. I was afraid that you might do something foolish, and I am the man here. Mary, I will provide, and I'll care for you both somehow, I mean it."

A soft smile curved Marissa's lips as she listened to the passion and vehemence of his speech. That was Jimmy. He could not really even hope to take care of himself and Mary, but he was willing to promise to care for her, too.

"'Tis too late, Jimmy," Mary murmured. "Marissa's gone off and married the Yank."

"What!" Jimmy exclaimed, horrified.

Marissa sighed. "Jimmy, it's all right—"

"You've married the old bloke!"

"He's not old, Jimmy."

"He's still a strange Yank!"

"Whatever, Jimmy, the die is cast."

"We'll annul it!" Jimmy announced.

Marissa stood and faced them both. "We'll do no such thing. I barely managed to get what I wanted, and now that I've got it, we're going to live with it. I imagine—"

She broke off because there was another knock at the door, crisp and hard this time. Shivers danced over her spine because she was certain that it was Ian.

Jimmy, unaware, headed for the door. "Wait!" Marissa called out, but it was too late. Jimmy had already opened the door, and it was, indeed, Ian standing there.

He had bathed and changed. And shaved. His hair was damp, the dark wave still rippling over his forehead. He wore an off-white suit that enhanced his dark good looks.

Dark and glowering. He looked at Jimmy with his jaw set at a harsh angle, his blue eyes shooting off sparks, and yet with a harsh, cold control about him. Then his gaze fell upon Marissa across the room, and it was condemning to such an extent that she had to grip the back of the needlepoint chair to keep from visibly shivering.

She could not let him intimidate her so! she told herself fiercely.

"What the hell is going on here?" he demanded, his voice a low, warning growl.

Jimmy backed away from the door, and Marissa bit hard upon her lip, willing him her strength. Tremayne was probably ten years Jimmy's elder, taller and broader, a formidable man. But Jimmy moved back, she knew, because of Ian's dress and confidence. Jimmy was accustomed to poverty, and to giving way to the rich. And she was suddenly very angry for Jimmy, and angry that Tremayne was assuming Jimmy was the lover she had denied she had.

"I am entertaining friends, Mr. Tremayne!" she snapped.

"Lady, you had best not be entertaining—"

"Mr. Tremayne, if you don't mind!" she managed to murmur with incredible presence, her head raised regally. And then before she knew it, a lie was upon her lips. "I thought I'd lost you," she said. "Please, do come in. I'd like you to meet my very good friends, Mary and Jimmy O'Brien."

His gaze went quickly from her face to Jimmy's, then to Mary's. Jimmy seemed to be frozen. When Ian looked at Mary, his gaze grew more gentle. It had to be something about Mary's face, Marissa thought, and she wondered if she resented Mary for having this affect upon others, or whether she should be grateful for it. There was a gentleness about Mary's beauty. She had the look of a Madonna, as if nothing more than kindness lived in her heart. Her smile was always genuine.

Mary stepped forward, taking his hand in a firm shake. "How do you do, sir. It is indeed our pleasure."

Ian smiled suddenly, bending over her hand. He brushed it with a kiss. "Forgive me, Mrs. O'Brien. I am afraid that I am still fatigued from the journey here, and not in the best of temper."

"Sir, we are not offended."

Yes, we are! Marissa wanted to cry. But Ian's gaze had moved to Jimmy.

Jimmy had removed his cap. He wound it uneasily in his hands. He wanted to speak, Marissa knew, but he was tongue-tied.

"Jimmy, dear!" Mary persisted. "Come meet Mr. Tremayne."

Jimmy stepped forward and shook hands with Ian. Marissa watched as Ian Tremayne quickly assessed the man, and to her surprise seemed to like what he saw.

"Mr. O'Brien, Mrs. O'Brien. The pleasure is mine." He looked across the room at Marissa. "No, my dear, you did not lose me. I simply had some arrangements to make. But I see that I should have waited. I assume that these are your friends?"

"Yes, my very good friends," Marissa admitted without moving. "They—they wish to come to America, too."

His gaze fell upon Mary, and Marissa was certain that he read her ill health in a matter of seconds. "It's a long journey," he said.

"I know," Mary told him.

"What do you do, Jimmy O'Brien?" Ian asked.

Mary cleared her throat. She was standing behind Marissa, and gave her a light prod. "You must ask your husband to sit down, Marissa. And offer him a drink."

"Of course!" She had promised to be such a wonderful hostess and she seemed as incapable of movement as Jimmy. After the angry way that Ian had left her, he seemed calm enough. He seemed almost charming. Once he had decided that the door hadn't been opened by her supposed lover, he had seemed to acquire a keen interest in her friends.

"Mr. Tremayne, please do have a seat. Would you like a whiskey or a brandy, sir? Would—"

Mary was prodding her again, then whispering at her ear. "You've married the man, Marissa. You must call him by his given name, not 'Mr. Tremayne' or 'sir'!"

Ian was staring at them both, smiling. She thought again that at the very least, she seemed to amuse him often enough.

"A brandy would be fine," he told her, lounging comfortably upon the settee. "Mr. O'Brien, join me. Tell me about yourself."

Jimmy was wringing his cap in his hands once again but he moved tentatively to the settee. He sat, or perched, near Ian. Then he seemed to realize that the man had a genuine interest in him. "I'm already an immigrant, to be sure," he said. "Irish," he explained, as if his name and looks didn't give him away in a second.

Ian's grin deepened. "There's plenty Irishmen in San Francisco, Jimmy. What do you do?"

"I was a farmer, but . . ." he shrugged. "Well, it seemed we were all tryin' to make a livin' from potatoes where there was no living to be made. And I'd always wanted to be a shopkeeper. I could read and write and cipher fair enough, for the village priest, he did see to that. He said that we'd not throw off the yoke of the English if we didn't concentrate on the like." He flushed suddenly, realizing that he was in England.

"It's all right, Jimmy, go ahead," Ian encouraged. "So you wanted to be a shopkeeper."

"Aye."

"But it takes capital," Ian said.

"Aye, that it does."

"Well, Jimmy, if you're sure you and your wife have the will and determination to come to America, I think that I can help you."

"I can't take your money—"

"And I don't intend to give it to you," Ian said. He took his brandy glass from Marissa without looking at her, and she felt curiously like the downstairs maid again even as she watched the hope dawning in Jimmy's face.

"You see, Jimmy O'Brien, my father and grandfather were shop-keepers. They had years and years to build up, to gain experience. We've a really fine family emporium in the heart of San Francisco. I don't spend the time there that I should. I'm not a merchant at heart. I'm a builder. But if you're willing to take the time to learn my business and gain some experience, well, I'm certain that we could arrange a salary that would provide you with the savings to open your own place after a while."

Mary gasped with pleasure, her eyes glowing. Jimmy stared at the man as if he had just handed him a thousand pounds in gold.

"Well, Jimmy?"

"I'd work hard, Mr. Tremayne, I swear it! You wait and see, sir!"

"I know you will."

"I expect to start down at the bottom, sir—"

"And that you will, too. In the basement. It's the stockroom, and everyone has to learn the stock."

"I'll learn it upside, downside and all around, sir!" Jimmy vowed.

Ian smiled again. "I'm sure you will." He gazed past Jimmy to Mary, who stood behind him, her hands resting upon his shoulders. His voice grew more gentle. "You will enjoy San Francisco, Mary. It's one of the most beautiful places on earth. I don't think you will miss your home too keenly."

"I cannot miss my home, Mr. Tremayne," Mary said. "Where Jimmy goes is home. And of course, we will be near Marissa. That is all the home that I need."

Ian rose, studying her. Marissa bit her lip, thinking that Ian admired and liked Mary very much. Perhaps they all might have been much better off if they had never planned to deceive him.

But as she had said, the die was cast.

She was the one who had lied and deceived him.

And married him.

"Marissa."

She grated her teeth at the sharp sound of her name upon his tongue. He spoke to her as if she were a child. As if she were still the downstairs maid. And yet he was as polite and gentle to Mary as a man could be.

She gave him her attention, waiting, but did not reply. He stood. "I'd have a word with you alone, madam."

"Oh!" Mary murmured. "Really, Jimmy, dear, we must be going. Mr. Tremayne and Marissa must have an awful lot to discuss."

Jimmy stared at her blankly.

"Jimmy, come on."

"But—"

"I'll make your travel arrangements and advise you of them, Jimmy," Ian told him. He shook Jimmy's hand, then bent his head low over Mary's. "We'll meet again soon enough."

"Yes, of course, and thank you! Thank you so much for everything, Mr. Tremayne."

"Ian, please. We are to be friends."

Mary smiled slowly, beautifully. "Ian, then." She withdrew her hand from his. "Jimmy, come, please."

Marissa watched them depart, Mary determined, Jimmy dazed. As the door closed upon the two of them she was painfully uncomfortable once again, face to face with the man she had married.

"I had thought that we should both leave within the next few days—" he began.

"But I can't!" she interrupted him. It was one thing to play the grand lady in London. But she couldn't just leave the country. She had to say goodbye to Theo, and she had to convince him somehow that she had fallen in love and married and that her husband was very rich and that she would send him checks every month. And then she had to try to convince him to come to America eventually, but that could wait. Maybe she could even travel back for him herself. Beautifully bedecked, magnanimous, a heroine to the mining community where she would see that a school was set up. . . .

That was all in the future. At the moment, she had the piper to pay.

"Admittedly, madam, I have not up until now trusted you," he told her. "This morning, I would have said no."

"But?" she murmured, watching him.

"But I find your friends very responsible, and therefore perhaps I misjudged you."

Resentment flared inside her, but she kept her lashes lowered, determined not to argue. "So you will give me some time?" she said.

"Yes. You and your friends can come on the liner *Lorena*. She leaves London ten days from now. That should be sufficient for you."

"Ten days!" she murmured in dismay.

"It is unusual enough, Marissa, that a newly married man should return without his wife. Ten days is what I can give you. The *Lorena* will take you to New York. From there you will take the train to California and San Francisco. It is a long journey. You will be on the ship for about a week and the train for as long again. It would have been much better if you could have prepared to travel with me."

No! She was tremendously grateful that she would not have to travel with him. They would eventually have to establish some kind of relationship, she knew. But she was willing, very willing, to play for time.

She raised her eyes to his. "Sir, I am competent, even if you've little faith in me. I will manage the journey, with transfers and pitfalls, I promise you."

He smiled slowly. "Yes, I believe that. You don't lack courage, or strength. For a young woman of your birth and privilege, you're really quite extraordinary."

Marissa wasn't at all sure that it was a compliment, not the way he gazed at her. But then he turned away, pacing the small parlor. "I do apologize for my manners this morning. You caught me quite off guard." He spun and stared at her. "After all, you went from attempting to remain in England to insisting upon marriage. Quite a difference."

"Perhaps," she murmured, watching him uneasily. Mercurial seemed to be the best word to describe him, from the depth of his dark blue eyes to the tone of his voice to his energy. He was constantly in motion. He accused her of change, yet one moment his manner verged upon tenderness, and the next moment the air could be rife with hostility.

"Well, it is no matter now. The deed is done. I'll admit that the haste of the situation was born of impatience and anger. I walked the city for some time after, wondering what I had allowed you to goad me into doing."

"So it is all my fault!" Marissa cried in protest.

He laughed. "Fault? No. I'm still not so terribly sure that you really knew what you wanted. No, if there is fault, I think that I take it myself. But it is done now, you see. And I thought that I should tell you a few things."

Marissa walked uneasily around the settee, using it as a barrier between them, though he offered her no physical harm. She still could not forget the wedding kiss he had bestowed upon her. She would never forget it, she thought, or the way it made her feel.

And with him, alone, she discovered herself watching his mouth and remembering far too much about it. She scarcely knew him, and already she was learning far too much about him. She could close her eyes and remember the curve of his smile. Remember the mockery, remember a gaze of tenderness. She could close her eyes and see his eyes upon her. She knew she would walk down a busy street and remember the timbre of his voice. And the touch of his hands.

Her memories made her grow warm. She swallowed slightly, afraid that he would touch her again and somehow afraid that he would not. It occurred to her that he had never really made any agreement about their marriage; she had no idea of what it was to be like.

"You've already told me quite a few things," she murmured coolly, seeking a refined distance between them. "You don't want a wife, you think it's amusing that I might protect you, and there is no such thing as an unwanted advance since you admittedly and eagerly seek the company of—" She paused, the word "whores" upon her tongue. She amended her words with a bitter note. "Dance-hall girls. San Francisco does have the finest."

His lip curled, but he was neither amused nor pleased with her recitation. "My dear Mrs. Tremayne, but you've got a quick and dangerous tongue!"

"I'm repeating what I've heard," she said tartly.

"I didn't come here to fight with you," he said easily enough. With a lazy stride, though, he was moving toward her. "However, madam, I do find it tempting to remember my deep and solemn vow of guardianship and see to the mending of your reckless ways."

"Oh! And what did you intend?" Marissa gasped, but she thought it wise to move quickly, even while challenging him.

"Oh, something mild. A sound thrashing, perhaps."

"You most certainly can't be serious!" she assured him.

"Can't I?" he demanded. His arm snaked out and his fingers wound around her wrists, and she suddenly found herself drawn tight against him. He was taunting her, she knew, but he was also tense with anger. "Take care, Marissa, for you do not know me at all. I do not always know myself. Take this morning. I certainly had not intended to wed, and you began to speak and I found myself engaged in the deed."

"You said—"

"I said that it was my fault, most assuredly. For no man can be so twisted and manipulated unless he allows it to be so. But I will not be twisted or manipulated any longer. Still, I did not mean to tell you that."

"Please," she murmured suddenly, twisting her wrists in his grasp. She could not bear to be so close to him; she had discovered that this morning. Warmth seemed to leap and sizzle from his body into her own, and she felt too keenly the form and shape and strength of his body. And she felt the rivers of warmth that invaded her, entering her blood, her limbs. The racing fires left her weak and uncertain, wanting to escape, wanting to fling her arms around his neck so she could continue to stand.

"Marissa, I wanted only to tell you that you would find the city beautiful, and my house an easy one to dwell within. You may take the later ship, as I have told you. It will be an easy enough life for you, I daresay. Leave me to my peace and remember I cherish my name and would harshly revenge the misuse of it, and we may get on better than most."

Her head fell back as she ceased to struggle. She was suddenly caught by the deep blue command of his eyes, and she could fight no more. Nor could she speak.

And he fell silent, too. He was gazing into her eyes. She did not fight him, but neither did he let her go.

Then suddenly he released her, turning away. "I shall see you again directly before I leave. I'm taking the *Princess of the Seas* the day after tomorrow. I shall have all your necessary travel papers and instructions on how to reach San Francisco prepared for you. Oh," he added. "And for your friends, of course."

She nodded. Now he was brisk and cool once again, all business. He reached the door, and suddenly she found herself moving after him. "Mr. Tremayne!" She hesitated as he turned. "Ian," she said softly.

"Yes?"

"I—I didn't thank you."

"For what?"

"For Mary and Jimmy. For accepting them so cordially. For—for giving him a job."

He shrugged. "He seems a likeable enough lad. And he's wed himself a true lady. I'd not make your life a living hell, madam, no matter what your beliefs on the matter."

He turned and started to leave again.

"Ian!"

She was startled when she called him back a second time. He held the doorknob somewhat impatiently and awaited her words.

His given name still felt so strange upon her tongue, she was amazed that it had slipped from her lips so easily.

"I—I do not wish to make your life miserable, either, sir."

She thought that she detected a hint of a smile just barely curving his mouth. "Well, thank you for that," he told her. "Good night."

He left for good this time, closing the door firmly behind him.

She did not call him back.

She leaned against the door and closed her eyes, thinking that she had survived the day.

And then she remembered that she had married him. Legally married him.

She remembered his kiss, and her fingers brushed over her lips. She felt a swift, searing warmth sweep along her spine.

She tried to close her mind to the memory, to the feel of his hands upon her, to the power within them. He could be very kind . . .

But he also had a sharp and mercurial temper.

And she had lied to him. She had more than lied to him. She had played a monstrous pretense upon him.

If he ever discovered the deception . . .

She didn't dare dwell upon the thought. She pushed away from the door with resolution and poured herself a very small sherry, sat down and began to daydream of the trip to see Uncle Theo, when she could tell him that he would never have to step foot inside a mine again.

It was all going to be worth it. Everything. She could do so very much. She had succeeded in the charade. She had learned her lessons well. Everyone was going to be so very happy.

She swallowed more sherry.

If that was the case, then why did she see visions of his searing blue gaze upon her every time she closed her eyes?

And why did she remember so constantly the feel of his hands, the warmth of his touch . . .

And tremble?

CHAPTER FIVE

The London fog was rolling in, but it didn't disturb Ian. He was accustomed to fog, and he loved it. A lot of London reminded him of home—the sight of an expanse of bridge, the swirl of the mist and the coolness of the night against his face.

He had met with a Scottish wool merchant for dinner, and had chosen to walk to the boardinghouse rather than take a hansom cab. He was enjoying himself. There was a great deal of beauty and elegance here in the heart of the city. He paused before a new house going up and critically studied its lines. It would be a beautiful home.

He frowned then, thinking of the postponed meetings he was going to have to reschedule when he returned home. He'd been hired to design an office building. The site was to be upon some of the newly reclaimed land in the marina area, and he was having a hell of time convincing the owners that if they chose to build there, their costs would go up. He felt uneasy about building on the land—it was all fill. Deep pilings would be necessary, and a great deal of steel. And it would also have to be a building capable of sway. Tremors often swept the city, and a certain amount of sway was necessary to keep the structures from cracking. He had been watching buildings go up ever since he was a boy. And he had known even then that more than anything else in the world, he wanted to build. And he had hated the store for standing in the way of that dream.

It was late, he realized, really late. He started to walk in the direction of Hyde Park, and as the moon flared its soft light upon him to join with the glow of the gas lamps, he suddenly raised his hand to note the thin white band around his pinkie where he had removed the signet ring in the middle of his wedding ceremony.

He stopped cold, feeling ill, feeling a heat sweep over him. For what seemed like the thousandth time that day he demanded harshly of himself just what in hell he had done.

And why, in God's name, had he done it?

He paused and leaned against a fence and closed his eyes tightly. He had vowed on the day when he had stood in the drizzling cemetery and watched as Diana's coffin was sealed into the family mausoleum that he would never marry again, never call another woman his wife. They had loved one another too deeply, too fiercely. She had been the most gentle woman he had ever met, so gentle that she had left life behind her with barely a whisper.

It had been a long time before he had managed to touch another woman, and then, perhaps, he had managed to rationalize things in his mind. It was all right to find women entertaining and amusing, and it was even all right to form certain relationships, as long as they were kept in their proper perspective. As long as the women were never his wife, as long as he need never rouse himself to offer love.

And he had been managing just fine. . . .

Now there was this chit of a girl in his life. He had accepted the responsibility that Sir Thomas had begged of him, but he had never expected this.

His mouth set in a grim line of anger. She wanted her inheritance enough to beg and plead. She had sold herself, just as surely as the finest courtesan in London or the most jaded street girl in San Francisco. She'd used logic, indignation, a touch of pathos and even fury, and somehow, she had sparked something dark and dangerous in his heart. He had said no, he had meant no. And then suddenly he had been out pounding the streets in a state of total dishabille, digging up the Honorable Mr. Blackstone—

And exchanging wedding vows.

What was it that she did that could cause him to feel such a passion of fury in his heart and soul? He didn't want to hurt her. By God, she was Sir Thomas's daughter.

No, he didn't want to hurt her. He didn't want to be near her. He had just wanted to go on living, allowing her to roam his house and giving her the freedom of her own life. And she, in turn, should have politely avoided him, stayed out of his way, and behaved graciously and kindly to guests within his home. It could have worked.

But he'd lost his temper and married her . . .

He pushed away from the fence, still furious with himself as he strode down the street, heading for his room.

He hated her, suddenly and intensely, and what she had goaded him into doing.

He paused again, inhaling, exhaling. No, he didn't hate the girl. He hated his reaction to her. He hated the curiosity she drew from him when he looked into her eyes. She could appear so haunted. As if she was desperate to reach out and grasp things, and hold them tightly, simply because they had always eluded her.

She could have a look about her, as if she had witnessed serious nightmares.

She had just lost her father, he reminded himself. And yet there was more. She could be regal and supreme, she could speak with a voice that rang cool and imperious, and yet, caught unaware, there could be that beautiful and haunting appeal in her eyes. Those cat's eyes, green cat's eyes, proud, spirited, beguiling.

His wife, he reminded himself, and tasted the bitterness on his tongue.

At least she was beautiful. Maybe she had a point. She would be an asset to his home and to his business. He imagined that she could throw an elegant dinner party, and wear mink or silver fox to the opera with panache.

It could be a bargain well met.

And along with her came that young Jimmy O'Brien. Ian was impressed with the lad. Oh, he was raw, but his eyes held honesty, and he was earnest. And he was seeking the American dream, something that Ian believed in deeply. No kings, no queens, no royalty. Just a tough but beautiful land where hard work and ambition and dreams could be realized. O'Brien could be trusted, he felt.

And O'Brien could save Ian a great deal of time. Ian knew he could have sold the emporium, but it would have seemed like a betrayal. His father and grandfather had loved the store.

And if Diana had survived, and their child had been born, perhaps his own son or daughter would have loved the merchandising business, too.

But now there would be no children, no heirs, ever, he promised himself. He could sell the bloody business.

But he would not.

He had returned to his lodgings, and he quietly let himself in the front door of the boardinghouse.

Just as he reached his room on the second floor, he heard a sound and looked down the stairs. A woman was standing there. A tall, handsome blonde with a full figure and proud carriage. She was dressed in red silk with a matching feather-ornamented hat. Her name was Molly, and she played the piano and sang at the Gray Friars, a pub down the street. She could be elegant, and she could be discreet, and he had shared a pint or two with her during trips to London. He had even mentioned vaguely that he might see her when he had first arrived two nights ago.

She smiled slowly, and he was tempted to call her up. But before he could open his mouth, he felt as if he were suddenly blinded by a pair of flashing green eyes. He could hear Marissa's voice, painfully scornful and dignified despite the very sweetness of her tone, as good as telling him that he was welcome to his harlots and his whores and his dance-hall girls.

Desire seemed to surge within him, along with a sizzling of fury. But when he looked at the tall, handsome blonde he felt only weariness.

"Good evening, Molly," he called to her.

"Mr. Tremayne!" she murmured.

Ian knew she expected more, but he merely said, "Good night, Molly," and entered his room.

He sat at his desk. He had spent last night with the brandy bottle to warm him. It seemed that tonight he would do the same. And he would drink until he could drown out the sight of those haunting emerald eyes.

His wife's eyes.

He groaned and took a long, long swallow of the burning liquor.

Then he leaned his head back and prayed for a decent night's sleep.

At two-thirty the following afternoon Marissa stood before the altar at Saint John's to witness Mary's and Jimmy's wedding.

They had both come to the hotel not long after dark the previous night, blushing, happy, so blissful that they appeared to be a pair of fools. And they had announced their wedding to Marissa. Apparently Jimmy had seen a minister the moment they'd come to London. The banns had already been called.

Marissa had been startled and hurt that they had kept it a secret from her, but then she realized that Mary had not wanted her to know, had not wanted Marissa to feel that added pressure.

Jimmy and Mary both hugged her fiercely, thanked her again— and then assured her that they both thought the very world of Ian Tremayne.

Marissa said tartly that that was quite nice, since Mary really should have been the one married to the man, but they were so very happy that she couldn't put a damper on their tremendous enthusiasm.

She loved them both, and she was delighted that it was because of her they could be so very happy. But watching them that night gave her the first pang of emotion regarding all that she had given up.

Mary and Jimmy sat together on the sofa, held hands and gazed into one another's eyes. And there was such a look of adoration between them that she felt as if she was an intruder, and then she realized that she was. She retired quickly and left them alone.

In bed she lay awake staring at the ceiling and relived every moment of her own hasty wedding, then thought about the man she had married. He was definitely not Jimmy, she thought with a sigh. He would never sit before a fire, gazing adoringly into her eyes.

And yet she could not forget his touch, his kiss. And the more she remembered their encounters, the warmer her thoughts made her grow, the more she felt a quaking within, a sizzling of apprehension . . .

Of excitement.

In the morning, Mary seemed more beautiful than she ever had before. Her eyes sparkled and shone, her cheeks were flushed, and there was no sign left of the fever that had so seriously plagued her just weeks before.

She had dressed in a day dress of soft ivory satin with an elegant Spanish veil that had been left to her by her mother. Her enthusiasm and happiness were contagious, and Marissa could not resist her good humor. They very decadently decided to order champagne for breakfast, and by the time Jimmy came for them in a hansom cab, they were both giggling and giddy.

"So you have to be tipsy to marry the likes of me, eh?" Jimmy teased Mary, but she laughed and uninhibitedly reached her long fingers around his neck and dragged his head down to hers and kissed him so long and sweetly that Marissa finally had to clear her throat to remind them of her presence.

Jimmy laughed a little huskily, and he offered an arm to each girl. They arrived at the church and spoke to the reverend, and Jimmy checked that all their papers were in order. The minister's plump and beaming wife came out to play the organ and sing, and she did both beautifully.

And then the ceremony began, with Marissa and the minister's wife as witnesses. It was small, as small as her own pretense of a wedding had been.

But it was different. So different.

Marissa thought that she had never seen such love in anyone's eyes as that which shone in Mary's and Jimmy's eyes. She had never seen a couple so devoted.

Their vows were barely whispered, but their hearts were in their whispers. When the minister told Jimmy to kiss his bride, and Jimmy did so, Marissa felt she was about to cry. She didn't understand why; weddings did not usually make her want to cry. She realized that she was witnessing something she had never considered might exist. Something that was far, far out of her own reach.

And then some curious inner sense made her turn around.

She inhaled sharply, feeling a cold shiver sweep over her.

Ian Tremayne was at the back of the church, leaning against one of the huge white pillars. Casually, comfortably. She had the feeling he had witnessed all of the ceremony.

The blood drained from her face. What was he doing there? How had he come upon them?

She had lied to him, introducing Mary and Jimmy as man and wife. And now here he was at the back of the church, watching the ceremony.

He was standing in the shadow. She could not see his eyes; she could not begin to fathom his thoughts.

But she knew he was staring at her. And she seemed frozen, unable to tear herself away from that gaze.

"Mrs. Tremayne!" the minister called to her. "If you will, please, we need your signature!"

Those words propelled her into action. Mary's real name was on those papers. She had to get them signed and put away. What if Ian should chance to see them?

She sped down the aisle to the side pulpit and quickly scratched out her name, K. Marissa Tremayne. Ian was walking down the aisle.

Mary caught Marissa's eyes and realized that they didn't dare allow Ian to see the papers. She rushed forward, blocking Ian.

"Mr. Tremayne!"

"It was a lovely wedding, Mary. Really beautiful," he told her.

"Thank you. If I'd known you were planning on coming—"

"Well, Mary, I wasn't planning on coming. It was my under-standing that you and Jimmy were already wed."

Mary blushed furiously. "Ah, that's Marissa! She was trying to—defend us."

"Defend you?"

"Well, it must have appeared that we . . ." She let her voice trail away delicately with a note of distress. "She did not wish you to think ill of us."

"Oh, Mary, I did not think ill of you or your young man for a moment," Ian said smoothly. He looked up and smiled crookedly at Marissa over Mary's shoulder. "I did not think ill of you at all."

Jimmy was rolling his set of papers into his jacket while the min-ister shuffled his. Jimmy, flushing, paid and thanked the minister and his wife, then he, too, hurried down the aisle.

Marissa remained by the pulpit, stiff and straight.

Ian congratulated Jimmy, and Jimmy began to stammer. Ian waved a dismissing hand in the air. "You did nothing wrong, Jim O'Brien. And I did truly enjoy witnessing the ceremony."

"How did you come to be here?" Mary asked him at last.

"The parlor maid from the hotel sent me here when I arrived at Marissa's room with your traveling papers. Since I did make arrangements for a Mr. and Mrs. O'Brien, I'm glad to see that you are man and wife in truth."

He stepped past them and walked down the aisle to the pulpit where he faced Marissa. He didn't say a word to her, but his eyes were hot upon her and she felt the simmering anger within him.

He wasn't mad at Mary or at Jimmy. He was furious with her. She had lied to him.

He reached out to take her arm. She almost flinched from his touch, but managed to refrain.

"Ah, so this must be Mr. Tremayne!" the minister said jovially. "Elizabeth, had we known Mrs. Tremayne's good husband was going to be here, he could have served with his wife as witness!"

Marissa paled slightly, thinking of the trouble they would have been in if Ian had seen papers that joined James O'Brien and

Katherine Mary Ahearn. Ian greeted the reverend and his wife solemnly, adding, "I'd really no idea that I was attending the wedding; my wife did not invite me."

"Oh!" the minister murmured, distressed.

Ian offered him the slight curl of a smile. "It was quite a service, though, and I am very glad that I did not miss it. Good day to you, sir."

He doffed his hat and spun Marissa around. She wanted to wrench free from his hold, but it was firm, and she was swept along without making an effort to escape him.

In the middle of the aisle they reached Jimmy and Mary. "Well, it seems we've quite an occasion here," Ian murmured. "Would you be so kind as to accept a wedding supper from your new employer, Mr. O'Brien?"

Jimmy's mouth worked for a moment without sound. Then he managed to speak. "Sir, it's kind, but I can't accept more from you—"

"Nonsense. Any man can accept a wedding dinner from another. Come along while the night is young. Neither Marissa nor I would want to intrude upon too much of this special time, yet neither would we have you begin this new life without proper celebration. Eh, Marissa?"

Was he serious, or was he taunting her? What was his game? His eyes were still filled with fury when he touched her. His grip was tight with tension.

"Marissa?"

"Of course," she murmured.

He was always in control, she thought. On the street he quickly hailed a cab and asked the driver to take them to an exclusive but expensive club near Parliament, one that was patronized by members of the royal family. Jimmy did not know the name. Mary's eyes widened. "Mr. Tremayne, you needn't—"

"Mary, indulge me," he said.

Soon they were at the club. The doors to the hansom were opened for them, and Ian was lifting Marissa down. A doorman swept them into the club, greeting Ian by name. He spoke with the maître d', and they were quickly led to a table in a private room.

Potted palms adorned the room. The chairs were huge, elegant with carved lions' feet. The table was covered in snowy white linen, and the flatware upon the table was golden while the wineglasses were of the finest crystal. Soft light shimmered from candles in a chandelier.

Ian seated Marissa. Jimmy did a fair job of imitating him as he seated Mary. Ian ordered rack of lamb from the waiter, who obviously knew him. And champagne.

When the champagne came, Ian lifted his glass to Mary and Jimmy.

"To a lifetime of health and happiness!" They all sipped champagne.

"Aye, and thank you!" Jimmy exclaimed, leaping to his feet to toast in kind. "And to you, sir, and to Marissa! A lifetime of—"

He choked at the end, realizing that there was really little to wish them. The slow, taunting curve came to Ian's lip, and he lifted his glass to Marissa. "A lifetime of wealth," he murmured, "and health and happiness, too, of course."

Marissa smiled coolly. "Thank you so very much."

He turned from her with a shrug and spoke to Jimmy. "I'll be leaving tomorrow morning." He reached into his jacket pocket and produced a parcel of documents, which he handed to Jimmy. "Tickets, transfer points, the address and phone number for my home in San Francisco, everything you might need, I hope. I plan on being at the train station when you arrive, but should something prevent me, a carriage or a car will meet you."

Jimmy nodded gravely, accepting the packet. "Thank you, Mr. Tremayne. Thank you."

"Ah, another toast!" Ian said. He lifted his glass again. "To a long and prosperous business relationship between us!" he said.

"Hear, hear!" Mary cried, delighted.

Ian filled the glasses. Marissa discovered that she was acquiring quite a taste for champagne. It went down so easily, and it smoothed out the rough edges of discomfort and unease.

And fear! she thought unhappily. He had come so very close to seeing the name on Mary's wedding papers today!

Ah, but he hadn't really thought to look at them. He didn't suspect. He thought he remembered Marissa at times, but he didn't realize she had been the maid in the shadows or the child in the mining village. And still, tonight, each time he glanced her way, she knew he was condemning her for the one minor lie he had caught her in . . .

Her glass was empty. He filled it. She felt the sharp probe of his blue eyes, and lowered her lashes to study her crystal glass.

The food was brought and it was delicious. Marissa was saved from much conversation, for Ian questioned Jimmy, and Jimmy talked about Ireland, and wool—he knew wool very well. Ian told him how alike San Francisco and London could be at times, blanketed in fog, mysterious, beautiful. And through the fog you could see the bridge and the bay, and the houses with their gingerbreading and pastels and colors, and they were beautiful. Marissa listened to him, and was suddenly afraid again.

She didn't want to leave England. She didn't want to sail the distance of an ocean, then travel across a continent.

She looked up. Ian was watching her again. She flushed slightly, and her lashes lowered.

She toyed with dessert. The check was signed, and they were soon out on the street. "I'll hail you a cab," Ian said to Jimmy. "And see Marissa to her rooms."

She glanced up, startled, then realized that Jimmy and Mary were married. Legally. Naturally Ian presumed that Mary would be staying with Jimmy. But the thought of being left alone with Ian terrified her.

"Oh, but it's early yet!" she said hurriedly. "Perhaps they'd like to return to my suite for a while."

"For more champagne?" Ian asked politely.

How much champagne had she already swallowed, she wondered. Not enough. She felt dizzy, and guessed she would have a headache later, but at least she felt a little more capable of dealing with him.

"Champagne, sherry, conversation—" she began.

"They are *true* newlyweds, my dear. And surely seek their privacy," he said. He lifted his hand and flagged down a hansom.

There was nothing Marissa could do. She quickly hugged Mary, not wanting to let her go. She kissed Jimmy, and perhaps clung to him too long.

Ian's arms disentangled her. "I'll see you in America!" he called to Jimmy.

"Aye, sir, in America!" And the bay horse pulling the cab clip-clopped into the night.

"Come on," Ian said roughly. He tugged Marissa's arm and she saw that a second cab was awaiting them.

"I can see myself to the suite," she said with what casual aplomb she could manage.

"You can scarcely walk," he said flatly, "and I wouldn't dream of allowing my dear wife to travel the streets of London alone."

He lifted her up and set her into the cab, then climbed up beside her, calling the address to the driver. They didn't speak but she felt the warmth of him beside her, the flex and movement of his every muscle. She felt the tension that had stayed with him, no matter how smooth his manner, since he had seen her in the church.

They came to her suite. When she had entered the parlor she tried to turn swiftly and thank him for the meal and for escorting her back.

He none too gently pressed her forward, entering determinedly behind her, then closing the door behind himself.

Marissa swept off her cape and moved into the room, dropping the cape upon the settee. Ian leaned against the door, his blue gaze searing.

She fought the champagne, for it was making her dizzy, and her vision was blurry. Perhaps it was for the best, when he stared at her so.

No! She needed her wits to deal with him.

She yawned extravagantly. "Really, Mr. Tremayne, it is late—"

"You were just saying that it was early."

"But I am suddenly so exhausted."

"Well, exhausted or no, Mrs. Tremayne, you've an explanation to make, haven't you?"

"Have I?"

"About your newlywed friends."

She shrugged. "I don't—"

"You lied to me about them."

"It seemed easier to introduce them as man and wife. I knew they were marrying the next day. Why on earth are you so angry about them?" she demanded, determined not to show her fear.

"Oh, I'm not angry about them at all," he said softly.

"Then?" she murmured.

He moved into the room at last. He was stalking her, she thought. She moved back. A quivering seized her. She was angry; she was uncertain.

And she knew that he was going to touch her, corner her and touch her and hold her to his whim. It was in his stride, in his eyes. And she shivered because she did not know if she despised the idea . . .

Or anticipated it.

"Then . . . ?" she repeated on a note of desperation.

"Then . . ."

She was backed against the wall. He laid a hand flat on either side of her head, imprisoning her without touching her, except with that blue fire in his eyes.

"What I want to know, my dear Marissa, is just what else you've lied about to me."

"Really, there's nothing—"

"I will have the truth, Marissa. And I will have it tonight."

CHAPTER SIX

I haven't lied to you about anything else!" Marissa protested. She slipped away quickly, moving around the room to keep a distance between them. Coming to the little silver tray with the decanters of brandy and sherry and whiskey, she paused, pouring out a snifter of brandy. She needed to be very calm. "Would you like something?" she asked him politely.

"Yes, I'd like the truth."

She sipped the brandy, studying him over the rim of the glass. "Your Yankee manners are atrocious, Mr. Tremayne."

He moved toward her. She swallowed the contents of the brandy glass, and it was suddenly plucked out of her hands. "Have I married a little drunkard as well as a cunning little liar?"

"A drunkard!"

"Lady, you've had enough champagne today to sink a ship."

"How dare you! You Yankee—"

"Yeah, yeah, us Yanks. It's been like this ever since we finally won that war in 1812."

She tried to move away, but he caught her arm. His touch was forceful, but not painful. She could feel his determination. She wasn't going to escape him again.

"Let's talk," he said flatly.

She didn't have much of an opportunity to resist; she found herself sitting on the settee with him beside her. Close beside her. His eyes blazed into hers.

"Let's have it, Marissa."

She raised her eyes to his. He was so damned determined! She suddenly wanted to spit out the truth and beg for mercy.

No. She wouldn't let him intimidate her. The truth could do nothing for any of them now.

Jimmy and Mary were legally wed.

And she was wed to this man.

She shook her head, allowing her lashes to fall over her eyes. Dear God, she should have left the brandy alone. The champagne had been bad enough. And she needed so desperately to be in control.

Especially tonight. Some fierce fever burned in Ian Tremayne tonight. His eyes seemed ringed with it, both fire and ice, burning hot one minute and cold the next. She'd seen him gentle, tender, amused and angry, but never so tense as this.

All because she had lied to him.

But the life she was living was a lie, and there was no way out of it, no way to tell him the truth. There was nothing to do but play her part, that of the spoiled and willful child of a very rich man.

She stared at him, chin high, eyes level. "I'm sorry that you are so affronted over such a very minor thing as the precise hour and date of a marriage."

"A lie is never a minor thing, Marissa."

"This one was," she insisted. "I knew that Jimmy and Mary would be married, and I wanted you—to accept them as man and wife. I couldn't have left here without them, you see."

"Your lives are so entwined, then? I'm curious. How?"

His eyes were maddening. So dark, so blue, so demanding. She felt pinned to the settee. Desperate. She didn't like the feeling. The warmth emanating from his body encompassed her. The clean scent of his soap hinted warmly of the man's masculinity, and the soft feathering of his breath when he spoke touched upon her face. The sensations were pleasant. She suddenly wanted to laugh and touch his face, no matter how hard and forbidding that face.

It was the champagne, she thought. Do not touch, for he bites!

She closed her eyes and rested her head against the settee.

"Tell me about these very good friends of yours, Marissa."

"I can't. I'm quite exhausted. I need you to leave. I shall explain everything that you desire at some later time."

"Will you?"

"Indeed."

"I think not."

He caught her hands and pulled her up. Her eyes flew open, blazing with fury. "If you were any kind of British gentleman—"

"Well, I'm not. I'm not British at all. What I am is a Yank, remember, and therefore, according to you, my manners are by nature atrocious."

"All right, all right!" She snatched her hands free from his and leaped to her feet. There was a sudden blackness before her and she wavered. She caught hold of an oak table to remain standing. "Her father, Mary's father, was the vicar of our parish. As children, we were very good friends. And not long after her father died, she came to live with us. It's very simple, sir!" she announced scornfully.

"And Jimmy?"

"And Jimmy?" Marissa found that she was smiling slowly. "Why, she met him, and she fell in love with him. There's no mystery there, Mr. Tremayne."

"Ah, but your life seems to be shrouded in mystery, Mrs. Tremayne," he taunted softly.

"It's quite amazing that you should feel so, sir," she said sweetly.

"I want to know what else you've lied about," he returned.

"I've told you—"

"And I've warned you," he snapped.

She meant to walk by him very smoothly. Chin high, shoulders square—with a firm upper lip. But she had barely moved from the table when the swamping dizziness came over her again. She tripped—she was rather certain that she tripped right over his foot. The next thing she knew she was falling and, reaching out, she came in hard contact with his chest.

He half rose to catch her, then her impetus threw them onto the settee, her fingers curled into his starched white shirt, her body draped across his lap. His arms had wrapped instinctively around her to break the fall. Startled, she gazed into the blue depths of his eyes. She meant to jump quickly away, but she could not. She suddenly seemed to be enveloped in the strength and scent of the man, and in the power of his eyes. She did not move at all, but met his gaze. Heat seared through her. A sweet trembling began in her stomach and traveled like wildfire to her limbs. Delicately she moistened her lips with the tip of her tongue, seeking to speak, to break the curious hold.

And she was suddenly certain that he meant to speak, too. But he did not. Not really. Instead an oath shattered the air, and he bent down to her. He was going to kiss her again, she thought. She should rise, protest.

Instead she awaited the touch of his mouth. The sensations were again spiraling wildly through her. Something molten, something delicious, churned deeply within her. She had felt his kiss before. And she anticipated it now.

It was the champagne. Or the brandy. She could not think.

Or perhaps . . .

It was just the man.

And then his lips touched hers, forming over them with a practiced and fierce demand. Hot and moist and so very sure, they drank in the fullness of her mouth, touching, invading, exploring, eliciting more fervent sensations to swirl and play wickedly within her blood. She felt again the urge to touch him, and this time she did, her fingers uncurling from his shirt front to touch his cheek and feel the texture of his bronzed flesh. She pressed closer against him, instinctively responding to the overwhelming sensuality of the man. Some small voice warned her that she was catapulting into danger with a stranger, with the enemy. But intelligent thought had long since eluded her. She felt only the sweep of his tongue, the molding of his lips, the pressure of his hands, holding her leisurely to his will.

His lips parted from hers.

"Indeed, madam, what other lies have you spoken?"

She fought his grip suddenly, furious, her head reeling.

"None!"

She struggled to rise, slamming her fist against his chest. "None! I am weary, I am exhausted, and you plague me endlessly while you pretend that we can live amicably in the same house. Please! I am too tired—"

"You are too drunk," he said dryly.

"Oh! And you didn't drink champagne as if it were water yourself!"

"I did not drink champagne out of fear."

"I am not afraid of you."

"You are afraid of some truth, and yes, Marissa, therefore you are afraid of me. Very much afraid of me."

"Oh!"

He released her and she leaped to her feet, pointing dramatically at the door. "Tremayne, we shall speak of this some other time, I tell you!"

She started for the door, but he stood and caught her arm. "We'll speak of it now! And take care, madam, that you never again show me a door before we are finished."

She heard his words, but she was suddenly too weary to fight him. She fell into his arms. Her eyes closed and she clung to his shoulders. She groaned softly. "Please, I cannot stand."

"You will stand. It's all a trick with you!"

"No!" she whispered. "No. This is no trick."

He carried her to the settee and set her down on it. He leaned over her, and though she had allowed her eyelashes to drift softly closed over her eyes, she was suddenly aware that he was concerned.

She had told him the truth, her knees had buckled, and she had been able to stand no longer. But now she realized that perhaps this was the best game to play with him.

Her lashes fluttered open and she discovered that he was studying her intensely. She found herself returning his gaze, unable to look away. His left hand lay upon her hip while his right hand sat upon her shoulder and his face was close, bronzed, tense, close. She inhaled the clean scent of the man and felt the sudden rush of his breath against her cheek. She wanted to look away; she could not. A sweet cascade of sensation suddenly ran throughout her limbs, hot where he touched her and hot where his eyes seared into hers. It swept her breath away, and caused her heart to quicken its pace until she could feel the maddening pulse within her mind.

"Leave me—" she started to murmur, but her voice broke off for she realized that he was going nowhere.

His mouth was slowly descending upon hers.

His kiss was not gentle. No, not gentle at all.

His lips seared hers with a simmering anger just barely held in check. He did not hurt her, nor did he allow her any room for escape. There was force behind his touch, and still . . .

And still, somewhere within it, was the sweetness of seduction, of coercion. His left hand lay upon her hip while his right one caught her cheek, his thumb stroking her flesh while his kiss found its own haunting leisure. Her heart began to pound more fiercely. She didn't know if it was the sweet fire of the champagne or of the man entering into her blood, warming her, filling her with the same anger.

And the same passion.

She meant to protest. But instead her lips parted to his fierce demand, and she felt the intimate foray of his tongue, tasting her lips, delving into the dark and secret crevices of her mouth and seeming to enter into her soul. She felt the fascinating sweep of his tongue with her own. Her heart pounded. Darkness seemed to descend. The clean male scent that swept evocatively around him touched and stirred new sensations within her.

Her hands lay against his chest. She needed to push him away. She did not. She let her fingers roam over the fabric of his vest and felt as if she held tight while some whirlwind caught her. Then his lips raised from hers at last, and his eyes were upon hers again, sizzling with anger and fire, and she realized that no tenderness or pity had stirred his actions. Furiously, she shoved with all her strength against him and got to her feet.

"It's time for you to leave, Mr. Tremayne!" she gasped, shaking, wiping his kiss from her lips with the back of her hand as if she could erase the passion between them.

He didn't move. "I still haven't gotten an answer," he told her. "Or perhaps I have."

"I don't know what you're talking about. Now get up and get out."

"You are a rotten little liar," he told her softly.

"Meaning?"

"That was no innocent kiss."

"I did not kiss you."

"Ah, but you see, you returned the touch."

"I was trying to be polite."

"Polite!" he exclaimed, then he burst out laughing. "Dear Lord, how often are you polite? And with just how many men?"

"Oh, you are horrid!"

"Merely American."

"Is it one and the same?"

"I'm wounded, deeply."

"No, dear sir, you wound others deeply."

His voice remained light, but there was underlying danger in his tone. "I'm seeking the truth, my love."

Desperate, she cried out to him. "I haven't lied to you! Oh, dear Lord, help me! I'm trying to tell you—"

She broke off. He was on his feet at last, and heading toward her. Then she realized that he only meant to sweep past her on his way to the door. She inhaled quickly with relief, and he turned.

"I—I haven't lied to you!" she cried, but she faltered. And then she suddenly panicked as his hands came to rest upon her shoulders.

She slammed her fists against his chest. "Damn you! Can't you just leave it be! You want your life; I want my privacy!"

But even as she spoke, her lips were still burning where his had touched them, and she shook with tremors from the intimacy they had shared. She hated him, and yet she longed to touch his face. She wanted to feel the contours of that hard, angry jaw. She wanted to soothe the anger away and see him smile with tenderness.

His voice thundered with anger. "You'll have your privacy when you've answered all my questions, Marissa, damn you!"

"You'll leave now!" she snapped. And then dizziness burst within her mind just as he pulled her into a hard embrace. She tried valiantly to straighten and free herself, but she fell into his arms. Her anger drained from her suddenly. Her eyes, wide and uncertain, stared into his. "Ian, please, I—"

"Ah, yes, you are falling again!" he taunted. "Poor sweet innocent! It is the champagne. You need nothing more than to be left alone. Out of the clutches of your cruel guardian—and husband."

She looped her arms around his neck, protesting. "Truly. It is the champagne. I should not have drunk so freely."

"That damnable champagne is there whenever you want it, Marissa. You are not so inebriated as to act out whatever role you choose to play. I want the truth."

"What truth?" she cried out. She was within his arms, held there easily as he stared at her. She returned his gaze, fascinated by the color of his eyes, by the rugged planes and angles of his face. She wet her dry lips with the tip of her tongue and felt a sizzling tremor streak through her. She wanted to taste his kiss again. It was amazing, for she resented him, she could not care for him, and yet she did. "Ian," she murmured, and no other word would leave her lips.

Suddenly he was smiling, and some of his anger drained away.

"Perhaps I shall just discover the truth for myself," he said.

The truth about her, he thought. There was one way to know if she had entertained a lover before. And with the blood seeming to shimmer in his veins and the pounding in his head, he knew that discovering more about her was suddenly necessary to him. He had never wanted a woman more. "If I'll not have something from you in words this night, then by God, lady, perhaps I will have a wife! My manners are already considered rude, and as you claim the champagne, sweet, so can I claim the brandy!"

He unerringly found the route to the bedroom, long strides bringing them into the darkened room. She knew where they traveled. Winds created by his impetus stirred over her face, and she was vaguely aware of what she was doing. It was insane. So were the fires that stirred within her body and soul. She longed to taste his lips again, to know again the fever of his arms.

And more.

"You really must put me down," she told him.

"I intend to," he promised.

They entered the darkened bedroom, and he laid her down upon the bed, then sat beside her as glimmers of moonlight played in the room. She felt her breath coming quickly, but she did not close her eyes. She sought his in the strange surreal light, and found he was looking at her hair.

It was splayed upon the pillow in the moonlight, shimmering like a thousand fires. His fingers moved quickly within it, removing the few pins she had used to secure it from her face. And when it stretched in burning, golden cascades around them, he lowered his face to hers, catching her chin softly between his two hands. "Earth and fire," he whispered softly. "Passion, tension, spirit. God forgive me, for I'll not forgive myself."

His words stirred a great unease within her soul, but his kiss quickly wiped that unease away. In the darkness it was suddenly magic. He tasted the rim of her mouth, and plunged and delved deeply within it. He whispered against her throat, against the lobe of her ear.

And then his hands were moving expertly over the tiny pearl buttons of her elegant blouse. She barely felt the sheath of silk whisper against her flesh as it was whisked away.

His kiss burned a sweetly forbidden fire against the length of her throat, delicately, erotically pausing at the point where her pulse beat wildly.

This was what a woman did when she was madly in love, Marissa thought vaguely. Lose all sense and reason, and hunger for a man. She was not in love. She was wary, as an intelligent lamb might be of an experienced, sometimes world-weary wolf . . .

No, she was not in love. But she was fascinated, as she had always been fascinated by him. Angry and fascinated. Careful and suspicious and fascinated. Furious and fascinated.

Taunted and seduced and fascinated . . .

Taken in by the spell of his gaze upon her, by his very touch. The subtle, masculine scent of him was stirring fires and hungers within her soul. She was fascinated by the gentle, callused brush of his fingers, by the strength within them, by the power of his hands. Stirred and tempted and challenged by the dark lock of hair that fell over his forehead in the mystic near darkness of the room. She was aware of what she did, of where they were, of where this new intimacy would take them. And it was wrong.

But it was also right. Something had been awakened within her. Something secret and beautiful, something of the dreams that Mary had spun, the dreams in which she had never believed. In the shadows, in the night, there was something beautiful and exciting. Something growing that she could not deny. She wanted to hold him, and hold him tight, and pretend that he did love her, to know just a taste of an emotion so rich and fine.

But this was not a dream! She struggled to remember that, but she felt drugged. She slipped into danger, and she saw the flames, yet resisting the sear of the fire seemed impossible. She had to stop him. She had to remind him that theirs was not the customary marriage.

That he did not want her . . .

She inhaled on a sweet shudder as his fingertips moved over her breast, untying the silken ribbons of her chemise, releasing the ties of her corset. She felt her breasts spill free of the restraint and the burning pressure of his lips low against the valley between them. She had let this go too far, oh, way too far. No, she had not let it, she had encouraged it, she had brought him here, to her.

Ian felt the first protest on her lips when he kissed her again, but he thought it more of her taunting, more of her game. He didn't understand what core of anger had burned so brightly within him, except that she had tricked him, she had lied, and he was suddenly damned sure that she had lied about more.

There *was* a lover. She had married Ian, perhaps planning all the while to turn to her lover. Perhaps to bring him with her across the ocean.

And he wondered what it mattered, there was so little that he could give her. He shouldn't be so angry, he should understand. He couldn't love her; he couldn't give her tenderness; he didn't even want to be near her. She was his wife, not a dance-hall girl.

But there was more to it than that. At least this night there was. There was that never-ending challenge in her beautiful green eyes, and there was the firelight that played within her hair. There was the impudence in her voice, the spirit, the anger, the laughter. The tilt of her chin. And now . . . the softness of her skin, the sweet taste of the champagne upon her lips, the subtle scent of her perfume.

Yes, the scent of her perfume.

He groaned aloud, taking her breast into the palm of his hand, gently covering the shadow-haunted peak with his mouth, curling his tongue over the nipple as his palm caressed the fullness of the mound. Again he felt her shudder, felt the faint murmurings of protest upon her lips. But even as she murmured, a fire of desire and longing stronger than her words, stronger than his own denial, swept raggedly through him. And again he kissed her lips, kissed them hungrily, angrily, then tenderly, bathing away any little hurt he might have inflicted with the stroke of his tongue.

He moved his fingers along the smooth silk of her stocking from her ankle to the lace of her drawers just above the knee, and there his fingers found the sleek softness of her bare thighs beneath the fabric. He teased her flesh, feeling her body move against his. And he felt again the protests bubbling to her lips, and silenced them with his tongue. He was not unaccustomed to women's finery, and easily found the ties to loosen the lace, and in seconds he had stripped the garment from her.

Alive with the fire of desire, he paid little heed to any other barriers between them. He seared her flesh with the hungry force of his kiss as he briefly adjusted his own clothing, then moved his weight against her body, between her thighs. She had ceased to protest, but trembled incredibly in his hold. Her pulse beat frantically at her throat when he touched it with his tongue. And when he paused, stroking her cheek to look down upon her, her eyes were emeralds, brilliant, stunning against the darkness, both dazzling and dazed. Her lips were parted softly, damp with his kiss, and her hair, that majestic hair, was still splayed in fire and splendor across the pillow. Her throat was long and white and elegant, and her breasts, bared and yet framed in lace and silk, were glorious, rouge peaked in the near darkness, shadowed, and still as tempting as original sin. Her eyes met his with some sudden and strange recognition, and she suddenly inhaled and cried out. "Ian, I did not intend—"

He did not know what she intended—he knew only that he did not intend to let her speak. There was a mystique in the darkness. He had ceased to think or reason or remember. He threaded his fingers through her hair, holding her to his will as he forcefully kissed away her words.

And as his tongue invaded her mouth, he found the sweet petals of her sex, teasing first with the thrust of his desire, then plunging hard with the spiraling depths of his need. Then he stopped, stunned, waiting.

Not even his kiss could drown out her cry.

Tears stung Marissa's eyes, and she bit hard on her lip against the sudden pain.

Ian had grown still, dead still.

The magic of the night had slipped away, the beauty of the shadows, of the dreams within the room. Suddenly he was very real, and flesh and blood, a man, and not a dream of love. Marissa realized that she had brought him here, that she had been seduced, perhaps, but that she had seduced in turn. And his hand lay against her face, his thumb moving over her cheek.

And feeling the dampness of the tear that lay against her flesh.

"Marissa!" She felt the warmth of his whisper there, and she wouldn't allow him compassion or pity, not now.

"Dear God, don't!" she cried.

And he grew still again, but the pad of his thumb moved gently over her face, smoothing away the dampness. Then his lips touched where his thumb had been, ever gentle. And she longed to scream, to cry out, to toss him from her.

But he did not leave her. He kissed her again and again. Finding her brows, her throat, her lips, her earlobe, her lips again.

And then he moved.

Slowly, so slowly, she was barely aware of his thrust at first.

And she was keenly, achingly aware, because slowly, so slowly, the magic was evoked once again.

She didn't know when she fell within the twilight swirl, not when she felt the budding excitement begin anew. It eased the burning at the apex of her thighs, yet created fire all over again. It came like lava, lustrous, sleek, sweet, moving through her limbs. It stretched out like lightning from the center of her being, and it warmed her, and returned again to that center, making her rise ever higher with the growing wonder of sensation.

And then the softness was gone, the slowness of his motion cast away. He moved like lightning, hard, fast, demanding. His arms were tight around her, and she realized that sounds were escaping her again, no longer protests, but exhalations and sweet, sweet moans. And he urged her to rise against him, and she did, arching to meet his every thrust, twisting, undulating, thinking that she could bear no more, take no more . . . yet ever reaching for the stars.

And then it seemed that those stars exploded above her and around her. The darkness was shattered with light, and then the light was plunged into darkness. She felt him, hard and powerful, driving deeply into her and shuddering as a hot lava seemed to fill her again. Tremors had seized her, too. Little tremors, bringing again the wonder, the stars, the darkness and the light. And when they left her at last, she was shivering.

It was cold, for he had lifted his weight away. And even as the magic she had barely glimpsed began to fade from her grasp, she realized that he was leaning upon an elbow, staring at her.

And the darkness was no cover against the probe of his eyes. She was in complete dishabille; he still wore his elegant jacket.

She turned aside, groping blindly for the covers, swept into a tempest of emotion. She wanted to hate him, but she knew that she did not. And that was a bitter thought, for she felt again the nagging pain of what she had done, what they had done, and it tore at her heart.

"Why didn't you tell me?"

His voice was a rasp. He seemed so angry still. He seemed angry! It was surely her place.

"Tell you what?" she snapped.

"I assumed—"

"You assumed!"

His hand touched her shoulder, and she wished that she dared to turn, to look into his eyes. But she lay there rigidly, her shoulders tense.

"I'm sorry," he said simply.

"Please, don't be."

An impatient oath escaped him. "Marissa, I did not force you—"

"No!" she cried, flinging back the covers, then swearing as she tried to rise and tripped over the shambles of her clothing. "You did not force me."

He rose quickly, which did not please her, for he appeared so respectable. The disarray of his hair, that dark lock lying over his forehead, was the only sign of all that had passed between them. He was coming around the bed to her, she realized. She wrenched the cover from the bed and swept it regally around herself like a cape. And she backed away, trying to escape him, but he quickly caught up with her, taking her arm.

"What do you think you're doing?"

"I'm leaving—"

"It's your room, you little fool."

"But—" She tried to break free from him. He released her, much to her surprise. Off balance, she fell against the wall.

And she was in his arms once again. And then she saw his eyes, blue, burning into hers. "Damn you!" he said softly. "It's the champagne, right?"

"Oh! Leave me alone!"

"I will."

He laid her upon the bed, but made no move to join her again. "Go to sleep," he told her harshly.

"Sleep! I cannot sleep—"

"You wanted to be alone. I'm leaving you alone. Cherish the privacy, my love. And sleep!" he snapped.

"You must leave—"

"Come the daylight, I am leaving. On a ship across the ocean, remember?"

"With any luck, you will be swallowed within it!" she hissed, trembling.

He paused. "Ah, but luck does not seem to be with you lately, does it my love?" He did not seem to expect an answer. He turned on his heel and left the room.

For long moments she lay there, numb.

Then Marissa felt again the burning that would not ease completely from her body. She closed her eyes, and remembered his kiss, his touch.

And it seemed that her flesh burned everywhere as she remembered the sweetness that had invaded her, the ecstasy. The sounds that had escaped her, the way they had been. She was angry with herself, unable to believe what she had done with her eyes wide open.

I tried to protest! she told herself.

But she had not. Not really. Perhaps she could not have gotten him to leave her rooms, but she could have stopped him from this.

It was the champagne . . .

No, she had clung to the champagne. It had been an excuse, and she could not deny it.

She wanted to scream. She wanted to claw at his face. She wanted so badly to hate him. And then she realized that her cheeks were damp again, that she had been crying.

And she had been crying because she did not hate him at all.

She craved things she had never imagined wanting before.

A home. A husband, a real husband. Happiness.

And more.

She wanted love.

CHAPTER SEVEN

Ian strode to the parlor of the suite and poured himself a generous portion of brandy. The heat of the liquor burned his throat and seemed to shudder its way through him, and still he felt at a loss. He sank down on the settee, studied his glass and swore softly to the night.

What the hell had he done?

Well, you wanted to know if she was lying, he reminded himself. You wanted the truth about the lover the squire had said would destroy her life.

And while she might have lied about half a dozen other things, she had definitely never bedded with the boy.

And that was what you wanted to know, wasn't it? he asked himself mockingly.

And now he knew. Now he had touched and tasted and entered into the realms he had forbidden himself. She had goaded him into it, damn her. Damn her a thousand times over.

His fingers constricted so tightly around his empty brandy glass that it shattered within his hand. Absently he began to pick up the pieces, scarcely aware that he had cut himself, that his palm was bloody.

He dropped the pieces of glass on the table and stared at his hand. Then he swore suddenly, feeling the ragged pain that tore at his heart.

He had betrayed Diana, and he had betrayed himself.

Damn the girl. She had goaded him.

But he couldn't really blame her, he realized, closing his eyes against the headache that was beginning to pound at the base of his skull.

No, he couldn't blame her.

He had breathed in the sweet scent of her perfume, he had touched the softness of her flesh. And he had fallen into the green fire of her eyes, and there had been only himself to blame. He had wanted her.

She was his wife, he reminded himself. And she had given him what he so rarely found these days. Moments of forgetfulness. More. She had poured over him like a gentle balm, and she had given him a taste of fire. She had eased him in a way that he could not remember being eased. They had made love in a tempest, and the tempest had been good and sweet.

There could even be peace between them.

He swore violently, raking his hair as he came to his feet. No, there could be nothing between them. Nothing at all. Tonight was a mistake that would not happen again.

He heard a soft rustling and rose quickly, turning toward the bedroom door.

Marissa was there. She had changed to a very prim and concealing nightdress, white cotton with blue flowers and a high laced Chinese collar. She seemed composed, and he almost smiled, for it seemed that whatever happened, she held her chin high. Her eyes mirrored the fire in her hair. He swallowed, feeling his fingers clench into fists at his sides, the whole of him constrict with tension. She was very beautiful, willful but proud, and he realized that he admired her. A curious tenderness tempered his rage. Perhaps the anger would not be so great if she did not elicit such a staggering desire. In all men, he imagined, not just himself.

But he had misjudged her; he knew that now.

Words hovered on her lips as she met his eyes, then her gaze lowered. A frown puckered her brow, and she seemed to have forgotten what she had intended to say.

"Your hand!" she exclaimed.

He looked and saw that tiny drops of blood were falling from his clenched fist onto the elegant Persian carpet beneath his feet.

He lifted his hand against his chest. "It's nothing."

But she walked to him and took his hand. Her touch was electric, and he nearly wrenched his hand from her grasp.

Why the hell wasn't she angry with him? Screaming again that he had to get out?

She had been angry, he realized. Furious. Until she had seen the blood. Then it seemed as if some instinct of caring had set in. What a complex creature she was! Cold as ice, hard as nails when she was determined to have her way. Soft at times, capable of laughter.

And still, though he knew her innocent now of certain things, he was still convinced that she was hiding something from him. Every once in a while the emerald fire would leave her gaze, and he would know that she was afraid of some discovery.

But now her gaze was innocent. There was no anger in it, no fear, and for once, no defensive challenge. Her eyes were wide as they touched his, wide and surprised.

"My God, you've really cut it quite severely," she murmured.

"It's nothing," he said curtly, but she had already headed for the bedroom, only to return with a white swatch of bandage and a pharmacist's bottle.

"You might need stitches," she said. He stared at her blankly. "Will you give me your hand, please?"

"I don't need—"

"It will sting, but not that badly," she said. "Give me your hand. Do you want an infection in it? A fever?"

He gritted his teeth and stuck out his hand. She opened his fingers, surveying the cut.

"If you're so anxious for me to sink to the bottom of the ocean, why not choose a deadly infection instead?" he asked wryly.

"Too slow, and not nearly dramatic enough," she returned quickly. She dabbed at the cut delicately.

"Not true at all. I could die slowly and painfully, and at the last moment, you could rush to my bedside, hold my hand and be a virtuous, loving wife for all to see."

"Um . . . but I should have to come to America for that. If you disappear to the bottom of the sea, I won't have to leave at all."

"And the money will be all yours."

She looked up at him, startled. "If you—if you were to pass away—my inheritance would fall to me?"

He smiled slowly and leaned against the settee, watching her. "Planning my demise?"

"Maybe." She liberally applied the red stuff, and caught off guard, he let out a gruff oath. "Oh, come!" she cried. "Children are painted day and night with this medicine, and they do not protest."

"Really? I think that you are planning my demise."

"Um. Death by iodine solution." She deftly wound the white bandage around his hand, tucking it in neatly. He stared at his hand, somewhat surprised that she had learned to tend to minor injuries so competently and swiftly in the secure world of her father's manor. He looked from his hand to her face, and their eyes met. And her cheeks were suddenly flooded with red, reminding him that it had been only minutes since they had met upon the most intimate level possible.

Marissa leaped to her feet and Ian realized that their thoughts had traveled like paths. He was startled by the rise of heat that swept through him when he recalled her touch. Thoughts came unbidden to his mind. Sweet carnal thoughts of the volatile pleasure she had created, though she knew very little. Thoughts of her softness and her beauty. Of mist and shadows and forgetfulness. Given time, given tenderness, she could be a lover like no other with her firebrand hair a tangle to entwine them . . .

No. He tightened his jaw against the heat and the anger and the pain that knotted and twisted inside him. He stood also, and she backed away, and he smiled, glad that she had done so. Things were becoming too easy between them. Laughter had come too easily. And there had been a curious closeness between them when she had tended his hand. He didn't want it; he had to break it.

"Marissa, I apologize for this night. My American manners were truly faulty. But you needn't fear. Such an evening will never occur again."

Something flickered in her eyes, but other than that, her expression did not alter. She scarcely seemed to breathe. "Marissa, did you hear me? I said that I was sorry."

"I heard you."

"Well?"

"What does it matter? The harm is done."

He exhaled impatiently. "I'm telling you that—"

"I don't care what you're telling me. It doesn't matter. Weren't you leaving?"

"I had left you alone, my love. You followed me out here."

"I wanted to see that you were gone."

"Well, I'm not." He was anxious to leave. Why did she bring out everything perverse in him? "It's nearly morning now. I might as well wait for the day."

"You can't stay here!" she protested.

He arched a single brow in challenge. Her eyes narrowed. They both knew she hadn't the strength to throw him out.

She circled behind him. He heard her voice at his back, innocent, soft. "Is it true, Mr. Tremayne, that if you do sink to the bottom of the ocean—or die that long and painful death of infection—that my inheritance falls straight to me?"

A smile curved his lips. "So I believe." He turned quickly, catching her hand. "Would you add murder to your other sins, my love?"

She snatched her hand away. "Surely, never, sir! But then again, you do not know me well—"

"Well enough," he interrupted smoothly, and was rewarded with a slight coloring in her cheeks again.

"You'll have to wonder, won't you?" she said sweetly.

"My eye will ever be upon you," he promised pleasantly enough.

Her lashes lowered demurely. "I'm sure that will be entirely unnecessary. I shall pray for divine retribution instead."

"Ah, but I am truly curious. Which of us is it that the divinity might bring retribution against?" he queried softly.

Again her cheeks colored softly. "Perhaps we both need to thank the divinity that it will be quite some time before we meet again." She turned regally and headed for the bedroom.

Thank God, indeed, he thought, wincing as tension seized him. He knotted his fingers into fists again, bringing a fresh wave of pain to his hand. She was too adept at whatever game she played.

And too damned superior. He had expected tears and fierce repercussions. He had meant to remind her brutally that it had been as much her fault as his own.

But she had never implied that it had been anything other than something they had both created. She had kept her dignity beautifully.

"Don't think, Marissa, of changing any of the plans I have made for you. You will arrive via the transportation I have arranged, on the proper date."

She paused and looked at him, surprised. "I hadn't intended to change anything. I will arrive just as you have commanded."

"Ah, yes, I imagine that you must. You'll be wanting your allowance."

"Yes."

"What a pity! The sacrifices you must make for money!"

She shrugged, and something about the way she stood ignited his anger and his passion. The challenge was alive in her eyes, just as the fire burned in her hair. "I had nearly decided that you were not so crude and terrible a man."

He found himself walking swiftly toward her and taking her by the shoulders. He wanted to shake her. Fighting for control, he realized that he wanted to do much more than shake her, that he wanted to drag her into his arms again, taste her lips, force his way to her very soul.

He did not shake her; he defied the violence within himself. He merely held her, his eyes dark and narrowing. "Don't deceive yourself, my love. I am very crude, and terrible. Don't ever deceive yourself otherwise!"

She did not flinch, but returned his stare, her head, as always, high, her eyes dazzling, moist, as if there might have been a hint of tears within them.

No, she would not cry.

He released her, fighting the urge to shove her from him. He turned and strode angrily toward the door, but once there, he paused. He did not turn to her.

"I will meet your train when it arrives, my love. See that you are on it."

He flung open the door and strode out.

And he wandered into the depths of the London fog, wondering just what web it was that she could spin that could evoke such a tempest of emotion within a man.

He walked in the fog to forget.

But when he stripped down in his own room for what remained of the night, he was haunted with dreams.

Dreams of Diana.

But Diana's face faded away, and new dreams came to haunt him. Dreams in which he held her—Marissa—and met her emerald gaze. Touched her naked flesh.

And felt the whisper of her words against his flesh. A whisper so soft he could not hear the words . . .

No.

He tossed in his sleep, and the whispers became louder. Whispers of tenderness, of love.

He would never love again.

He could never touch her again.

She was his wife.

He jerked up, covered with sweat, and slammed his fists into his palm. He inhaled sharply as pain assailed him, and he was glad of the pain, for it released him.

Thank God it was morning. He would soon be on a ship headed for home. Feeling the ocean breeze, letting it cool his head.

And his loins.

He would forget her, forget the night they had shared. By God, he would.

"You look grand, Marissa!" Theo told her. He stared at her with obvious pride as he looked her over, still holding her shoulders after the hug with which he had greeted her. "So very grand. I can't seem to get over just how wonderful you look!"

Marissa smiled at him as the cool morning breeze lifted the tendrils of hair at her forehead and set them gently upon her face. It was a beautiful day. The sky was a radiant blue with just a few puffs of clouds. It was Sunday, so there was no dynamiting to be heard. The world seemed quiet, and the landscape, with its mauves and greens and browns, rolled in the gentle silence. Sheep and cattle grazed the fields that stretched beyond the ramshackle cottages of the village. The few creatures that added substance to the life eked out by the miners.

But then she turned toward the cottages, small, one-room residences for the most, pathetically reaching toward respectability as the miners' wives placed what fall flowers they could find upon the windowsills.

Grand. Theo thought she looked grand.

And here, perhaps, she did.

She had spent money on herself. Mary had warned her not to appear in San Francisco without a proper wardrobe, and had convinced her that they couldn't keep on sharing a wardrobe. "You've sacrificed your soul for the money—and for us, of course!" she had reminded Marissa. "You should have something for yourself."

Mary would never know all that she had sacrificed, Marissa thought wearily, for Marissa would never tell her, no matter how close they were. But she did need clothing, so she had allowed Mary to guide her to the shops in London, but she had used her portion of the inheritance allowance very carefully. She had been far more careful of price than she had been of style, yet still, she had managed to select some very elegant pieces at very reasonable prices. Today she wore a simple cotton dress with a crocheted collar, but the designer had created a very elegant bustle just the right size for fashion, and she had found a charming bonnet with an egret feather that perched at an angle upon her forehead.

And perhaps, she thought, she appeared grand because there was no hint of coal dust upon her person. . . .

She had no right to be ashamed of the coal dust, she told herself. The miners were good people.

Far better than she. Most of them would probably look upon her deceit with horror.

She couldn't think about that now. She linked her arm with her uncle's, her smile still firmly in place, and started walking toward the house. "Uncle, I'm going to America with Mary."

"America!" He stopped on the pebbled path and stared at her. "Marissa, so very far! Why, child! I'll never see you again."

"Don't say that!" Marissa cried. She couldn't bear to hear such words. His slim face, haggard and worn and yet beautiful in the love and wisdom within the lines and crevices, was very dear to her. "You'll come to be with me soon enough." It was a lie; he couldn't really be with her. Not for years.

Unless Ian Tremayne did sink to the bottom of the sea. And despite the tangle of emotions she felt for the man, she realized that she did not really wish his demise—by fair means or foul.

Just thinking of him brought color to her cheeks, and tremors raced along her spine. She lowered her face and quickly spoke. "You're to retire, Uncle, and I mean it. Mary has given me a fantastic salary, and I've more than enough to spare for you."

"You're not to take care of me, child," Theo told her, pushing open the door to his cottage. Marissa preceded him in and sat at the rough-hewn table before the cooking fire. A black pot sat above the flames, and a kettle sat upon a heated rock. Water for the kettle came from an outside well. There were no conveniences here.

Nothing elegant, nothing fine, she thought, but her eyes were stinging with tears. Except love, for Theo loved her, and wasn't that worth more than anything elegant or fine?

She exhaled, pulling off her gloves, and smiling at her uncle. She meant to keep him alive to love her, she reminded herself. He was staring at her worriedly, and she was suddenly afraid that she had changed somehow, that all the things she had done were emblazoned upon her features. No, that couldn't be, she assured herself. "Uncle Theo, be reasonable. You cannot continue in the mines."

"Marissa—"

"Uncle Theo, do you love me?"

"Marissa, you know that I do!"

"Then you'll stay alive, for me."

He made a sound of impatience, then his cough seized him and he doubled over, wheezing for breath. Marissa jumped to her feet and patted his back, then quickly poured him a glass of cool water from the clay pitcher on the table. He sipped it gratefully, eyeing her all the while. She made him sit. "Theo, you must listen to me. I mean to set up a little school. I went to see the new young curate about it and he assured me that I had provided amply to bring in a teacher. And they said that the old storage building could be suitably made over, but the teacher will need help with the people here, and with odds and ends and such. Uncle Theo, you must be the one to give the help, to be my representative, don't you see?"

He was still wheezing, and it took him several minutes to answer. "So you are moving to America," he finally said softly.

"But you will come soon!" she insisted.

He didn't say anything, and she knew suddenly that he didn't want to come. This was his home, despite the soot and poverty. His friends lived and worked and had died here, and he had always thought to do the same.

Well, he wasn't going to die. And there had to be a better life for the others here.

"Uncle, you will come soon enough," she said.

He nodded, and she squared her shoulders. One day she would have to find a way to come back for him.

"There's rumblings of protest against the shareholders, you know, Marissa," Theo said. "The men are trying hard to find a way for better conditions."

"And so they should," Marissa agreed. "But, Uncle Theo, you're out of it now. Protest is for the young men."

"Wait until the shareholders learn about your school," he warned her.

"The vicar will not let the school be closed," she said, praying that it was true. Not even Mr. Lacey dared defy the vicar, who had caused tremendous havoc when a lad of ten had died from over-work in the tunnels a few years past. "Uncle Theo, you have to make sure that the vicar hears about any trouble Mr. Lacey might decide to cause."

Uncle Theo sat and stared at her, then sighed. "All right, my girl," he promised softly. "I'm out of the mines, and living on your charity."

"It's not my charity! What is mine is yours, Uncle."

"Ah, but you work to earn it!"

"Working for Mary is no hardship," she said uneasily.

"And glad I am that you're her companion, so fine and sweet a lady. At least I rest assured that she asks nothing difficult or ill of you, lass. She's indeed a great and moral lady, and I rest easy, know-ing you're in her company."

Marissa folded her hands in her lap and looked at them, feeling a burning sensation invade her once again. Mary was a very fine lady. And no, Mary would never ask anything ill of her.

The lies and deceit were all her own. And so was the night in which she had cast away her pride and innocence. For a stranger. A stranger she had married in a massive lie.

A stranger who seemed to hate her. Ever more deeply since the tempest and tenderness . . .

"Marissa, are you all right? You're pale as death!" Theo exclaimed.

She looked at him in dismay. "No, I'm—I'm fine, Uncle, honest." She smiled quickly. "I'm simply famished, and the pot is sending off the most delicious aroma! Come, let's eat! You always could create the most wonderful meals from so very little. And, oh! I've got to get the coachman to bring in the things I've brought from the manor."

"Ah, Marissa, did you take more from Miss Ahearn on my poor behalf?"

"We'll be leaving, Uncle. The larder was overstocked. You sit now, and I'll serve our supper."

"Marissa—"

"Come, Uncle, please? I'll not be able to be with you for months and months now. Please, sit down and tell me the gossip and let me serve the soup!"

So coaxed, Theo sat, and as Marissa dished up the soup and made tea, he entertained her with stories about the mines and miners and their children. He told her about the day they had managed to "accidentally" knock over a bin of coal dust right on Mr. Lacey's head. "He was madder than a hornet, he was! But he couldn't find no one to blame, could he, and so we all had a good laugh at his expense!"

Marissa laughed, too, imagining Mr. Lacey's fat jowls covered in coal dust. Then she managed to give Theo more pounds sterling than he usually saw in a year, and his awe as he looked at the money suddenly made everything she had done seem worth it all. And there would be more. There would be a school that might save some child from this life, just as Mary had saved her.

No matter how tragic or humiliating her life might prove to be, it would all be worth it.

She sipped her tea, finding that her hand was shaking. Ian was gone, she reminded herself. He was somewhere on the Atlantic right now, and she still had weeks before she would have to see him again.

But there were so many things she couldn't forget! So many things that plagued her! Even now, sitting here, in Uncle Theo's cottage, she could see Ian's face. His eyes alive with fire in the shadows and the darkness. Sizzling with the heat as he moved within her . . .

She couldn't breathe, and she forced herself to see another picture. His eyes with the fire of fury within them as he warned her,

"Don't ever deceive yourself. Don't ever deceive yourself. I am a crude and terrible man . . ."

She'd married him; she'd bedded with him. For money? What did that make her?

She felt as if she was going to be sick.

"Marissa, you're as pale as a ghost again. You can't be going to America if you're ill—"

"I'm not ill, I swear it! And I'll write, every week, I promise, Uncle Theo. Oh, Uncle! I do love you so much!" She threw herself into his arms and hugged him fiercely, and willed the memories away. She had done what she had to do, and nothing more.

"And I love you, child. Oh God, I do love you, more dearly than you shall ever know!" he promised. His gnarled hands moved over her hair tenderly, and she suddenly wished that she had never known a different life, that she could stay with him, sheltered in his arms and by his love.

She yearned to close her eyes and pretend that she had never gone to London with Mary, never seen Ian there. Never married him, and never been—touched by him.

But she could not. The die was already cast. And no matter what his anger toward her, she knew he would come after her if she did not arrive in San Francisco.

She could not betray Mary or Jimmy or her uncle.

"What is it, Marissa? What's wrong?" Theo asked her gently.

"Nothing. Just me, Uncle Theo. Hold me tightly, please."

He held her until night fell and it was time to go.

Alone in Mary's handsome coach then, she waved goodbye until Uncle Theo was only a speck in the darkness. Indeed, all the mining village was nothing but a speck in the night . . .

Like a particle of coal dust.

And then she wept, silent tears streaming down her cheeks. She wept for Theo, for the village and for herself. And then she remembered again the first time she had seen Ian Tremayne, the very first time, here in this same dingy, little town fast disappearing into the night.

She remembered her fury, and her thoughts.

She would be a great lady. She would show him.

Ah, yes! She would show him!

She dried the tears from her cheeks and sat straight in the carriage.

And by the time she reached Mary and Jimmy and the manor, no sign of her distress remained.

She would show Mr. Ian Tremayne. She would never shed another tear.

One week later, at the appointed time, she, Mary and Jimmy stood by the ship's rail.

And this time, it was England's shore she watched disappear.

Mary cried softly. But Marissa was true to herself. She did not shed a tear.

She looked away. Toward the west.

To America.

And to the new life.

CHAPTER EIGHT

San Francisco
January, 1906

A tap sounded on the door to Marissa's compartment, and she paused in the act of pinning her hat at a jaunty angle that defied the dread in her heart. When she did not respond to the knock, the porter called out cheerfully, "San Francisco! Next stop San Francisco! Five minutes now, Mrs. Tremayne."

Five minutes, Marissa thought, a mere five minutes, and a journey that had seemed epic in its length and scope would be over. She had crossed the mighty Atlantic Ocean, traveling first class on a great ocean liner. Then she had boarded the first of the several trains that had taken her across the entire American continent.

There had been so very, very much to see, to assimilate. She was English, and proud of England.

But this country . . .

There could be nothing like it. A land of such startling contrasts and beauty. Earth that was green and covered with forests, and then deserts that were orange and gold and mauve and fascinating.

And then there were the people. Everyone seemed to live here.

Everyone. German, Dutch, Scandinavian. Black, red, yellow. Oh, London was a melting pot, but this . . .

She felt such an excitement for the country. She loved each new day.

Until the end.

Today had brought them to the Bay, and to the train ferries, which had brought them into the city. Five minutes and they would arrive. And Mary and Jimmy would set up housekeeping in marital bliss, and she . . .

She had cast herself into a prison of her own making with a man who never ceased to infuriate . . .

And fascinate . . .

She closed her eyes. It was difficult to breathe.

She hadn't cared, she reminded herself. She had sworn to Mary that she wanted nothing more than security. That she had no patience with sentiment. And she had received all she wanted. Theo would be well, a school was under way, she was dressed in silks and laces, and she had traveled the North Atlantic and the great width of America, all in style.

And still, she could feel the bars of her prison closing in on her now. She could almost hear the clang of iron and feel the reverberation as it trembled deep within her soul.

Soon, very soon.

Her time of payment would begin.

Madam Lilli's was unique, even among the endless supply of waterfront dance halls that graced some of the lesser streets of the city.

The house had been there since before the gold rush. With the Victorian era, fine gingerbreading had been added to the quaint Colonial architecture. And Lilli, being fond of colors, had added paint and trim until the house stood out like a gilded lady herself, both tarnished and beautiful.

Lilli, arrayed elegantly upon a settee, twitched a feather boa over her shoulder and studied Ian with wide gray eyes as he stared out the window. "That's the third time you've pulled out your watch, Ian. And you haven't paid the slightest heed to a single word that I've said."

He spun around, pocketing his watch, and leaned against the windowsill. "You're the one who said you had no need of conversation," he told her, far more sharply than he had intended.

She seemed to flinch, and he was sorry. He swore inwardly once again at the wife arriving at the station this evening.

The wife who had best be arriving, he reminded himself. He wouldn't put it past her to fail to appear. And then what would he do? He'd have no choice. He'd have to find her.

"I don't recall asking a lot of you," Lilli said evenly, the hurt evident in her voice. "I don't mind your Nob Hill mistress, and I don't expect to go to the opera or the theater with you. However, I do appreciate it when you at least pretend that you care who you are with."

He exhaled slowly. "Sorry, Lilli."

Lilli nodded, her lashes sweeping low over her face. He had hurt her, and he knew it, and felt the worse for it. There were no pretenses about Lilli. She was a showgirl with a place to run. She was careful when she selected her lovers, but she made love with a rare talent that bespoke her experience.

She wasn't anything like Diana. Indeed, she was the farthest thing in the world from Diana, with her voluptuous figure and tinted red hair. But it was the very fact of the difference and her forthright honesty that had brought him to Lilli—and the fact that she asked nothing of him, not even simple caring.

"Why do you keep pulling out your watch?" she queried softly. "It's none of my business, of course, and I'm not demanding conversation—"

He strode away from the window and kissed her on the top of the head. "My wife is arriving today."

"Your wife!" She swept the boa around her and leaped up, stunned. "Wife?" she said again. Then she started to laugh, sinking down on the crimson day bed. "You're meeting your wife this evening and you came to see me this afternoon?"

"She's not a wife for real, Lilli," he said flatly. He lifted an arm, looking for an explanation. "She's—she's a ward, really. I'm her guardian."

"So you married her?" Lilli said, fascinated. "It can't be money, you've plenty of your own. I admit—I don't begin to understand."

"Neither do I," he muttered.

She smiled broadly. "Not that I mind. But the charming widow, Mrs. Grace Leroux, is going to mind terribly. In fact, I think I shall enjoy the way she will mind. Hmm. Guardian. Ward. How—how European. Tell me, what's she like? I conjure up images of a school-girl with pigtails. And perhaps buck teeth."

"No, I'm afraid not. In fact, she's quite stunning."

"You've a stunning wife arriving, and you're here?" Lilli said, her voice suddenly very soft.

He was here *because* his wife was arriving, he realized. Because he was damned determined he wasn't going to change his life. His voice hardened again.

"It was an arrangement, Lilli, nothing more. You know my feelings about marriage."

"Yes, I know them," she said, smiling ruefully. "But you see, I never expected you to marry me. Now Grace, she is going to have her problems. She's never believed that you wouldn't marry again. And of course, she was right, since you've a wife arriving. It's just that she assumed that she was going to be the wife."

"Well, she shouldn't assume things, should she?" Ian said. To his annoyance, he realized that he had drawn out his pocket watch again. Irritated, he shoved it back where it belonged.

"It's all right—you can run out," Lilli told him.

"I'll be damned if I'm running anywhere," he said.

"You'll be late."

"Then I'll be late," he said flatly. He'd be as late as he wanted. He'd while away the evening with Lilli's sweet brand of forgetfulness.

But he hadn't come today for forgetfulness, he realized.

He'd come because he didn't want to remember the feel of the golden-haired girl in his arms. He wanted to assure himself that he'd never fall beneath her spell again. There were other women to make love to. Women like Lilli.

"Tell me," Lilli said huskily, sweeping him into her embrace as he sat beside her on the day bed, "is the new Mrs. Tremayne aware of this open marriage? Does she, too, intend to find her own brand of entertainment?"

He stiffened: "What?"

"Ian, I was teasing you."

He stood and straightened his cuffs, suddenly impatient to be on his way. He kissed Lilli's cheek and strode toward the door.

"Ian!" Lilli called after him anxiously. "I've a new show opening Saturday night. Will you come? Please? Your patronage brings in so many others."

"Yes, surely, if you think that it will help," he promised. Then he paused. "No. I'd wring her pretty little neck."

"What?" Lilli said.

"No, she's not part of any open marriage, Lilli. I'd wring her neck."

Lilli laughed softly. Ian walked out the door, closing it quietly behind him. Then Lilli's smile slowly faded. A quiet ache formed within her heart. No, she had never deceived herself. She could have never been his wife. His feelings, what he gave her, had been real enough, but he was deceiving himself now.

The marriage meant more than he was willing to admit, it seemed. Far more than he was willing to admit.

A wife was one thing. A wife who mattered was quite another.

And so the ache in her heart.

She sighed softly and rose and walked to the window and looked out at the fog as it rolled in.

She'd still stand by him, as a friend.

She smiled slowly. It might even be amusing to see the very grand Mrs. Leroux meet the new Mrs. Tremayne.

Lilli spun around quickly, calling for her maid. She was suddenly very determined to see the new Mrs. Tremayne herself. Maybe she would even meet her.

Ah, the girl wouldn't want to meet a woman from her husband's past. But she should, for Lilli was not the real competition. And if the girl seemed to warrant it, Lilli just might be willing to offer her a certain assistance when she met the real dragon lady in her husband's past.

Marissa inhaled sharply. The train was braking. They were pulling into the station.

Mary burst into the compartment, breathless, her cheeks flushed. "This is it! We're here!"

They stared at one another for a minute, then they hugged fiercely. "Oh, Marissa! You've done so much for us!" Mary said.

Afraid that she was going to choke or cry, Marissa answered quickly. "Don't be silly. I'm the one living in the lap of luxury. And I'm afraid that we'll all sink if we're ever caught."

"Don't you be silly," Mary protested. "This is America. We're never going to sink."

Marissa nodded. She should have been the one so determined.

Jimmy burst through the narrow doorway. "Ladies, come on, we're here!" He was carrying Mary's small travel bag and picked up Marissa's. Smiling, Mary turned to follow him as he hurried down the train aisle. He moved with confidence, Marissa thought. Both he and Mary had changed over the long journey. They'd found a new strength in one another.

And she had been losing her own determination in silly daydreams.

She squared her shoulder, dreading the moment when she would see Ian Tremayne again, yet curiously longing to do so, too. He had said that he would come to meet them. Had he done so? Or had he forgotten the wife he had not wanted?

She hurried after Jimmy and Mary. It was a new world. And she'd sworn to herself once that she would show Mr. Tremayne her mettle.

At the steps to the platform she paused for a moment. Twilight and fog were falling over the city. There was little she could see beyond the station, but as her eyes adjusted to the gaslight and the coming night, she became aware of the man standing on the platform.

He was framed in light and shadow, and she saw nothing but his silhouette at first, tall and dark. Even the shadows became him, enhancing the breadth of his shoulders, the leanness of his hips, the fit of his clothing.

She didn't need light to realize that he had not forgotten her. He had come to the station.

Her heart began to pound too quickly, and she was furious with herself. Yet she could not move for a long moment, but remained frozen at the top of the steps.

He must have seen her, for he stepped forward into the light. A hat sat rakishly low on his forehead. It was cream-colored like his suit, and the color contrasted with the black ribbon tie around his throat. As he walked toward her she realized that he was being followed by a young Chinese couple. The man was handsome, the woman extraordinarily beautiful with perfect skin, sleek raven hair to her waist and huge, dark eyes with an exotic, sensual twist. Both were dressed in loose trousers and orange silk Chinese jackets.

Marissa looked at Ian, meeting his eyes. They seemed to sizzle with the same blue fire that had ruled them the night he had left her. The night he had touched her, and somehow destroyed the blind determination that had brought her through a lifetime. She still wanted to hate him. And instead she felt a dizzying heat sweep through her, then tremors seized her and she stiffened, determined to show him no weakness. He was an autocrat, she reminded herself. He was the man who had knocked into a simple maid, heedless of the destruction he had caused.

Even then he had told her to come to America.

Well, then, she was here.

"Mrs. Tremayne?"

The porter was waiting to help her down the steps. She smiled, blushing, and took his hand at last, reaching the platform just as Ian reached her.

He made no pretense of a loving—or even polite!—greeting. He walked straight to her, staring at her still. "So you've made it," he said.

She stiffened her spine and smiled sweetly. "And so have you."

"I promised I would be here."

"And so did I."

"Perhaps I had reason to doubt you."

"I have very great reasons to doubt you," she reminded him, far more sharply than she had intended.

They were barely a foot apart. Marissa suddenly realized that the small space of air between them was thick with tension and that Mary and Jimmy and the porter and Ian's servants were all staring at them wide-eyed, trying to read the innuendo and cool reproach in the words they shot at one another. Perhaps Ian came to the same realization, for he turned to Mary with the smile that could be entirely charming when he wanted it to be. "Welcome to San Francisco. I hope your journey was not too difficult."

"It was wonderful," Mary assured him.

Then Ian remembered his companions and quickly brought the couple forward. "Marissa, Mary, James, may I introduce John and Lee Kwan, who tend my house. John, Lee, my—" he paused, then continued evenly enough "—my wife, Marissa, and her friends, Mary and James O'Brien. Mr. O'Brien is going to come to work for the emporium."

Marissa wasn't sure what she expected, but she was surprised at the Chinese man's melodious, accentless speech as he greeted them. "I, too, would like to give you all welcome. Welcome to my city. You will see, she is one of the most beautiful on earth."

Then the woman spoke, and her voice was soft with a musical flow to it. "Indeed, we welcome you. Anything that you might require, you've only to ask."

"Thank you," Marissa said, then she realized that the girl's beautiful, exotic eyes were nowhere near as warm as her voice. She seemed nearly as hostile as Ian.

"I'll get the bags," John said. "If someone will direct me to the proper pieces?"

"Aye, of course," Jimmy quickly volunteered. "And there's plenty of them, I am afraid." He grimaced at Ian. "Women, sir, you know."

"I know, and I imagine that it will take the three of us, Jimmy," Ian said, flashing him a quick, easy smile. It was a captivating smile, Marissa realized. Mary was watching him with a curious affection and admiration, and when Marissa studied the beautiful and exotic Lee Kwan, she saw that the Chinese girl was staring after him, too.

He had his charm, indeed. She had discovered that herself. It was in his manner, and in his eyes, and even in his anger. She should know. She had fallen prey to it easily enough.

But she would not fall again, she promised herself, feeling her temper sorely tested. The girl kept his house, indeed. She gritted her teeth and reminded herself for the thousandth time that she had received everything she wanted from the bargain.

But she felt the clang of iron and steel again. And she thought that her prison might well be a torture chamber.

"We shall go to the carriage," Lee told her and Mary. "Come, I'll show you the way."

Marissa and Mary followed Lee through the crowded station and out to the street beyond. Leaving the station behind, Marissa paused. The cool air, rich with fog; touched her cheeks. The remaining daylight was dim, yet it made the scene all the more enchanting.

She could see the hills that looked down upon the bay, and the magical, beautiful homes that sat atop the hills. Painted in soft and rich hues, the city seemed filled with elegance. Victorian row houses, enchanting in their ginger-breading, lined some streets. More elegant grande dames looked down from rich, tree-laden properties. Gas lamps burned with a yellow glow against the growing darkness, and the fog gave it all a picture book quality. It might have been a fairy-tale land. She inhaled quickly, a deep breath, heedless of people passing by her.

It was beautiful. So beautiful. She had been awed by sophisticated New York, and had wondered at bustling Chicago, but here she felt a sweet trembling of excitement deep within her heart. This felt like home. This beauty was soft and enchanting, like the gaslight glow. It beckoned to her and seduced her. She loved the very feel of the air, the color of the night, the kiss of the fog.

She felt someone behind her, but paid no heed.

"It's magnificent!" she whispered.

"Indeed, she's a very great lady," said a rich, husky voice.

She spun around. Ian stood there, carrying a bag in either hand. His gaze had lost something of its anger as he watched her; his eyes were probing hers. She could not speak as he stared at her. "Come on. You've had a very long trip. I'll see you all settled for the night. Tomorrow will be time enough for you to see something of the city." He indicated that she should proceed, and she hurried ahead to his carriage. It was a large, handsome vehicle, drawn by two matching black horses with hides that shone under the lights as beautifully as Lee Kwan's hair.

A horn honked nearby, and an automobile chugged by in the street. A horse drawing an ice cart suddenly reared in fear of the motorized carriage. The auto veered onto the sidewalk. Another horse reared, and a cart of apples and produce went spilling into the street. The automobile sputtered to a halt.

"Progress!" Ian laughed.

"I believe greatly in progress, and I adore automobiles," Marissa told him.

He watched her for a moment. "Good. May we go now? I'd like to get home."

She hurried toward the carriage. She would have ignored him, but he set her bags down, and before she could mount the step, he had set his hands on her waist and lifted her up. John Kwan helped him with the bags, then Ian was beside her.

His scent was rich with leather and soap and his own masculine mystique. She was startled at the vehemence with which memories of a closer time between them returned to haunt her. She caught her breath, determined not to look his way, not to feel the heat and strength of his thigh so tight against hers.

"Ian, the city is wonderful," Mary said. "Which way do we go?"

He pointed in the night. "Nob Hill." He smiled at her. "The city *is* wonderful. There will be a lot for you to see and to learn."

"Why is it called Nob Hill?" Mary asked.

He smiled, and Marissa felt his gaze upon her once again. "Some say that it's from the word 'snob.' But it's not; it comes from the Indian 'nabob.'"

Marissa gazed at him. His eyes were inscrutable, but she felt laughter in his tone, as if he thought she belonged in a place called snob hill!

She was determined to ignore him. Her eyes met his. "I'm sure I shall be very happy upon your Nob Hill, Mr. Tremayne."

"Will you, my love?" he queried politely. "Well, we can only hope."

Marissa started to turn, then thought she saw someone in the crowd watching them. She frowned, staring hard through the fog. She was right; someone was watching them.

It was a woman. Tall, with blazing red hair. She was dressed in a fashionable blue velvet gown whose well-cut lines hugged her stunning body like a glove. The woman realized Marissa was watching her, and she seemed to start. Then she smiled. It was a surprisingly warm smile.

Beside Marissa, Ian turned. Marissa looked at him and saw him frown when he noticed the woman. "Lilli!" he murmured. "What on earth is she doing?"

"A friend of yours?" Marissa asked sweetly. Oh, yes, a friend! Marissa thought, and she wondered why she should be so infuriated.

Because one of her husband's mistresses had come to the station to study her!

She felt a flush of red climbing up her cheeks and she wanted so badly to swallow her bitterness. Why should she care? She wanted nothing from him except a chance at a new life for herself and Jimmy and Mary. And that chance was now hers.

But he'd seduced her, then been furious with her because of it. It had devastated her life, taken over her dreams and her every waking moment. And it had meant nothing at all to him.

She suddenly wanted to tear out his hair.

"A friend?" she repeated.

"A friend," he agreed flatly, staring at her hard.

Marissa turned and waved to the woman. "Lilli, hello!" she called cheerfully.

"What the hell do you think you're doing?" he demanded tensely, for her ears alone.

"Inviting your friend to the house. You do want to keep her, I imagine," Marissa said innocently.

He swore, heedless of Mary, Jimmy and the Kwans. "Lady, you don't invite anyone to my house, do you understand? You don't know who the hell you're talking to!"

"A dance-hall girl, I imagine. But then, this is America. Land of opportunity—and equality," she told him. His fingers were knotting, she realized. He was probably longing to wind them around her throat, and was just barely controlling the urge to do so.

"But I shall ask into my house those whom I choose, madame, not you!" he returned. His voice was soft but his tone warning, near savage. She fought the urge to draw away, and remembered her own fury.

"Do forgive me," she whispered. "I merely wanted to show your—friend—that I intend her no harm. Mistresses are not always fond of the arrival of—"

"Wives. But then you are not the customary wife, are you, my love? No," he answered himself. "Certainly not customary. My dear, dear lady."

Not a lady at all, Marissa thought. A brat from the coal mines, with less financial potential, surely, than the red-haired woman who stood and watched her.

The anger within her grew. Perhaps he wanted to throttle her. She longed to give a good cut to the hard angles and planes of his face.

But Mary was staring at her.

"Not customary at all, I promise you," she told Ian.

And he swore softly, then gritted his teeth and called out to John. "Let's go, please. Just circle around the confusion up ahead."

The carriage jerked as John Kwan flicked his whip in the air and the fine matched blacks started up at a trot.

"Head straight for home, John," Ian instructed, leaning past Marissa.

She closed her eyes, catching her breath. Home. It was his home. But her home now.

No, his home. To which he could invite whom he chose when he chose. It would not really be her home. He had made that very clear.

She felt a strange fluttering in her heart.

The bars were closing tightly around her prison.

It would be a beautiful prison, she thought. The city had found a place in her heart already.

But still . . .

No matter how beautiful a prison it might be, it would still be a prison. She would live shackled by the agreement she had forced, furious with Ian Tremayne, fascinated by him.

Jealous.

No! Her eyes flew open. She felt him watching her. She turned quickly to him, and saw she was right. Bright against the darkness, his gaze was hard upon her.

Her jailer . . .

A shudder touched her soul.

Her jailer, her husband. A husband who did not want her here.

She turned and looked toward the station. The beautiful red-haired woman was still standing there. She lifted her hand and waved.

Fury entered her heart. He had told her he had women in his life. He had made it very clear.

But that was before he had touched her.

She wanted to be away from him! She had barely seen him again, and it seemed that already the night and her life were filled with tempest and pain. Oh, it was a lie, it was all a lie, and she had created it.

And there wasn't anything she could do.

It was time to begin living the lie.

CHAPTER NINE

The house was magnificent.

Jimmy and Mary had been left at the entrance to the grounds, where a caretakers' cottage had been done over for their privacy until they chose to find their own home. John and Lee Kwan had quietly disappeared on their arrival at the grand Victorian entryway, and Marissa was alone with Ian when she walked up the steps to the huge elegant porch with its engraved and beveled windows. He said nothing, but merely opened the front door, allowing her to enter first. And she did so, drawing her gloves from her fingers as she stared at the foyer. It was huge, with a grand chandelier hanging from a high ceiling. The ceiling allowed for the entire length of the extraordinary stairway of hewn and curved wood. The flooring was a light marble, taking away any sense of heaviness that might have been found in the elegantly carved doors leading to other parts of the house.

Marissa stared at the stairway, then realized that Ian was standing behind her, watching her.

"Will it suffice?" he asked.

She swung around to look at him. What was he expecting from her? Maybe she had forced the issue, but she couldn't see offering him eternal gratitude.

Not when she could still remember the woman at the station all too clearly.

He was proud of this house, she thought. And he had a right to be; it was elegant, it was beautiful, and it was still warm. He couldn't have built it himself, for it was far too old a structure, but he had probably added to it.

If she hadn't seen the redhead at the station, she might have been tempted to praise the house, to tell him with warmth and laughter and enthusiasm just how wonderful a house it was.

But she had seen the woman at the station.

He warned you! she taunted herself. And she stepped farther into the room, playing for time. She had fallen prey to him once. She would not do so again. She wasn't sure what she had expected from him, but not this distance and coldness. She was surprised at the way it hurt, and she was suddenly furious again over the last night she had seen him in England. If only he had never touched her!

"Yes," she said quietly, without looking his way. "It will suffice."

"I am so glad," he told her. And the resonance of his voice showed her she had touched some chord deep within him.

She turned to meet his dark and enigmatic gaze. "It's been an extraordinarily long journey. Perhaps you'd be good enough to show me to my private quarters?"

A dark brow shot up, and his lip curved in a hard smile. "Your private quarters?"

"I should remind you, sir, that you were the one so insistent that your private life should not be disturbed in any way."

"Very true. But may I remind you, my love, that you were the one so very insistent on marriage."

"Indeed. And you were so very—kind—as to agree to marriage on my behalf. Yet you were very careful to remind me that you did have your own life. A fact you managed to demonstrate most amply this evening, and therefore I shall be incredibly happy to see that you are not disturbed in any way."

"How very kind," he murmured dryly, and indicated that she should precede him up the stairway. Above her, a stained-glass window graced the landing. It was dark now, but by the gaslight of the chandelier and the hall candles she could see the colors within it, beautiful blues and reds, then the white of a rearing unicorn that seemed to look down upon the stairway.

She reached the landing, with Ian upon her heels. His hand touched the small of her back and he urged her to the right where the hall split in two directions. He paused before a set of carved double doors and pressed the brass handle downward, opening one door. He turned up a wall lamp and soft light filled the room.

It was huge. A massive bed against one wall was covered with a white, gold-trimmed spread and set against a beautifully painted bed frame. The high ceilings were molded, and the walls were papered in a light yellow and mauve print. The hardwood floor was enhanced by an elegant Persian rug in complementary colors. One corner of the room was a hexagonal turret set with windows. A glass table and several chairs covered in a rich gold brocade had been comfortably arranged there. And there was a fireplace. With a marble mantel, two armoires, and a beautiful Art Nouveau dresser and elegant brocade-covered seat. There were two doors within the room, leading to opposite sides.

Tears suddenly stung her eyes. The single room was far larger than the entire cottage she had shared with Theo. The bedspread alone was worth more than Theo made in a year.

Ian pointed to one door. "There's a dressing room and bath beyond, and beyond that, a library, office or sitting room, whatever you choose. All are your private quarters. But by the way, madam, just what is it that I so amply demonstrated this evening?"

Marissa was startled by the sudden question. He hadn't seemed to notice her words downstairs. Apparently he had chosen to ignore them until now. And while it had been easy enough to set little barbs into conversation downstairs, she was annoyed to discover herself at a loss up here.

"As I said before, it was a very long journey—"

"Therefore I suggest you talk quickly," he said politely, only a hint of warning to his words.

She walked over to the Art Nouveau dresser, studying her image as she unpinned her hat and set it down. Her hair was coming loose in wild strands and tendrils, and she suddenly wished she'd left the hat alone. Then she saw Ian's face in the mirror behind her, his handsome features taut, his eyes dark and demanding upon hers. A lock of black hair hung loose over his forehead as he, too, removed his hat, tossing it on the bed. "I've all evening," he told her.

"Ian," she said, speaking to his mirrored image, "if you'd be so kind—"

"Well, I wouldn't be. We've gone through this before. I'm an American, crude, no gentleman. So let's finish this."

She swung around furiously. "Yes, indeed, let's. You poor dear thing! You're mourning your wife, your one and only real wife. And so you want your complete freedom to play with your whores. We agreed to that. I just thought that perhaps you might have better manners than to bring them to the station on the night you were to meet me!"

She had never imagined a man could go so white, or that every muscle within him might tauten and flick with such violence and fury. He took a sudden swift step toward her, his hand raised as if to strike her. Marissa cried out, suddenly and regretfully aware that she had gone a step too far. She had wanted to wound him. She had done so. Swiftly, precisely and well.

"No!" she gasped, ducking low, feeling the blood drain from her own face.

He paused. His hand fell. She saw the long, deadly fingers close into fists, and she tried to run past him.

He caught her, and his fingers threaded through her hair, pulling her to him. She cried out in pain, her eyes stinging with tears. Caught against him, she looked into his eyes that seemed obsidian, and though he hadn't said a word, she found herself apologizing. "I'm sorry! I'm sorry! I didn't mean—"

"Don't ever, ever mention my past again!"

"Let me go! I didn't mean to mention your past! It's your present I find offensive!"

His eyes narrowed sharply. His fingers, entwined in her hair, tightened upon her upper arms. "Why, you little witch! I told you from the very beginning—"

"Let go!" she insisted, pounding against his chest. She could feel his heartbeat, and his heat. The situation was becoming all too reminiscent of an earlier one. She didn't want to be so close to him as a man. It evoked new hatreds and furies, and longings.

"I told you—"

She tossed her head, meeting his gaze with flashing eyes. "Who do you think you are! Don't you think that anyone else has ever been hurt before? I'm sorry about your wife. I'm damned sorry about your wife. But you with your grand house and your store and your building and your disgusting money, you don't begin to understand what real hurting can be. You—"

He shook her suddenly, and she broke off, horribly aware of everything she had been saying.

"What the hell are you talking about?" he demanded heatedly. "What hardship have you ever known? Threatened with a world in which you would have to survive on your own, you married me for money. So don't you ever—"

"I'll not spend my life tiptoeing—"

"What are you talking about!" he thundered.

"I lost my father!" she snapped. "And I—" Again she broke off, not because he touched her harshly or with violence, but because his gaze was so very probing, because it felt as if the room were stifling hot. Pressed so close to his chest, she felt each slam of his heart against her breast. She couldn't breathe, and she wanted more than anything to escape him. But he was staring at her so intently that she thought he could see through the sham of her elegant clothing, that he knew everything that lay beneath. Had she given herself away?

"Tell me!" he thundered. "Tell me what the hell gives you the right to judge me. What hardship have you ever known?"

He no longer accused her of having a lover; the truth of that had been given to him on that night in London. But in her anger she had given much more away, and she was still doing so. "I've seen—I've seen Mary's life. I've seen the miners where she lived cough away their lives, and I've seen their children dressed in rags, starving, no more than skin and bone and wide eyes. I've seen children so covered in mud and smut that they were unrecognizable!"

Oh, Lord! She had to pray, and pray fervently, that she had been unrecognizable. He didn't remember her as the muddied waif in the village, did he? He would never, never associate his wife with that poor creature! Or would he?

She was shaking, her teeth chattering, and her eyes fell from his. "You're not the only one who has ever been hurt!" she repeated.

He didn't move. He was silent, staring at her for so long that she began to feel the pain of his knotted grip upon her.

Finally he released her, but she cried out as he turned away, for tendrils of her hair were still entangled about his fingers. To her surprise he did not jerk free from her, but paused to carefully untangle every last hair. Then he strode toward the door opposite the dressing room and bath. When he spoke, his voice was level and flat, curiously detached.

"John will soon bring your belongings," he said, "and Lee will bring you something to eat. There's a tub with hot and cold running water in the bathroom. If there's anything you need, you've only to ask Lee or John. There's other help in during the day, but only the Kwans live in the house. They've an apartment on the third floor should you need them at any time."

"I'm usually quite self-sufficient, thank you," Marissa said. She watched as he walked to the door and opened it. She could just see a large room past it, completely different from her own. There was a huge bed within it, covered in dark black and crimson pattern. The floor there, too, was hardwood, and covered with a beautiful Oriental rug in lighter shades to ease the darkness of the bed and draperies. The fixtures were in brass, and a very heavy long oak desk stood before one window.

"My God!" she gasped suddenly. "That's your room."

He paused, turning to her. "It is."

"There's a lock on the door, I assume."

His lip curled with taunting humor. "My dear Mrs. Tremayne, I thought you were distressed because of my, er, friends. Yet knowing that I have those friends would seem to keep your private quarters quite safe from unwanted visits. And if I do recall correctly, just this evening you invited one certain friend into this house!"

"I don't mind your friends," she assured him.

"Then just what is your difficulty?"

"That you—" she began, then paused, inhaling deeply. "I mind that you had that woman at the station."

"I didn't have her there. It is a free world, remember?"

"Will you please just get out so I can lock the door?"

He smiled pleasantly. "Yes, by all means, lock the door. But remember, Marissa, it seems that you are fond of attacking me and my life. You say that it is my present that disturbs you, but you felt it right to comment on my past. So bear in mind that this is my home. My door, my lock. And if for any reason I felt the need, I would shatter the wood from the door to enter any room in this place."

"That wasn't the agreement—"

"No!" he snapped, dispassion gone. "I made no agreements, and no promises. Bear that in mind, lady, and if you would have your precious privacy, then I warn you most strenuously—stay away from me, and keep your judgments and opinions to yourself!"

He stared at her one moment longer, then turned.

The door slammed in his wake, so hard that it seemed the wood already shattered.

She stared at the closed door, swore softly, then sank down on the foot of her bed, alarmed as she felt the threat of tears sting her eyes.

This was a new world, her new world. She already loved the city, and she would have respectability here, for she was the wife of a very rich man. She had so much here.

And she wasn't going to let him ruin it!

She blinked furiously and hurried through the door to her bath and dressing rooms. Each was as elegant as the bedroom. The huge bathroom offered a large white porcelain tub with lions' claw feet, racks of snowy white towels, lovely Dutch tiles on the walls. She opened a cabinet to find soaps and lotions and a large pink bottle of French bubble bath. She closed the cabinet and leaned against it. She couldn't wait for her bags to arrive, for total privacy, to sink into the tub.

She hurried on to explore the next room—her study, library, sitting room, whatever she chose it to be.

She pushed open the connecting door and stared blankly.

My God, she could house half of the miners and their families in these few rooms! If only Mary were with her here!

But Mary wasn't with her. And she wouldn't even be at the caretakers' cottage for long. She and Jimmy would be moving on to their own household.

She was alone here. With Ian too close and too far away all in one. And with John Kwan and the beautiful Lee, who already stared at her with hostility.

Did the exotic Chinese girl offer her master more than domestic services?

As she taunted herself, Marissa felt her face burn. She pressed her hands against her cheeks. She didn't want to know, she told herself.

But she did. With a dread fascination, she wanted to know everything about Ian. Even the things that seemed to pierce so sharply into her heart.

Impatient with herself, she went into the room. It was set up as a library, and she thought that she liked it very much that way. There was a desk with a swivel chair, and there were two leather armchairs set before the fireplace. In the far corner, by a set of bookshelves, was a beautiful day bed, covered in a blue damask set off by the dark brown leather of the armchairs. It was a handsome room with the rows of books, and in a far corner, another turret set with a comfortable blue armchair and needlepoint footrest. The windows took the upper portion of the wall and were etched and set with brass. She imagined that in the day the light would pour in, and that it would be a wonderful place to curl up with a book. And if it rained, and if the wind blew, and the weather turned cold, there was always the fire to come in to.

She had curled into one of the leather chairs when she felt a presence behind her. Holding back a scream, she turned to see that the woman, Lee Kwan, was standing still and silent behind her.

"I startled you, madam. I am sorry."

Marissa leaped up. "You might have knocked," she said, unnerved by the woman's appearance.

"The doors were open. I just wished to let you know that John has brought your things, and I have left you a covered tray. Shall I unpack for you?"

She shook her head, then realized that she did not want to be enemies with Lee Kwan. Not until she knew more about her home, at least.

"Uh, no, thank you. I appreciate the offer, but I prefer to unpack myself."

Lee Kwan's inscrutable dark eyes lowered as she bowed to Marissa. "As you wish."

She was going to turn and leave, Marissa knew, and she was startled when she called the woman back. "Thank you for bringing the tray," she said quickly. The woman nodded, offering Marissa nothing more. "Have you and your husband been with Mr. Tremayne long?" she asked.

"My husband?" Lee asked.

"Yes, John."

"Oh." Lee's lashes flicked over her dark eyes. "He is not my husband. He is my brother. Is there anything else that I can do for you, Mrs. Tremayne? May I draw you a bath?"

"No, thank you." She wanted a bath but she wanted Lee Kwan gone more. "I'll take care of myself this evening, thank you."

"It was a long journey for you," Lee offered.

"Very."

Lee bowed again and turned to leave. Marissa did not call her back.

And when the woman was gone, Marissa followed her to the bedroom, locking the double doors to the hallway. She did not want to be surprised again. It would probably be a long night. As tired and travel worn as she was, she would probably never be able to fall asleep here tonight. In his house.

She stretched out on the bed, running her fingers over the beautiful gold and cream spread. It was such a wonderful house. Or it could be, she thought, if it could be brought to life.

She closed her eyes and tried to imagine what ian's first wife would have been like. Maybe a very delicate blonde, with no hints of red within her hair. And her eyes would have been a soft blue, and she would have been really beautiful, a lady in every sense of the word. And they would have reigned here together with love and laughter, and then the house would have been truly alive.

She sighed softly. Life would be good here for Jimmy and Mary. Jimmy would flourish at Ian's emporium. He was smart, he could work tirelessly, and he loved Mary with all his heart. Mary would be happy.

It was her own life that would be so very empty.

She wouldn't allow it to be, she told herself. She was going to wallow in the luxury. And write long letters to Uncle Theo, and to the vicar, and she was going to be certain that everything went well with her school.

Uncle Theo and the school were across a continent and an ocean. And life stretched out long before her here.

She was exhausted, she thought. That was why she continually felt the hotness of tears behind her eyelids. She was going to start with luxury, an endless bath with sweet-smelling bubbles in the huge porcelain tub. Then she could put her things away, her beautiful new things, and it would begin to feel like home.

But she never took her long bath that night, never glanced at the tray of food that she had been brought. She didn't even take her shoes off. She closed her eyes, stretched out on the silky cover.

She had no trouble sleeping in her new home, Ian's house, at all.

Nor did dreams trouble her. She wasn't aware when the door between the two rooms, the door she had not remembered to bolt after demanding to know if it could be locked, opened.

Ian walked in quietly and stared at her face for a long moment. He sighed softly, unlaced her shoes and pulled them from her feet. Sweeping back the covers, he laid her upon a pillow and started to loosen her blouse.

The act was too reminiscent of one he had performed before. He felt the muscles tighten in his jaw and despite himself, he smoothed his knuckles over her cheek. She seemed so innocent, sleeping. Beautiful, with her fair skin, softly parted lips, flawless oval face and lovely features. The passion within her was silenced now, but he remembered with discomfort the vehemence of her attack upon him. He turned away from her, lowered the gas lamp and returned quietly to his room.

He stood overlooking the downtown area of the city far below. Lights flickered and gleamed, and the fog was softly swirling in, like a magical dragon, from the bay.

What hardships had he known? he taunted himself. He'd been a fighter, he told himself, always a fighter. He'd gone his own way, he'd fought to build homes and offices that would be both beautiful and safe. He'd never taken the rich man's way out, and despite his father's advice, he'd enlisted in the Navy.

He'd fought for Diana, fought as long and hard as any man could fight.

But he hadn't really known hardship. Marissa was right. Not the way she had made him see it so briefly. But she was a child of privilege, too. How could she bring the suffering so vividly to life?

And why did she have such an effect upon him?

He sighed and kept his eyes upon the city he loved. It wasn't late. By the waterfront, the dance halls and theaters and bars would be going strong. He should don his coat and escape this house tonight.

But he didn't. He continued to stare at the magical city within the magical fog. And when he turned from the windows at last, it was to strip off his clothing, turn down the lamps and crawl into his bed.

He had wanted to hold her tonight, he thought gravely, fingers laced behind his head as he stared at the darkness of the ceiling. It had been something different than the raw desire that had sparked him in London, something deeper than the sexual desire that could still plague him because of her beauty. He had wanted to hold her, to ease away the hurt.

And for the first time, he realized, he had been startled from his depression. He was not the only man to suffer a loss. From the tone of her voice, he had sensed a loss, a pain, different perhaps, but as deep as any pain he had ever known.

She had lost her father recently.

But the anguish he had seen in her eyes seemed to go deeper than that. As if she had truly understood a different world.

He has seen that world himself, and it had, indeed, been dismal. Once investors had encouraged his father to buy into the mine. The squire had warned James Tremayne that he would despise the place, and James had indeed despised all he had seen. Life was hard for the common worker. It was a lesson Ian had learned that day.

But even in that darkness, there had been a curious beauty. And pride. He suddenly remembered the little girl he had seen there. She had been so clean and white. So determined. So different from the other black-faced waifs, covered in dirt and grime and coal, who had reached out small grubby hands for any little pittance that might come their way. She had been angry, and proud. He smiled. It was strange. She'd had eyes like Marissa's, startling, vivid green eyes. Or maybe he was just remembering the child as having his wife's eyes, because both had been determined to give him battle.

The village had been a terrible place. He had sensed death, and pain, and a raw struggle to survive.

Marissa must have felt for her friend greatly.

And tonight, Ian had wanted to hold Marissa, to smooth her hair. To give her security against . . .

He didn't know.

Shrugging, he ground his teeth together hard and turned over with a vehement twist, pounding his pillow. He was tired; he should sleep. He had a meeting with the men tomorrow about the new buildings for the waterfront district. And he had to show his new wife and her friends something of the city. And there was young James to see settled in at the emporium. He was weary; he should sleep.

But he did not.

Ian was the one to lie awake most of the night.

It taunted him to know that Marissa lay just beyond the door.

A door she had not remembered to lock against him, despite her words.

There had been something about her, that night in England. Something that still teased and haunted his senses, something that made the present seem suddenly more important than the past. Something in her eyes had challenged him, something in her heart had awakened him. Something in her innocence still laid claim to him.

And she had not locked the door. It was his house, he had told her, his door. And he'd never made any promises or agreements.

She was so close. All he had to do was step through the door.

He turned again, closing his eyes tightly. She could not take Diana's place. He would not let her. He could not let her be a wife in truth. And if his flesh burned and if his dreams were fraught with images of her, he would learn to get past them. That was why he had gone to see Lilli.

But Lilli, even with her pretty face and stately form, could not compare with Marissa. The lift of her chin, the emerald blaze of her eyes, the cascade of her hair. Her passion, so visible in her anger . . .

So sweet when she allowed it to flow and undulate in his arms. He could not forget the scent of her skin, the silk of her hair, entangling him.

Desire . . . It was natural, for she was beautiful, and she was young. The sparks of fury that flowed between them could so easily become more.

But tonight . . .

Tonight he had listened to her cry out to him. And she mocked him and railed against him.

But her words had been true, and she had awakened more in him than desire. He'd never intended to be a self-pitying monster. He had just missed Diana with all his heart.

He'd married Marissa; he'd made no promises. He had only to burst through the door, lift her into his arms and carry her in here, to his bed. He'd not force her. He'd make love to her, and her protests would die softly away as they had before. And he would ease the rage in his loins and the tension in his limbs.

He rose, sleek and naked in the night. He took two steps toward the door between them, then paused.

He might ease the tension and desire, but he'd create a new tempest in his heart. He could not bring her to this bed, for it had been Diana's bed. He could not sweep Marissa into any world he had shared before.

He had married Marissa. He still could not allow her to be his wife.

The fog settled over the city, and the moon rose high above it to create a soft, surreal glow.

And Ian stood there, muscles knotting, his head cast back. He nearly cried out as pain and longing knotted together within his soul.

Minutes passed, long, aching minutes. He padded to the window and looked out again on San Francisco. He inhaled and exhaled slowly. It seemed that he stared out at the city forever.

A foghorn sounded and he started, then smiled, with just a hint of tenderness curling his lip.

She had just arrived. She was close, and it was his own fault. When she had still been endless miles away, he had not thought that having her so near could wreak such havoc upon him.

She slept in exhaustion. So innocently.

No, he thought wryly. He would not disturb her sleep, no matter what decision he had made within his heart.

He would leave her be.

He realized suddenly that light was breaking through the fog. He had stayed awake for hours, staring into the night.

He laughed ruefully.

He'd leave her be . . .

Maybe.

And then again . . .

Maybe he'd let her live in just a bit of the tempest that was nearly driving him to distraction!

CHAPTER TEN

Marissa awoke with a sense of disorientation. She opened her eyes to see her fingers stretched over embroidered cream sheets. Across the room, she could see the door to the bathroom slightly ajar. The morning light was streaming through the etched and beveled windows, and the entire room was cast in a soft glow.

The night's sleep had done her a world of good, and she smiled slowly. This was all hers. These rooms were her domain. With their soft and subtle beauty, they were where she lived.

She rose, frowning for a moment as she tried to remember taking off her shoes, then she shrugged. She had been so very tired, she couldn't even remember falling asleep.

Her bags were still on the floor at the foot of the bed. She rose, found her overnight case and searched diligently for her toothbrush and cosmetics, then headed into the bath. She doused her face and scrubbed her teeth and smiled to the image in the mirror over the porcelain sink. "A prison not so tortuous, I think!" she told herself. She was ready to wrestle with Ian once again this morning. With a vengeance.

She turned on the gold spigots for the tub, thinking of home. This house offered everything. At Uncle Theo's, a bath had been a time-consuming chore. She had to heat endless pots of water, drag out the tub, fill the tub, empty the tub! Even at the manor there had been no running water. There had been several "necessary" rooms, but nothing like this.

She took bubble bath from the cabinet and added it liberally to the water. Then she quickly disrobed and stepped into the tub, luxuriating in the heat.

The bubbles rose around her and she was delighted. She sank down as the water rose, drenching her hair, rubbing her scalp. She inhaled the sweet rose scent of the bubbles and doused herself again, feeling like a child. Then, with a soft sigh, she settled back, her head resting on the edge of the tub, her arms elegantly draped over the sides.

"Not so horrid a prison," she murmured. And she lifted a hand, pointing as she might to make something clear to a schoolboy. "Mr. Ian Tremayne will be made to see that it cannot be had both ways, and then I think that I shall settle in very nicely! He will be put in his place, I swear it!"

"Really?"

The quiet, amused challenge of his voice coming from behind her was the greatest surprise of her life. She almost bolted from the bubbles, then managed to twist around beneath them to stare at him where he leaned against the door frame, his arms casually crossed, brows arched as he stared at her. He was dressed for business in a pin-striped suit with a gray silk vest and white pleated shirt beneath. Hatless, and with the errant lock of hair falling over his forehead, he was striking. Her heart began to pound, and she forgot for a moment that she was ready to wrestle with him. He was definitely one of the most handsome men she had ever seen. Yet it wasn't just his looks that made him so arresting; it was that air of confidence, the energy, the tension. There was danger in his eyes, in the fire within them. And despite her pride, it was far too easy to flicker close to the flames burning there.

She remembered her pride at last. "What are you doing in here?" she demanded sharply.

"Oh, just listening to how you'll put me in my place," he replied with a casual smile.

Flames crept to her cheeks, but she remembered she was the one with the right to be indignant. "These are my private quarters—"

"I knocked, but you didn't answer."

"Then you weren't given leave to enter!"

"You might have been drowning here, my love. I had to make sure you were all right. Indeed, I thought at first that you *were* drowning, since your head was lost in the foam."

"Well, I wasn't drowning, and I'm quite all right, and you've no business in here at all!"

"I own the house."

"But you gave me the bath!"

"I did not give it to you!" he protested. "I loaned it to you." He took two long strides into the room and knelt beside the porcelain tub. Marissa tried to maintain her dignity by drawing the bubbles around her.

They were breaking up at an alarming pace.

She narrowed her eyes. "Out!" she told him sharply.

"I really don't understand your distress," he said, a leisurely smile curling his lip. "We're adults, man and wife—be honest here! I've seen in the naked flesh all that you would hide behind those elusive bubbles—"

"In the dark, in London, a long time ago—and during a mistake, which you yourself apologized for!" she interrupted, her temper growing. He was so near. And the curve of his smile and the humor in his eyes were nearly akin to tenderness.

He touched her, drawing a soft line from her throat to her shoulder. "It was not so dark, what matters the city, not so long ago, and an apology would do nothing to alter my memory of every piece of your—of you. Dear Lord, those bubbles do not last long when you want them to, do they?"

If she was losing them anyway, Marissa determined in a flash of fury, she might as well use them well. She dipped a hand into the water and sent a spray of bubbles flying onto his face and chest. She was rewarded with a sharp oath and a sea of sputtering. "Marissa, you little witch—"

She leaped up, thinking to escape, remembered she was naked, and decided she had best run anyway.

He caught her just as she reached the bedroom. His hands slid over the length of her flesh, but she eluded him, for the soap that remained on her was slick and slippery. "No!" she shrieked, torn between panic and laughter.

"You've destroyed my suit!" he thundered.

"You destroyed my bath, and my privacy!" she retorted. The bed was behind her. She turned to grab the sheet, but he was moving again, striding quickly across the room. He caught her with an energy that sent them both flying down upon her beautiful bed. She was soft and slippery, the essence of the bubbles still upon her flesh.

"Off!" she commanded. "Ian, you rake—"

"Ah, but you were well warned to stay away!"

"I was in my own bath!"

"You saw fit to wage war."

"I saw fit to defend myself!"

She had entered this marriage knowing everything.

But the texture of his tongue upon her flesh was rough and sleek and exciting, and the flames that had touched his eyes were growing to burst into a fire at the center of her being. She could not allow this.

This was too much like falling in love with him. She seemed to need the laughter in his eyes, the curve of his smile. She hated him because he had others in his life, and not because of the way he had manipulated her own life.

His kiss moved lower. His tongue tasted a patch of bubbles that remained high upon her breast. His fingers curled over hers and entwined, and his kiss moved farther down. Slowly. So slowly. The tip of his tongue just moving over her naked flesh, lower and lower upon her breast.

"You—you do not want me," she reminded him.

His face lay within the valley of her breasts. He paused, pressing a kiss there, running his tongue lightly over that valley. She ached for more. Longing to have him take her deeply into his mouth. She wanted to run her fingers into the darkness of his hair and draw his face to hers and kiss his lips. And she wanted to strip away the soaked pin-striped suit and feel the naked tension of his body.

She swallowed hard and repeated her words, "You do not want me here, Ian. Ian!" She tried to escape his hold, twisting in a fury. But she could not fight his weight and his hold, and he had not released her. As she twisted she was only wedging herself more closely to him. His lips were pressed deeply against her breast, and the fire raged more deeply between her thighs. "Ian!" Taut and still, she called his name.

He was silent for a long moment. Then the husky, muffled velvet of his voice came to her. "Ah, but I do want you," he murmured.

"Let me go!"

"Is that what you want?"

His head rose above hers. There was no laughter in his eyes, only darkness. His features were tense, his jaw hard as his gaze sought hers.

"Ian—"

"What of you, Marissa? Do you want me?"

She caught her breath, unable to speak. His eyes were dark and demanding upon hers. This time they were not doing battle, nor were they jesting. And yet she was too afraid to answer him. She could not spill out her feelings, even if she could completely understand them herself. Then they came clear to her.

Love me! she wanted to cry out. For I have fallen in love with you, in love with a memory, perhaps. And even in love with the anger and the challenge and the arrogance. For I've seen the care, and the tenderness, too. And I've seen the beauty of what can lie between two people, and I never knew that my heart ached for that loving, too.

But he could not love her. He was in love with a ghost, and he made love with faceless women who did not count.

And she couldn't say she loved him, for she was living a lie. She wasn't the woman he thought he had married.

And still she wanted to touch his face, to draw it to hers, to taste his lips upon hers.

She did. She reached out, her fingertips falling upon the curve of · his cheek and the bronzed contours of his face. Then she cried out, alarmed at herself, incredulous that she could forget her pride.

"No!" She twisted from beneath him, and he let her go. She sat with her back to him, her spine straight but her head lowered. "No!" she said, and the sound was more desperate than angry.

Not when you long for a dead woman! she added silently. Not when I would be nothing more than a dance-hall girl. She couldn't say those things to him.

"And I meant to taunt you!" he murmured.

She looked at him. He was propped on one elbow, watching her with a wry smile.

"Pardon?"

He shook his head. "Nothing." His eyes closed, and a ragged shudder swept his body. He stood, and to her amazement he stripped the cover from the bed with a fluid motion and set it around her shoulders. "Breakfast is a buffet downstairs. We do share the dining room, since I haven't two, I'm afraid. We need to get started, it's a busy morning. Meet me there as soon as you can."

She rose uncertainly, holding the cover around her. He grinned, came to her and stared into her eyes, then gave her a firm smack on the derriere. "Get cracking, lady. I'm American nouveau riche, a Yank, remember, not British gentry. I have to work to maintain my bank accounts."

He didn't wait for her answer, but left her, slipping through to his own room. She rose and followed him, meaning to lock the door. But she hesitated and did not touch the lock.

She turned pensively instead, and walked slowly to the bath-room to dress.

Ten minutes later she found him in the dining room.

A walk down the curving stairway brought her to the entry. She discovered, by walking to her left, that the dining room was there, beyond a large parlor with huge bay windows looking down the lawn to the street. Ian was sitting at the end of the table with a cup of coffee and a newspaper. He looked up when she arrived. He had changed into a navy suit with a paisley vest, and his errant hair had been combed.

"Biscuits and eggs are on the buffet," he told her, and he reached across the table, where a place had been set for her, and picked up her cup. A coffee urn was sitting before him, and he looked at her before pouring from it. "Would you prefer tea?"

She shook her head and slid into her seat. "Coffee is fine, thank you."

He poured her coffee. "You need to eat something. We'll be out all day."

"I'm not very hungry—"

"You need to eat. Lee, would you kindly fix Mrs. Tremayne a plate?"

Marissa started, unaware that the Chinese woman had been standing in the corner. Lee came forward to do as she was bidden, and Marissa stood, determined that she wouldn't require any help from Lee.

"Thank you, Lee. I can manage myself."

Exotic dark eyes touched her for a moment, their hostility still evident, then they fell as Lee bowed her head. "As you wish, Mrs. Tremayne."

Marissa walked to the buffet and helped herself to fried eggs and biscuits and bacon and sat at the table. She had come down intending to be as mature and reasonable as she could. She had wanted to talk, to form some kind of a livable relationship between them.

But with Lee in the corner of the room, she couldn't talk. She sipped her coffee, which was delicious, and bit gingerly into a piece of bacon.

"I'll try to show you and the O'Briens something of the city this morning," Ian said, glancing at his paper as he spoke. "But I'll need to bring James into the emporium after lunch, and I've an appointment myself. John will be at your disposal to drive you around should you choose."

Lee cleared her throat, as if waiting for permission to speak. Ian glanced her way curiously.

"Perhaps Mrs. Tremayne and her friend would prefer exploring on their own. The cable cars are wonderful."

"Yes, Lee, they are. But perhaps they should become a little more familiar with their surroundings before exploring on their own. It's a beautiful city—it can be a dangerous one, too."

Marissa buttered a biscuit, smiling sweetly as a touch of resentment rose within her. "Um. I understand that the Barbary Coast offers all manner of entertainment, theaters and the like."

"I think you are mainly thinking of years past, when brothels were thicker than flies, my dear."

"They've all gone then?" Marissa queried innocently.

His eyes were hard. He sipped his coffee, then set his cup down. He leaned forward with a pleasant smile. "Not at all. But then, my love, I mean to show you the finer sights of your new city. Are you ready?"

She wasn't ready at all, but it was apparent that he was determined to go. He was on his feet, pulling her chair out for her. "Tell John to meet us at the emporium around two, Lee, to pick up Mrs. Tremayne and Mrs. O'Brien."

Lee nodded. "Will you dine at home, Mr. Tremayne?"

"Yes, we'll be home for dinner, thank you. Come on, Marissa, let's go."

He caught her hand and led her to the foyer, then frowned. "You'll need a cloak of some kind. The weather here changes quickly. Hurry."

She raced up the stairs and dug in her bags for a lightweight cape, then swept up her small reticule with her comb and money. She couldn't have moved faster, but when she reached the entry, he was pacing.

He pushed open the front door and led her down the steps. "If you'll wait here, I'll bring out the car."

"The car?" she asked. He'd picked her up in a carriage. In all her life, she'd never been in a motorcar.

He smiled. "You're not afraid of automobiles?"

"No, no, of course not." She hurried after him, almost crashing into his back when he stopped.

"I said I'd pick you up."

"I know, but I'm anxious to see it."

"It?" He smiled. "Them, my dear." He started walking again, around the main house to the carriage house. The doors were open. To the left were stalls with horses, among them the matching blacks that had drawn the carriage that had come for them at the station. Near the stalls were several different carriages from a row of three motorcars, all shining even in the dim light.

She stared at them until he beckoned to her. "Do you know much about them?" he asked her.

She shook her head.

Ian caught her hand and took her to the rear of the carriage house, to an automobile painted a deep green. It barely resembled a carriage, and had a huge nose. "She's French," he told Marissa. "A Levassor-Panhard, with her Daimler motor here in front." Marissa paused to study the vehicle, but he was already moving on to the next. She followed after him. "This is a Renault, also French. And in front of us is an American car, a 1901 Olds." He opened the passenger door and took her hand, helping her up. She smiled with excitement. Perhaps her smile was contagious, for he laughed. "Had I only known you would have come here without the slightest argument if I had commented on the automobiles!"

He cranked the engine. Marissa jumped as the auto burst into life, then chugged its way out of the carriage house and down the driveway. The breeze swept by her and she turned to him. "It's wonderful! But how very odd! I had thought that you were such an avid horseman. Why, you were riding when I saw you—"

She broke off quickly, hoping he did not remember the time she was thinking about, when he had come riding up so heatedly to the Squire's the year before the Squire died. She tried desperately to remember if he had ridden to meet her in the city of London, but her mind had gone blank, and she could feel a nervous flush rising to her cheeks.

"Was I riding?" he said.

"Oh, maybe I was wrong. I don't remember," she said quickly, looking at the road.

"I do love horses. And I've a few magnificent animals in my stalls."

"I know. The blacks are gorgeous."

"I've riding horses, too." He shrugged. "I love horses, but I do see motor vehicles as the way of the future. Eventually, I daresay, the cars will outnumber the horses."

They had come to the caretakers' cottage. Mary appeared at the front door, waved, then reappeared with Jimmy behind her. Both were as awed with the Olds as Marissa had been, and Ian allowed them the time to walk around it as he answered Jimmy's questions about fuel and speed and mileage. Then the two crawled into the back, and Ian told them they had a little time, and he'd show them all he could of the city of San Francisco.

From Nob Hill they drove to Union Street and Pacific Heights, then by Russian Hill and Telegraph Hill. They took a detour through Chinatown, then headed toward the waterfront. Along the road, Ian stopped the car atop a hill where they could look down on much of the city. They left the car to stand on the cliff, and Marissa was startled when Ian's hands fell on her shoulders and he pointed out at the city, lightly dusted in fog this morning. Marissa felt a glow of warmth. The morning had been pleasant, she thought. Her excitement over the Olds had pleased him, it seemed. It almost had seemed as if they might be friends this morning. But she couldn't let that happen. She was too haunted by the life he had led, by the things she didn't know—and by the things she hadn't told him.

"It's so beautiful!" Mary said, slipping her arm around Jimmy's waist.

Ian released Marissa and turned to the car. "Think you'll adjust?" he asked Jimmy jovially as they all got back in.

"Aye, that I will. It's a wonderful place, and you're proud of it, I think, Mr. Tremayne," Jimmy replied.

A slow smile curved Ian's lip. "That I am indeed, Jimmy. She's a grand place, never too hot, never too cold."

"Paradise," Marissa murmured.

"Yes, except for—"

He broke off, frowning.

Except for the tremors that sometimes shook the earth, he added silently.

He shrugged. He didn't know why he had avoided mention of the quakes that had shaken the city in 1865. Except that his meeting this afternoon was with the businessmen who wanted to build by the waterfront, in the landfill area.

"Except for what?" Marissa asked him.

"There are no exceptions," he said.

"But you just said—"

He was suddenly curt and impatient. "It's late. We must hurry if you want lunch before going to the emporium."

Marissa fell silent. Ian was quiet as they drove down the hill, then entered the city traffic. Horse-drawn conveyances vied for space with the autos, and Marissa saw her first trolley car. Then Ian pulled up by a curb, and they exited the car. She didn't need him to point out the emporium—it couldn't be missed.

It was a large three-storied building with "Tremayne's" written across the bricks of the top floor in large black letters. But Ian took her arm, guiding her away from it. "We'll lunch here."

There was a large building in front of them. One window advertised the telegraph company, another advertised a bank. Between them was a doorway leading to Antoine's. Ian led them in.

A stairway went to an elegant basement dining area. Snowy white cloths adorned the tables, and candles were set in glass and brass holders. There was rich carpeting on the floor, and the aromas that mingled in the air were appealing. The diners were more arresting in their finery than the restaurant. Ladies in silks and taffetas with elegant little feathered hats sat across from men in their business best. A pianist played soft music from a dais, and the black-jacketed waiters were as proper as the clientele.

The maître d' knew Ian well, and led them to a table by a railing overlooking the piano. He greeted Ian by name, and didn't try to hide his excitement at seeing Marissa.

"Madame Tremayne, *je pense, monsieur*?"

"Yes, Jacques, this is my wife. Marissa, Jacques. And Mr. and Mrs. O'Brien. If you're ever wandering around and in need of a meal, come see Jacques. He will see that you are well cared for, whatever the rush. Isn't that right, Jacques?"

"Oh, *mais oui*!" Jacques agreed. The handsome little Frenchman was smiling widely, with a keen sense of humor and excitement about him. As he seated them and handed them menus, he added, "Madame Tremayne is very young, and very beautiful. *Elle est très belle*!"

Marissa felt a soft blush touching her cheeks as Ian looked at her, too, as if debating the Frenchman's words.

"Yes," he agreed wryly. "She's young."

Marissa had thought that Jimmy might plunge in with something complimentary in her defense, but Jimmy was still busy staring around the restaurant, while Mary was studying her menu.

"Jacques, what on earth is going on with you today?" Ian demanded, exasperated.

"Nothing, nothing," Jacques said quickly. "Monsieur Tremayne, Raoul will wait on you today. I shall send the wine steward immediately, also, yes? Raoul!"

The man was quickly at their side, and seemed as fascinated by Ian's wife as Jacques had been. Marissa was wryly glad that she did not seem to disappoint, yet she was truly curious at the air of excitement she was causing.

"May I order for us all?" Ian asked politely. He was impatient, she realized. He had taken her around the city on her first day, and now he was anxious to get lunch over with and move on to business.

"Please, do," she said, and Ian looked at Jimmy.

"Oh, aye, please do!" Jimmy said quickly, after a moment.

The wine steward poured burgundy into their crystal glasses, which Ian tasted and approved. Marissa noted with a smile that

Jimmy had studied his every move, and that Mary watched Jimmy fondly as he sought to learn. Ian ordered and started to tell them about Golden Gate Park, which they had not seen. "A Japanese tea garden was erected there during the Exposition of 1894," he said. "Perhaps the ladies will want to make an excursion one day—"

He broke off suddenly. Marissa turned to discover why.

A woman was walking toward them. She was tall and slim, with fine, delicate features, large, dark-fringed eyes, and hair so deep and lustrous a brown it was like sable. She smiled, and her chin was held elegantly high. She was dressed in mauve, and a fashionable feathered hat sat jauntily upon her head. She was elegant and sensual, and it was apparent Ian knew her very well.

And it was equally apparent that she was no dance-hall girl.

Ian stood as she approached. He did not seem wary or distressed, and Marissa felt her cheeks burning despite her determination that they should not. Ian had made no promises to her.

"Hello, Grace," he said as the woman approached.

"Ian, dear!" The woman took his hands and rose on her toes to delicately kiss both his cheeks. Her eyes were warm, and she seemed as gentle and fragile as an angel.

Then she turned to Marissa, and her gaze was deadly.

"You must be the new Mrs. Tremayne . . . child. What a lovely girl, Ian. My congratulations. Oh, I am sorry. Ian has horrid manners at times, doesn't he? Well, perhaps you don't know him quite as well as I do yet. I'm Grace Leroux. We're old friends."

The woman at the station had been one thing—this woman was another. Marissa forgot that at one time she couldn't have cared less what Ian Tremayne did with his life. She wasn't anyone's child, and she wasn't about to let this sweet-faced harpy best her in any way.

She rose, offering Grace Leroux her hand, and smiling serenely. "Very, very old friends, I can see," she said sweetly. "And indeed, my husband's manners can be quite atrocious." She flashed Ian what she hoped was an adoring and intimate smile. She gritted her teeth, hoping he would not step in and make a fool of her.

He did not. His brows rose, his lip curled and he watched her with growing amusement as she continued.

"Mrs. Leroux—or is it Miss?"

"Mrs.," said the woman, her dark eyes narrowing, the hint of a hiss in the word.

"Mrs. Leroux, my friends, Mr. and Mrs. James O'Brien. Mary, Jimmy, Ian's very old friend, Mrs. Leroux."

Jimmy was already on his feet. Mary smiled demurely. Marissa cast a quick glance at Ian, and discovered that he seemed annoyed with the situation.

"Grace, are you staying? Would you like a chair brought?"

"Yes, what a lovely idea," Grace agreed. Ian motioned to their waiter, who quickly brought a fifth chair and seated Grace. She nodded across the table. "Mr. and Mrs. O'Brien," she acknowledged with little interest. She turned her back on Marissa. "Ian, the picnic for the Orphan's Fund is next week, or have you forgotten? Our most influential businessmen will be coming during the day. I do hope that we can count on you to attend." She turned to Marissa. "Oh, dear, it really isn't for wives. Ian, you will be there, I hope?"

"I always support the Orphan's Fund," Ian said with a sigh of impatience. "Of course I'll be there."

"Why isn't it for wives?" Marissa asked with a mock innocence.

"I'm curious myself," Ian murmured, crossing his arms idly over his chest as he watched Grace.

"Well, it's rather a workaday thing, dear. Boring, if you're not involved. And it's a traditional thing, really. Ian has been very involved. He usually escorts me. I am so sorry, dear," Grace purred to Marissa. "You will forgive me for stealing your husband?"

"If I allowed you to steal my husband, I would have to forgive you," Marissa said pleasantly. She folded her hands on the snowy white tablecloth and smiled at Mary. "Mary and I were longing to see the park, so I imagine that we'll explore it on the same day. That way you won't have to feel guilty about my husband, and we won't disturb your tradition."

Grace was still smiling, but the effort seemed to be growing difficult. She stood swiftly. "Well, we shall see," she murmured. "Ian, dear, we'll speak later. It was such a—surprise, meeting you," she told Marissa. Then she waved elegantly and left the table. Marissa noted that she turned and stared at Ian moments later, and that there was cold fury in her eyes. But Ian was not paying any heed, for the waiter had brought their food.

Marissa found herself very quiet during the meal, until the subject of the picnic came up again. Mary asked about the Orphan's Fund. Marissa watched Ian, and was startled when he suddenly turned his head and caught her in the act.

"Should we see the Golden Gate Park that day?" she asked him.

He shrugged, but didn't look away. "If you choose. I've no idea what Grace's tradition is. There is no reason you shouldn't both attend, you and Mary. I plan to have Jimmy busy at the emporium by then."

Marissa lowered her eyes quickly, not wanting him to see that she was inordinately pleased with his words.

Yet when they left the restaurant and Jimmy and Mary preceded them down the street, she could not help but challenge him again.

"You mentioned to the maître d' that you were married. Yet I had the feeling that Mrs. Leroux had no knowledge of me until we met."

He shrugged. "I made luncheon reservations for myself, my wife and friends. I had no reason to inform Grace."

"Yet you almost defended me against her."

He case her a long, dry look. "You seemed to be defending yourself, my love. I've acquired a cat with claws, so it seems."

Marissa stopped in the middle of the sidewalk, and Ian turned impatiently. "I've an appointment this afternoon—"

"She is your mistress, isn't she?"

"Marissa, I told you—"

"You didn't bother to tell your mistress that you'd acquired a wife?"

"It's really none of her business, is it?" he asked her smoothly.

"But it is. I like to be aware of the situations I find myself cast into."

"She's an old friend." He grinned. "Very old, as you were so quick to tell her."

Marissa flushed, but she felt her temper growing. "I don't care to have lunch with your intimate old friends."

"I didn't invite her. Now, would you please come on?"

She didn't move, and he suddenly caught her arm. "Come on!"

She had little choice, for he was nearly dragging her down the street. And when she would have balked again, he paused and turned to her in a sudden fury. "Damn you, girl, you're the one determined on your private quarters!"

"Which you ignored!"

"Ask me in, then." His eyes burned, seeming to bore into her and sweep away the rest of the busy world around them. "I told you, my love, I want you. It was a wretched discovery, but a damned true one. So my affairs, or lack of them, are quite up to you."

"It's not enough!" she cried, trying to shake free of him.

"What?"

"I want—" she began. "I want more than just to be wanted!" she cried out in a rush. She jerked free and hurried ahead, leaving him standing on the sidewalk, reflective, furious.

Then a slow smile crossed his face, and finally he laughed out loud.

CHAPTER ELEVEN

That night Marissa sat at the dining table alone. She picked at an expertly prepared duck à l'orange, and wondered if it was true that Ian had been detained on business.

He had been quick to desert them that afternoon. Well, perhaps he hadn't deserted them. He had turned Mary and Marissa over to one of his clerks, a freckle-faced girl named Sandy O'Halloran, and he had disappeared with Jimmy. Sandy had a natural friendliness and enthusiasm that was instantly endearing, and Marissa felt immediately comfortable with her.

She was the first woman Marissa had met in San Francisco who seemed honestly pleased to meet Ian's wife.

And she obviously loved the emporium. She spent the first hour dragging them from department to department. The emporium seemed to sell absolutely everything from furnishings to garden tools, foodstuffs to recreational paraphernalia. There were bicycles and baseballs, canned goods, the latest in chemises and nightwear, spades and hoes, fine English Chesterfields.

And in the basement there was a cafeteria where the employees had their meals. Though they had already had lunch, Marissa and Mary had tea with Sandy and watched as the employees went through the line for their meals. The cafeteria seemed busy and productive, and the employees were relaxed, talking among themselves as they ate. Marissa caught the occasional covert glance at herself, but she felt that the interest was friendly and open enough, and she smiled in return when she could.

"What do you think?" Sandy asked, seeing Marissa's interest as she surveyed the area.

"I think it's very active!" Marissa laughed.

"Oh, well, then, you should see it on Sunday mornings!" Sandy told her.

"Why?"

"The children from St. Kevin's have their breakfast here after church."

"What is St. Kevin's?" Marissa asked.

"Well, St. Kevin's is the Catholic church, and there is an orphanage, too. Sundays are wonderful."

"You work on Sundays?"

"Oh, no. It's strictly volunteer service, but I do love the children. There are about fifty of the little hooligans. I'm the oldest of twelve, you see, but my sisters and brothers are all back in Ireland. I miss them, and I make up for it on Sundays. Mr. Tremayne supplies all the food, and whoever cares to shows up to help see that it's all ladled out. The children love it. There are griddle cakes and ham and huge sausages and fish—it's a wonder for the children, it is, all the jelly and sweet maple syrup they can eat!"

"Is it in connection with the Orphan's Fund?" Marissa asked her suspiciously.

Sandy gave a little sniff. "No. Mr. Tremayne started his Sunday breakfast long ago. Her Highness Leroux just started with her charity appeals after she learned that Mr. Tremayne—"

She broke off in distress, her eyes very wide as she realized that she was gossiping about her employer's mistress to her employer's wife.

"It's quite all right, Sandy," Marissa said smoothly. "I'm anxious to see this Sunday breakfast. We'll meet you again, I'm certain."

Marissa realized soon after that Mary was wan and exhausted. John Kwan had come for them. Jimmy was busy in the offices, they learned, and Ian had gone to his afternoon meeting.

Marissa accompanied John to see Mary home, but she was determined to explore more of the city herself.

"If you'll bring me downtown, John, I can take a cable car," she told him.

He seemed uncomfortable. "May I show you some of the homes on our hill, Mrs. Tremayne? It will grow dark soon today. Tomorrow you could explore in the morning."

"And you've been told not to let me out of your sight, right?" she asked him wryly.

She could see no reason to cause John distress, so she smiled and agreed to see more of the hill. And after they drove down the hill, where he showed her the magnificent Fairmont Hotel, not yet completed, on the brink of Nob Hill, overlooking the Bay. She was surprised to have thoroughly enjoyed both the impromptu tour and John.

But when she had returned to the house, she discovered that Ian had sent a message home; he would not be there for dinner. And so she was left in the huge dining room alone, with Lee Kwan—whom she did not one bit enjoy—serving her dinner in a stilted silence.

Lee liked her no more than she liked Lee, Marissa realized.

Marissa hovered downstairs as late as she could, but Ian did not return. Finally, when the clock had struck eleven, she gave up and went to bed. Ian still had not returned.

Nor did he disturb her in the morning. She awoke late and found that he had left the house long before she came down to breakfast.

She and Mary spent the afternoon taking a cable car ride. Mary sat on one of the seats, but Marissa could not help but hang on at the entryway, holding her hat on her head as they moved up and down the hills. The cool wind fanned her cheeks. Staring around her with fascination, she decided she loved the city more and more.

On Saturday morning, she awoke once again to find herself alone except for Lee in the beautiful Nob Hill house. More hurt than she was willing to admit, even to herself, she left the house, not mentioning a destination to Lee inside or John by the carriage house. She determined to walk downhill.

She had almost reached the nearly completed Fairmont Hotel when the sound of horse's hooves close behind her startled her. To her surprise, Ian, mounted upon a huge bay, had reined in just behind her.

"Where in God's name do you think you're going?" he said with a frown.

She stepped back, surprised that her heart should hammer with such vehemence. "I am going for a walk. And don't you speak to me that way."

He arched a brow, then leaned low over the horse's neck. "I'll speak to you however I choose, my lady. You scared me half out of my wits."

"I scared you? I do beg your pardon! You're the one who came pounding down upon me."

"I didn't pound—Jinx here trotted."

"Then Jinx here can trot away!" she retorted pleasantly and turned to keep walking.

Jinx didn't trot away. Ian leaped from the horse's back and halted Marissa with an arm around her waist, turning her to face him. His voice had a rough edge to it. "You didn't tell anyone where you were going."

"I didn't know I was required to tell anyone where I was going," she said smoothly, lifting her chin and raising her eyes to his in an emerald challenge. "You never do," she reminded him flatly.

"I'm hardly likely to be the victim of kidnappers or thieves!"

She wished her heart would not pound so loudly, and that the whisper of excitement would not sweep so heatedly throughout her just because he was near, because he touched her. She swept her lashes over her eyes, fearful suddenly that she would give away too much of that excitement.

"Thank you for your concern. Now that you've voiced it and you know I'm out for a walk, I'll thank you to let me proceed."

He stopped her before she had taken a step. "You'll not proceed, young woman!" he snapped. "What foolishness is this? You don't know a thing about the city. You just presume yourself above it all, and you go strutting off not knowing if you're waltzing into danger—"

"Danger!" she taunted him. "Here? On Nob Hill? I hardly think I'm walking through dens of cutthroats and thieves!" She laughed, but her laughter faded at his murderous glare. She slipped free from his arm and backed away. "Ian—"

"Get over here, Marissa."

"I will not!"

"You will!" He promised, taking a step toward her.

"I will not!" He was still coming. She took another step, both dreading and fascinated by the blue fire in his gaze. "You don't bother to speak to me for two days, and then you come riding down upon me like some hound from hell! I will not tolerate it, I'm telling you right now that I simply won't tolerate it!"

"You could have told Lee—"

"I needed air! And I owe nothing to Lee, it is none of her affair—"

"But it is my affair!"

"No, it is not! Not when—"

She broke off with a cry. He had wrapped his arms firmly around her and was setting her up upon the bay with such vehemence she was afraid she would go right over the other side of the horse. But before she could do so he was quickly behind her, and his arms were around her as he took up the reins. Her skirt was not made for riding, and she was forced to fall between his thighs upon the English saddle or lose her balance. Her shoulder rested firmly against his chest, and as he nudged the horse into a smooth canter, she gasped and put her arm around his waist.

"Where are you taking me!" she cried out.

He leaned low. His whisper mingled with the rush of the wind. "You said you needed air!"

And she certainly received it. She could not say that he was careless, for he was an excellent horseman. Yet he rode with a certain recklessness, a wildness, that was exhilarating and exciting. She could feel the heat and energy of the stallion and the man as they rode pell-mell down the street. The wind tore at her hair and plucked at her skirt, chilled and caressed her cheeks. Where his arms touched her, though, she was warm, and deep within her, she felt a rising heat. Tiny laps of fire kissed the base of her spine and radiated like the sun's warmth through her loins to her heart.

She didn't know where they traveled; she didn't care. She closed her eyes and immersed herself in the grace of the animal and the strength of the man. She felt the beat of the horse's hooves. They slowed at last, and the horse moved at a more moderate pace.

As they walked, she opened her eyes and realized that he was staring at her, intently studying her face.

"Where are we going?" she asked him softly. She didn't move her cheek from his chest or her hand from where it lay against his jacket.

He smiled slowly. "For air."

Then he reined in, and, regretfully, she straightened. They were in the midst of a busy world, on a road where the trolley moved, where cars honked, where carriages jangled past.

"The Palace Hotel," he said, indicating the handsome structure before him. His voice had a whimsical quality to it. "General William T. Sherman and President Ulysses S. Grant have stayed here, among others. Caruso will come here on tour soon." He leaped down from the horse and reached up, his hands warm and firm around her waist as he lifted her down beside him. "But there is much, much more to make her great."

He was clearly talking about something that mattered to him, and Marissa was surprised he was doing so to her. He took her hand and walked closer to the hotel, sweeping out an arm to include all of the construction. "She is built on massive pillar foundations that go twelve feet deep, and iron-reinforced brick walls are two feet thick. There's a huge tank of water in the basement, and there are seven more tanks upon the roof. One hundred and thirty thousand gallons of water to fight fires, and five miles of piping to distribute it. Each of the eight hundred rooms is fitted with a fire detector that triggers an alarm in case of fire, and watchmen patrol every floor every thirty minutes. There have been a number of small fires here, and all successfully fought." He fell silent.

Marissa, her fingers curled in his, knew nothing at all about building. But it suddenly mattered very much to her.

"Ian, how do you know all this?" she asked softly.

He shrugged. "It's my business to know." His hand still holding hers, they strolled along the street. "I'm just so damned frustrated. This is the way things should be built. In San Francisco, at least. And those fools who have asked me to design their offices on the waterfront don't seem to realize that. They don't mind paying for an architect, but when I start telling them about pilings and hoses and water tanks, they start crying poverty."

He fell silent, and Marissa walked quietly beside him. "What are you going to do?" she asked at last. "They couldn't possibly—compromise you."

He stopped and turned to her with one of the slow, lazy smiles that had captured her heart when she had not been aware. He brushed a stray strand of hair gently from her forehead with the back of his free hand. "No, Marissa. They will not—compromise me," he said with a soft laugh that held a stirring note of curious tenderness. "I won't build the damned thing for them unless they're willing to do it my way."

He was suddenly in a hurry again, full of energy. She had to run to keep up with him as they hurried back. A doorman held the horse at the entrance to the Palace Hotel. Ian lifted her up by the waist and leaped expertly to his seat behind her. They trotted with the traffic to the rise of Nob Hill, and there Ian gave the horse free rein so that they raced again.

Marissa closed her eyes and leaned against him. When Ian reined in the horse she opened her eyes with a start.

They were not far from his house, but it was a different home they had come to. It, too, was large and beautiful, with stained-glass windows and moderate gingerbreading, two matching turrets, and graceful ells that gave the house both size and beauty.

"It's one of mine," Ian said simply.

"You built it?"

"Yes. Do you like it?"

"It's—wonderful," she admitted.

"Thank you," he told her. He nudged the bay, and they walked in silence to the house.

Marissa had never known that she could be both excited and content at once. Her veins still seemed to leap when he touched her. But it was comfortable, so very comfortable, to rest in his arms.

But her contentment wasn't meant to last. When they reached the house, John was out front waiting for Ian. "What is it?" Ian asked, still mounted upon the bay and holding Marissa close against him.

"A problem with—logistics, Mr. Tremayne," John said. He glanced at Marissa. "Mrs. Leroux says there's an emergency with the finances for the new children's wing at St. Kevin's. They need you immediately."

Marissa's spine stiffened. She pulled from Ian's hold and leaped down from the bay.

To her distress, her skirt caught upon the saddle. She nearly catapulted over, but Ian caught her. She wrenched angrily at her skirt.

He released it for her.

"Marissa!" he called as she strode toward the house. She didn't answer him.

And to her growing rage, she heard his laughter follow her to the house.

That afternoon she lay carelessly in a steaming bubble bath. She leaned back and closed her eyes, despising Grace Leroux, the woman at the train station, Lee Kwan—and herself. Once upon a time it had been easy to despise Ian, too. But now, though her temper simmered and steamed, she could find no outlet for it. She wanted to shake him and hurt him . . . and make him look at her. She wanted to share things as they had this afternoon. He had dreams, too. Perhaps he had buried the art of loving someone when he had buried his first wife, but he still knew how to dream. And he loved something. He loved building—with a passion.

She started as she heard a door slam. She thought quickly—she was certain that she had locked the door to the hall. She had no intention of being surprised by the silent Lee Kwan.

But she hadn't locked the door between hers and Ian's rooms. And he was coming in now, still in his riding clothes.

A flush that had nothing to do with the heat of the bath flooded her features as she frantically swished the water to make more suds. She wanted him, yes. She was falling in love with him, yes.

But she was not going to let him know it.

Heat pressed behind her eyelids and she felt ridiculously as if tears would sting her eyes again.

Not unless he fell in love with her. Not unless he could rid his life of the Grace Lerouxs and the dance-hall girls and the Lee Kwans . . .

She looked up, and saw he was carrying a silver tray with two teacups and a beautiful samovar.

Marissa stared at him blankly, then swore with a sudden fury. "What are you doing?"

"Bringing my darling young wife tea," he said. His tone was pleasant, but his eyes carried a satyr's gleam.

She sat up, trying to hold on to her bubbles. "I don't want tea."

"Certainly, you do."

He set the tray upon a wicker stool, poured the tea and brought her a cup. She clung to her bubbles, glaring at him. "I do not want tea."

"Suit yourself." He leaned against the wall and sipped the tea.

"Would you please leave?"

"I came with a gesture of goodwill."

She leaned back, smiling sweetly. "How's Grace?"

"Aha! So there we are. That sweet edge of jealousy!"

She wished he weren't quite so appealing with the gleam in his eyes, the rakish fall of his hair, even the laughter within him.

"I'm not jealous," she said demurely. Her bubbles were popping quickly.

"You're not?"

He was so darned sure of himself. It seemed time to test her own power.

She stretched out a leg prettily, soaping it with an oversize bath sponge. "Not a bit," she said. "Why should I be jealous? This marriage is in name only, right?"

"It's what you've said you want."

She lowered her leg slowly and gracefully, watching it. Then she met his eyes. "You don't want a wife," she reminded him very softly.

He set his cup down on the tray and strode to the tub, staring at her. "Perhaps I've changed my mind."

She smiled, stretching her arms out elegantly before her. "Oh, I think not."

"And why not?" He lowered himself, hunching down beside the tub, his fingers idly moving over the water.

She watched the play of his hands, thinking how very close they were to her naked flesh. She caught her breath, watching him, unable to answer at first. Then she met his eyes again. "You were too eager to run to the beck and call of—" she hesitated a minute, then finished sweetly "—that old bat."

He burst into laughter, and the spark of fire remained in his eyes as he continued to swirl his hand through the water. "Not jealous?" he murmured.

"I merely call a spade a spade," she said innocently.

His laughter faded, and his ink-dark lashes covered his eyes. "But you see, I didn't leave my wife to run to that old bat. The wife, you see, went huffing off without a single question, giving the husband no recourse."

She gently but firmly pushed his straying hand to the edge of the tub. "No recourse but to run to the old bat?"

"Indeed, I saw the er, old bat. But it was necessary to talk to a friend and assure him he needed to spend his money for a new wing for the children. I had to convince people that all we needed to do was come up with the price of the materials and labor, since my services would cost nothing. And they would all be praised for their generosity, with so little needed!"

She smiled. "I don't believe you."

"It's God's own truth, I swear it," he told her.

"The lady is only a friend?"

A slight curl touched the corner of his lip. He reached out, setting his thumb beneath her chin so that her eyes met his. "Not always. I would be a liar to assure you that nothing ever was. I painted you no half truths in London. But I do admit, the old bat pales mightily in comparison to the young vixen."

She could not draw her eyes from his. She started to smile at his words, then her smile suddenly faded for he had stood up and was drawing her to her feet.

When she was standing, still in the tub with the water and the bubbles sluicing from her body, he wound his arms around her and his lips met hers. His kiss was hot and filled with a passion that invaded her being just as his tongue invaded her mouth and all the sweet crevices within.

His fingers moved over her naked spine as he kissed her. And he pressed her close against him as his lips deserted hers to roam over the arch of her throat, to find the pulse that beat heedlessly there, to linger, to roam again.

She caught his cheeks between her hands. She felt the masculine texture of them, somewhat rough and exciting, and she met his eyes again. And she stood on tiptoe to press her lips against his, to taste the rim of them, to delve within them herself, shyly taking the initiative at first, then boldly pressing forward.

The scent of him swept her. A rich scent of leather and fine brandy and man. And then she could no longer hold him to her for his kiss was pressed against her shoulders. The searing heat of his mouth curled around her breast as his passion plucked at one rouge crest. Then his lips were buried in the valley between them before moving on.

He fell to his knees, and the flickering motion of his tongue moved in and out of her navel. Then he turned her and a gasp escaped her as his kiss centered upon the base of her spine, as the fire of his tongue moved up and then down again, until a fire seared all the flesh of her buttocks, and she was certain she would fall.

He turned her yet again, and now his kiss was searing the center of her being, boldly, intimately, completely. Shock and excitement wrapped her, and she grasped desperately for his shoulders. She was going to fall. She could not fall. Sensations she could not endure began to sweep through her. Sweet, so sweet, hot and sweet and so unbearable that she could surely die.

She cried out, she had to protest. But it was no cry of protest that left her lips. The cry was sweet with growing wonder, growing desire . . .

Then startling, shattering knowledge. So quickly, so wonderously, so heatedly, a startling, shimmering lava burst within her. She cried out again, stunned, shivering, gasping, almost falling.

He swept her into his arms, and his lips touched hers, and she was so stunned with the wonder that had seized her, she could not kiss him. She was barely aware that he carried her into the bedroom, barely aware that she lay on the bed, stretched out, waiting for him.

And then he was with her. Naked this time. He crawled atop her and found her lips again. And suddenly she was clinging to him, shivering. Her eyes met his, he smiled, she closed her eyes, and he kissed them, then kissed her lips. And her arms went naturally around him.

And as he kissed her she began to explore his flesh. Her fingertips moved over his naked shoulders and back. She heard the sharp inhalation of his breath as she touched him. And touched him.

She shivered, awakened anew as his weight sank between her thighs. She buried her face against his shoulder as he teased her with his touch, creating a new rise of desire, of heat and dampness. She wanted to cry out, but she could not. He brought her fingers down and wound them around him, and she started at the pulse and boldness of his body. She cried out as he wedged himself hard between her thighs, then entered deep within her in a slow, sensual thrust.

The rhythm of the world took flight. In his arms, she soared. She felt the fullness of him within her, she felt the texture of his thighs, the caress of his hands, the heat of his whisper. And she felt, too, the wonder, the soaring . . .

And the final caress of the magic. Deep and shattering, filling her body, coursing through her. Stars seemed to burst, and disappear, and there was nothing but blackness, and she was drifting . . .

Until she heard her name, the whisper of her name, upon his lips.

She opened her eyes, and he smiled. The slick dampness of their bodies was still hot between them. He had not moved, but remained deeply imbedded within her even as little tremors remained to touch their bodies.

The tremors faded away, and still their eyes met. And he spoke to her again at last.

"I have learned something, Marissa," he said, his voice amazingly tender. "I have learned that I do, after all, want a wife. I want her very much."

Her heart seemed to slam against her chest. And she started to smile, and he caught her lips in another deep and shattering kiss.

And with that kiss, she surrendered all.

CHAPTER TWELVE

M arissa would remember little that was precise about that afternoon. Rather she would remember the sensations. There had been sweet comfort in the quiet between them when ecstasy faded to gentle bliss and she lay beside him, her hair a tangle upon his shoulders and chest. There was the sound and the cadence of his words as he spoke to her. He never said he loved her. She wouldn't have expected him to do so. It didn't matter. She had more than she had dreamed, for he wove a future for them. He spoke of the opera, of the ballet, of the waterfront. Of sunsets and sunrises, trips to Sausalito and Carmel, of riding along the coast to see the majestic sights.

Then the quiet and the comfort faded as passion was rekindled. And in the next sweeping wave of fire, she began to learn to explore herself. She began to dare new things, to discover the man. To run her fingers through the soft, dark hair upon his chest, to touch and stroke . . . to tempt. She was amazed at the laughter between them, at the breathlessness, at the closeness that blanketed them as her inhibitions were shed.

Twilight came, and a soft fog wafted over the city. It seemed to enter the windows, to wrap them in something mystical. Marissa could almost feel it, cool and caressing against her naked flesh. Within its embrace she rose over Ian, smiled and met the curious fire in his eyes. Then leaning low against him she sensually swept the soft length of her hair slowly over his chest, following each silken sweep with the damp heat of a lazy, luxurious kiss. And so she made her way down his body, delighting that he could tremble so beneath her, until he caught his breath in amazement and excitement, going rigid beneath her bold touch. He swore softly, then lifted her above him to impale her swiftly and surely.

The gentle fog tempered her cries and whispers, and caressed her still when she lay exhausted and sweetly sated and amazed once again.

Marissa drifted into sleep, curled by his side, her hair blanketing his chest, her fingers resting lightly upon his naked flesh. She heard a rapping sound, as if far away. Then she started, for the hard-muscled cushion beneath her head moved. "What is it?"

"Lee is at my door," he said. He rose, sleek and handsome in his nakedness. He found his trousers and started for the connecting door.

Then the rapping came at Marissa's door. In the hazy twilight that blanketed the room, Ian cast her a wry grin that caught at her heart. He opened her door.

Lee was there. Marissa heard her softly spoken words, but could not understand them.

Ian closed the door and came to the foot of the bed. His hair was dark and tousled over his forehead, and the shiny dampness of his chest enhanced the muscled structure of it. Marissa started to stretch out on the bed, heavy-lidded, lazy and luxurious.

"Oh, no!" Ian told her with a laugh, snatching up the sheet. "We've company."

"Company!" She bolted up. She was a mess, hair everywhere, naked, and slick with a slight sheen of perspiration.

He smiled easily at her panic. "Take your time—you've at least five minutes. I'd forgotten, Sullivan and Funston are here for supper."

"Who?" she gasped.

"Dennis Sullivan, the fire chief. And Frederick Funston, Brigadier General Funston, that is, acting commander of the Presidio. He and his wife, Eda, have a beautiful home here on Nob Hill. I'm afraid you caused it to completely skip my mind, but they're downstairs now. Lee will serve drinks, I'm sure."

"We've company, and you're standing there like that!" she gasped.

He laughed and headed for the door to his room. "I'll be back in five minutes."

"No, I can't dress in five minutes and meet people! Ian, you must wait—"

But he was already gone. Hastily she went to the bathroom. Biting her lip, she doused herself with cold bathwater then dried off furiously. She raced to her room, rummaged through several drawers to find underclothing and proper attire, then tried to brush, arrange and pin her hair.

Her hair was civilized, she decided, staring into the mirror. Her eyes were still very wild.

She heard a low whistle and turned. Ian was back, dark, handsome, immaculate in black. His blue gaze took in her appearance from head to toe. She had chosen a white ruffled silk blouse with a high collar and a watered silk skirt. The white of her outfit was offset by the jet beads and drop earrings she had chosen, and the fine black brocade jacket.

"Am I all right?" she asked anxiously.

"Positively—virginal," he told her. She flushed, and he arched a brow with a curious smile. "It's just Dennis and Freddie and Eda," he said, "not royalty."

She glanced at him quickly and remembered that although it had seemed that she had been changed completely and forever by their lovemaking, she hadn't been. She might be in love with him, but that didn't change the fact that she was living a lie. She could tell he was thinking that she was accustomed to meeting the upper crust of British society.

She looked at the dresser. Not even the lie really mattered now. She was a good actress, and she had learned her role well. "They are your friends, aren't they?"

"Yes."

"Then they are very important to me," she said softly.

He was across the room to her with a few long strides, raising her chin with his thumb and looking into her eyes. He studied them carefully and slowly smiled. "My love, you are such an enigma. So very proud and determined, fighting all the way. And yet when you choose, the pride is stripped away, and the heart can be laid bare, and it is a beautiful heart."

"Don't!" she whispered.

"Don't?"

"It is not so beautiful a heart," she murmured quickly. She backed away from him. "You've been very good to my friends." She stood still, then raced to him, throwing herself into his arms and looking into his eyes. "Ian," she began hurriedly, "I started things badly, I forced this on you, but I mean to try to make things work, I want very badly to be what you want—"

"Shh!" he whispered, puzzled, as he caught her face between his hands and kissed her gently. "Marissa, if I had been completely against the idea of marriage to you, I wouldn't have married you, no matter what. I could not have been forced to do so. And since I met you, you've been surprisingly many things that I want, many."

She flushed, her lashes lowering.

"Modesty now?" He chuckled, then moved his thumb gently over her lower lip. "Marissa, you caught my heart the other day. You made me see that I was creating my own hell. Marissa . . ."

He pulled her against him and held her close. Then he broke away, his eyes sparkling. "Our dinner guests await." He caught her hand and led her from the bedroom, down the stairway and to the dining room, where their company awaited them.

A short red-haired man stood beside a lively little woman with dancing blue eyes. By the buffet, which was doubling as a bar, was a taller man with a lean face and a haunted gaze.

"Eda, Frederick, Dennis, welcome," Ian said quickly, drawing Marissa around. "My wife, Marissa. Marissa, I give you the true heartbeat of San Francisco and Nob Hill, Mrs. Eda Funston, and her husband, Freddie. And by the buffet, Dennis Sullivan."

The gentlemen assessed her silently; Eda's blue eyes sparkled as she greeted her effusively. "So this is the new bride that has the city abuzz!" Eda said. "Marissa, welcome, welcome. What a lovely addition you are to this house. It has not seemed quite so alive in positively ages."

"Thank you so much," Marissa told her, glancing at Ian. Eda was wonderfully warm. She felt very welcomed, indeed.

Lee appeared. She remained silent until Ian noticed her, then she announced that dinner was ready.

They were soon seated. Lee returned to serve the soup, and Ian poured wine, and the conversation remained casual. Then Dennis Sullivan almost curtly asked Ian, "Have your clients received the permits for the new buildings from City Hall?"

Ian stared at Dennis, then lifted his glass and stared at his wine. Then he looked at Dennis again. "Yes, the permits were received."

The fire chief slammed a fist upon the table and the dishes rattled. He apologized profusely, but he was still vehement when he looked at Ian again. "I'm telling you, this is more corruption! Those codes are insane! It's Mayor Schmitz and that kingmaker of his, Reuf, collecting under-the-table money on these things. Just like the Barbary Coast, feet from our door! Reuf makes money every time he hands out a license for a French restaurant!"

Marissa had no idea what was going on. Eda Funston gently put a stop to the conversation. "Gentlemen, we are at the dinner table!"

"Yes, we are at dinner." Ian offered Marissa a wry smile, then looked at the fire chief. "Dennis, I have turned the project down in no uncertain terms. They'll have to find themselves another builder."

Eda turned the conversation, chatting easily about the upcoming tour of the Great Caruso and his famed temper. When the meal ended and the gentlemen had disappeared into the study for cigars and business, Eda and Marissa wandered across the entry to the parlor, and Marissa asked Eda what was going on.

Eda sighed, taking a seat before the window. "Corruption, my dear. I'm afraid this city is filled with it! My dear Freddie and Dennis and your Ian are quite disgusted with all of it."

"But what, precisely, is going on?" Marissa demanded.

"There's not so very much that we can prove, but we know licenses and permits can be bought. The insurance underwriters have given us reports. It's amazing—and entirely through the diligence of the fire department, they have said—that the city has not burned to the ground. Dennis wanted to train men to use explosives to fight the fires, and he thought a supplementary saltwater system to fight fires was necessary. The War Department in Washington was willing to send men to the Presidio to be in readiness to help with the fire department. All they wanted was for the city to provide a thousand dollars to build a brick vault on the Presidio grounds to house the explosives. Mayor Schmitz managed to thwart his plans."

"But if the city has been warned—"

"The board cannot enforce changes, only recommend that they be made."

"What is wrong with a license for a French restaurant?" Marissa asked her.

"Oh, my dear!" Eda said, and laughed softly, a look of mischief in her eyes. "The restaurant is usually there, all right. Downstairs. And then upstairs . . . well, French restaurants are often the facade for . . . well, for bordellos. Er, houses of ill repute. Do you understand?"

"Yes, I understand," Marissa told her, hiding a smile. She understood quite clearly. She might not have known the names of such places, but from the first time Ian had discussed his life with her, she had been well aware that he knew the location of many a dance hall and house of ill repute.

"And the building codes?" she said to Eda.

"Building permits can be bought, you see. But Ian has never been fooled by Mayor Schmitz. He is far too brilliant a builder not to love the quality of his work. I knew he would never agree to work unless his own codes were met!"

She smiled proudly at Marissa, then added softly, "Of course, it is a shame. Someone will be willing to build using those permits. Then heaven help us all if there ever should be a problem!"

Marissa was startled to feel a curious little tremor seize her heart. She shrugged it aside. Whatever happened, Ian would not be involved. And that was all that seemed to matter.

"Well, now, that's settled. Now, tell me more about your life in England, dear. You've the softest, loveliest accent! You're from the country, and your father was a squire, and now you're here. So, does that make you Lady Tremayne?"

Marissa lowered her head quickly. Guilt riddled her. "I'm Mrs. Tremayne, Ian's wife," she said. That, at least, was true. She managed to describe the manor in England, and to avoid any other direct questions.

Eda was sweet and pleasant, and Dennis Sullivan and Freddie Funston were charming when they joined them in the parlor.

And she knew she did well. The evening should have been a triumph.

But listening to Eda talk, Marissa realized bleakly that, for her, every night of conversation might be a tightrope walk. She would always have to lie and hedge and take care.

It was a sorry thought.

She glanced up and realized that Ian, standing by the fire, was studying her very carefully. Something of her unease must have shown on her face, and it seemed as if he was reading into her soul. She was betraying her own guilt.

She looked away from him quickly, her heart thundering.

She was coming to know him so very well. His eyes were still upon her.

And even when someone asked him a question and he turned aside, she knew that he had not forgotten what he had seen in her face.

And later, there would be a reckoning.

She wasn't expecting it as soon as it came.

She was the last at the door, saying goodbye to Eda, when their company left. Returning to the parlor, she felt at first as if her heart were warmed despite the cool winter night. There had been the wonderful afternoon, when she had begun to believe that she could be cherished. And then there had been the evening, when she had begun to believe that she could really become a part of her husband's life.

But as soon as she walked into the small parlor and saw the way Ian looked at her as he stood before the mantel, she was forced to remember that she was living a lie.

She wanted to run for the stairway, to escape to her room, slam and lock the door. Just fighting for the courage not to do so kept her heart hammering hard.

Perhaps cowardice would serve her well at the moment. It was strange how she had once dreaded being too close to him. Now she longed to be close. A passionate kiss could spark the magic to make them both forget that secrets lay in her eyes.

He was staring at her darkly and broodingly. She opened her mouth to speak, but words would not come. She picked up an elegant little pillow from the sofa and plumped it, seeking easy, casual words.

"Your friends are very nice. I enjoyed them thoroughly."

He didn't say a word. "It does seem a shame that you've got this beautiful city and then problems in the City Hall."

He still didn't speak, and she felt her nervousness growing. She set the pillow down. "Well, it seems very late. I think I'll retire for the evening—"

"I think not," he interrupted softly.

There was nothing soft about his gaze.

Marissa straightened her shoulders, swiftly deciding that indignation would be the best way to play the scene, with perhaps a touch of pathos. "Really, Ian," she said very quietly. She lowered her lashes to flutter over her cheeks. "After everything, that you can still accuse me—"

"I'm not accusing you of anything," he said flatly. "And yet that you answer so quickly and defensively disturbs me." His gaze was hard and penetrating still. "And you are not guilty. Then what?" he demanded.

"I don't know what you're talking about!" she snapped.

A wry, suspicious smile curved his lips. He left his stance at the fire and strode toward her.

"I'm going to bed!" she announced haughtily, spinning around, but too late. She knew him; she should have known he wouldn't have allowed her such an arrogant retreat.

He grabbed her by the shoulders, and then his fingers were raking through her hair, holding her head so that her eyes met his relentless blue stare.

"Ian, really—" she began impatiently.

"Yes, really, my love. Tell me what it is that you keep from me?" His voice was low, but intense and passionate. She felt a trembling begin within her, and she shook her head.

"Damn you, there's nothing!"

"There's nothing," he repeated softly.

"Bloody nothing!"

"Ah, but then why is your gaze so haunted? You can no longer fear me, I am certain."

"I never feared you!"

"So what is it that you do fear?"

"Nothing!"

She bit her lip, meeting his hard, hostile gaze.

He couldn't have ceased to want her so quickly! she told herself. She had not ceased to want him!

If only he would hold her close, kiss her hard, let it be! She longed to cry out, to sweep her arms around him, to forget that she lived a lie. She wanted so badly to tell him the truth at that moment.

But she couldn't. Not now. Maybe the time would come. Perhaps she could earn his trust, his affection, even his love.

"Marissa?"

"There's nothing!" she repeated, trembling. And then she wrenched away from him, certain that he would come after her. And then she would hold him, and make him forget his demands upon her.

But he didn't follow her. He walked to the tall mirrored hall tree by the doorway and picked up his black cape and top hat. "We'll discuss it when I return," he told her briefly. "Have an answer by then." He tipped his hat to her and turned.

Startled, she stared after him. He strode through the beautiful entryway to the front door.

Marissa forgot she was on the offensive and tore after him. "Where are you going?" she asked in amazement.

He smiled. "Out, my dear," he said, and threw open the front door, then headed toward the carriage house.

Marissa felt a blush rush to her cheeks. She couldn't believe the pain and jealousy that seared through her. After the time they had spent together, after the uninhibited abandon she had learned, he was leaving her!

Heading for the Barbary Coast. And French restaurants!

She caught the front door before it could close and followed him out in absolute fury and indignation. "Ian! Ian Tremayne!" she called from the beautiful Victorian porch.

He stopped and spun around.

"Don't dare think to question me again!" she warned him, her eyes alive with an emerald fire. "Don't think to question me—don't come home, for that matter!" she snapped, forgetting that it was his home. Before he could respond, she turned and slammed her way into the house. She leaned against the front door. She couldn't believe it! She was about to burst into hysterical tears. How could he leave her? She had fallen in love, and she had given everything to him, and it had meant the world to her, but nothing to him!

She heard horse's hooves upon the drive, and she knew he was gone.

Marissa glanced up just in time to see Lee Kwan slipping from the entryway to the dining room. She didn't know what the girl had seen or heard, but embarrassment suddenly rippled into her pride just as viciously as pain had torn into her heart.

She turned and slammed out of the house. She would walk down to the caretakers' cottage and see Mary and Jimmy, she thought.

But she didn't really want to see Mary. She didn't want to bare her shattered heart or pride.

She walked into the night. She was startled when the door opened and closed quickly behind her. She spun around to see that Lee had followed her out.

Lee, with her exotic beauty and mysterious face! Marissa felt even more battered.

"Mrs. Tremayne! Please."

"Please what, Lee?" she responded, watching the woman with wary suspicion.

"It's late. Sometimes men—drunk men—wander this way from the dance halls. We are perhaps too close, as the Funstons think. You must come back in the house!"

Marissa smiled suddenly. "Where is he going, Lee?"

Lee's dark lashes covered her exotic eyes. "Just for a ride."

"You're lying. Why do you bother to defend him from me? I could have sworn that you hated me."

Lee looked straight at her then, and slowly smiled. "I did hate you," she admitted.

"You did? Meaning that you don't anymore?" Marissa demanded.

"No, I do not hate you anymore," Lee said quietly.

"Well, I admit to being confused. But then, you know where he has gone, don't you? And I do not." It was a wild shot, but it seemed that her conversation with Ian's servant had taken a curve that her heart demanded she follow.

"Yes, I know where he has gone."

"To see the woman by the train."

"He is doing nothing that will hurt you."

Marissa threw up her hands, ready to laugh, and ready to cry. "How can you possibly know what will hurt me?"

Lee shook her head and lifted her chin. "I know him better than you."

"Obviously. At least, you have known him longer."

Lee shook her head again, vehemently. "You are wrong, Mrs. Tremayne. Your husband has never made me his concubine, though I might well have been willing. He has always been a friend to John and me. He treats us as people, when many blame the Chinese for every ill within the city. We had nothing, we starved. We worked for pennies a day, and John was ill when Ian found us in Chinatown and gave us jobs here. So, yes, I love him. But not as you think. I hated you when I believed that you meant to hurt him. Now, if I am not mistaken, you are in love with him. And you will not hurt him. So I bear you no ill will."

Marissa stared at the Chinese woman for a long moment, amazed. Lee was not speaking as a serving girl was supposed to speak to her mistress.

But then Marissa had been a serving girl herself, and she had never forgotten her own pride. Lee had much of it. She stood with the gentle evening breeze just plucking at her turquoise silk shirt and black pants. Her fabulous black hair moved in the wind, as inky dark as a raven's wing. Her chin was lifted; she was prepared for anything.

"You have the right to dismiss me now," Lee told her.

Marissa shook her head. "Dismiss you?" Then she laughed, and she almost wished that she could tell Lee the truth about herself. "I have no desire to dismiss you, Lee. And if I did," she admitted, "Ian would certainly not tolerate the act!" She walked toward the woman, smiling, and offered Lee her hand. Lee hesitated, then took it.

"Thank you," Marissa told her.

Lee nodded after a moment.

"But where did he go?" Marissa asked her. Lee was quiet and Marissa said again, "He went to see that woman. The one at the train station."

"There is a show opening tonight. He has gone to support the show, and nothing more."

"How can you know that?"

Lee shrugged. "I know, that is all." Marissa wanted more, and Lee knew it. "Because he cares for you now. I believe he went because his patronage helps her business. So he will go to see the show."

"Why didn't he tell me?"

Lee smiled. "It will take him time," she said. "He is his own master."

On an impulse Marissa laughed and hugged Lee. For a moment the Chinese woman was stiff, then she warmed and hugged Marissa in return.

"Thank you!" Marissa said, then she fled to her bedroom.

The hour was very late. Marissa changed to a nightgown, then began to pace the room. In a sudden fit of anger, she locked the door between the rooms.

And then she paced the floor again.

She curled up at the foot of her bed and ran her hand over the spread. Lee had been in the room, it seemed. She had managed to serve dinner and clean the room.

Marissa hugged her knees to her chest and wondered if Lee was right, if Ian had come to care something about her. She smiled, beginning to weave dreams.

Then she gasped and leaped to her feet as the door between the rooms suddenly seemed to thunder, then came bursting open.

Ian had returned.

She stared at him, and at the door, and he offered her a wry, challenging smile. "It's my house, my door. I warned you, remember?"

She met the challenge with fury. "Your house, your door. My determination for privacy!"

He stripped off his cape, and tossed his hat aside and came striding into the room. She cried out, determined to escape him, but he was too quick. His fingers had already laced around her arms. She began to shake, furious, yet glad that he had come at last. Wanting to shake him, and wanting to hold him.

"How dare you!" she whispered vehemently, fighting his hold. "How dare you go running to your brothel and come back to me!"

He swept her into his arms. "I went to no brothel!" he swore, and tossed her hard upon the bed. She started up, but his weight came down upon her too quickly, pinning her there. And his blue gaze was full of both ice and fire.

"Don't—" she began, but equally vehemently, he challenged her. "How dare you, madam!"

"How dare I what!" she cried indignantly. She felt the power of his arms, of his thighs. Beneath his trousers she could feel the heat of his body, and more. Against the flimsy fabric of her gown, she could feel the pulse of his desire, growing, insolent, demanding . . . exciting.

"Lie to me," he whispered.

"I did not run to another!"

"Nor did I."

He caught her lips in a passionate kiss. She surged against him, trying to escape. She was desperate that he understand he could not go to other women and have her, too. She twisted and tossed, and only managed to come closer against him, to become more aware of the promise that lay so boldly between them. She broke free of his kiss. "Ian, I'll not—"

"By God, would you still fight me!" He gazed at her with a fire in his eyes that sent her mind reeling and her heart drumming. A pulse ticked hard in his throat, and she felt the rigid pressure of his muscles.

"I'm not fighting you!" she gasped suddenly. "I'm fighting her!"

"Her?"

"That woman."

"Madam, there is no one to fight."

She believed him. She wanted to believe him. "And—" she whispered.

"By God, and what!" he thundered in sudden torment.

"The questions," she said softly, meeting his eyes.

A breath escaped him. His head fell back, then he stared at her again. "Damn the questions, Marissa. Just hold me. Let me make love to you."

A soft cry escaped her. She wound her arms around him, and when his lips caught hers again, she parted her own beneath him and gave way to the passion of his arms.

CHAPTER THIRTEEN

In the days that followed, Marissa made no further mention of Ian's night out. And Ian did not haunt her with questions.

It was a fascinating time for them both, a time for discovery, a fragile time in which they wanted to relish the amazement and wonder of one another. In her wildest fantasies, Marissa had never imagined what it could be like to love such a man. There were wonderful, tempestuous times in bed, and there were times of laughter, too, such as the occasion he crawled fully suited into a tub with her. And there were the gentle times, the slow, lazy, sensual times when they would sip champagne and eat tiny bites of fruit and cheese in bed.

There were evening rides, when Marissa discovered more of the city she was coming to love so very much. And there were the times they would go to the emporium. Marissa loved the store, she was terribly proud to see how very well Jimmy was doing, and she and Mary both became good friends with their one-time guide, Sandy, very quickly. Marissa was particularly fascinated with the orphans at the Sunday meal, finding that the little urchins with their feisty pride reminded her very much of herself when she was a child.

The more she learned about her husband, the greater the pride she came to feel for him. Perhaps he lived on Nob Hill, and perhaps he was welcome among the very best of society. But Ian drew his friends from people he liked. They included builders and policemen as well as the most influential businessmen. He abhorred the politics at City Hall, and would have no part in the bribery that went on there.

He was as willing to sip tea at the caretakers' cottage with Jimmy and Mary as he was to attend the most elite function.

As much as he loved San Francisco, he was not immune to the dangers within the city. One night when they rode, he showed her how close the wildness of the Barbary Coast lay to the quiet of Nob Hill.

"It's a city in which to take grave care," he warned her. They had reined in atop the hill to look down upon the city below. "Murder can be bought for the price of a cheap bottle of whiskey," he told her. "The police have started using automobiles now to patrol the city better, and it seems we have a decent chief in at last, but this is a place where there is a certain amount of crime. Shanghaiing occurs daily—"

"What's that?" she asked him.

He glanced her way quickly. "Ah, my love, you are an innocent! Shanghaiing is kidnapping. Young men and women are taken, sometimes to work on ships—more often to enter the brothels of the Orient. That's why the Barbary Coast is a place you should definitely avoid. I imagine that you'd be worth a fortune, with your hair and eyes, to some potbellied old geezer out there."

"Well, I like that! I'd be worth a fortune only to a potbellied old geezer?" she demanded.

He laughed then, huskily, and the bay pawed the ground as Ian moved his horse closer to hers. "No, my love, though I don't think I'd dare tell you what your value is to me. It might be dangerous information in your hands, and it might well go to your very pretty head."

Marissa smiled, pleased with his response. Their marriage still seemed fragile, but it was enough for now.

"Then you must stay away from the Barbary Coast, too," she said sweetly.

"But there are certain pursuits there to be enjoyed by gentlemen."

"My curiosity is awakened. Since it is not safe for me to go alone, I shall have to come in your company when you next seek your pursuits."

"You, madam, are going to have to learn your proper place as a lady and a wife."

"And you as a gentleman."

"A Yankee," he reminded her.

She sniffed, but after a moment she met his eyes and asked him softly, "Are you then resigned to having a wife once again?" Then she wished she hadn't spoken, for shadows seemed to cross his features.

"I'm sorry," she said quickly. "I didn't mean to cause you pain." She nudged her horse and started off at a trot toward the house. Seconds later he was pounding up beside her, then he caught her horse's reins. Startled, she looked at him.

"I am much more than resigned to having a wife," he told her. "I am grateful, for you made me see that I lived in a dark cavern of self-pity. You have given me the delight of the sun once again."

"Oh!" she murmured, stunned by his words.

"I'm delighted to have a wife. Indeed, come along quickly. Let's return to the house, and I will show you just how delighted."

Ian smiled at the soft flush that touched her cheeks. He was amazed at the change she had wrought in him.

From the first she had appealed deeply and sharply to his senses. And then she had wedged her way into his soul with her haunting passion and mystery.

He was in love again. Sometimes it was painful, because he felt that he betrayed Diana. But there was something more, for Marissa had taken him from his misery, and now, though he had not ceased to love the memories of his first wife, he had discovered that he had something to offer the new.

She had made his life full again.

And now, as he watched her, he felt the familiar hunger gnawing at his loins. She was part witch, he decided, part vixen to best the harlots of the Barbary Coast, part angel to spread her heavenly hair across the sheets and still blushed a virgin's rouge when she read his mind. He could not remember ever being so sated and content, then so aroused and thirsting from the sound of a whisper or a brush of her cheek.

"Come on—home!" he said, and nudged the bay, and suddenly they were both racing pell-mell for the house. He called to John to take the horses as they neared the carriage house, then he swore suddenly. "I gave them the evening off!" he said. "Ah, well!" He leaped down and helped Marissa from her sidesaddle. She followed him as he led the horses to their stalls. The light in the carriage house was muted as he closed the stalls. The scent of the new hay was sweet.

She had swept off her elegant little bright green riding hat with its dashing feather, and her hair was neither pinned nor tied, but streaming free and wind-tossed down her back in a cascade of gold and flame. In the dim light, her eyes were a beautiful emerald fire. She was very proper in her green riding habit, yet the excitement in her eyes and the curve of her smile were anything but innocent.

She stood several feet from him, watching him, waiting for him. He leaned against the stall door, and allowed his gaze a leisurely stroll down the length of her.

"Ever made love in the hay?" he asked her.

"No," she told him, warily backing away.

"We can correct that."

"No, no, I'm not starting now. You can wind up with hay in your hair and hay in your clothing and—"

She broke off. He had caught up with her and crushed her into his arms. His mouth closed on hers and he tasted the sweetness of it. He buried his face against the streaming silk cascade of her hair, and the lilac scent of her shampoo evocatively pervaded his system.

He lifted her into his arms and carried her into the carriage house, to the rear left corner, where fencing hid the loosened hay. He set her down and swept off his riding cape, laying it over the hay. Throwing himself down on it, he looked at her, certain that he was going to have to do a bit more coaxing.

He was not.

The simple light bathed her. She had cast aside the green jacket and skirt already. She wore only stockings and a silk chemise and pants, fabrics that molded to her body.

Her eyes met his, and she stepped toward him, smiling beautifully. He rose to his knees and circled his arms around her waist. Again, her sweet scent assailed him. He laid his face against her belly, holding her close. Then he kissed her stomach, teasing the soft silk over her body. He drew her down and closed his mouth over her breast, teasing the hardened pink crest beneath the silk, running his tongue over it again and again. She moaned at his touch. He felt the quiver of her heart, the movement within her, felt her surge to his touch. Her lashes had fallen over her eyes. He kissed them, then laid her down, his hands finding the hem of the chemise to pull it over her head. Her breasts, pale and glimmering as perfectly chiseled marble, came free in the night. He touched and caressed her, and found the ribbons of her pants. He pushed them down slowly, and as he bared her flesh to his eyes he bathed it with leisurely kiss after leisurely kiss. Beneath him, she moved more erotically with every teasing flick of his tongue. Mesmerized he watched her. Watched her head toss lightly in the hay, her hair like tangled fire. Watched the rhythm of her hips, her growing impatience, her growing desire.

Then he stripped away his pants, and settled between the sleek temptation of her thighs. He paused to gaze at the beauty of her face. "Marissa, open your eyes," he commanded her. And when she did so, he teased no more but boldly kissed and caressed the heart of her womanhood. With each cry and surge against him, he felt the hammering of his desire rise hard and hungry. She begged him to come to her, to take her then. He did not. He loved her as she quivered and trembled and whispered until the whole length of her exquisite body tightened and shuddered, and seemed to explode like quicksilver. Until she cried out with ecstasy and anguish. And only then did he shed the rest of his clothing in the hay and come to her.

She had risen to her knees. Hungry for him. Eager to hold him, to press kisses against his shoulders. To nip at them lightly . . . run her tongue against him. To bring sweet ecstasy and anguish to him as he had brought to her. He groaned, casting back his head as she caressed and teased and tormented his body, her tongue like sweet laps of burning honey, her hands and fingers deft and demanding. She slid lower and lower against him until the longing was something he could bear no longer. He cried out, lifted her and laid her flat upon her back. He parted her thighs and sank deep, deep within her.

She wrapped him in her arms and thighs. The glory of her hair entangled them both in a golden cloud. She gave everything, and he marveled at her beauty even as the shattering passion rose to strip away thought. He felt her movement, felt her rise against him, meet him, dance with him, accept and caress him. He whispered words of longing to her, and told her graphically how she made him feel. He rose to a volatile, shuddering climax, pulled away from her, then sank deep, deep within her once again, and there he held.

And as the night cooled them, he thought that he loved her indeed, and the words were on his lips, but he could not say them. Not yet. For now, it had to be enough to hold her, to love her in the silence of the night.

But then he fell to her side, and he heard the soft sigh of her whisper. "Ian?"

"Yes?"

"I . . ."

"What?"

"I . . ."

What was she going to say? He rolled over her, supporting his weight upon his hands. "What is it, Marissa?" he persisted.

Her lashes shielded her eyes. "I like making love in the hay," she said at last.

He smiled, but he felt the disappointment in his heart. Had she been about to whisper softly of love?

No, it would have been deeper than that. She would have told him why that haunting misery so often came to her eyes when she did not know he was watching.

He lay down, holding her. He couldn't press her. It would do no good. When she was ready, she would tell him.

And she would whisper that she loved him.

The next afternoon Marissa sat upon a blanket on the grass next to a lovely little pond in Golden Gate Park. There were people everywhere, Ian among them. Mary and Jimmy sat beside her, Mary busily throwing dry bread to the ducks in the pond and Jimmy watching Mary while he chewed on a blade of grass, a look of absolute adoration on his face.

They'd met a number of people, among them the mayor, Eugene Schmitz, the man she had heard so much about already. He had been charming, absolutely charming. But his smile did come a little too easily, she thought.

And then Grace Leroux had discovered their little haven on the blanket, and she had most pleasantly managed to take Ian away.

Marissa hadn't minded watching the ducks for a minute or two, for it was a beautiful park and a wonderful day, but when Ian didn't return, she grew restless. "Oh, she is so much trouble!" she whispered in a sudden fury to Mary.

"Shh!" Mary told her. Marissa had never said much about the change in her relationship with Ian. There had been no need for her to do so. Mary had watched the changes in her. "You mustn't let anyone know that she bothers you in the least."

"Why not? I'd like to rip her dyed hair out!"

Jimmy laughed and brought his opinion into the conversation. "You must not let anyone know that she bothers you, Marissa, because she wants to bother you, don't you see that?"

"But she is so pointedly after Ian!"

"She can't have Ian unless Ian agrees, and that's a fact, Marissa."

That was true enough, Marissa decided. "It seems like there are just so darned many of them!" she murmured, thinking that he had left her once to see a show with Lilli. She had learned a little about the woman from Lee, and she had also learned that Lee liked Lilli a lot more than she liked Grace Leroux. "Why are men always so fooled?" she said to Mary.

Mary, looking over her shoulder, suddenly turned a dark shade of red. Marissa swung around to see that Ian had returned at last. "I don't think that they're so easily fooled," he said, smiling as he settled down beside her. "It just depends on what they want at the moment."

Marissa arched a brow at him. "I wonder what you were wanting when you met our dear Mrs. Leroux." Her voice had a purr in it. Even Jimmy laughed.

"She has a way about her," Ian said.

"Um. As does a black widow," Marissa agreed pleasantly.

"I can see this is heading us nowhere good," Ian said with a laugh. He rubbed Marissa's shoulders and pointed through the crowd. "See there, my love. That's Phineas Van Kellen."

"It is?" Marissa asked. "Who is Phineas Van Kellen?"

"A very smart man. I've just agreed to build a place for him downtown. And he's just agreed to do it my way."

"Oh, I'm so very glad, Ian!" Marissa declared happily.

He flashed her a smile, and for a moment she thought they shared the world.

If only she could tell him the truth about herself! She had almost done so that night in the carriage house. But it wasn't just her own life she held together with a lie—she had Mary and Jimmy to consider, too. And if Ian did despise her for the lie, no matter what their lives had become together, then the others might be hurt.

"See, Marissa?" Ian was saying. She had missed something, and she didn't know what. "Here—"

He had rolled over on the blanket, and Jimmy and Mary were doing likewise, she in her fresh white cotton dress and stockings, he in his light beige suit and handsome new Italian shoes. Bemused, Marissa joined them and laughed as Ian showed them the proper way to construct buildings with blades of grass. "Now see, when the earth shakes, you need a building with some sway. You must have pilings, and you must have steel, but you must also be careful to have that sway!"

He was so passionate about his creations. Marissa loved that in him. She smiled.

"Does the earth really shake so badly?" Mary asked Ian, sitting up.

He looked at her, but never replied, because Grace Leroux was standing over their blankets. "Ian, and dear, dear—oh, I am sorry! It's dear little Myrtle, isn't it?"

Ian had risen and helped Marissa up. "My wife's name is Marissa, Grace. And Mr. and Mrs. O'Brien, you must remember them."

"Oh, yes! Of course." Grace knew their names, Marissa was sure of it. But she could be so very rude with such an innocent demeanor!

Marissa forced herself to smile as Grace sweetly told Ian about certain men he needed to see. Then someone else called Ian, and he excused himself and stepped away from them. He turned back to point out the way to the tea garden.

Mary and Jimmy started toward the garden, and Marissa was momentarily left alone with Grace.

"You think that you've won, don't you?" Grace said. Her smile was gone and her eyes were hard and there wasn't a thing pleasant or innocent about her. "Well, mark my words, little girl, you haven't even begun to play."

There was such venom behind her words that Marissa felt a tinge of unease, but she managed to smile. "Grace, should you forget my given name again, please feel free to call me Mrs. Tremayne."

And then she stepped past the startled woman and hurried after Mary and Jimmy, her smile growing all the while.

Grace was wrong, she thought. She had won. And she won because Ian had allowed her to do so.

But later that night she wondered if she had been right after all. She had won for the moment.

But if she was caught, living out her lie?

That lie and the way she had to live because of it were the only things marring what was quickly becoming an otherwise perfect life.

And Ian had to wonder what she was doing with the allowance when he signed the papers for her each week. She lived in his house and, other than her excursions with Mary, it would seem she really had little to do with the money. He knew that she was still helping Mary and Jimmy, but he had no idea of just how much money she was sending home, and he certainly knew nothing about the long letters she wrote to Uncle Theo.

Ian did know, however, that she was making a contribution to the Orphan's Fund, although he didn't know that she had discussed it with Mary first. There was one little rascal, Darrin MacIver, of whom she had grown very fond during the Sunday meals at the emporium.

He was ten years old with the street wisdom of a hardened adult, huge brown eyes and long lashes, and a gaunt, haunted face that might one day be very handsome. Father Gurney had told her that his mother had been "a poor fallen angel" in the Barbary Coast area, and the poor wee lass had died there, leaving Darrin on his own. The child knew every vice game in town, played poker and could swear like a sailor. He had sassed Marissa one day, and all the training of the lady who had become Mrs. Tremayne had fallen from her shoulders and she'd given him a brisk talking to in turn. He'd grown quiet, but on his way out that morning—sweet rolls stuck into his pockets—he had paused to tell her that she was "an all right fellow."

She had spent some money buying Darrin a new suit of clothing, a corduroy cap, flannel breeches, two cotton shirts, long socks, vests and shoes. His delight at the presents had brightened his eyes like lamps, but then the shine had faded and he had pushed the boxes toward her.

"Don't need no clothes, Miz Tremayne."

"But you do need clothes, Darrin. You've holes in your britches, young man!"

"I can make it on what the old man gives me."

"Father Gurney, you mean."

"Yeah. The old man."

"Father Gurney."

"Weren't never a Catholic," he said stubbornly.

"Well, we English are not customarily Catholics, either, Darrin, but I respect such a man sincerely, and therefore he is Father Gurney!"

"Father Gurney," Darrin agreed at last. "But I'm not a charity case!"

If ever there was a charity case, it was Darrin, Marissa thought. But no matter how sweet life had become, she would never forget the taste and smell and feel of coal dust, and she understood him in a way that he must never know.

"Darrin, I need letters mailed every so often. And I'd like them kept quiet. The clothes don't need to be charity; you can mail the letters for me in return. You can start this Tuesday—meet me around the corner from the entrance to the emporium at about ten o'clock."

He still didn't trust her, but at last he agreed. Just in time, it seemed, for Ian was coming toward them, interested in the boy who had seemed to capture so much of his wife's attention.

"You like the lad, eh?" he asked her.

"Yes, I do, very much." She smiled at Ian. "Don't you like him?"

"Yes, I most certainly do. He reminds me of you. It's in the eyes."

He was teasing her. "Ian, Darrin has very handsome brown eyes. Mine are green."

"Yes, that's true. But upon occasion, it seems that you both have a very haunting shade of gray within them." He walked by her without further comment, and she watched him.

He was not going to persist, she realized. He had just reminded her that he had not forgotten that he had many questions he might still want to ask her.

That night she was nervous through dinner, and uneasy when he came to her room.

But he didn't ask her any questions about her past. She stood looking out the windows in the turret of her room, her silk nightgown touched by the moonlight. He came to her there, and swept her into his arms, then carried her to bed.

And again, the night passed in magic.

She and Mary met Darrin by the emporium the next Tuesday, as she had planned.

The scamp was there, waiting for her in his new outfit. She greeted him, then handed him a letter for Uncle Theo.

He stared at the letter. "You could mail this yourself, you know. Quite easily."

"Maybe. But I'd like you to."

He shrugged. "Sure." Then Marissa realized that he was looking over her shoulder, and that a hostile expression had come to his face. "It's the wicked witch, it is!"

She turned to see that Grace Leroux had just come around the corner. The woman stopped, surprised to see them.

"Darrin!" Mary said, startled by his comment.

"She's someone to keep a firm eye on!" Darrin warned Marissa.

"I can't stop her from shopping in the emporium," Marissa told him. She realized that Grace was watching her intently, with a curious and cunning expression. Then she smiled suddenly.

Darrin was right—it was a wicked smile.

But it was a smile. Grace liked to play social games. Fine. Marissa waved. Grace hurried on.

"She is a wicked witch!" Darrin insisted.

"Darrin, she's so involved with the Orphan's Fund—" Mary began.

"She's involved to impress people, and that's all!" Darrin insisted. "Well, I'll be on with my business then, ladies. Good day to you."

Darrin walked on, and Marissa suggested lunch.

They dined at Delmonico's, and Marissa ordered champagne. Sipping it, Mary looked around the restaurant at their fellow diners, the women in their beautiful gowns, the men in their frock coats and morning suits. She smiled and leaned closer to Marissa.

"Can you believe this, that we've come to be here? And everything is so wonderful."

"Yes, things are wonderful."

"I have never seen you happier," Mary told her. "But then, I've never seen you in love."

Marissa flushed and Mary laughed. "All right, so I have never been happier!" she agreed with Mary. Yet even as she spoke the words, she felt a chill settle into her spine. "And sometimes I'm frightened," she murmured.

Mary set down her glass. "You've got to tell him the truth."

"I can't tell him the truth! I don't dare."

"You must."

Marissa shook her head. "There have been times when I wanted to tell him. Times when the words have been right on the tip of my tongue. But then I remember that I cannot. Mary, I must think about all our lives! About you and Jimmy and Uncle Theo! Oh, Mary, what if he would not tolerate the truth?"

"He loves you!"

"He has never said that he loves me."

"But he does love you! Oh, Marissa! It's in his voice when he talks to you, it's in his eyes when he looks at you. And dear Lord, Marissa! He has proven himself to be such an extraordinary man! Strong and ethical, and so very handsome and sure of himself!"

Marissa smiled. Oh, he was sure of himself! And they could still argue themselves silly, for she was jealous and he wouldn't lie. . . .

And there was still the fear that he might find her out.

"Shall we order?" Marissa suggested, giving her attention to the menu.

"Mmm. But what if he catches you? Wouldn't it be better to tell him yourself?"

"Yes, and if I can just find the right moment somewhere along the line, then I shall do so." She looked at Mary, and saw that her friend still seemed to have a keen sense of excitement. "What is it?" she demanded.

"Oh, Marissa! Jimmy and I are going to have a baby."

"A baby!" Marissa cried with delight. Mary had so much love to give. She and Jimmy were wonderful together. They would love a child and give it so much!

"Oh, Mary!" she cried, grabbing her friend's hand. Then she gasped. "Oh, Mary, what has the doctor said? Are you well enough to have a baby?" She couldn't forget how sick Mary had been in England.

"Yes, I'm quite well enough, and—I'm having a baby one way or the other, Marissa! Oh, Marissa, be happy for us!"

"I am happy for you, so very happy!" Marissa promised her. She squeezed her friend's hand again, then lifted her glass and offered a toast.

But when she lowered her head to the menu again, she realized almost bleakly that she couldn't tell Ian the truth now. More than ever before, she had to protect the secret they all shared. Mary was going to have a baby.

Mary had said that she felt well, but the next Tuesday when Marissa called upon her to come downtown, Mary was still in her nightdress, not feeling at all well.

"It's morning sickness, and nothing more! You and Jimmy must stop worrying!" Mary told her.

Marissa was worried, but she had to go downtown anyway. Darrin would be waiting for her.

Lee was upset that she wanted to go alone. "John can drive you downtown. You should not go alone."

Marissa was surprised. "Lee! I know the area very well now. I'm going to ride down by myself, and I'll be just fine!" The last thing she needed was to have John Kwan with her, wondering what she was doing!

Lee was still unhappy, but Marissa smiled and ignored her. She was touched that Lee seemed to care, and pleased with the affection that had risen between them now that Lee knew that Marissa loved her husband—and Marissa knew that Lee did not!

She rode the small black mare, Jet, that she had taken over for her own. She left Jet in the livery stable by the emporium and visited the store. Ian was not in, she learned. He was due soon, but he was visiting a building site. She stopped by to see Jimmy, and was pleased to see how happy he was among his coworkers and how well he was doing as a buyer and manager. She left him to hurry down and have morning tea with Sandy, and was thrilled when Sandy told her that plans were afoot to open the cafeteria on several early mornings during the week for the orphans.

It was nearly ten o'clock when she kissed Sandy's cheek and hurried out to the corner. She glanced nervously up and down the street, hoping that Ian would not come upon her. Then she saw Darrin hurrying toward her along the walk. She smiled and waved. A minute later, he was with her.

"You're all alone, Mrs. Tremayne."

"Yes, Mrs. O'Brien is not feeling very well."

He frowned, and Marissa was both annoyed and amused. "Darrin, I'm quite able to take care of myself, you know."

"Sure, I know." He shrugged. "I put your letter in the post within half an hour last time," he told her proudly.

"Then here's the next."

He took the letter from her. "You've still got kin in England, huh?"

"I—I've people back home, yes."

"That must be nice," he said. Then he quickly corrected himself. "No, I guess not. Kin lie to you and betray you—and leave you. It's better just to be on your own, that it is. If there's anyone you can believe in, it's yourself, and that's that, I do say!"

He took the letter from her. "Good day to you, Mrs. Tremayne." He walked on and then stopped and turned back. "Take care of yourself, Mrs. Tremayne. We're not far from the Barbary Coast."

She nodded and waved, her heart breaking. She wanted to talk to Ian about the boy. He was such a prickly little lad. Maybe they could find something for him to do up at the house. They could feed him well and give him a good home without offending his pride.

She started walking idly, unaware that she had turned from the main street into the quiet alleyway behind the shops. She was so preoccupied with thoughts about Darrin that she didn't pay much heed to the sound of footsteps behind her.

Then she sensed that she was being flanked. She glanced quickly to the left and right. On one side was a tall man with a dark mustache and a bowler hat worn low over his forehead. On the other was a clean-shaven blond man with a smile that made her skin crawl.

Too late, she realized that she was in danger. She opened her mouth to scream, but before a sound escaped from her, the mustachioed man caught her around the waist and shoved a soaking handkerchief over her face. She breathed in a sickly sweet smell, and the world began to spin.

She fought desperately for reason, fighting the drug that assailed her senses. She had always fought so very hard! And now she could not kick or claw or scratch. She was powerless, and her body was very, very heavy. She could not even scream.

The street careened before her as she started to lose her grip upon consciousness. She could not even feel the arms of the men who held her.

She had fought so long and so hard, and now that happiness was hers . . .

She could fight no more.

Her last conscious thought was that there had been no one to see her. She would leave behind no sign of a struggle. No sign at all. She had wandered off alone.

Then she could think no more. All the world was black.

But she was not as alone as she had thought.

Darrin MacIver, suspicious street-smart child that he was, had not walked away.

He hadn't thanked her for the clothes, he told himself. Then he muttered out loud that he didn't need to thank her for the clothes, he was working for her now, wasn't he?

But there was something about her that he liked. She was young, and she didn't seem so awfully much older than he and some of the boys. Yet she seemed to be a real lady, not like that Mrs. Leroux. When Marissa Tremayne talked to him, he felt that she really wanted an answer. He felt she cared.

And she had changed *him*, too. Tremayne, the man with the money. Not that he had ever been mean or anything to any of the boys. It had just seemed as if it hurt him to look at them now and again. He'd lost a baby when he lost his wife, Darrin had heard. Funny, life was. A nice rich man with good intent like Mr. Tremayne, and his wife and kid up and die. And down in the brothel, the prostitutes had kids like him in the squalor every damned day.

He felt a sudden guilt at his language. Neither the good priests nor the brothers had ever made him feel guilty. "I'll bet she knows a few swear words herself!" he thought, kicking a rock in his path. Oh, she probably knew a few, all right. Just like she seemed to know him, what was in his mind and what was in his heart. And she was so pretty, so beautiful, with all that golden red hair of hers, and those huge green eyes. He liked her. He liked her a lot. She had changed his life.

He turned, suddenly determined to say something. Thank you, maybe. Something.

He started to follow her.

He was just in time to see the two men sweep up Mrs. Tremayne in her elegant green riding habit and shove her into the rear of small black carriage.

He stood dead still in the street, his mouth open. Then he shouted, "Hey! Hey, you let her go! Hey!"

The carriage moved into the street. He started to run, then he realized that he would never catch it. He stopped again and looked around blankly.

He saw the large sign. Tremayne's. He started to run again. Mr. Tremayne had to be in. He just had to be in by then.

He started running to the store. He hesitated only once.

And that was when he saw her, the wicked witch, Leroux. He didn't know why he paused. He just wanted to know what she was doing where she was, on the sidewalk, coming around the corner. Pulling a glove up her wrist, and smiling. Oh, smiling. With such great pleasure.

Darrin couldn't worry about her. Not at the moment. He shoved past her. "Mr. Tremayne!"

He was shouting the man's name long before he burst through the doorway.

CHAPTER FOURTEEN

Ian had just settled into the swivel chair behind his desk. He was congratulating himself about Jimmy O'Brien—the Irish lad had proven himself to be an invaluable asset already. In time, he could take over a great deal of the management. And the more management Ian could hand to others, the more time he had left for architecture and building.

And Marissa, and a personal life that had suddenly become very important.

"Hey, there, young sir! You can't just go barging in on Mr. Tremayne! What's the matter with you, lad?"

Ian frowned. His secretary, Arthur Mount, had shouted the words. Through the frosted glass of his office window he could see the silhouette of Mount holding a squirming youngster by the collar.

"I've got to see him! Let me go! It's an emergency! You let me go or I'll—"

Mount groaned with pain. The youngster fell to the floor, then came crashing through Ian's door. It was the orphan boy, Darrin.

He rammed his cap down hard over his forehead. Ian stood, coming around his desk just as Arthur Mount limped in, following the boy.

"I tried to stop the little hoodlum, Mr. Tremayne, I did! Give me just a minute and I'll box his ears and—"

"No, no, that's all right, Arthur," Ian said, somewhat amused by the belligerent boy and the indignant, limping secretary. "There must be some serious problem for Darrin to be so anxious. What is it, lad? Can we help you?"

"They've got her!" the boy burst out. And suddenly the toughened street kid was stuttering. "They—they've taken her. Mrs.—Mrs. Tremayne. Two men. Outside on the street corner. I met her like I was supposed to, and I turned away. And they had her. Two men. They rode off in a carriage."

Ian stared at the boy blankly for a moment, unable to assimilate and unwilling to comprehend his words. "What?" The single word exploded from him like a rocket; he gripped Damn's shoulders in a vise, staring at him hard. "What?"

"Two men." Darrin was thinking fast, desperately. He still trembled inwardly, but he gritted his teeth. "One tall with a handlebar mustache. Dark. Pin-striped suit, red vest. The other was blond, not as old as the other guy, maybe about twenty-two. No hat. No whiskers. They took her in a small black one-horse carriage pulled by a small bay, and rode down from the corner eastward—"

"Barbary Coast," Arthur supplied.

"Chinatown, I think," Darrin said, his wide eyes solemnly on Ian.

Ian dropped the boy's shoulders and headed for the door. "Call the police, Arthur. Get someone here quick. I mean quick!"

He went out onto the street, ran the length of the store and tore around the corner. There was no sign of anyone there. No sign of a scuffle, nothing. Frantically he stared down the alleyway, feeling as if cold fingers had clamped down hard around his heart. The boy had made the whole thing up, he tried to tell himself. But he hadn't. Darrin was beneath her spell, Ian had seen that easily enough. The lad adored her.

He swung around. Darrin was there now, he had followed behind him, close, hopeful.

"From here?" Ian demanded. "They took her from here?"

Darrin nodded.

"All right," Ian said. "Get my horse from the livery stable. Then wait at the store and tell the police everything that you told me. Everything. Any little detail might be important."

Darrin fled to do as he had been told. Ian stepped out into the street. There were tracks everywhere, but he could just barely discern where a small carriage had been pulled in close to the buildings in the alleyway. Chinatown. He knew where they were heading. Into the brothels and opium dens, where beautiful women definitely had a price.

Darrin was already coming down the street with his horse. He stared at the boy and he knew they both realized something.

Marissa had to be found quickly, or she would never be found at all. That was the way when a woman was shanghaied.

"Meet the police," he told the boy. "And find Mr. O'Brien in the store. Tell him to get hold of John and Lee Kwan. Perhaps they can discover something. I'll be in Chinatown." He leaped quickly upon his horse. With a nod, he raced down the alleyway, heedless of traffic.

The news of Marissa's kidnapping spread like wildfire. She was the wife of one of San Francisco's most prominent, affluent and respected men. Also, one of its most popular and charming, for in his days as a widower he had both shocked and excited the mamas of the society belles who would have gladly become his wife by his escapades in the dance halls of the Barbary Coast. Wickedly handsome in evening attire, he was apt to leave an opera for a late show and more decadent companionship. He was loved for his passion for certain ethics—and his total ignorance of others.

In her mansion on Nob Hill, Grace Leroux heard the news from a neighbor with shocked distress.

Then she turned into her doorway and smiled.

Down near the waterfront, in the Barbary Coast, Lilli Reynolds heard the news, and her heart went out to Ian. Few people knew how deeply he had already been hurt.

She called a special employee to her room.

He was a man with a long scar down the left side of his face. He had small eyes, a cavernous face, and was surely as ugly as sin.

But no one knew the dens of the Barbary Coast as well as he. His name was Jake Breed. He'd been in the Barbary Coast as long as anyone could remember. He didn't work for Lilli because he needed money, but because she was the only person he had ever loved.

From her settee Lilli lit a long cigarette and indicated the outside world. "Mrs. Tremayne has been taken. The police seem to imagine that she's in Chinatown somewhere. She was taken by two men." Lilli gave him the description Darrin had so meticulously given to Ian and then the police. "Find out what you can." Lilli hesitated only a moment. "I have a feeling that this was no accidental job."

"I won't come back without something," Jake told her.

Lilli offered him one of her warm smiles. "I know that."

Marissa awoke very slowly, the drug seeming to take a long, long time to fade. She was aware first of a sweet scent in the air. Then she came to realize that she was lying upon silk. She could feel the elegance, and the softness, and for long moments, the feel of that silk was deceptively comforting.

It was difficult to open her eyes. When she finally managed to do so, she was stunned to realize that she was looking up a very long way at a very fat man.

His hair was straight and black, and he had a long, straight black beard, and a mustache that fell over the beard with the same astounding length. He wore a Chinese coat and dark trousers, and he studied her, rubbing his bearded chin so that the long strands of hair shook.

"Green eyes," he murmured. Then he turned to someone behind him. "Yes, she is worth much. But you are overanxious—and greedy.

We will discuss the price. I will send for tea and a pipe, and we will finish our business."

The price. They were talking about her. She wanted to leap up and rip out that black beard by the handful. She still couldn't move. She could barely keep her eyes open.

She decided to close them and try to fight off the sick dizziness that remained. She heard whispers.

"The price doesn't matter! We've already been paid!"

"Right, damned right, so whatever we make now is pure profit, and I want some of it!" came the response. The first voice had been deeper. Marissa was certain that it belonged to the dark-haired man who had seized her. The second voice had been higher, more youthful. The blonde.

And then the large Chinese man returned. She heard him ordering someone around, and heard the sound of liquid being poured into cups. She smelled something, a cloying, sweet scent, and she wondered if it was opium.

The Chinese man gave her two abductors an offer for her. Apparently, it was shockingly low. "You must be insane! Not only has she green eyes, but she has golden hair! She's young and beautiful. She has superb lines, wonderful breasts—" the blond man began.

"And the word is on the streets as to who she is. The police are seeking her already."

"Ah," interrupted the darker of her abductors. "But you have the resources to get her on a ship within the next hour. And once she is gone . . ."

The Chinese man haggled. Marissa slitted her eyes, desperate to survey her surroundings.

She was in the corner of a large room. There were only two windows, and those were beyond the men who were haggling at a low round table. Straight across the room from her sat a woman, her head low, her back bowed in absolute submission. She was beautiful, a little China doll. She was there to serve the tea, to light the opium pipe, Marissa thought.

She would not be difficult to elude. . . .

But the men were there. If she tried to rise, to escape, they would be down on her in seconds. Carefully, unobtrusively, she tried to gain strength, flexing her fingers, then her toes. The feeling was coming back to her. She stiffened an arm, then a leg, then relaxed them. She started to inch over to the window. They weren't paying the least bit of attention to her. If she were not too high up, perhaps she could jump out. And if she were high up . . .

At least she could scream. She had to do something!

They had come to some kind of an agreement. The men were rising. "They will take her to the ship right now. You will wait for your payment below until she is safely on the ship," the heavy Chinese man said.

Now . . . right now. They were coming for her now. They might drug her again, and she would be helpless, unable to protest.

Marissa could afford no more finesse. She leaped to her feet and raced for the window.

The blond man shouted and jumped. He was almost upon her. She turned and kicked him with all her strength. He bellowed in pain and fell to the floor. Marissa reached the window. She tore open the drapes.

She was high, very high. On the third floor. If she jumped, she would kill herself.

But the streets were crowded. The citizens of Chinatown pulled their little wagons through the street, or walked quickly, some with their papers, some with carts of vegetables and meats.

Some were criminals.

And some were good people.

A hand touched Marissa's shoulder.

She leaned out the window and screamed. "Help! Help me! Oh, dear God, somebody help me!"

She was wrenched into the room with such force that she fell, stunned, upon her back.

"Perhaps we should renegotiate, gentlemen," the heavy-set Chinese man said. "You neglected to inform me that she is an incredible amount of trouble!"

Ian had toured the streets, one by one, stopping to ask questions, growing ever more determined and desperate. Passing by a market, then a
known opium den, Ian saw a man called One-Eyed Charlie who was a
notorious—and extremely slippery—criminal. Charlie dealt in hash-
ish, the best, and in female flesh, the most pathetic. He'd been taken
downtown to jail a score of times—he had always managed to avoid
conviction. Evidence disappeared, just as women disappeared.

Seeing Charlie, Ian didn't hesitate. He shouted the man's name.
Charlie cast his one good eye in Ian's direction, then started through
the narrow alleyways, plunging through the crowds. Ian shouted
again, leaping from the horse, and racing after Charlie.

He caught up with him in the middle of a narrow alley where
clothing and animal carcasses hung in profusion. He catapulted
onto the man's back, then dragged him to his feet, nearly strangling
him as he shook him by the collar. "Where is she, where the hell is
she, Charlie? If she's gone, you aren't going to get off this time! I'll
break your neck here and now if I don't get something!"

Charlie burst into a spate of Chinese. Ian shook him, and Charlie switched to English as he began to turn blue. "I don't know, I
don't know what you're talking about—"

"My wife, Charlie! The whole damned city knows, and you're
going to tell me that you don't?"

"I don't have her, I swear, but I'll find her! Put me down, I'll find
her. She could be in a few places. I'll find her—"

"Ian!"

He heard his name shouted as he held Charlie by the throat. He
looked at the street and saw Lee Kwan coming toward him quickly.
"Ian, we've got something. Drop Charlie. We've got something!"

Ian looked at Charlie then dropped him. Charlie sprawled on
the ground, then picked himself up and dusted his loose trousers,
staring at Ian suspiciously.

Then he bolted and ran like a rabbit.

"Lee, what?" Ian demanded anxiously.

"Lilli called. She said she sent feelers out, and she was able to get
an address. She said to warn you that it could be dangerous."

"The address, Lee, give me the address."

"I've called the police—"

"And they might be too late! Give me the damned address!"

She had scratched, she had clawed, she might have cost a few of the heavy Chinese man's helpers a new dynasty of children, but in the end it had done her little good.

Marissa was carefully trussed and wound into a carpet. She could scarcely breathe, and she was afraid that she would lose consciousness when she most desperately needed her senses.

She was thrown over the shoulder of a man who bore the imprint of her nails from his brow to his chin. She could see nothing. Her arms were caught to her sides by the carpet, and she thought she would die if she couldn't breathe soon. But she could hear clearly.

Her assailants were gone, and she had been left to the mercy of the Chinese flesh merchant. She could understand nothing of the language, but she knew that she was being sent to a ship. She was leaving the house in Chinatown, and the man she had so ignominiously wounded was making no effort to be gentle as he carried her downstairs. Her face, wound in the heavy carpet, thudded hard against his back again and again. She could not brace herself for she could not move her arms.

She heard the shouts as they reached a rear alley. She was pretty sure the man who carried her was flanked by three others, wiry, strong young men who carried sharp knives and knew how to use them. She had fought them all until she had felt the blade of one of those knives at her throat. And the heavy Chinese man had warned her then that her value would not decrease too dearly should she bear a scar or two here or there in discreet places.

It was impossible to contemplate what was going to happen to her. She'd been warned but she hadn't wandered into any dangerous neighborhood. She'd been taken anyway. And now God alone knew where she would end up, she thought bleakly.

Did it matter? She would lose everything of importance to her. This life, Uncle Theo, Mary, Jimmy . . .

Ian. Love.

All her life she had been searching. Even when she hadn't known it. And she had finally found everything. God had given her not just a way to survive. He'd given her far more than gowns and beautiful things. He'd given her Ian. He'd given her love.

Perhaps this was justice. Perhaps she'd been given too much. Perhaps, like Icarus, she had wanted to fly, and so God had seen to it that her wings were melted and that she came crashing to the ground.

No! Tears stung her eyes. She could not accept defeat so easily!

She began to slam her body back and forth. Someone had to notice the movement! The carpet began to loosen around her.

"Stop!" Hands clamped down upon her brutally. She ignored them, squirming like a worm. It would do her no good, she thought desperately.

Then she heard the voice.

"You! You there! Stop this instant."

It was Ian. She could have sworn it. Her heart began to hammer, and she writhed with greater determination to make the package of carpet and herself move more visibly.

The man carrying her did stop. Marissa felt him whirl around, and then she was dropped carelessly to the ground. There was a challenge spoken, and then she heard a thunder of footsteps.

Frantically, she rolled out of her carpet and staggered to her feet.

They were in the alleyway, Ian, the man who had held her and the others. The others, with their horrible, wicked knives.

The man who had carried her roared like a lion. Then he bore down on Ian like a steam engine. Marissa screamed, but Ian paid no heed. He was assessing his enemy. He stepped aside just before the man could butt him, then slammed his joined fists down upon his attacker's back. The man crumbled at his feet.

But the others were encircling him now. The eternal fog was settling upon the city, and the streetlights were winking on. The knives were caught in that glow, twinkling as their owners twisted and turned them in warning.

There was another cry and one of them broke from the group, leaping for Ian, his knife high and poised. Marissa screamed a warning again. Perhaps she was in time; perhaps he had already known. He caught the man's arm. They plummeted to the earth together and began to roll. The two other men ran after them. Marissa gathered up her tattered skirts and did the same. In the fog, she could see nothing but the entwined figures thrashing upon the ground.

And then one man was up.

Ian.

"Ian!" She shouted his name.

"Get out of here, Marissa! Get the hell out of here!" he shouted to her.

She couldn't go. The other two men were taking no chances. They were approaching him together. He backed away, a careful eye on the deadly knives. One rushed him. The second started to do the same.

"No!" Marissa shrieked. She ran forward, leaping upon the man's back. She grasped his face, blinding him. She heard a growl burst forth from him. His hand was upon her, groping, trying to dislodge her.

His knife went clattering down to the cobblestones. She felt herself wrenched free. In the night she saw his murderous dark eyes. And then it was as if she was flying as he hurtled her aside to deal with Ian.

Somewhere in the night, she heard a police whistle. She tried to rise, and she staggered against a wall. She heard a gasp, and the sound of steel ripping into flesh. She screamed, doubling over.

Ian!

Then there were footsteps everywhere. The police had arrived.

Suddenly arms wound around her, lifting her swiftly. She cried out, then her eyes widened. Ian, his face blackened with the grime from the street, blood streaming from a cut near his eye, looked at her. "My God!" she breathed, "I thought it was you!"

"No," he said softly. "Don't look back."

But she had already done so. One man lay in a hideous arch over his own knife. Police officers were hurrying around his body and the others.

"Mr. Tremayne!" One of them called after him. "Mr. Tremayne, we've questions—"

"And you can ask them tomorrow!" Ian answered. "I'm taking my wife home now."

She smiled and leaned against his chest. He carried her out to the street. Lee and John Kwan were in a carriage there. Lee helped her up, and Marissa leaned against her while Ian tethered his bay to the rear of the carriage. Then Ian held her again.

"How did you ever find me?" she asked.

"We moved quickly. Darrin saw them take you. Still, I would never have known where to look if it weren't for Lilli," he admitted.

Marissa nodded. "Then I must thank her," she murmured.

The rest of the ride home was made in silence. It didn't matter. Marissa felt so very comfortable. So loved. She was home with John and Lee.

And she was cherished by Ian. He had fought for her. Risked his life for her. Killed for her. She would never question his feelings or his past again.

Darrin and Lilli were waiting outside the house. Marissa descended from the coach and hugged the boy first. Then she looked at the woman.

"I just wanted to see that Ian brought you home safely," Lilli said. Her dress was subdued. She wore no makeup. She had carefully chosen her attire to come to the house, and now she was speaking very shyly.

Behind her, Ian didn't say a word.

"Lilli, I can never thank you enough. Please, come in," Marissa said.

"Oh, but I can't—" Lilli began. "It wouldn't be right—"

"You're always welcome," Marissa assured her. She glanced at Ian, who looked at her approvingly. "There is no way that it could not be right."

Both Lilli and Darrin were pressured into coming in. Marissa described the house, her assailants and the day, and Ian commented that in the morning, she would have to tell the police. Lee served cold meats and fresh bread and lemonade.

Ian insisted that Darrin take a room in the house for the night, and called the orphanage to say he would be with them. Lilli bid Ian good-night, but Marissa walked the woman to the door.

"Thank you," she whispered again.

Lilli touched her cheek. "No, thank you. I was never your enemy, my dear. I never could have competed. I won't come again. It wouldn't be right. But I am your friend. If you ever need me."

"Thank you again," Marissa told her. "And we will see one another again."

Marissa closed the door on her. Lee was waiting, and insisted on making her a hot toddy, and setting her into a warm tub. And when she was there, Ian, freshly bathed and in a smoking jacket, came for her.

For the very first time, he brought her through the doorway and made love to her in his bed. She lay beside him, sated, miraculously content, feeling so very cherished, and so very blessed.

His arms were strong around her. His lips brushed her forehead. She inhaled the rich scent of his soap and his warmth, and snuggled more closely against the crisp hair of his chest. She closed her eyes and savored the rugged feel of his hair-roughened legs entwined with hers. Thank you, God, thank you! she repeated in silence over and over again.

And she knew then that she had to tell him the truth.

"Ian?" She whispered his name.

But to her surprise, he was asleep beside her. Deeply, contentedly asleep. His face was strikingly young in repose. And very, very peaceful.

Marissa bit her lip. There would have to be another time. She could make him understand, she could tell him that she loved him too much to live a lie anymore.

And she had to believe that he would love her enough for it not to matter.

She smoothed his hair. She couldn't wake him. Her time would come.

Or so she serenely believed that night.

Fate was destined to betray her again.

CHAPTER FIFTEEN

Three days later Ian was at his office in the store, looking over the police reports. The Chinese flesh dealer, Lau Wang, had been closed down. One of his men had been killed in the fight; two others were in jail. But the men who had originally kidnapped Marissa were still at large, and once she had been with him in safety for the night, she had remembered the curious conversation that had gone on between the two men.

"They said something to the effect that they had already been paid, Ian. That whatever they made from Lau Wang would be pure profit."

Lilli hadn't been able to help her. Her man had only been able to discover that Marissa was being held at Lau Wang's. She had promised, though, to have her people keep their eyes open.

Ian had let it be known on the street that he'd pay well for information regarding the kidnapping. It might have been a mistake. He'd already entertained a number of drifters and seedy characters in his office. When Arthur told him he had another visitor, Ian sighed and assumed the man had come seeking some reward.

He leaned back in his chair as the newcomer entered the office. Surprise touched him briefly, for this man was decently, conservatively dressed in a bowler and a suit.

"Mr. Tremayne?" As soon as the man addressed him, he heard in the words the man's English accent, so similar to his wife's, and his curiosity was aroused.

"Yes, I'm Ian Tremayne. Have a seat, sir." He indicated the chair across from his desk. "How can I help you?"

The man cleared his throat. "My business was really with your wife, you see, but there's a very handsome Chinese woman at your home who is guarding the door like a lion."

Ian smiled. Lee did have the heart of a little lioness, and she was extremely loyal to Marissa. More loyal to Marissa than she was to him these days, he thought in wry reflection.

"We've had some trouble recently," Ian told his visitor. "Miss Kwan is understandably nervous."

"Yes, of course. I understand. But for the sake of your wife's uncle, it's imperative that I reach her."

"Her uncle!" Ian said with surprise.

"Theodore Ayers."

Ian shook his head. "I"m sorry, I've no idea what you're talking about."

The man seemed as confused as Ian. "Let me introduce myself. I'm Lawrence Whalen, curate of St. Giles's parish."

"And?"

The stranger shook his head. "I can't understand that Marissa has never said anything to you, she is so very devoted to Theo. And to her home. You must know that she is supplying funds to the parish."

"No, I didn't know," Ian said quietly. He wondered why he was experiencing such a bitter sense of unease. It seemed that a huge rush of water was spilling by him, a cacophony in his ears. "Please, explain."

"It's imperative that Marissa come for Theo, Mr. Tremayne. He joined with certain men in a strike against the mine owners, and he's being held by the law right now."

Ian still didn't understand who in hell the man was, but he asked, "If he's being held by the law—"

Lawrence Whalen, his face mirroring his unhappiness with the situation, leaned toward Ian. "There were men killed during the riots that followed the strike. The mine owners intend to prosecute Theo for murder unless Marissa will take custody of him." He was quiet for a minute, then he sighed. "And have her swear that she'll keep Theo out of England for the rest of his life."

Ian stared blankly at Whalen. "Are you quite sure you know what you're talking about? My wife has no living relatives." He knew that for certain. That was why the squire had been so determined Ian should marry his daughter.

It was Whalen's turn to look surprised. "Well, sir, Theo was Marissa Ayers's only living relative."

"Ayers? My wife's maiden name was Ahearn."

"Oh, no, sir! The squire's name was Ahearn."

He was losing his mind, Ian thought. "Right. Squire Ahearn's daughter, Marissa, is my wife—"

"No, no, sir. The squire's daughter's name is Mary. Katherine Mary Ahearn. I had quite a time tracing them both to you, Mr. Tremayne. Seems Marissa never told her uncle she had married, only that she had come to the states with Miss Ahearn. Indeed, this has been a headache that has cost us a great deal of time, but a man's life is at stake, a good man's life, and Marissa has certainly given her all to the parish, and therefore the vicar was especially concerned. I'm sorry; I seem to have given you quite a shock. If we had not cared so deeply—"

"No, no. It's quite all right," Ian interrupted him quietly. He held a pencil and it snapped in his hand. Lawrence Whalen jumped, startled. Ian gave him a bloodless smile. "If my—my wife's—uncle is in danger, then something must be done. Perhaps, Mr. Whalen, you will be good enough to accompany me to my home. The handsome lioness who greeted you at the door is also an exceptional cook."

"Well, I'd be quite delighted, sir," Mr. Whalen agreed.

Ian excused himself and went out to speak with Arthur, telling him he'd be gone for the rest of the day. He returned for Lawrence Whalen and rented the man a horse from the livery stable when he went for his bay.

Ian was amazed to discover that he could point out certain of the city's sights to the man. A glance at his own fingers upon the bay's reins showed him that his fingers were shaking. Inside and out he felt the staggering heat of his rage taking hold of him. It seemed incredible that he could still function normally.

Well, he had known she kept some secret in her heart. He had even suspected that she had lied. He'd never realized just how great her lie, that she had managed to make a complete fool of him. Nothing in his life seemed real anymore. He'd been a fool to trust her. A fool to let her into his heart in any way.

A fool to love her.

They reached the house. John Kwan, as always, seemed to have anticipated his arrival. He ran outside, ready to take the horses into the carriage house.

Ian preceded Lawrence Whalen up the steps to the foyer. Lee opened the door, looked suspiciously at Whalen, then at Ian. "It's all right, Lee. Mr. Whalen has come on important family business. Would you call Mrs. Tremayne down, please. Mr. Whalen, the parlor is to the left, if you would join me there. May I interest you in a brandy?"

Lawrence Whalen thanked him and accepted the brandy. Ian offered him a sweeping smile and said, "Can't join you in brandy, no, I think not. I'll have a whiskey. No, maybe I'll just have the bottle."

He was pouring a drink when she entered the room. She was in white, beautiful, eyelet white, a dress with a high collar and sleek lines, a straight skirt except for the very small bustle at her rear. Her hair was drawn up with just a few ringlets to curl by the side of her face. Her eyes, those fascinating emerald eyes with their curious blazes and flames, were on him. Wide, interested, innocent. So damned innocent, his wife.

But was she his wife? He wasn't even sure about that anymore. What the hell was legal and what wasn't?

It didn't matter. What mattered was that his hands were still shaking. It felt as if the whole of his body was on fire. The witch. Entering his life so completely. Listening to his dreams. Wedging her way into the hearts of the orphans. Captivating his employees. Stealing his heart, making him think he could live again.

He'd been better off with whores.

He smiled icily. "Hello, dear."

"Ian, what—"

And then she saw Lawrence Whalen, and it was apparent that she must have realized that the gleam in Ian's gaze was absolute fury. She fell silent for a moment, then she quietly greeted Whalen.

"Mr. Whalen. What—what has brought you all the long way to America?"

"It's your uncle, Marissa. I've explained to your husband."

"Oh, my God!" The color drained from her face. If anything could be said to her credit, she loved this uncle. That much was true. "Mr. Whalen, is he all right? Has something happened? Oh, dear Lord—"

"Now, now, don't distress yourself, Miss Ayers. I'm sorry, Mrs. Tremayne. Marissa." Lawrence Whalen was on his feet, patting her hand. She was going to fall, so it appeared.

But then she was such a wonderful actress.

Ian used a foot to drag a chair up behind her. "Sit, my love. Do take a chair. Mr. Whalen will explain." She stared at him for a moment, aware of the edge to his voice even if Mr. Whalen was not. She had to be wondering just what course he would take now that her deception was discovered.

He didn't blink. He wanted her to worry.

And at the moment, he didn't have the least idea of what he wanted to do. All he knew was that he was more furious than he could remember being in all his life.

And hurt.

Damn, but why hadn't she told him?

Because everything between them had been a lie, from the very beginning to the bitter end.

And he was so damned angry because he was so damned hurt. He wanted to reach out and shake her. He wanted to hear her cry, just as he wanted to cry out even as he stood there, staring at her.

She tore her eyes from his at last and gave her attention to her guest, and she seemed to understand a great deal more than he about what was going on.

"Please, Mr. Whalen, what happened? Uncle Theo was not supposed to be working! I left him plenty of money—"

"I'm sure you did," Ian commented dryly. He saw her color, but she did not look at him.

"It was a matter of his friends, Mrs. Tremayne," Whalen told her quietly. "They were striking against conditions. Theo joined them. He wouldn't have it any other way. He's one of their leaders, always has been, working or not. You know your uncle. That Mr. Lacey had been terribly hard on the miners, you see. He cut the wages. Well, you know what those wages were to begin with!"

"But what did Uncle Theo do?" she asked. She sounded like a lost girl, Ian thought. She could so easily have drawn his sympathy. He stiffened. No, she had done that already.

"Lacey had brought in men, and there was a scuffle, and some of the men were killed. He wants to charge Theo with murder." He was quiet for a minute. "And ask for the death penalty."

"No!" Marissa cried.

And Ian almost reached out to her. Almost.

"The vicar went to Lacey, Mrs. Tremayne. And Lacey will drop the charges if you'll just come for Theo—and swear that he'll not set foot in England again."

"But he couldn't have been guilty. Uncle Theo is not a murderer—"

"Mrs. Tremayne!" Whalen interrupted very softly. "You've been gone awhile now. But have you forgotten the power Lacey wields?"

She stood, clenching her fingers into fists at her side. "There is no problem, Mr. Whalen. I'll come for my uncle immediately. Mr. Lacey has nothing to fear from us," she added bitterly.

"No," Ian said flatly, leaning against the cherrywood liquor cabinet. "You won't be going anywhere."

She stared at him, startled, her eyes growing very wide. He could almost see the desperation washing over her. "Ian, I'll do anything. I'll—I'll do anything," she repeated. It must have been very hard to talk with Mr. Whalen there. "I must go for my uncle."

"I repeat, my love," he said with an edge. "You'll not be going anywhere. I—"

"Ian, for the love of God, please!"

"Well!" Mr. Whalen said, nervously twisting his hat with his fingers. "I can see you need some time alone. Mr. Tremayne, I can leave—"

"You've been invited to dinner, Mr. Whalen, and you must not leave. However, my wife and I do have a few matters to discuss. If you'll excuse us . . . ?"

"Of course!" Whalen said.

Ian looked at Marissa, then indicated the door to the foyer and the stairway. She stared at him blankly for a moment, refusing to accept the fact that he was going to force them into an immediate confrontation.

"Ian—"

"Marissa, if you will, please?" The last was not a request in any way, but a sharp command. She swallowed sharply, lifted her chin and excused herself to Whalen. Ian smiled to the man. "Please, make yourself at home. Have another drink—there's a daily paper in the rack by the door. This discussion just might take some time," he said pleasantly. Then he followed Marissa as she hurried through the foyer.

"That was very good, Marissa," he commented as they reached the stairs.

"What was good?" she hissed.

"Your manner with Whalen. You're beginning to believe that you were born a lady yourself, aren't you?"

She swung around, a hand raised. He caught it before she could begin to strike. "Aren't you worried about Uncle Theo?" he queried her sharply.

A deep blush colored her cheek and she wrenched her hand free and hurried up the stairs. She stood still in the hall, and he shoved open her door. She didn't move, and he pushed her through the doorway none too gently. She almost stumbled, straightened, and took a seat regally at the foot of her bed, staring straight ahead.

He leaned against the door for several moments, then exploded. "My God, don't you have anything to say to me yet?"

She stared at him. "No! No, you're not going to believe or understand anything I have to say anyway!"

"Try me."

She leaped up, staring at him. "Don't you see? There was no other way. We had to lie to you, Mary and I. There was no other choice."

"Because you had to have the money."

"Yes! Oh, God, how can you be so angry? You always knew I married you for the money."

"Yes," he said softly, deceptively softly. "But before, it was your money!"

"It's Mary's money."

"No, no, it's not!" he exploded. "You made me a party to fraud! She's married to James O'Brien, and I'm married to you. Hell, am I? I don't even known if we're legally married or not!"

Marissa lowered her head suddenly and walked to the turret window. "It's legal," she muttered.

"What?" he thundered.

"It's—it's legal." He was staring at her, and she looked at him at last. "The squire had seen to it that you had a license, but there was nothing filled in on it. I signed my own name."

He swore and hit the wooden door. "Thank you, madam! You have made me as guilty in this little scheme as you are yourself. Why the hell didn't you tell me?"

"You wouldn't have married me!" she exclaimed.

He leaned against the door, hands crossed over his chest. "You're the maid," he commented suddenly. "The maid with the tea tray and the burning eyes. How in God's name did I miss that?"

She swung around on him. "Because I was a maid! Just a maid! No one for the rich and wonderful American Ian Tremayne to bother about!"

He started to laugh, a dry, humorless sound. And the laughter was directed against himself. "And you weren't just the maid, were you? Oh, no! Had I begun to imagine such a deceit, I'd have known so easily. Ah, yes! You knew all about the hardships in the coal mines! You were the little girl all dressed in white who fell into the mud. There are no other eyes like yours, none other in the world. You've known me for a long, long time—"

"I'm amazed that even now you could associate the coal rat with your wife!" she cried out.

He shook his head, earnest, still furious. "Madam, the prejudice has been yours, not mine! I couldn't care in the least where you came from. Coal dust washes away. But lies and deceit do not!"

Marissa barely heard what he said. She heard only the condemnation in his voice. "I had no choice!" she cried.

Ian continued to stare at her, the depth of his fury evident in the coldness of his eyes. "So you knew me, you knew me all along. And you knew why you looked so familiar to me!" He started walking into the room, closing in on her. He could see the fury of her pulse beating against the beautiful flesh of her throat. "You knew all along. And you never, never said a word to me."

"I couldn't—"

"Yes, damn you, you could!" he thundered. "You had chance after chance."

"No! You don't understand!"

He had reached her. Maybe if he hadn't been stricken anew by her beauty he wouldn't have been quite so angry. He reached for her arm, pulling her against him. Her eyes rose to his. Her emerald eyes. Dazzling, green, damp and appealing even now. He wanted to throw her from him. He had longed so desperately to believe in her.

"You scheming little liar! My God, did you use me!"

She tried to wrench free from him. "No! Let me go, Ian. I couldn't—"

And then he did push her away, with a force that sent her flying onto the bed. Stunned, she stared at him. Her eyes were damp. He gritted his teeth, trembling, and he strode to the door, anxious to leave her.

"Ian!" She cried out his name and rose. "Ian, I know you hate me. And I know you want me gone, and I know I owe you a fortune. But please, please—"

"Please what?" he snapped, spinning around.

"You—you have to let me go for my uncle!" she told him. "He's not guilty of any of this. You must let me go—"

"No."

"Ian!" She raced to him. He caught her wrists. Her hair was tumbling free, falling down her back. He wanted to run his fingers through it, bury his face in the red-gold cascade and breathe in the fragrance. "Ian, please! I'll do anything."

"Anything? You do sell out easily," he told her coolly.

"Bastard!" she whispered, and the tears were hovering on her lashes. He could see her grit her teeth. "Anything!" she snapped again.

The tension between them sizzled. He didn't know when the fury and the hatred had turned to desire, he only knew that he would have sold his own soul at that moment. And she was repeating the word to him.

"Anything . . ."

He drew her hard and tight against him, and he gave his fingers free rein to thread through the hair at her nape. He tilted her head to his and found her lips. Angry, he ground his mouth to hers. Still furious, he forced her lips apart, and kissed her.

She started to protest, but he lifted his mouth from hers briefly and stared into the glistening green inferno of her eyes. "Anything!" he repeated.

She inhaled sharply and stepped away from him, those hypnotic green eyes were still upon his. She tossed back her head, pulling a pin and freeing her hair. And she loosened the pearl button at her throat. And then another, another, watching him with a heated defiance all the while. With elegance, with grace, she dropped the white gown. It fell to her feet in a swathe of innocence. With dignity still, with mesmerizing grace and beauty, she dropped her chemise upon the dress, her petticoats, her silk drawers. And she stood before him, challenging him, taunting him. She was like some goddess as she stared at him then, her eyes liquid and emerald and undauntable, the shimmering sweep of her hair evocative as it curled over the marble rise of her breasts.

"Anything," she murmured.

He smiled slowly and removed his coat, tore at his tie and ripped buttons from his shirt. Shoes and trousers were quickly abandoned and he set his hands upon his hips. Her gaze flicked just once, and he laughed aloud.

"Anything," he agreed, and he swept her off her feet and carried her to her bed. And then his mouth found hers again, found it with hunger and need and fury . . .

From somewhere deep within, he tried to control the tumult rising with the rush of his blood, the heat of his body. But it suddenly seemed that there was no need, for she was meeting his kiss with a fury and passion of her own. Her fingers tangled in his hair, her lips sought his. Her hands moved down the length of his naked back, light, delicate, haunting, over his spine, kneading his buttocks, soft as a whisper as they stroked his flesh. He deserted her lips to press his mouth against her throat, and he left that soft white column to caress her breasts with the heat and moisture of his lips and tongue. She arched to his touch, cradling his head to her. He drew soft, fascinating trails down the soft flesh of her abdomen, and he stroked her thighs with his fingertips, whispering against her flesh.

He loved her, he knew then. He loved her still, no matter what she had done. He couldn't sweep away the anger, but he loved her. Loved the beauty of her flesh, the fragrance of her. Loved the spirit, and loved the taste of her kiss. Loved the way she moved against him.

And her eyes, open, clear when she made love to him. Challenging and innocent. Framed by the magic sunburst of her hair. He caught her gaze and moved lower against her, bringing his body against her, bringing his kiss intimately upon her.

Sweet cries escaped her, and she touched him in her turn, her fingers closing upon the hardness of his desire. Molten, hot, trembling, they came together. He made love with a rhythm that was fast and furious still, the culmination of all the love and hatred and anger simmering between them.

The end came quickly, explosively. He shuddered fiercely, felt the heat and fury and passion seep from him in a little shower of his seed, deep into her body. And he felt her trembling beneath him, and he knew that she, too, had found a physical release, even if there was nothing that could bridge the gulf that stood between them now.

He eased his weight from hers and sat on the edge of the bed for a moment. Then he rose and padded silently to the turret windows. The fog was rolling in, thick, rich. He felt as if his thinking processes were rolling with that fog. He still loved her. He was still furious. He could feel his muscles knotting anew with the tension.

Watching him, Marissa bit softly upon her lower lip, wishing that she dared rise and walk to him. She wanted to whisper that she loved him, but it was probably too late. She pulled the sheets to her breast and fought tears. His anger was so great she had felt it in his touch. And yet she had been glad. She had wanted him with an equal desperation. It had been all she had to hold on to.

His shoulders squared, straightened, fell. "Well, it seems that I must say that I'm sorry again," he muttered, his back still to her.

He had told her that once before. And it hurt more deeply now.

"You needn't be sorry," she whispered.

"Indeed, I must," he said coolly.

"Ian, damn you!" she cried, and she hesitated and added softly, "I love you!"

He swung around, naked, masculine, and suddenly very terrible in his anger. "You, madam, needn't conjure up such a pathetic lie. It doesn't become you."

She gasped, feeling as if she had been slapped. "Oh, you—bastard!" she hissed. She was going to burst into tears. She had dared to bare her heart, and it meant nothing to him at all. She had to hold on to something.

"Is that a way to talk when you still want something from me?" he demanded sharply.

She tossed back her hair, hating him very much at that moment. "I'm going for my uncle. If I beg on the streets or steal, I'm going—"

"You are not!"

"Dear God, they'll kill him! How can you be so cruel?" she demanded. He couldn't mean it. He had to let her go.

"No one is going to kill him."

"Don't you understand? I have to—"

"You're not leaving San Francisco. I'll go for your uncle."

"But your work—"

"You're not leaving. God knows where you might wind up, and for the moment, you're still my wife. If you want to help your uncle, you can follow a few simple rules until I get back. You don't leave this house alone. Ever. Lee or John must be with you. You are limited to the store, the carriage house, and an occasional social function in my absence. Is that understood?"

He was going for Theo. That was all that she could allow to matter. But the cold way he spoke to her cut into her heart, and she was still afraid that she would break down if he did not leave her soon.

And she wouldn't even mind burying the very last vestiges of her pride, except that it wouldn't matter. He wasn't going to believe anything she had to say to him.

"Yes, I understand," she said flatly, staring at the sheet.

"Then get dressed. Mr. Whalen will surely miss us soon enough. And I intend to leave with him on the evening train. I want this done."

"Tonight? You're leaving tonight?"

"Yes, it might quell my urge to throttle you."

She flushed, still staring at the sheet. "You can start divorce proceedings," she murmured, "and be plagued no more." Then she gasped, raising her eyes to his. "None of this was Mary's fault. It was my idea, solely my idea. She—she's going to have a baby. You wouldn't—"

"No, Marissa, I wouldn't cast Mr. and Mrs. O'Brien out on the streets," he said.

"You won't fire Jimmy?"

"Jimmy has proven himself useful," he said, a definite edge to his voice.

She stiffened. "And I have not, I take it?"

"Oh, no, Marissa. You have proven yourself useful enough, too. But then, so have other women."

She forgot that she was completely at his mercy and leaped to her feet. But she had barely slammed her hands against his naked chest before he caught her arms and held her still against him. She felt again the masculine heat of his body against her own, and she wanted so desperately to lay her head against his chest. To make love again. To be held.

Cherished.

She cast her head back and met the cold blue ice of his gaze.

He would never cherish her again.

"Remember Uncle Theo, love," he reminded her. He smiled and touched her cheek. "You really are so beautiful, love. A fool's undoing, so it seems." He smiled bitterly, and his fingers tightened around her arms. Then he released her and started for the connecting door.

"Ian!"

He turned back.

"What are we going to do?" she cried.

"I don't know, Marissa. I just don't know," he told her. "Get dressed so that we can get this fiasco of a meal over with, and I can be on my way."

He didn't bother with the clothes on the floor, preferring to stride over them and through the door.

He closed it behind him with a very definite slam.

In misery, Marissa sank down upon the foot of her bed and bit down hard against the threatening onslaught of tears. What was going to happen?

He had already told her.

He didn't know.

CHAPTER SIXTEEN

Marissa! It's a telegram for you!"

Sitting at the tea table in the little terrace at the caretakers' cottage, Marissa felt her heart begin to pound quickly. She leaped up and hurried through the sunny kitchen and parlor to meet Mary at the doorway. A young uniformed man tipped his hat to her. "Mornin', Mrs. Tremayne. I went up to the big house, but I was told you were down here, so I came on to find you. Hope that's all right."

"That was very thoughtful of you, thank you," Marissa murmured, eager to snatch the telegram from him. It was mid-April, and Ian had been gone over six weeks, and she had received only one message from him, that having come about three weeks ago. It had been short and terse. "Theo fine, in my custody. Leaving soon. Ian."

Her fingers shook as Mary bid the telegram man good day. She tried very hard to hold the paper steady enough to read this message.

"Arriving San Francisco evening train on April sixteenth. Have John at station. Ian."

"What does it say?" Mary demanded.

Marissa read the message out loud and sank down in one of the needlepoint chairs that flanked the door. "Oh, dear Lord, Mary. He'll be home tomorrow night!"

Mary knelt beside her, covering her hands with her own. "Well, that's wonderful!" Marissa didn't comment.

"Marissa, it is wonderful, things will be all right!"

No, things would never be all right again, Marissa thought. She could still remember the night he had left. They had both sat through dinner very politely with Mr. Whalen.

Afterward she had tried to speak to him; she had tried to tell him that she appreciated the fact that he was going for her uncle. But her words had been stiff, and Ian had been cold, and it had been alarming to realize just how desperate he was to be away from her. One minute it seemed that he wanted to strangle her, the next he wanted nothing to do with her. He didn't want to hear her voice.

It was the distance that frightened her. The coldness.

During his absence, she had clung to little things. She had been bitter at first that Ian had clearly ordered John Kwan to follow her everywhere she went. She could only assume that he didn't trust her in the least. But when she had assured John one day that it wasn't necessary to trace her every step, John had solemnly assured her that it was.

"No one knows what happened, the day you were kidnapped, Mrs. Tremayne. I have given my solemn word that nothing will happen to you while your husband is gone. I am not the only one that watches."

She had been startled by his answer, and then she had begun to tremble—with pleasure that Ian had at least been concerned about her physical well-being.

He might have been anxious for some enterprising soul to shanghai her now.

But then again, he was a man of certain ethics, and perhaps those ethics would not allow him to let evil fall her way.

But his two messages to her had been very cold and terse. It didn't seem his feelings had softened one bit since he had been gone. And it seemed that she had lived on pins and needles since that night.

Not that the days and weeks had passed in any outside torment. Society had discovered her. The wives of many of San Francisco's most influential men had come to call on her. She had been very careful at first, but it seemed that the women's interest in her had been natural and real. It had made her uneasy, however, to realize that she was beginning to move in a circle with Grace Leroux.

And she had felt like a fraud with every movement she had made in Ian's absence. It had been Mary who had insisted that she must keep up his social front for him while he was gone. Whatever he chose to do when he returned would be his decision.

Marissa remembered now with what assurance she had told Grace that she had won. Well, the game had changed.

But at least it seemed that she had not taken them all down with her.

Ian had contacted his secretary, Arthur, before he had gone, and Jimmy had been given a great deal of the management power in Ian's absence. Marissa had taken to spending a great deal of time at the emporium, helping with the breakfasts. She and Darrin had formed a fast bond, and she spent many afternoons with him. She'd tried to coax him into living at the mansion on Nob Hill in the servants' quarters on the third floor, but Darrin had steadfastly refused. He wouldn't do so until Mr. Tremayne had returned, and only maybe, then. He wasn't beholden to anybody, really, and he liked Mr. Tremayne really fine, but he wanted to know Mr. Tremayne's mind before taking on a job or a room at his place.

Marissa had to swallow hard on that one. She wasn't sure if Ian intended to keep her at the mansion, much less let her make any of the decisions regarding life there.

Sometimes she tried to mask her fear and heartbreak with anger. He wanted nothing to do with her now because he had discovered the humiliating fact that he had married a servant girl. The maid. The coal-miner's brat. She told herself that Ian was a snob, a member of the American aristocracy, and that she should hate him for the arrogance she had discovered that first time she had seen him.

But his arrogance was in his boldness, and in his temper, and in his passion. And they were all things for which she had come to love him.

There was no easy way to hate him. Especially when she lay awake and dreamed by night of that last evening between them.

And especially when she was slowly becoming certain that that particular evening had led to certain results. She hadn't said a word to anyone yet, not even Mary. She told herself that she wasn't sure, even though she was. And then she wondered somewhat bleakly just what she should do, and what it would mean. She couldn't tell Ian, not until they had come to some kind of an understanding about their future. If he meant to divorce her, she wouldn't stop him with the news that she was expecting a child.

And it frightened her, too, to know that his first wife had died in childbirth. That she was alive and well and expecting might make him despise her all the more, and surely he would draw comparisons between his beloved Diana . . .

And the English maid who had tricked him.

"Marissa," Mary murmured, her voice concerned, "you can't worry so much! You've gone absolutely white. I'll bring you something. You just stay there for a moment!"

Mary disappeared into the kitchen and returned with a small glass of sherry. Marissa took it from her gratefully and swallowed it. "Sorry," she murmured.

"Don't be sorry, just don't be so nervous," Mary told her. "I'm sure that he won't take my—our!—allowance from the bank anymore, but Jimmy's income at the store is quite sufficient now. And—"

A wave of cold had come over Marissa. "Mary, don't you understand? We all fooled him. What if he fires Jimmy?"

"Why would he have put him in charge of so much if he meant to fire him?" Mary demanded with serene wisdom. "And he left word with Arthur to make sure that he had good seats for four to see Caruso."

"Ah, but what four?" Marissa murmured. "He might be intending on taking Grace—"

"Oh, no! He's taking us, I know it. He told Jimmy."

"Maybe he's taking you and Jimmy and Grace," Marissa murmured.

"He's not going to ask for a divorce," Mary insisted. "He simply wouldn't."

"Because of his social position?"

"No." Mary laughed. "He'd snap his fingers at his social position, surely you know that."

"But if he doesn't divorce me, it just might be a greater hell," Marissa said. She stood and paced nervously. "I couldn't endure living the life I once thought I wanted. I couldn't stay with him in name only and watch him head off to the Barbary Coast or to the opera or theater with his good associate, Grace, on his arm."

"You must stop being such a pessimist, Marissa," Mary insisted with a sigh. "It's not like you at all." She smiled. "You're the fighter, remember. You definitely put up a fight when Jimmy and I were down."

"It was easy to fight then," Marissa said.

"Because you weren't in love then," Mary told her. "But being in love, Marissa, you must fight for him even harder."

Marissa smiled after a moment, the glitter of the challenge coming to her eyes. "You're right, Mary. I am in love with him, and I will fight for him. I'll even fight him, if that's what it takes."

Mary smiled serenely. "Things will work out. Have faith."

Marissa tried to have faith. She kissed Mary and hurried to the house. She had just called John to make him aware that they must be at the train station the following evening when Lee came to tell her that she had a visitor.

"Eda!" she said warmly when Lee brought her into the parlor. She wasn't sure if she had wanted a visitor or not, but maybe it was best not to be alone. "How lovely to see you," she told the woman. "What can I get you?"

"Not a thing, dear." Eda stared at Lee pointedly and then waited for the beautiful Chinese woman to leave the room. Marissa offered a barely discernible shrug to Lee. Lee smiled, quickly lowered her head and left the room.

"What is it?" Marissa asked.

Eda Funston was not the type of woman to beat about any bush. "Marissa, you've suddenly become the talk of the town."

Her brows shot up. "More so than Mayor Schmitz and the arrival of Caruso?"

"Indeed, I'm afraid so. I imagine I know where this rumor started, and it's simply abhorrent, but still, the rumor is around, and I thought you should be warned."

"What is the rumor?" Marissa asked her.

"That Ian Tremayne's wife is not the daughter of an English squire. That she is a fortune-digging little maidservant who tricked him into marriage."

Marissa felt cold. As cold as ice. She folded her hands and stared at them, then looked evenly at Eda. "I *was* a maid, Eda." She couldn't admit that the rest was the truth as well.

To her surprise, Eda waved a hand impatiently. "This is America, San Francisco more precisely. There's nothing wrong in being a maid." She smiled. "Half the occupants of this hill come from good old robber baron stock! Don't you let any of this get to you, not one single bit! I'm quite sure I know where this all started!"

Where? Marissa wondered, and she felt ill, wondering if Ian hadn't told someone himself.

"It's that wretched Grace Leroux. She was always asking questions about you. She must have hired an investigator to dig into your past."

Had Grace done so? Or had Ian told her himself, because he was tired of his wife?

"Keep your chin high, my dear," Eda told her. "I didn't mean to upset you, merely warn you. Forewarned is forearmed, so they do say!"

Marissa smiled. "Thank you, Eda. I do appreciate your coming to forewarn me. Please, won't you stay for dinner?"

"Oh, no, thank you. Freddie will be expecting me. But you take care. Ian is due soon, isn't he?"

"Tomorrow night."

"Well, he'll soon set things straight. Whatever you were, dear, you're his wife now."

Eda gave her a hug and hurried out in her efficient way.

Marissa stood in the foyer and suddenly felt that she was not alone. She looked up and saw Lee watching her.

"It seems there's quite a rumor about me," Marissa murmured.

"I've heard," Lee told her.

Marissa quirked a brow, but she wasn't really surprised. San Francisco was a big town, but news traveled very quickly.

"Well, it's true, Lee. I am no lady."

Lee cocked her head and smiled. "You speak to John and me as politely as you speak to your friends. You tend to the children because their lives matter to you. I would say, Mrs. Tremayne, that you are indeed a lady." She turned and disappeared through the dining room door, leaving Marissa in the hallway to ponder her words.

Finally Marissa smiled, then wearily climbed the stairs to her room. She stood in the turret, staring out the window at the fog blanketing the city.

She had been there a few seconds when Lee tapped on her door. She had brought a message. "There's a boy outside awaiting your reply if there is any."

Marissa thanked her and ripped open the note.

She smiled as she looked at the words, then she laughed.

The note was from Lilli, and it warned her that a smear campaign had sprung up against her. And Lilli, too, told her that she must snap her fingers at the rumors and keep her chin high. "Someone else is on your side, Marissa. It seems that a few well-aimed tomatoes were thrown at Grace as she walked out of her favorite hat shop the other day. Thought you might appreciate that. Oh, and I thought you might also appreciate the information that the little scamp who hurled the tomatoes was not caught."

"Is there any answer?" Lee asked her.

"Yes!" Marissa told her, still smiling. She penned out a thank-you to Lilli and sent it with a tip for the messenger.

Then she stared out at the city again. The city she was coming to love so much for its raw beauty and its recklessness. She had friends here. Good friends. From all walks of life.

And it was Ian's city.

She started to tremble, then she willed her hands to be still. Mary was right. She was a fighter, she had been born a fighter.

And she was going to fight for Ian.

The next night she stood on the platform at the station, waiting for Ian's train.

The train was late, and she tried to still her nerves by reading the paper. There was trouble in Russia again; the czar had put down a revolt. And a reader's poll showed that most people were convinced that the automobile would never be an alternative to the horse-drawn buggy. She tried to read further but she couldn't give anything her full attention. She was fooling herself. She couldn't give the paper any attention at all.

There were a large number of people waiting for the train. Marissa recognized a few of the matrons who lived not far from her on Nob Hill. Mrs. Nancy Masterson was down the platform from her. She had heard that her son was coming in from his college in the east. She caught the woman's eye and started to smile, but Mrs. Masterson turned from her quickly.

She was doomed, Marissa thought. Hold your chin high, she reminded herself. And she did so. Then she heard the train's whistle. She had to brace herself to keep from shaking.

The great brakes squealed and steam rushed around the wheels.

And then she saw Ian, standing by the rear of the third compartment, waiting to detrain. And behind him was Uncle Theo, looking tall and gaunt but dapper. And Marissa held her breath, waiting to see what would happen.

Please, Ian, please! she wished in silence. Don't ignore me before Mrs. Masterson! Then she realized that she didn't give a damn about Mrs. Masterson; she just didn't want Ian to ignore her. Should she rush to him? She didn't know what to do. It didn't matter. She seemed incapable of movement, as if her feet had been nailed to the platform.

It didn't matter. "Marissa!" She heard her name shouted with Theo's soft, slurring accent and she didn't have to run because he was running to her. Then she was crushed in his arms, and she hugged him fiercely, feeling tears running down her cheeks. Whatever else happened, she would be grateful. Theo was all she really had, and Ian had saved him for her. She looked into his eyes and saw the happiness there and the glistening of tears and she cried out and hugged him again.

"Marissa, oh, my God, love, but it's good to see you again! Thank you, thank you, girl, for sending that young man of yours. I owe the both of you my life," Theo murmured, holding her closer.

"You're here, Uncle Theo, safe and sound, and that's all that matters," she said softly in reply. But he had slowly slid her to her feet, and now she could see over his shoulder and she knew that that was not all that mattered in her life, not anymore.

Ian was almost upon them, tall and striking, and drawing attention within the station as greetings were called to him. He responded, but his eyes remained on Marissa.

Then he did seem to hesitate, and Marissa saw a frown darken his brow. And she realized to her horror that Mrs. Masterson was talking about her to someone, talking loudly.

"Why, she's nothing but an upstart, so they say. The downstairs maid. Tricked him into marriage, seduced him, I dare say."

"Oh, my, no!" came an outraged reply from a tall, heavy-bosomed dowager in dove gray. She looked down a very imperious nose at Marissa. "And our own Mr. Tremayne was such a prize!"

"Perhaps he'll find a way to rid himself of her," Mrs. Masterson said firmly, in her whisper that carried halfway through the station.

And despite her staunchest resolve, Marissa could feel the color flooding her cheeks. She prayed that Uncle Theo hadn't heard the things being said. If he did, he pretended not to.

And suddenly Ian was walking again, a slow smile curving his lips. He paused by Mrs. Masterson and took her hand. "Nancy!" he greeted her pleasantly, brushing a kiss over her hand. "How nice to see you. Edgar is due home for the break, eh?"

"Oh, yes, Ian!" She was positively tittering, Marissa thought.

"That's good, Nancy. He's a fine lad." Ian tipped his hat to the dowager at Nancy's side. "Edith, how are you? A fine evening to you, ladies." He started away, but then he turned back. "Oh, by the way, Nancy. My wife did not trick me into marriage. Anyone has only to look at her to discern why I was quite determined to marry her from the moment we met. Good evening, then."

He walked away, leaving the women to gape after him. And it was only when he had almost reached her that Marissa could see the sparks of anger flying in his eyes. Eyes that touched her with hostility still, when she would have greeted him with so much gratitude. Indeed, she had almost thrown her arms around him in happiness.

But seeing his gaze upon her, she held still. "My love!" he greeted her loudly for other ears. And he set an arm around her shoulder, and kissed her cheek.

His lips were cold.

She looked at him. "Welcome home, Ian."

"You needn't have come to the station."

He was playing out a charade for the ladies, Marissa thought. And all she wanted was to go back to that brief time of complete happiness when she could have thrown herself against him, breathed in his cologne and the clean masculine scent of him, rubbed her cheek against the texture of his coat. Well, appearances mattered. He was playing for them. She could do the same.

She faced him with a radiant smile, running her fingers over his lapel. "I'd not have dreamed of it! I had to see you as soon as possible!"

"And your uncle, of course."

"Oh, yes, and Uncle Theo, of course!"

She looped one arm through Theo's, and the other through Ian's, and she allowed her voice to slip huskily low for the benefit of Nancy Masterson. "Do let's hurry home, Ian. Dinner will be waiting, and you must feel that it's been a long, long time since you've slept in your own bed!"

"Mmm," he agreed, placing a hand upon her arm. "Do let's get home." There was a definite edge to his voice.

As they left the station, Marissa swallowed hard. They had escaped Mrs. Masterson, but Uncle Theo was an intuitive old soul and could surely sense the sparks between them. What would he think?

But what anybody thought didn't really matter at all.

Ian mattered.

And Ian was home.

Uncle Theo stood in the doorway of the house in Nob Hill and stared, jaw agape, at the chandelier and the marble flooring and the staircase rising high to the second floor. Marissa swallowed hard, thinking that Ian must be very aware of her roots now. But then he had to be aware of her past already—he had been to pick up Uncle Theo, he had seen the tiny cottage, he had breathed in the coal dust.

"Uncle," she murmured, urging him forward. Then she was ashamed of herself for having been ashamed of him. And she was suddenly furious with Ian for making her feel so miserable.

Not that Ian had done anything, or indicated in any way that Theo was awkward in his rich surroundings. He walked in and called to Lee that they were back. Then he turned to Theo. "May I take your coat, sir?"

"What? Oh!" Theo let Ian take his coat. A new coat, Marissa saw. Ian must have bought it before they left London. Theo seemed unhappy to let the fine woolen garment go, but then Marissa realized that the men had done a great deal of shopping. Theo was newly clad from head to toe. He was wearing handsome black leather shoes, and a dove-gray suit with tiny charcoal-gray pinstripes. His shirt was white with a pleated front, and his vest was a charcoal gray that matched the pinstripes on the suit.

She realized suddenly that her uncle was a handsome man, tall, gaunt, very dignified.

"This—this is your house?" Theo said to Ian.

Ian smiled at him. "Yes, and I think you'll find it comfortable enough in time. John will see your trunks up to your room, and after dinner you can settle in."

Theo took his hand and shook it heartily. "Thank you, Mr. Tremayne. Thank you so very much."

"Ian, Theo, Ian. Please."

Theo turned to Marissa and swung her into his arms, trembling. He looked over her head at Ian. "My God, I cannot believe you, sir! I am so grateful for Marissa, that this is her life. Ah, Marissa, but you did well."

"Indeed," Ian murmured dryly. "Very well."

She stiffened, but then Lee came and said that dinner could be served immediately.

It was the most difficult meal of Marissa's life. She tried to comment on things that had been happening. Ian replied stiffly. Theo stared from one of them to the other.

At last the meal was finished. Ian suggested that Lee show Theo to his room. Suddenly unwilling to be alone with the man she had waited so desperately to see, Marissa jumped up and said that she would show her uncle up.

And upstairs, when Theo had seen the space that was to be his and his alone, he hugged her fiercely again and whispered, "Marissa, but this is fine. You've found yourself a fine, fine man. And all this, too! But God has smiled upon us. And bless God, girl, for you've deserved this!"

No, this was God's irony for the deceit she had practiced, Marissa thought. But she laughed and hugged her uncle in return. She had to give him this first night in San Francisco. Whatever Ian chose to do, Theo would at least have this night.

But when she started for the door, he suddenly called her back.

"Marissa."

"What is it, Uncle?"

"Whatever is wrong, you can solve it. I know you can."

"Nothing is wrong, Uncle Theo."

"Ah, but I can see it, girl! I can see it in your eyes. But you mustn't be disturbed. You mustn't let some little quarrel upset you. He loves you, lass."

"Did he say that, Uncle Theo?" she asked.

He shrugged. "No, no, he didn't so much as say it, but then I've spent some time with the man. He came to the jail and I was made to understand just who he was. You might have told me that you had married, Marissa," he said, wounded.

"I'm sorry, Uncle Theo. I really thought I knew what I was doing. Good night, now, Uncle. I love you. And I'm glad to have you here."

"Marissa, we'll get on, you and I. We always have."

"Yes, Uncle, we always have." She ran to him and they hugged tightly once again. Then she left him, still staring around his room, and retreated to her own.

She sat on the foot of her bed and bit hard into her thumb and waited. Ian would come; he would have something to say to her soon.

He didn't come. She stood and began to pace the room. She sat down on the foot of the bed again, and then she stretched across it. Maybe she should try to find him. But it seemed that he didn't want to see her.

She closed her eyes, and she must have dozed for a while. She checked the time by the clock on her mantel and was startled to realize that it was four-thirty in the morning.

She stood and pulled the pins from her dishevelled hair. In front of the mirror she brushed it out, fighting tears and a feeling of desperation. He hadn't even wanted to talk to her.

He hadn't wanted to touch her, even in anger. That was the most frightening. If she had lost his passion, she had lost everything.

She stared at her reflection, her eyes wide and haunted, her hair flowing thick and free down her back and framing the pallor of her cheeks.

Then she started, aware that John Kwan and Ian were outside in the hall.

"I can't imagine what's gotten into them!" Ian was saying.

"I've never seen the beasts so restless, sir," John agreed. "But it does seem that you've got the bay settled down for the night. Thank you. I'm sorry you were disturbed on your first night back."

"Curious night, John. I noticed the dogs barking downtown when we came in tonight. Oh, well, maybe the stars are aligning in a peculiar fashion or something. Who knows. Get some sleep, John, whatever you can."

He was still awake. Marissa waited, holding her breath. But he entered his room from the hallway, and she could hear him shedding his coat in his room. She waited longer, hearing nothing but silence. And then she couldn't stand it anymore. She burst through the connecting doors to accost him face to face.

He was stripped down to his black trousers and white pleated dress shirt. It was open at the throat. He stood at the window, staring out at the night, or at the coming morning. Very soon, the first hint of dawn would streak across the sky, and the misty beauty of the city below them would be visible.

"Marissa," he murmured, and his mouth took on a crooked, taunting smile. "What a time for a visit. And when your uncle is already here, and you've nothing left to bargain for."

She gasped, stunned. "Oh, how dare you!" she snapped in fury. Fists clenched at her sides, she strode across the room to stand before him. "How dare you! I came here to thank you for what you did for him, and that's all. I can promise you, Ian Tremayne, I'll never come for anything more! I'll never touch you again, I—"

She broke off as his fingers shot out and circled her arm, dragging her to him. "But you're my wife, Marissa. Just where you wanted to be."

She was so close to him. She felt the bitterness and the tension that had not died. She wanted his fingers to move across her cheeks with tenderness. She wanted a whisper of love, and if she could receive it, nothing else would matter.

But she wasn't going to receive it.

"You didn't want a wife, Ian. You made that clear enough. But then it seemed to be all right until you discovered that you married the maid. Not good enough for a scion of Nob Hill!"

"Why, you little witch!" he snapped heatedly, and she was jerked closer against him. The warmth of his breath fanned her cheeks, the scent that was inherently his filled her with the rampant heat of his body. "You lied to me! I gave you every chance, and you just kept lying and lying. You married me to climb a ladder."

"I didn't—"

"You married for money. We both knew it. It was just that I thought it was your own damned money."

"Then let us both out of this! I don't want your money, I never wanted your money. I just want out. And then you won't have to worry about what people think or say—"

"I don't give a damn what people think or say."

"Then go ahead—divorce me!"

"There will be no divorce."

"But you just said you don't give a damn about propriety, about the things people say—"

His vise around her arms was so tight that she nearly cried out. His eyes were the silver-blue of a dagger as they pierced into her heart.

"There will be no divorce, Marissa. And it hasn't a thing to do with others, it has to do with a vow. Till death do us part."

"So you will let us live in this agony!"

"I would let us live in hell, madam!"

She stared at him in silence for a second and then she cried out. "I cannot! I cannot! I cannot live with you when you—"

"You will live with me. And as a wife!"

She trembled with hate and fury and excitement, and with love and hope. At least she could still anger him, still arouse him. She could have his touch this moment if she so desired.

No.

"No! I can't live this way because I cannot bear it!" she told him. "I—I love you—"

"Liar!" he thundered.

But he seemed so startled that his hold on her loosened, and she wrenched free from him. They stared at one another for a moment, and then she cried out and ran from his room.

"Marissa!"

His voice bellowed after her. She ignored him, and tore down the stairway. She burst outside, knowing that he would be after her.

And now she didn't want to see him. She had bared her heart and soul once again to try to convince him that she loved him. He didn't believe her, or else it didn't matter. She couldn't endure his mockery right now.

She raced to the carriage house and into her mare's stall. The animal bolted, nervous, skittish. "Oh, please, what is the matter with you!" she whispered to the horse. What was wrong with all the animals? She soothed the mare quickly, then bridled her and leaped upon her back without bothering with a saddle.

The first streaks of dawn were becoming apparent in the far east as she trotted out of the carriage house. Ian was on the lawn.

"Marissa!"

She nudged the animal into a canter, knowing that he would follow her soon. She'd had no plan, but now she realized that she could race for the store. It would be open because Sandy and others would be preparing for one of the orphans' breakfasts today.

She raced recklessly through the streets, seeing the city as she began to come to life. Most people would still be in their nightshirts, but several grocers were setting up their produce. Newsboys were already on the streets. Some sleepy soul swore at her as he jumped out of her way.

Feeling guilty, she plowed on, and soon reached the store. She jumped from the mare and tethered the animal. She looked up the street to see that Ian was already thundering down upon her.

She quickly flung open the door and nodded to the security guard who greeted her retreating back. Then she hurried down to the basement, anxious to be with others.

Across the room she could see Darrin. His freckled face broke into a broad grin and he rose to greet her. He began to frown, taking in her wild hair and disheveled appearance.

She couldn't hide behind children, she thought. If Ian was angry enough, he'd drag her out of the basement and demand a confrontation. She had no right to be here. She should have faced him, no matter what.

"Mrs. Tremayne!" Darrin called to her.

And then there was a rumbling beneath her feet.

"What the—" someone cried.

"Shaker!" Darrin shouted. "Shaker! It's a shaker! A big one."

The rumbling became a cacophony, and it seemed as if the world began to crumble and break.

CHAPTER SEVENTEEN

The most amazing thing to Ian was that he saw the quake. Saw the way it ran up the street, tearing the ground apart, saw it rend the earth asunder.

There was the sound, a rumbling, a moaning.

The bay reared, nearly unseating him, and Ian leaped quickly from the animal's back. Even as he soothed the horse, he looked down the street. And he could see it.

The great buildings, waving, undulating, engaged in a macabre dance. And the rip . . . the rip itself, slashing its way down Washington Street, undulating, sweeping, cascading, coming toward him like the massive and powerful waves of an ocean.

"Marissa!" he screamed. The desperate urge to protect her, to see her, to hold her, at all costs, assailed him. But it was too late. The street was ripping in half. Steel pipes were bending and snapping. Wood, cement, concrete, metal . . . everything buckled beneath the gigantic tear . . .

It reached him. The bay screeched as it was picked up and hurtled toward the building. Ian could give the horse no comfort for he was suddenly flying himself, picked up as if he were no more than an ant, thrown in a high arc then slammed down flat. He braced himself against the wall he touched. It was the brick wall of the emporium.

He stared across the street. Facades were crumbling, buildings were falling. He braced himself as the world continued to shiver and shake. Marissa! She was inside the building . . .

The building would hold! he promised himself. His grandfather had built it well, and he had personally seen to all the modifications over the years. The store would hold.

Before him, a wall came crashing forward. Great chunks of cement came hurtling through the air, and he rolled just in time to avoid being crushed. A wood frame building came crashing down as if it had been wrecked by dynamite.

And the street continued to undulate, the buildings to dance.

Ian heard screams, horrible screams.

And then suddenly, the earth went still.

The bay was down; he ignored it. Screams were rising from all around him. He barely heard them. Picking himself up, he ran to the emporium entrance.

Only one thing gave him pause.

He could hear a hiss. A slow, almost lazy hiss.

But he knew what it was. Gas. The pipes beneath the city had been split by the quake. At any moment, explosions could start up.

"Marissa!"

He tore into the store and found a security guard on the floor. Ian stooped beside the man and quickly noted the smashed display case by his side. It was Bobby Harrison, a young Irishman who had been with the emporium since his sixteenth birthday.

The latest in French pottery had downed him.

Ian lifted him. The man began to blink. "Mr. Tremayne. I'm sorry, sir. There was a shaker. Oh." He grimaced. "You must know that. The case fell. I—"

"Yes, Bobby, it was a shaker, a bad one. My wife just ran in here, before the quake. Where did she go? Who else is in here, and where?"

"Just the folks down in the basement. No one's been up to the offices, and no one's come to work on the floor. Only some of the kitchen folk to cook, and—" he paused, his eyes opening wide "—the kids. There's about ten kids down there already. Two cooks, a priest, er, Sandy is in, and that's it, I'm sure." He stared at Ian. "You needn't worry, she's going to stand, sir. I'm sure of it. Some merchandise went flying around, to be sure, but the building, she's as good as gold."

"We've got to get them out of here, Bobby," Ian said. "The gas mains are broken. We've got a sprinkler system, but if the pipes blow . . ."

Bobby understood. Despite the jagged cut on his forehead, he was quickly on his feet. "I'm right with you, sir." Ian was already racing along the corridor for the elevators. He pressed the call button, then realized that the elevators might have been hurtled off their tracks. He turned and started for the stairs to the basement.

"You need to do something about that shoulder, sir," Bobby told him.

"What?" He hadn't realized he was bleeding; he hadn't felt a thing. He looked down to see that blood was bright and very red over the white cotton of his shirt sleeve. "It's all right," he said briefly.

He threw open the door to the stairs and ran down them. He started to press through the door to the cafeteria and discovered that it wouldn't budge.

"Dammit, give me a hand here, Bobby," he said. He threw his shoulder against the door, but nothing happened. Bobby joined him, and together they threw all their weight against the door. Nothing happened. "What the hell?" Ian demanded, his anxiety growing.

"Ian!"

Softly, faintly, he heard Marissa's voice.

"Marissa!" He thundered against the door, calling her name.

"Ian, we're trapped! A beam has fallen, and brought down some of the roof." Marissa sounded calm, and she sounded unhurt.

"All right! I'm going to get to you. Is everyone all right? Has anyone been hurt?"

"Ian, you must hurry. Sandy was struck by a cart. She's bleeding very badly. We've a few other injuries, too."

"Are you hurt?"

She hesitated, then said, "I'm fine."

He hoped she really was. That she wasn't just being brave, as she knew so well how to be.

She'd handle what was happening in there. She'd bind up the wounds and keep the others calm. Not because she was his wife.

Because of the person she was. The proud and beautiful downstairs maid from the coal mines who had learned all her lessons the hard way.

"Ian, do hurry, please!" He could hear that she was trying hard to stay calm. Things were clearly worse than she was letting on.

Much worse. He could still smell the gas.

"I'll hurry," he promised vehemently. And he added a silent prayer. Dear God in Heaven, let me be swift!

Shaker. Darrin had called it a shaker. It couldn't have lasted for more than half a minute, but it had changed the world.

Ian was alive, he was near, and he was going to get them out. Those simple facts meant everything to her. They almost made her stop the trembling that had begun in her with the quaking of the earth. She had never been so terrified in her life.

In the basement, all hell had broken loose. Tables and chairs had seemed to jump and leap around with minds and purposes of their own. Shelves of china and glassware had crashed and shattered. Plaster had cracked and beams had fallen. For a split second she had looked up at the roof and she had been terrified that the entire building was going to cave in. But it did not cave in. Even as the walls trembled and shook, they remained firm. Screams and cries littered the air as the shaking continued.

And then the shaking had stopped, but the cries had not.

Trembling, jerking, she had dragged herself from the spot where she had fallen by the door, just two feet from the fallen beam. Ian! she called silently. She wanted to scream in raw, blind panic. She had left him on the street. Anything could have happened to him. Oh, dear God, dear God, she was going to shriek and scream hysterically . . .

She couldn't! She knew that; she couldn't. Some of the youngest of the little boys had been screaming, and she had tried to call out assurances to them. All the lights had gone, and darkness permeated the basement. "It's all right, it's over now, it's going to be all right!"

Was it over? She didn't know! she thought with a growing panic. If only she hadn't run, if only she was with Ian, she wouldn't be so afraid. He would know what to do.

"I'm cut!"

"Me foot's broke, I know it is!"

"Oh, Marissa, I'm bleeding! I'm bleeding badly!" That call was from Sandy.

"We've an emergency lantern, Mrs. Tremayne," one of the cooks, a heavy man named Ralph, told her.

"Wonderful—" she began, and then she broke off, for the smell of gas was slowly becoming obvious around them. "No, no! Ralph, don't."

"Oh! Yes, you're right."

She could not panic! And she could not lose all sense and logic worrying about Ian. She couldn't imagine that a building might have fallen, that the earth might have opened . . .

"It's going to be all right!" she said.

The slightest bit of daylight was beginning to filter in through the slim grates that were at street level. Her hands still shaking, she called out to the boys, asking who was hurt. Then she heard a deeper voice.

"'Tis Father Donohue, Mrs. Tremayne. I'm little help for the lads. I'm caught beneath a table here, and I cannot move. I think me leg's crushed."

There was only a slight quiver to the good Father's voice, and Marissa bit into her lower lip, applauding his bravado.

"All right, then, my good young fellows, I'll get to you one by one!" Marissa promised them.

"We're all going to die!" a lad babbled hysterically. It was Tiny Grissom.

"Tiny! We are not all going to die. I'm not going to die. I've still a great deal ahead of me to do!" she assured him.

And she did have a great deal ahead of her, she realized. She knotted her fist over her stomach and began to shake again. She was going to have a baby. And so help her, she was going to live to have that child. Ian's child. "We're going to be fine, Tiny. Just fine. Now you remember that, every one of you!"

"I'm—I'm here!" Darrin suddenly called out. "I'll keep to the left side, Mrs. Tremayne."

And so between them, she and Darrin reached the boys one by one, and those who were not trapped by some piece of fallen furniture or debris she grouped together. One of the youngest lads definitely seemed to have suffered from an injured foot, and she carefully wrapped it in a bandage she made by ripping up one of the tablecloths.

Sandy was the one who scared her. A food cart had fallen upon her, and there was a great pool of blood soaking her skirt. Feeling ill and praying for courage, Marissa ripped up Sandy's skirt and created a tourniquet for her leg just above the thigh. The trickle of blood seemed to stop, but Marissa still felt ill. Teddy Nichols, Ralph's assistant, arrived at her side with a large bottle of cooking sherry, and they encouraged Sandy to drink.

It was then that she heard Ian's voice. And in the first few seconds she couldn't even answer him, she was too busy whispering prayers of gratitude. He was not only alive, he was coming to their rescue.

"See? We're all going to be fine. They'll be with us any minute."

She hoped so. The scent of gas was still very strong on the air.

And only seconds later she began to smell smoke.

Ian found the emergency equipment in its slot in the wall and seized the ax. Bobby followed him, and he began to hack at the door. The wood gave easily enough, but once he had managed to slice through it, he realized that there was more than a beam blocking him. Tables had overturned, plaster had fallen, and some bricks had come loose. There was a high pile of debris between him and the people he was so desperate to reach.

"We dig through, I guess," Bobby said.

"Maybe there's help in the street," Ian murmured. "I'll be right back."

But there was no help in the street. There was the most curious mixture of panic and absolute detachment going on. People, some ready for work, some half dressed and some almost naked, wandered around aimlessly, almost like sightseers.

And still, the screams were rising. Two of the city's horse drawn fire carts were racing down the ripped-up streets.

The face of San Francisco had changed within seconds. Some buildings still stood; many did not.

And the screams were going on and on.

Someone was shouting orders, a policeman perhaps, trying to gather what folk he could to lift the debris of a roominghouse. He was managing to find some support. It wasn't that the people weren't willing to help, Ian knew. They were still in shock.

The firemen were shouting warnings to evacuate the area. Ian was well aware that he wasn't going to get any help, and he could understand why. The firemen were using everybody they could recruit to rescue the people caught in the tangle of fallen buildings.

Down the block, Ian could see the flicker of flames rising from a downed wooden structure.

He breathed out a silent prayer, then he felt a renewed soaring of hope.

The bay was up. His handsome horse was up and standing, bleeding only slightly from a wound on the fetlock. And despite the panic, the horse hadn't fled. Marissa's mare was nowhere to be seen, but the bay was standing firm and waiting.

"Good old fellow," he murmured, patting the animal's neck briefly. "Wait for me, I may need you."

Then he hurried into the emporium. "Bobby, it's you and me. We're going to have to arrange some kind of a pulley and lever system. Let's dig and get to it, eh?"

Bobby looked panicked for a minute. Then he smiled. "Sure, Mr. Tremayne. Let's dig, shall we?"

They started digging. In a while, Ian called out to Marissa again. "We're coming. How's everyone doing?"

Horribly, Marissa thought. Sandy was no longer conscious, and she hadn't heard from the Father in a while. The boy with the injured foot was softly sobbing.

"We're—we're holding out," Marissa said. But they weren't holding out, not well at all. Her eyes stung terribly. Darrin was coughing every other second. So were the others. Ralph was complaining that he couldn't breathe.

"Almost to you!" Ian called.

Marissa bit her lip. She could see them working. The door was down, and there was more light peeking in. Ian and Bobby were dark silhouettes against that light, silhouettes in constant motion.

And still, the time went slowly. So slowly.

They could hear the shouts in the streets. The warnings to evacuate the area.

And they could hear the screams, too.

"Marissa!" Ian called to her. "We've created something of a tunnel here. I need a boy to volunteer to crawl through first."

She looked at Darrin. He shook his head, his eyes watery, his breath a wheeze. "I'm not coming out until you come out, Mrs. Tremayne."

"I'll go," a lad named Peter told her bravely. His voice only quavered a little.

"Good boy, that's grand," Marissa told him. She found his hand. His palm was wet in hers as she brought him to the debris in front of the doorway. Once they were there, Ian started shouting instructions to him. He had to keep his weight upon the beam. When he was close enough, Ian would grab him and carry him through.

"You all right with that, young man?" Ian asked.

"Yes, sir, Mr. Tremayne!" Peter promised.

And so they all watched him crawl atop the broken table and plaster chunks and make his way to the beam. He moved slowly, carefully and with a natural agility. It still took him endless minutes to reach Ian.

But then Ian's strong arms grabbed him, and the entire room cheered.

"That's my lad!" cried Father Donohue.

But Marissa knew that they were still in very deep trouble. Father Donohue was trapped. And Sandy could never make such a crawl. She wasn't conscious.

"Billy! Billy Martin. You're next now!" she called out cheerfully. Then she backed away and found Ralph and Teddy.

"We've got to free the Father," she said. "Maybe with the boys out there, they'll be able to dig a larger opening. But we have to free him while they're trying."

The two cooks looked at one another. Ian was shouting to her, wanting to know what was going on. She hurried to where he could see her and tried to put the truth of the situation into her voice without alarming the boys.

"We've just got to move a few things to reach Father Donohue, Ian. Darrin will be here. I've got to help Ralph and Teddy."

She could see him looking at the little boy who had just made it through. "Peter, now you're on the safe side, lad. I need your help. Take up that broken spade there and help Bobby start digging again, eh?"

"Yes, sir, Mr. Tremayne, sir!" Peter promised.

Marissa, hearing him, smiled, but she blinked quickly. She was very close to tears, and she couldn't afford to cry.

She hurried to Father Donohue. At his side, Ralph and Teddy were surveying the huge oak table that trapped the Father along with a tangle of broken chairs. She saw their dilemma. If they shifted the table the wrong way, it could fall upon him and crush his lungs.

"Mrs. Tremayne," Teddy told her. "You get down there by the Father. When Ralph tells you to, pull. And pull fast. It's the only way we can see to clear him."

Tiny, the boy with the hurt foot, limped his way over to her. He was a small boy, thus the name, but he had a certain wiry strength about him. "I can help you with Father Donohue's shoulders, ma'am."

"Tiny, you could be hurt here," she warned. She wondered if Father Donohue was going to make it. His blue eyes were closed; his fingers rested upon the cross that lay on his chest.

Tiny was no longer caught up in his own fear. He offered Marissa a crooked smile. "He's been Mom and Dad both to me for a lotta years now. Can't see's how I'll have anything much left myself were I to lose him, too."

Father Donohue's eyes opened. "Ye've a lifetime ahead of you, me lad, and don't ye forget it! Now the two of ye take grave care there, for I've a fondness for me Maker, and I'm certain he's a fondness for me, so if I leave ye this day, it'll be fittin."

"Father, enough blarney!" Marissa told him with forced cheer. She looked at Ralph and nodded. Tiny and she each took hold of an arm.

"Yea, though I walk through the valley . . ." Father Donohue began.

And then there was a screeching sound as the two men shifted the desk. The sheared portion would come flying down in seconds, Marissa knew. She and Tiny pulled and pulled hard, and there was a thunderous crashing just a split second after they freed Father Donohue's legs.

Again, a rousing cheer went up in the basement. But when Ralph tried to help Father Donohue to his feet, the man buckled with a cry.

"'Tis no use. Me leg is definitely broken," Donohue said.

"We'll get you out," Marissa insisted. "Bring him some of the sherry, Teddy. I'll check on Sandy."

Sandy, stretched out on the floor, her head laid upon Ralph's apron, was still unconscious. Her breathing and her pulse were irregular. She needed help, and needed it soon.

"It's going to be all right," Marissa whispered close to the girl's ear. She knew Sandy couldn't hear her. It didn't matter.

"Mrs. Tremayne," Teddy told her. "The boys are almost out. We've got to do something about Sandy and the Father."

"Yes, of course," she murmured. They were looking at her to know what to do. She glanced toward the doorway. With a number of the boys helping from the other side, the tunnel through the bricks and beams and plaster was widening. She looked quickly at Ralph. "I need two tablecloths. We'll rig stretchers for the Father and Sandy. Between the three of us, we can get them to the opening, and Ian will have to pull them through."

"There's not enough space—" Ralph began.

"Then they'll have to keep digging," she said stubbornly.

She hurried to the opening. She could see Ian's silhouette, dark now against the full light of day. What time was it, she wondered? The quake had lasted only seconds, but it seemed that hours had passed. She was tired and thirsty and her throat was growing harsh and dry as the smoke in the basement steadily increased.

"Ian!"

"Yes. Can you come now, Marissa?"

"No, I can't. We're trying to rig stretchers. We've got to have the opening a little larger. Can you keep at it?"

He was silent. Silent so long that she knew they were all risking their lives.

And she didn't want to die. She really, desperately didn't want to die. And she didn't want the tiny life within her to expire without ever having had a chance.

For the first time she realized that a child would be a part of them both. She could have a tiny son with his father's ink-black hair and striking blue eyes, and their baby could even mimic his smile.

And dream his dreams of a better world.

"We'll dig, Marissa," Ian said, but then she heard him turning to a number of the boys who were already out "There's no reason for you lads to hang around here. You Billy Martin, you're in charge. Take the lads out of here Ask a fireman which way you should be heading. But move quickly now. Stay together, and get away as soon as you can."

"Yes, sir!" Billy told him, and then Marissa could hear Billy taking charge, lining up the boys from the youngest to the oldest.

And she could hear the sounds of digging again.

"You get out now, Mrs. Tremayne," Darrin told her. "I can help with Sandy and Father Donohue."

She shook her head. "No, I've got to see everyone out," she told him, and she hurried to Sandy's side. "We need to take care getting her on the tabletop, Ralph. We'll have to carry them to the hospital like this, too, so we might as well make sure we've got it right to begin with." She started to tell them how to roll Sandy, then how to see that she was tied properly on the tabletop. Ralph stared at her curiously.

"I've been around a mine disaster or two, Ralph," she told him with a rueful smile. "Do trust me, please. I know what I'm doing."

"I never doubted it," Ralph told her. "Teddy, grab that tablecloth like Mrs. Tremayne told you."

Soon they were ready with Sandy. Ralph and Teddy lifted the makeshift stretcher, and Marissa watched nervously as they moved to the tunnel.

"Can you do it, men?" Ian called to them.

"Yes, Mr. Tremayne. Teddy and I and the boy can get her to the opening. We're fine on this end."

And so they began. Trying to get their burden over their heads was difficult and demanded the men's concentration. Sandy almost started to slip once, and Marissa caught her breath. But the stretcher evened out high above their heads, and then Ian cried out. "We've got her! Get to the Father, and quickly."

It was just then that the ceiling sprinklers, triggered by the thick smoke in the basement, burst into action. Water spewed down upon them.

Startled, Marissa cried out.

"Marissa!" Ian shouted.

"I'm—I'm all right! Just surprised!" she called back. Drenched, she turned quickly to Ralph and Teddy and the stubborn Darrin. "We've got to get Father out, now!"

Quickly, nervously, their wet fingers slipping over fabric and wood, the four set to work on Father Donohue.

Despite the odds against them, they managed to secure him to a stretcher. Father Donohue groaned with pain as they lifted him.

"Stop!" Marissa said. "His leg, we should have splinted it first—"

"No, ye'll not stop! I'm firm to this stretcher and ye'll get me the hell out so that ye'll get yerself the hell out, excuse me, Lord!" Donohue insisted with thunder in his voice.

Marissa and Darrin smiled at one another, and Teddy and Ralph repeated the procedure with Donohue. She heard a soft moan, and she knew how desperately he was fighting the pain.

"Got him!" Ian called.

"Mrs. Tremayne—" Darrin said.

"After you, my boy, and I mean it!" Marissa insisted. "I'll be right behind you, and then Teddy and Ralph."

Darrin agreed at last, climbing nimbly. Within seconds, he had crawled up to the tunnel and passed through. "Come on, Mrs. Tremayne!"

"I'm coming!" Marissa called.

But she never got farther than taking the first foothold of her climb.

An aftershock suddenly seized hold of the earth, and she lost her balance and fell to the ground.

There was a ripping sound, and a shard of wood from the beam came loose.

"Marissa!" She heard someone scream her name, and she tried to roll away from the falling missile. She moved quickly, but not quickly enough. She felt a searing pain as the chunk skimmed by the back of her head.

"Marissa!" She heard her name again. It was Ian's voice, she was certain, and yet the sound too quickly faded. She closed her eyes, and fought the void that was opening to welcome her.

"Marissa!" Arms closed around her. She opened her eyes. He had climbed through the tunnel to reach her. She wanted to smile. She wanted to touch his face and tell him that he was always noble, even if he couldn't begin to love her anymore.

But she couldn't do anything at all.

Outside, fires were beginning to burn with a red and regal splendor.

But in her world, there was nothing but blackness.

CHAPTER EIGHTEEN

Ian dared take no time to ascertain Marissa's condition while they remained within the building.

The Tremaynes had built a fortress, but not even a fortress could stand in the path of the ferocious gas blaze surely eating its way to them.

There was no time for anything; he could only carry her through the tunnel space, locked to his body with one arm, while he used his feet and his free hand to drag them along. When he came to the end of the tunnel through the debris, Darrin was waiting to help him. He allowed Marissa to collapse into Darrin's arms, then slipped free himself, calling to Ralph and Teddy that they must hurry.

He jumped clear and swept Marissa into his arms, leaving the others to deal with Sandy and Father Donohue as he carried her fleetly from the building and into the daylight.

There was not much of it. The smoke was a blanket upon them now.

She inhaled and exhaled on a shaky note. Her eyelids flickered open, and she offered him a feeble smile. Then her eyes flickered shut once again. He set a finger upon her pulse and found it steady. He whispered her name and leaned closely over her, listening to the pattern of her breathing. It, too, was steady and deep. She was going to be all right.

"Mr. Tremayne!" Ralph was behind him, carrying the Father with the help of one of the lads. The other boys had already fled to safety, except for Darrin. And Darrin was never going to leave Marissa, Ian knew that.

"How's the lady, sir?" Ralph asked. Darrin had already come around beside him.

"She'll make it," Ian said. He rose, carrying his burden. No, no burden, ever, he thought. Her weight was easy to hold.

They hadn't made it, though. Not yet, he thought. The street was filled with refugees, fleeing the threat of fire. Some were dressed, some were not. Some carried belongings. And some abandoned them along the way.

"Mr. Tremayne!"

He heard a shout and turned to see that a horse-drawn hospital wagon was coming to their side of the street. Driving it was one of Dennis Sullivan's fire lieutenants, Matthew Montague.

"Matthew!" he called in return. The wagon came to a halt at his side. "Sir, you're needed down the street. A man with building experience. They've got to rig up some kind of a system to lift a roof. There's twenty people trapped. Can you help them?"

"My wife—" he murmured, looking at Marissa. Her clothes were sooty and bloodied, her face was blackened with smudges of dirt. She was so still, and so beautiful, in her dishevelment. So vulnerable. They couldn't ask him to leave her.

"I can take your injured to the hospital, sir. Your wife will be well tended, I swear it."

"I cannot leave her," Ian said.

Darrin stepped up behind him. "I'll stay with her, sir. I'll never leave her. I'll tend her, I promise."

Bobby touched his arm. "I'll come with you, sir."

Ian wanted to scream out against the injustice. He had crawled through hell to reach Marissa, and now they wanted him to abandon her.

But she was going to be all right. He knew it. And there were twenty people caught beneath a roof, and he could help. He couldn't let them burn. The death toll would be high enough today.

"All right, Matthew."

Darrin leaped into the wagon and Ian crawled up behind him. There were already injured aboard. People with hollow eyes and bloodied bandages. Ian glanced their way, then laid his wife down, her head cushioned gently upon Darrin's lap. With guilt he realized that Father Donohue and Sandy were in far more dangerous shape, and he helped to bring them to the wagon.

"Where is Chief Sullivan going to form his fire line?" he asked Matthew.

"I'm sorry, sir. I don't know much of the plan yet. I'm afraid the chief is in the hospital. He went to reach his wife and fell through the floor." He was quiet for a minute. "I'm afraid they don't think he's going to make it, Mr. Tremayne."

Ian felt ill. Dennis Sullivan had been the one man in the city truly aware of its strengths and weaknesses. A good man, who had fought for more.

"I've got to get going, Mr. Tremayne," Matthew said nervously. He looked at the flames that were clearly visible behind them.

Ian stepped back. Darrin looked over the side. "Take care of them!" he called to Matthew.

The wagon rolled away. Terror struck his heart.

He might never see Marissa again. He was going to walk in the direction of the fire.

He had to see her again. They had survived thus far; they had to weather the fire.

She had never understood him. When he had tried to tell her she hadn't listened. He didn't give a damn if she was the daughter of the greatest sinner or the finest saint, a child of riches or a waif born in poverty. He had fallen in love with her, and neither time nor distance had changed a thing. He had been angry because she had lied, and kept on lying. She hadn't trusted him. Even when he had cradled her in his arms and spun out his dreams for their future, she hadn't trusted him.

She had never said that she loved him. Not until she had needed him. And then he had been angrier still because it had seemed that she needed to buy his help. He would have gone for her uncle whether she had loved him or despised him. She should have known that.

But that was the only time she had said she loved him. Until this morning.

And then she had run away from him.

Away from him . . .

And into the fire.

"I'm with you, sir," Bobby said, clearing his throat and tapping Ian on the shoulder.

"No, you're not," Ian told him. Bobby was a young man and there were surely enough willing hands by the downed roof. Only a fool walked toward a fire.

"See that bay there, Bobby? He's my horse, a darned good one. Take him and follow the wagon. Make sure that everyone is taken care of. Do what you can. I'll meet you at the hospital."

"But, sir—" Bobby protested,

"Would you get the hell out of here so I can get where I'm needed?" Ian demanded impatiently. Then he turned and started walking into the stream of people. The going was hard. People, some half dressed, were surging down the street. They carried what they could, or dragged carts of household belongings. Some held nothing, and some looked dazed. Some wore bandages, and some chatted as if they were tourists out for a stroll. And some had eyes that seemed already dead.

Ahead of him, he saw the fallen roof, and half a dozen firemen and civilian volunteers trying to help. One of the men recognized him, and they all made way for Ian to survey the situation. He called for rope and pulleys, and explained that they were going to lever away a section with what equipment they had. Everyone set to work.

To Ian's amazement, he realized that the coming fire was casting light across the darkening street. Twilight was coming.

And the fire was coming closer and closer. And with it, a continual stream of humanity.

San Francisco was under military law, someone told them. Funston had taken over at about four in the afternoon.

Looters were being warned that if they were caught, the police and the military would shoot to kill.

There had been tremendous bravery.

And there had been events to shock humanity. Thieves chopping away fingers to steal rings from corpses. Scalpers demanding huge amounts of money for the use of their wagons. Grocers demanding fortunes for a loaf of bread.

And always, there was the fire.

By early evening, the roof was cleared away. They were able to pull three women, six children and seven men from the wreckage. Three men were dead; they had been crushed by the falling walls. And one woman had been suffocated by the plaster. They had probably died immediately, Ian thought. And he breathed a prayer of relief, for he had been hearing other tales, horrible tales. Stories about men and women trapped, and rescuers trying to help them but not being able to. Stories about people running from the blaze, hearing the screams of the trapped behind them.

There was one story about the man who had begged an army officer to shoot him before the blaze could reach him.

Ian stayed with the firemen and the volunteers as the dusk became darkness, and only the ferocious fire was left to light the city.

It was out of control. It didn't take a trained eye to see that. The fire was entirely out of control.

And so, it seemed, was the city.

He had been holding her. Holding her, looking down into her eyes. And his gaze had been blue-gray with anguish, filled with concern. He had held her, and she had known that things would be all right . . .

But even as she awoke, she sensed that he was no longer with her.

Everything around her was white. Incredibly white. She blinked and realized Darrin was sitting in a chair by her bedside. He saw that her eyes were open and leaped to his feet.

"Mrs. Tremayne! You're awake. The doc said you'd come to soon enough. Promised me that you'd be fine, he did. I couldn't believe him, I was so scared. Well, no, I wasn't really scared, you know—"

"It's all right, it's all right!" Marissa acknowledged with a weak smile. She tried to sit up. She felt a fierce pounding, but it quickly subsided. "Ouch!" she murmured.

"Oh, you are still hurt—"

"Darrin! I've a knot on the head and a bit of an ache, but I'm sure the doctor was right and I'll be just fine. I was never badly hurt."

"Well, you had us frightened enough!" Darrin told her. "You were out cold."

"But I'm awake now," she said gently. "Darrin, what about Father Donohue and Sandy?"

"They set the Father's leg and gave him some brandy and sent him on. Sandy is not doing so well. She lost an awful lot of blood, they say. But they've sewn her up, and they're crossing their fingers. Now, you hold on, Mrs. Tremayne. I'm going for the doctor—"

"Wait!" she called. "Darrin, what—what happened to Mr. Tremayne?"

"Oh!" He came back to her bedside. "They needed him. He had to stay."

"What?" she cried with alarm.

"Seems they needed somebody who knew something about the structure of a building to lift up a roof. Mr. Tremayne had to go back with them. I promised him, though, that I would stay with you."

Marissa nodded, feeling dizzy. He'd gone on. He'd pulled her through, but then he'd gone on. And she must have dreamed that he held her in his arms with such anguish and tenderness.

Darrin returned in seconds, but not with a doctor. One of the nurses, a black-garbed nun, accompanied him into the room.

"Ah, Mrs. Tremayne, I'm so glad that you're back with us. Dr. Spencer says you'll be fine, just as long as you take it easy. Except that I'm afraid you won't be able to take it quite so easy. We're evacuating the hospital."

"What?" Marissa gasped.

The nun grimaced. "I'm afraid the fire is coming our way, and doing so quickly."

"The fire has come this far?"

"Indeed, I'm afraid so. We're under martial law, and officers have just come to warn us that we must be out."

"Has anything been heard of my husband, Sister?" Marissa was already crawling out of the bed.

"Mrs. Tremayne," the Sister said with a frown. "Where are you going?"

"I've got to find my husband—"

"Mrs. Tremayne, there is no way to find your husband. He is working with the rescue crews, and he is a very smart man, I've heard. He'll find you when he's able. Don't you see!" she added with some frustration. "There's no way for you to find him! Mrs. Tremayne! There's looting going on out there. And police and army traveling the streets. Looters have been shot dead in the streets. Children have been beaten. Thievery and abuse goes on. You cannot find your husband, and he can take care of himself. He will find us, I promise you."

"But we're moving—" Marissa began.

"To the park, Mrs. Tremayne. He'll find us. Now, get back in bed until we've got the evacuation arranged."

Marissa shook her head. "No, Sister. I can't find Ian, but I'm not sick. And others are. I can help, and so can Darrin. Give us something to do."

"Mrs. Tremayne—"

"Sister, we can carry things!"

The Sister sighed, then smiled. "Fine! I can use some volunteers! Those who can walk will. We've wagons outside for those who cannot. Come, I'll assign you to patients to watch!"

Ian thought it had been the longest day of his life. He stayed with his crew, connected with what was going on in the city through messages from the policemen, the firemen and occasionally one of the army officers.

The main thrust against the fire had been the use of dynamite.

But the firemen had never really been trained to use dynamite. Though the rumor was subdued, it was out there that they were causing more damage than good. Improperly laid, the explosions were sending sparks on to untouched dwellings.

But they needed a good fire wall. A solid stretch of space with nothing to feed the flames.

Mayor Schmitz was calling meetings and forming a committee of civilians to help make decisions. People were saying that Freddie Funston had had no right to place the city under martial law.

But terrible stories were running rampant. Stories of men shot for looting, and left in the streets with placards attached to their bodies. "Punishment for looting! Thieves take care!"

There were stories about cowardice and wretchedness. Stories about the average man, and stories about the rich and famous.

Word had already come in from Oakland that William Randolph Hearst, the great native-born San Franciscan now living in the east, had sent out early morning editorials minimizing the damage and change to the city.

He would definitely be changing his editorials in his New York and Chicago newspapers. When the San Francisco *Examiner* started up print again, there would be nothing left to minimize.

There was terror in the streets, but there was also the greatest heroism.

Ian, so tired that he didn't even feel it any more, just kept on working. He moved along with the fire wagon, his pick thrown over his shoulder, traveling from site to site, wherever he was needed. Bobby had come back to him with messages. Marissa was fine, safely in the hospital. Bobby had ridden to the house on Nob Hill, and Theo and the Kwans and Jimmy and Mary O'Brien were fine. The house had stood well, and none of the animals had been injured.

Darrin was still with Marissa, and a Dr. Spencer had said that she would suffer no aftereffects. It was really just a bump on the head.

Bobby rode back, and Ian felt at ease.

Until he heard that the fire had come licking dangerously close to the hospital. Then he knew that he had to hurry. He felt desperate to reach Marissa.

He was afraid he might lose her forever.

By then, they were into the second day of the fire. Marines had been ordered in, and orders came down that the crew had to break for a few hours of sleep at the very least.

Ian didn't sleep.

He left the others and hurried through the streets to the hospital. He'd had a perfectly good horse, he reminded himself. He'd given the bay away, and now he'd have given everything to have him back.

He started to run, feeling that he wouldn't make it in time.

He didn't. The last wagon was drawing away as he reached the hospital.

The first lick of fire was touching the roof.

Ahead, Ian saw a man on foot, following the wagon. Ian raced after the man.

"Wait! Where have the patients gone? Where are they being taken?"

The man stopped and turned to him. He looked as weary and worn as Ian felt.

"They've all gone, sir. They've all gone."

"Yes, I know, but where?"

"The Golden Gate Park. They're setting up the hospital and more. There will be tents for those left homeless, and food lines."

He paused for a minute, looking at Ian. "Hope you find who you're looking for, sir. I sure do."

"Thank you," Ian said. "I'll find her."

Exhausted, he started walking toward the park.

He just wanted to see her face.

The hospital had almost been cleared when Marissa ran into Dr. Spencer in the hallway.

"I heard you were up and about, Mrs. Tremayne." He caught hold of her and led her beneath one of the lamps, inspecting her eyes. "Well, it seems that you look all right. Are you still dizzy? Nauseated?"

She shook her head. "I'm fine, really."

He sighed. "There's nothing much I could do about it if you weren't. Too many broken bones and bleeders and burn victims. Still, you ought to be taking it easy during the next few days."

"I—I need something to do," she told him.

"All right, then. I've got a broken ankle left down in the ward. A society belle, and I haven't the medical staff to deal with her. The ankle is splinted and set. She'll have to hobble along. She's the last to be moved except for a few of the critical patients, and I need to get her down to the wagon as quickly as possible. We're out of crutches, and we haven't a spare person to try to fashion anything makeshift at the moment. Want to take her on?"

Marissa nodded, and Dr. Spencer pointed down the hall. "Left door. You're on your own."

She wasn't exactly on her own. Darrin, her little shadow, was waiting for her even as she spoke to Dr. Spencer. Marissa grimaced to him as the doctor walked on to tend to his more serious patients. Then she started down the hall to the ward.

A woman was sitting propped up on the bed. She was clad in day clothes, with her dove-gray skirt split so that the ankle could be attended to properly.

She looked at Marissa as Marissa walked into the room, and then both women froze.

"You!" Grace Leroux whispered.

From down the hall came a scream. "The fire! My God, it's caught the roof."

"Hurry! It's catching fast."

Marissa saw the fear that flicked through the other woman's eyes. She clenched her jaw and walked into the room, Darrin following her.

"Come on. We've got to get you out of here," Marissa told the woman. And to her surprise, Grace started to laugh. There was something very near hysteria in the sound. "You're going to help me? I don't believe it. Don't you know that this place could incinerate at any minute?"

"Yes, I know, so let's hurry."

"Oh, aren't you just so kind!"

"Grace, let's go," Marissa urged.

And then the woman was quiet. "You're really going to help save me, after everything?"

"You spread rumors about me, Grace. That's not exactly murder."

Grace kept looking at her. It was Darrin who spoke. "Don't you understand?" he said softly. "Grace is the one who set you up. She paid those men to kidnap you, to take you to Chinatown. To sell you across the ocean."

Marissa inhaled sharply. Staring at Grace, she knew it was the truth.

"So what now, Mrs. Tremayne?" Grace mocked softly. "Are you still so willing to save me?"

Marissa took hold of her arm and pulled her up. "Yes, I hate the stench of burning flesh. Now, for the love of God, can we go?"

Darrin supported one shoulder, Marissa the other. It was very slow going, but she and Darrin eventually got Grace down the stairs and into the wagon.

Dr. Spencer came riding up to the wagon then. "Get in with the patients, Mrs. Tremayne—" he nodded to Darrin "—son."

"I don't think that there's room—" Marissa began.

"You're still my patient. Get in." He rode up close to her. "You're a reckless young woman, Mrs. Tremayne. Brave. But do you really want to risk the child you're carrying?"

She felt a flush cover her cheeks. Darrin had heard the man. She didn't know who else had. And she didn't know if it mattered or not. They were living in disaster. Who would even remember the doctor's words?

And she didn't know if Ian would come back so she could try to tell him herself.

Without a word, she crawled into the wagon.

But when they reached the park, she discovered she couldn't dwell on any of her own worries. People were streaming in from all over the city. Food lines were set up, and they needed people to man them. Children were running around, lost and terrified. There were minor injuries that need attending to.

Help was on the way. A train was coming in from the east laden with doctors and nurses. They would come soon.

But for the moment, she was needed.

Even Nob Hill had been threatened. The great mansions were catching on fire. A new worry awoke in her as she feared for Uncle Theo, Mary and Jimmy. She had to believe that they would get out all right.

Marissa found the woman in charge of the food lines. The heavy-bosomed matron had no difficulty putting her straight to work. She and Darrin were assigned the lost children.

Marissa immediately began to make plates for them, and bind up little injuries, and try to make them believe that everything would soon be all right.

She was holding one little toddler when she looked up to see Bobby. He was staring at her, as pleased as could be. "Found your uncle, Mrs. Tremayne. And the Chinese folks and your friends down the hill. And the horses are going to be all right, well, I think they are, they were confiscated by the city. Better than burning up for nothing, right? Anyway—"

He stepped back, and there was Theo. She leaped up with a glad cry and hugged and kissed him. Theo was fine; his eyes were bright. He was ready for this new battle. He took the toddler from her while she went to see Mary.

Mary was already ill. Rounded now with her baby, but pale, she was lying on an army cot in one of the little tents. Pale and beautiful. Marissa felt her heart go out to her friend.

Mary cried out when she saw her, trying to rise to embrace her. Marissa hurried to her side and sank down beside her. "Oh, Mary, I'm so glad to see you safe—"

"And you! Bobby told us you'd been hurt, and we were so worried, but here you are."

"We've survived it, Mary. And we're going to keep surviving."

"You're so strong. Always so strong. I don't know what I would have done without you through the years."

Marissa looked at Mary and smiled wryly. "Me! Oh, Mary, you've always been the one with the optimism, certain that things would work!"

"The weak one. So useless now."

"Mary! You're not useless. You're about to have a baby. Very soon. Oh, Mary! Strength isn't in anything that we can or can't do. It's in the heart! And you've the strength of a tiger, I promise you."

Mary smiled, her lashes low, not quite believing Marissa, but not about to argue with her. Marissa told her to sleep, that she needed to get back to the children.

When she returned, she realized that her group was growing. Someone had handed Darrin a six-month-old child for her to tend to, so now her charges ran from that babe to a sweet fifteen-year-old girl who was doing her very best to be helpful. There were about thirty in all. And all of them frightened and missing their parents.

Marissa made sure that they were fed. She set about tending to their little wounds again. It was easier now. She and Darrin weren't alone. Bobby was there to do her bidding, and Jimmy split his time between seeing to his wife and helping her with the children.

And she had Uncle Theo, too, and between them they got the children settled down for some sleep, despite the fact that it was still daytime. And between them, they sat in the large tent allotted them all, and spun out fairy tales to take the children's minds off of the disaster.

Toward the end of the night, she looked up to see that a man was leaning against the post at the entrance. She stared harder and she realized that the tall, blackened creature was Ian.

Her heart slammed hard against her chest, and then seemed to fly. He was alive.

And he was watching her. She didn't know how long he had been standing there. She thought that it might have been awhile.

She almost cried out, almost leaped up and rushed to his arms. But she was suddenly afraid. Maybe his wife shouldn't be here. Maybe she was showing the circumstances of her birth, both she and Theo, so at home in such conditions.

He was alive, she told herself, and nothing else mattered.

But Ian didn't move, and she didn't move. She stared at the little girl tugging on her ragged skirt, and she finished her story with a faltering voice.

And then she rose. She tucked the little girl into a cot. "Your husband's come, Marissa," Uncle Theo said. "I'll see to the rest. With Darrin, me fine lad. And then I'll be tucking him in, too. This has been way too much for a boy this one's age."

"Thank you," Marissa murmured. She smoothed her hands over her skirt and stared at Ian. They were a pair. He was black with soot from head to toe, his white shirt barely recognizable, his hands charred, his hair whitened with ash. And she was still in her blackened white, too, her skirt torn for bandages.

And then he walked slowly toward her. The blue of his eyes was startling against the darkness of his face.

"Ian!" she murmured awkwardly. She smoothed her hands down her skirt again. "I'm so glad that you're alive!" she whispered, and then she kept talking. Too swiftly, and defensively. "I shouldn't be here, I imagine. If you'd married a real lady, she wouldn't be among the bread lines and the waifs. I'm sorry, I—"

"Ian!" Jimmy burst into the tent. "Ian, can you come quick? We need some help."

CHAPTER NINETEEN

A new wagonload of injured had just come in, and every available pair of hands was being put to use to carry the burned and wounded into the tents.

Doctors and nurses were arriving in the city now; medication had arrived from Oakland, and from every town close enough to render quick assistance.

Ian carefully lifted and carried men, women and children. He had just laid down a small child suffering from smoke inhalation when he looked up to see a familiar figure bent over a woman toward the rear of the tent.

For a moment he was puzzled. Then he realized that the man was Lilli's employee, the very questionable and homely Jake.

He felt a tinge of unease sweep down his spine, and he hurried along the row of cots to reach him.

As he had feared, Jake was bending over Lilli.

The stout, ugly man looked up and saw Ian. He seemed relieved, and quickly left his place at Lilli's bedside, motioning for Ian to sit. Ian hesitated, and the man said, "Please sir. It'd mean so much to her."

Ian knelt down carefully by the cot and took Lilli's hand. He fought hard to keep from shuddering, thinking of the pain she must be suffering.

Half of her beautiful face had been hideously burned.

He curled his fingers around hers. She opened her eyes and saw him.

"Oh, Ian!" she whispered. She twisted to hide the disfigurement.

"Lilli, Lilli," he murmured. "They're going to help you." He glanced at Jake. "Have they given her something for the pain? I heard that they were very low yesterday on anesthetics—"

"She's had morphine. I saw to it," Jake told him.

Thank God. She wasn't suffering. But something about Jake's voice told Ian that the man didn't think Lilli was going to make it.

"Ian . . ." It seemed very difficult for her to speak. "You shouldn't . . . have seen me so. You'll remember me like this."

"Lilli, I'll remember that you were always there for me. A beautiful heart in a beautiful person. But I won't need to remember anything, Lilli. This is your city, just like it is mine. You're going to pull through. I'm telling you—you're going to pull through. And we're going to walk arm in arm down the waterfront again. We're going to watch the ships, and buy shrimp from the peddlers, and tea in the garden. Do you hear me, Lilli?"

She squeezed his hand. "You're a good man, Ian," she said. "I always loved you so. But she loves you, too. You know that."

"Does she, Lilli? It's what she says. How can you tell?"

"It's in her eyes, Ian. You'll walk on the waterfront with your wife, Ian. Not with me."

"We'll all live to see it grow again, Lilli."

She didn't answer him. Her hand no longer squeezed his. He leaned close to her. He could still hear the soft beating of her heart.

"The morphine," Jake said.

Ian nodded.

"If there's any change, Mr. Tremayne," he said, "I'll come find you."

"Thank you, Jake," Ian said.

Wearily, he rose. He was on his way out of the tent when he nearly plowed into one of the doctors. The haggard-looking man paused, watching him.

"You're Tremayne, Ian Tremayne. Not that there's much likeness now, but I've seen your picture in the paper often enough with your buildings and your political stands. They should have listened to you and Sullivan. The quake didn't destroy the city—the fire did."

"So it seems," Ian murmured. He was anxious to get back to Marissa. "Doctor, er—"

"Spencer. Adam Spencer. I saw your wife this morning."

Ian's interest was renewed. "They assured me that she was fine. Is there something I don't know?"

Spencer smiled. "I'm not really sure."

"What's wrong with her? If the bump was not a bad one, why did you let her up? Why is she—"

"Mr. Tremayne, please. The bump was not bad. And a garrison of soldiers couldn't keep her down once she determined she wanted to be up. But she should watch out for herself."

"Why is that?"

"Unless I miss my guess, sir, your wife is about two months pregnant."

Ian stumbled, as if he had been struck.

"You didn't know, I see," Spencer murmured. "I'm sorry, she surely wanted to tell you herself. Well, she might not have done so. And I'm sure she's still up. She has such an affinity for those children. Maybe it's for the best that I told you. The both of you need some sleep. I hear you've been trying to save the entire city. It can't be done. Get some sleep, Mr. Tremayne. And see that your wife gets some, too."

Ian nodded, numbed, elated, stunned, all in one. And frightened. He couldn't bear to lose her.

And he knew what the risks were. He'd already lost one wife and child.

"Thanks," he told Spencer, and he turned and strode through

the barrack-like tents that flourished like spring flowers in the once green park.

He got lost once, turning into a large tent where a number of the elderly had been brought. He realized that he was exhausted. He hadn't slept in forty-eight hours. He started out again.

Marissa. He wanted to throttle her. Shake her and throttle her. She was pushing too hard.

And he wanted to hold her. He wanted to crush her against him and hold her forever.

He was too tired to throttle or kiss her, he realized, but he kept on going, searching for her.

"Ian!"

He paused, aware that he had headed in the right direction this time because Theo was standing before him. "Ian, 'tis glad I am to see you back. I've managed a few extra blankets, and I've bound two of those army cots together in the rear of the tent—I know she won't leave the children, you see. But there's room for you both to get some rest, and that you must do. You look like hell, boy, if you don't mind me saying so."

"Thanks," Ian murmured dryly. "What about you? Where are you going?"

"Oh, I'll be here. There's just a shortage of cots at the moment. I've got the lad, Darrin, set up with blankets inside, and I'll join him. Him and me, we aren't so used to anything too comfortable, you know?"

"Theo, you're not a young man—"

"And don't you go making me an old one. I know you'll fix me up nice and fancy again soon enough. The ground's good enough for me tonight." His voice grew gruff. "I don't want that niece of mine on the ground, and you're the only one's going to get her to sleep tonight on a cot."

Ian smiled and clapped Theo on the back. Then he ducked into the tent.

Marissa was just tucking the baby into a makeshift crib. He walked over to her and touched her shoulder. She turned, startled.

"You've done what you can for the little ones tonight, Marissa. They'll need you again in the morning. Come on, now. You've cared for these babies, now give a care to our own."

Her eyes opened wide. She was surprised that he knew, but he intended to offer no explanations that night, and she was too weary to start demanding them. Indeed, she didn't say a word.

"Marissa, we need some sleep," he said firmly. He caught her hand and led her to the bed that Theo had made for them.

She was as grime-covered as he. As disheveled, her glorious hair blackened with soot and ash. Tonight none of it mattered.

He swept her up, laid her down and sank beside her. And setting his arm around her, he pulled her against his chest, holding her close.

And there they both slept.

When Marissa woke, she was alone. It was very early, still dark. It must have been about five o'clock. It was almost three days since the quake had struck.

There was activity all around her. The children were up and awake. Darrin was playing with the baby, and Uncle Theo and Bobby were handing out pieces of bread.

Ian was nowhere to be seen.

"He's gone out, Marissa," Uncle Theo said, stopping by her side with a bucket of milk. "They've fixed one of the main water pipes—there's some water again."

Even as he spoke, they heard a thunderous explosion, muted by distance, but still painfully clear.

"They're still dynamiting."

"Dynamite and cannons. They're trying to save the docks. If they can do that, well, then, maybe it will be over," Uncle Theo said. The city had burned for three days, Marissa thought. What could be left?

"Come on, lass. We need to get these little ones fed. They're going to be ferried over to Oakland this afternoon."

She smiled, because she could tell he wanted her to. Inside she felt a wall of misery building. San Francisco was nearly gone. These poor children would be lost.

And after she had helped to get something into them, she learned from Bobby how bad matters really were. Some of the streets were empty now. The magnificent Palace Hotel had burned, despite all the planning and care that had gone into it. Great mansions on Nob Hill had burned. The fire-fighters, too busy to deal with those already lost, had been told to cast the deceased into the flames of the burning buildings.

The Barbary Coast had burned, along with its Dead Man's Alley, Murder Point and Bull Run Alley.

Some thought it for the best.

There was a fear of the rats. Doctors were warning people that they could be looking toward an epidemic of bubonic plague.

But until the fire was put out, that had to be the primary concern.

Within an hour, the children were all off on the ferry, except for the baby. Marissa had decided to keep her until her parents could claim her. She was so very little. And she had finally offered Marissa a tenuous smile, and that smile had nearly broken Marissa's heart. Dr. Spencer had seen to it that she had proper milk for the little girl, whom she had decided to call Francesca.

There were many births there, in the open air, and at the hospital barracks at the Presidio, she heard. And many parents were naming their children after the circumstances, names as wild as Golden Gate, San Francisco and Presidio.

Francesca, the feminine of the saint after which the city had been named, did not seem so bad.

Darrin was with her. Darrin still wouldn't leave her, and Marissa was glad of it. She didn't know what the future would bring, but she wanted the boy to be loved and cared for. Surely, Ian would allow her to bring Darrin home.

If they had a home.

She was vaguely wondering about the fate of their house when Darrin returned from a trip for milk. "Marissa," he told her, accustomed at last to using her given name, "the lady from the, er—from the Barbary Coast is here. The one who helped find you. And she was hurt awful bad."

"Lilli?" Marissa said, startled.

Darrin took the baby and showed Marissa the way. She hurried to the tent. One of the newly arrived nurses pointed her toward a cot in the rear, and she hurried toward it.

Then she froze, for the cot was empty.

"Oh, my God!" The cry of horror escaped her in a whisper. Lilli was dead.

Lilli might have been the best friend she had in San Francisco.

Then someone touched her shoulder, and she turned. It was a gnarled, ugly man, but he had interesting eyes. "You're Mrs. Tremayne."

"Yes. Yes, I was—looking for Lilli."

"The doctor is seeing to her, changing her bandage."

"Oh! Oh, thank God! She's going to make it?"

Even as she spoke, a nurse came in, leading a heavily bandaged Lilli to her bed. Most of her face was swathed. Marissa hurried forward, nodding to the nurse. "Lilli, it's me, Marissa Tremayne. I'll help her," she told the nurse.

The nurse was busy and glad to hand Lilli over to Marissa. "Marissa!" Lilli murmured softly. She touched her face. "You're here, and well. I'm glad for you. For you and Ian."

"You're going to be fine, too, Lilli."

She sat Lilli down on the cot. Lilli groped for something, and the ugly little man took her hand. "I'm going to live, yes. But I'm going to be horribly scarred." She laughed softly. "And in my business . . . oh, I'm sorry. I didn't mean to offend you."

"You haven't offended me, Lilli. I just feel that you—that you deserve better!" she said softly.

And Lilli laughed, squeezing her hand. "I'm going to get better, Marissa. Seems it took a fire and a dreadful burning to find out that Jake here loves me. And he's been saving every penny I ever paid him. He's going to marry me, and I'm going to set up regular house-keeping. Of course, we'll never have respectability. No one will ever call on me. San Franciscans have long memories. But I'm staying. I am a San Franciscan."

"Oh, Lilli, I am so very glad!" Marissa said. "And someone will call on you. I will call on you."

Very little of Lilli's mouth showed, but her smile was radiant. "I believe that you will. But I think that you should hurry back now. When I was being bandaged, I heard all kinds of shouting and excitement. I think they quelled the fire on the docks." She was quiet, then added with exasperation, "Ian will be coming back."

"You knew that he—went out?"

"He came to see me last night and this morning," Lilli said. "Oh, for heaven's sake, Marissa! He loves you. He's just the kind of man who doesn't forget old friends, even when they are scarred and ruined and hideous."

"Lilli, you'll never be hideous," Marissa told her. She rose and very gently kissed the top of her head. She turned to Jake. "Congratulations!" she told him.

And then she hurried out.

People were shouting. Crying out, jumping up and down. A stranger suddenly swung his arms around her. "They beat it! They beat the fire! Seven-fifteen exactly, they say. They beat the fire from the piers around East Street, and beat it back to the area south of the Slot! Where it was born, lady, there it died! The fire is out!"

Stumbling, she hurried to the tent where she had spent the night. And as Lilli had suspected, Ian was back.

His face was nearly as black as his pants and the boots that he wore, but he was talking to Uncle Theo and doing so animatedly. His teeth and eyes flashed handsomely against all the darkness around him.

Then he turned and saw her.

It was over, she thought. It was true. The fire had died, and it was really over. She lost all thoughts of inhibition, and she cried out and raced over to him.

She saw his brow shoot up and for a moment she was afraid. So afraid that he would not open up his arms to accept her. But he did. She flung herself against him, and she found herself lifted and held, held so very close.

And then he gently let her slide down against his body.

"It's out?" she whispered.

"Pray God it stays out," he said.

She heard a motion behind her and turned to see that Jimmy and Mary were standing behind Theo with Darrin and little Francesca.

"I think that we should give these two a moment alone—" Mary began.

"Oh, no, no, no, wait, just wait a little minute," Ian said. His arms remained around Marissa.

"I think you've all been wondering and waiting. All the time that I was gone . . . and then nothing seemed to matter while the fire burned. But as long as we're all gathered here now, we should discuss a few things."

Jimmy cleared his throat. "We were guilty, Mr. Tremayne. Just as guilty as Marissa. More so. She'd have never done what she done if she hadn't loved Mary so much like a sister."

"Yes, you are guilty," Ian agreed flatly. "All of you. And you made me guilty of fraud, taking all that money. So here's what we're going to do."

Marissa felt a cold chill sweep over her even as he held her. A fear as icy as the fire had been hot. She fought it desperately. Lilli had said that he loved her, and Lilli knew him well. And he had cared, she knew that he had cared. Last night he had insisted on holding her while she slept . . .

Last night he had known about the child.

He had come riding after her the fateful morning of the quake. And he had dug through rock and rubble and wood to get to her. And he held her so securely now.

He had refused to think of divorcing her. She knew that. But the marriage wouldn't mean anything anymore, not unless she had his love.

"I'm going to put back all the money that has been taken out of Mary's trust fund. I don't think that people are lining up to prosecute us, but we are all guilty of fraud. If we repay the fund, then I will, at least, feel that we've not defrauded the squire, and if anything should happen in the future, we will only be guilty of having borrowed the money."

"But, Ian!" Mary gasped. "What will you have? The emporium is burned to the ground, Nob Hill has burned—"

"I've a lot of insurance, and all with very reputable companies." He smiled. "And haven't you heard? The world is helping San Francisco. Money is already pouring in from New York and Chicago and Boston and countless other cities. And I've been told they're collecting across the globe. This city will rebuild.

"And I will rebuild with it. Jimmy, you and Mary should survive very nicely on the salary that I intend to pay you until Mary reaches the legal age to receive her inheritance. Theo, you're one of the most admirable men I've met, and I'm delighted to have you continue on with us. Of course, you're the one innocent party in this group, aren't you?"

"Innocent as a babe," Theo said smugly. Marissa wanted to kick him.

"There's only one stipulation to all of this, of course," Ian continued.

"Oh, Ian! You've been far more generous than we'd any right to expect," Mary told him. "We'll do anything."

"You might want to think about it, after the past few days," he advised her. "Because this is the stipulation. I'm not leaving here. San Francisco is my home. There's going to be a lot going on when they sit down and try to figure out how to rebuild properly. I want to be a part of that building. You've just weathered an earthquake and a fire to rival the worst. Are you sure you want to raise your child here? This is my home—it isn't yours."

Theo spoke up quietly. "It is now, Ian Tremayne. Home is where you build, and where you hope, and where you dream. We've nothing left behind us. So here we are, and here we stay."

"Indeed," Mary murmured. "Here we stay."

"Then so be it," Ian said. "I've finished with all I've got to say to you all about the matter."

"Oh, Mary!" Marissa burst free from Ian to hug her friend. Mary hugged her back, but almost immediately, Ian had his hand upon her arm, pulling her back. "I've finished with them, my love. I did not finish with you."

Startled, and chilled once again, Marissa stared into her husband's face. She squared her shoulders defensively, meeting his bright blue gaze. It was fathomless, and far from reassuring.

"You'll all excuse us?" he said to the others.

"I've got the little one, sir," Darrin told him.

Marissa thought he winked at Darrin, but she was being pulled out of the tent. And then Ian had her hand and he was walking toward one of the ponds, far from the area where all the refugees were camped. And then he suddenly swung around and stared at her.

"And what about you?" he demanded.

"What—what about me?" she whispered.

"I'm well aware that you did what you did to help Mary. And Theo. And I know now about your school in England. But I also know that you were seeking a better life. You dreamed of a big house, of an easier life. Well, my love, I may not have a house anymore. So, what about you?"

She jerked her hand free, furious that he could still think so little of her. "Ian Tremayne, how dare you. I have had all that I can take! I—"

"Marissa, love, there's nothing wrong with wanting to soar!" he told her softly. "One of the reasons I love you so deeply is your determination to seek something better."

"I married you for money, yes, but I—" She stopped dead still, suddenly certain that she hadn't heard him right at all. "What?"

"I said, one of the reasons I love you—"

"You love . . . me?"

He smiled, the slow, lazy, taunting smile that had once so easily seduced her. "Yes, Marissa Ayers Tremayne. I love you. I wanted you from the very beginning. I started to love you because of that haunted quality in your eyes. Because of the mystery, the determination, the spirit. I fell so deeply in love with you that I couldn't stand the fact that you hadn't trusted me. Marissa, you little fool! It never mattered to me where you came from. I love what I've learned about your past. And I'm glad that you can't bear to see lost children without taking them under your wing. I'm glad that you can't be licked by catastrophe or fire. You are everything I could have ever wanted."

"Oh, Ian!" she whispered, staring at him, unable to believe his words, or the tenderness within him. But there was truth, wonderful truth in his eyes. And as he smiled at her, blackened and haggard, she still thought she had never seen a more striking man. There was strength in his tired form, in the set of his shoulders, in the handsome contours of his face, strength, courage, determination and love.

She threw her arms around his neck, rising on tiptoe to kiss him.

"Well?" he demanded. Even now, she thought wryly, disheveled and worn as he was, he carried that arrogance about him.

"Well what?" she whispered.

"You didn't answer me. What about you?"

"Ian Tremayne, I love you. I never deserved you, because I did lie and cheat to get you. And I did hate you. I hated you because you saw so many things in me too easily. But I wanted you, too. And then I saw how good you were to Mary and Jimmy, how good you were to all of us. And when I came here at first I was so very jealous, and so I was so furious! And I wanted to hate you. I wanted so much to hate you so that I wouldn't care about Grace and Lilli—"

"There wasn't anyone once I had met you," he told her.

She smiled. "Thank you for that. But there was. Diana."

"I'll always love her a little in my heart. But you even allowed me to let her go, Marissa. Can you understand?"

Her eyes glimmered with the threat of tears, and Marissa prayed that it was all right to be so happy when a great city lay in ruins beyond them. But God would understand, she thought.

She intended to help rebuild that city.

"Ian, I love you! So much!" Then she added, "Oh! Ian, I saw Lilli, and—"

"And she's going to marry Jake and live happily ever after," he told her.

"Yes, and I'm so glad."

"You don't mind her so much anymore?"

"She probably saved my life. No, I don't mind Lilli anymore. I promised her that I'd call on her, and I will."

Ian smiled. "Yes, I think that you will."

"But Grace—"

"Grace is taking her broken ankle and leaving the city," Ian said flatly.

Marissa's eyes widened. He knew what Grace had done. "Ian, how—"

"Darrin told me that Grace had arranged to see that you disappeared. I spoke to her this morning, briefly. She's not interested in staying. Not really. And after I had a talk with her . . . well, she can inflict herself upon Chicago or New York for a while."

Marissa laughed. "Oh, Ian, I do love you so very much!" she told him, her arms wrapped around his neck. He held her close against him.

"So you'll stay."

"I'm your wife, Ian. Of course, I'll stay. Like Theo said, it's my home now, too. It's where I can hope and dream and build. It's where I can be with you. Oh, Ian! It's the first real home I've ever had. Oh! There's just one thing. It's Darrin. Could we—"

He started to laugh, interrupting her. "I knew, my love, that we weren't going home without Darrin. And I'm beginning to imagine that we might also be going home with an infant we're calling Francesca."

"It's just that she's so very little, Ian. We'll keep her just until her parents can come for her."

"And then we'll have our own very soon," he murmured, stroking her cheek.

"Oh, Ian, do you mind?"

"I'm delighted, Marissa. So very delighted. A year ago, my love, I was a bitter and angry man, alone. And now I am surrounded by love and loyalty. And it is all because of you."

His lips touched hers at last. With warmth, with tenderness, with a fervor that defied the very world. His kiss held passion; it held promise; it held all the desire that she could ever imagine. And it held love.

And it went on and on.

"Mr. Tremayne! Mrs. Tremayne!"

Dimly, she became aware that someone was calling to them in a voice that was becoming more and more frustrated. It was Bobby.

Marissa broke free from Ian's kiss and turned quickly.

Bobby was mounted upon Ian's bay. His uniform was torn, and he had smudges of soot on his face.

But he was smiling.

"Your house, sir, it's standing! More than half the hill is burned clear to the ground or gutted, but your house is standing."

"I don't believe it!" Ian gasped.

Bobby leaped down from the bay's back. "Go on, sir, and take a look. There's not much else to do here, help is pouring in from all over. If you want—"

"If I want!" Ian exclaimed. He swept Marissa into his arms and sat her upon the bay's back. Then he leaped up behind her.

They moved slowly as they left Golden Gate Park. But then Ian gave the horse free rein, and they moved swiftly through the burned streets, cantering all the way to the hill, then up the length of it.

And there, as Bobby had told them, the house still stood. Around them, mansions had burned. The walls were scorched and blackened, but the beautiful house still stood.

Ian eased down from the bay and reached for Marissa. Laughing, she fell into his arms. "We've even a home to come home to! A place for this ragtag family you've created!" he exclaimed.

And then he kissed her again, and while he kissed her, he lifted her into his arms and headed up the pathway to the house.

"We've got to go back for the others," she reminded him, breathing the words against his kiss.

"Bobby will see that they come here," Ian told her.

Then he paused at the front step.

"I have everything," he said. "What more could God grant?"

He kissed her, and as he kissed her, he suddenly discovered what greater blessing there could be.

It began to rain.

Sweet, cool rain began to fall. And he lifted his eyes to hers, and they both began to laugh with delight.

His lips touched hers once again as the cleansing rain continued to fall, running down their cheeks, clinging to their lashes. Mingling with their kiss.

And then he hurried up the steps to the house.

Miraculously, they had both come from fire, and found their way home.